LIVING FIRE

OF THE ELEMENTS BOOK 2

LIVING FIRE

J.B. LESEL

This novel is entirely a work of fiction. Names, characters, places and incidents are either the product of the author's imagination or are used fictitiously, and any resemblance to any person or persons, living or dead, is entirely coincidental. No affiliation is implied or intended to any organisation or recognisable body mentioned within.

Published by Vulpine Press in the United Kingdom in 2024

Cover by Claire Wood

ISBN: 978-1-83919-533-4

www.vulpine-press.com

Dedicated to my mother, Helene. For being her, a great and supportive mother. Often hard at work, always so loving and kind, who loves flowers and sunshine.

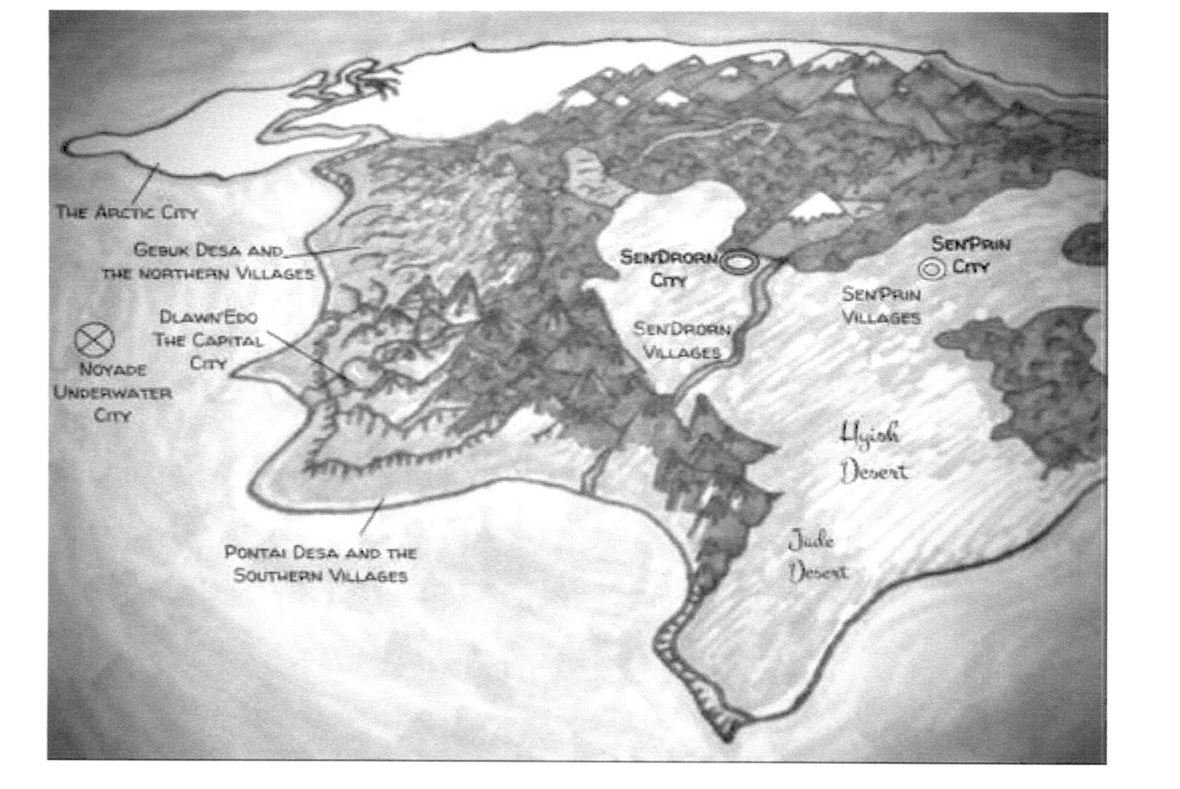
The Arctic City
Gebuk Desa and the northern Villages
Dlawn'Edo The Capital City
Noyade Underwater City
SenDrorn City
SenDrorn Villages
SenPrin City
SenPrin Villages
Hyish Desert
Jade Desert
Pontai Desa and the Southern Villages

CHAPTER ONE

Yulah rushed down the secret passageway that connected her flat to the Sen'Drorn fortress. She was heading to General Malotus's chamber. He had summoned her, his assistant, for a private meeting. While she had no idea what it could be about, she was anxious to meet with him as well. She'd been worried about him, The General of Tactics, for quite some time. He'd been acting unlike himself ever since the summer when Flax and the Meruyan girl had infiltrated the Sen'Drorn fortress.

Upon recalling the memory, Yulah burned with rage, her cheeks flustering with heat. What a fool she had been to fall for them, tricking her into acquiescing and playing their pawn so they could poison the top officials and steal their best engineers. That's what those Sen'Prin traitor-spies had done. That was the night she had learned the truth about Flax. To think, the deceit a man was capable of.

Worse, Malotus had warned her all along, and she'd snuck behind his back for months, a fool in love; trusting, silly, and base. That's how she felt now. Malotus had been right in warning her not to trust Flax. It humiliated her twice over, especially after she'd gone out on a limb for that boy. When she'd told Flax of a promotion for him and his father in their engineering shop, he'd used the information to leave his post and flee the city.

The slapping of her shoes on the stone floor filled her ears as she picked up her pace, unable to be alone with her dark plague of thoughts any longer.

Cautiously, she knocked on General Malotus's door. "May I enter?" she inquired lightly. He could be grouchy at times when things weren't done just so.

"Yulah, come in," came his voice. Usually so clear, it now sounded heavy, tired.

In fact, she'd known him all her life. He was not just the General, her superior. When she was six and her parents had died, Malotus, her father's brother had taken her in and raised her.

"Uncle Mal..." she breathed, slipping inside and shutting the arched chamber door behind her, the brass hinges squeaking. "You wanted to see me?"

He'd always been kind to her, and when she turned sixteen, he had made sure she'd been assigned to a good position in the Sen'Drorn government after her school years. It fulfilled her required duty to the state. She'd now served two years as Malotus's assistant, whereas most of her year-mates had been deployed to protect their assets far from home. She'd been given her own flat in the highest point of the city, specially reserved for top government officials.

He stopped and looked up at her. Were those tears flittering at the corner of his green eyes? That was not expected. His bushy black mane seemed wilder than usual. As if he'd been sleeping on the floor or pulling at it. He scratched at his broad horns, a horrifying act which she had never seen him do.

She trembled as she watched the eerie image of him.

"Yulah, I have been wrong," he confessed in a defeated tone. "I wanted to apologize for the way I'd been acting."

She stared blankly at him. *What was his plan?*

"Since eating the poison fruit, I am no longer fueled. My need for revenge against Arenay isn't enough. I do not know how to move forward under the loathsome emperor."

"It was only a poison, you can recover, uncle." she urged, hopefully.

"No...it was more than that, it showed me something. There are so many new questions, truths to explore. I saw something that day I must process. I must reconcile with myself, the hatred of others and the illogical nature of it which I saw."

"I'm afraid I don't understand..."

"I wanted you to be the first to know that I am resigning."

"*What?*" The ends of Yulah's long hair slipped from her hands. Her heart pounded in her chest like it was going to pop out and stop him. "What are you *saying*? You couldn't just *leave*...Could you?"

"I simply can't do this anymore. I need to get out of this city, to be alone for some time, and think about life."

Her ears filled with the sound of blood pounding, rising. Tears welled up, a sinking feeling hitting her. she put her head in her hands to wipe the tears from her eyes. "Oh, how could you!" Her hands pressured her eyes to wipe the tears down her face.

It was inconceivable. He was the highest ranking official in the strategy of Sen'Drorn! He couldn't simply *leave* now. Not to mention the terrible predicament the nation was in now.

The Sen'Drorn advantage was slipping. Now that the pendant and engineers were gone, so were their primary offensive strategies.

Even their resources, stable for a century, were threatened. The Meruyan who farmed their lands had ceased production and were now in open rebellion. The production of fresh goods to the city had been stalled for weeks. The people of Sen'Drorn were noticing and were asking questions.

Emperor Ryogrim had sent extra forces to regain order, but that meant the planned raid on Sen'Prin would not happen. The Sen'Drorn had been close to being ready to launch an assault on the Sen'Prin, a thorn in their side and threat to their way of life, and now they were running behind. The attacks had been pushed off indefinitely.

The Sen'Prin had split off from the Sen'Drorn and caused much chaos nearly twenty years ago. They didn't want to use the Meruyan resources for prosperity, but where had it gotten them? A life of survival. Like animals. Of course, the Sen'Drorn couldn't let them get away and ruin life for them as well. That's why the Sen'Prin had to be destroyed. Yulah hadn't been born during that time, but she had been a good student, she knew the history like any good Sen'Drorn child.

Malotus shook his head. "It wasn't just the fruit, I don't like who you are becoming, Yulah. You always held me back from my own acts of terror. I could rely on you to keep me in check. You have improved me, don't you see?"

Yulah shook her head. She couldn't be hearing this. Was he leaving her? Like her parents...It stung her deep inside: She knew they were dead, but in a way, it was the same. They had to go and die, and leave her alive, in need, alone.

"Mal, don't you see?" she appealed. "You were right, nobody can be trusted."

"Yulah, oh." Malotus said painfully and stared deep into her eyes. Her veins tingled with the way he said it, like a zap to her heart. "Don't become bitter like me. Unable to forgive or move on with my life. I kept myself down, I was the cause of my own unhappiness all these years."

"But uncle!"

That summer, it was like her world had come crashing down. Flax had left, he had broken her heart and double-crossed her. Malotus had been right all along; about people, about love. They were selfish, looking to gain, and then destroy each other. Her fingers plunged into her long hair and stroked it nervously. "Where will, or can, you go?" she asked him. "A Sen'Drorn village?"

"No. I don't know...somewhere I can go by myself, away from others. I wanted to say goodbye to you. Ever since I ate the fruit, I realized I was only causing harm. I need a break."

Malotus stood up and hugged her, which she was not expecting, but so needed in that moment. "My final advice to you Yulah, is don't let your mind consume you. Separate yourself from your mind, watch the thoughts that flow through it. It will allow you to think before reacting. That is how I have stayed calm under pressure all these years."

Then he went to the windowsill, where a beautiful view of the city below awaited.

"Grimley, come."

The green algae-tufted falcon screeched and flew from his perch to Malotus's level horns, protruding along the line of his shoulders, out of his black mane.

Yulah fell dumbstruck as Malotus flung himself from the window. He pulled wind from the air as he fell, diving toward the ground before swooping back up and rising over the city, Grimley flapping at his side. Yulah rushed to the window, a pain tightening in her, nervous, panic, as his form became smaller, until he was nothing but a distant speck.

What did he mean, watch your thoughts? As she questioned it, the sudden awareness of her own pain, noticing it, caused a startling change. To notice the feeling of her own pain, while she felt it, made it distant, leave with the shrinking speck of her mentor and only friend. What was this?

She watched the great winds above the city wall bending away for the General to pass. The never-ceasing hurricane which surrounded Sen'Drorn for defense, making it nearly impossible to leave the city. They wouldn't know they were letting a traitor pass, in the act of abandoning his post.

Her view became obscured by her tears, her legs like noodles, and she could stand no longer. She slid to the floor, cradled by the lower lip where the wall met the stone floors. The familiar metallic-earthy scent of the stone comforted her.

From sorrow, a rage began to bubble inside. *How could he leave me?*

And what would the Sen'Drorn do without their leader, their General, at a time like this?

How selfish of Uncle.

Cowardly.

She had fought Malotus's pessimistic beliefs all her life, and now... now she wanted to scream—pressure from inside demanding an outlet. It rang in her ears and she took a strange pleasure in the pain.

Then, another flicker bubbled up inside her. Watching it happen. How pathetic she looked on the floor like that. How weak she was. Did she have to stay that way? Noticing it, Malotus had been right. A wedge was created, just enough.

Scowling in indignation, she trembled to her feet, snatched up a lamp from his desk, and threw it with all her might until the satisfaction of its smash brought sweet release. She shoved the papers to the ground, toppled Grimley's wooden stand. She threw the books from their shelves.

"I'll show you control!" she screamed to nobody and continued to let out her rage. Panting, looking around at the destruction. A momentary clarity spoke to her, that she would have to clean this up, as his assistant. But then, without him, was she anyone now? Would she be dismissed from the inner council without General Malotus to serve? As the ward of a traitor, it could be worse even.

When she finally calmed down, she looked through stinging eyes at his oaken desk. She thought she'd cleared it of its contents, and yet there was something there. A folder, clinging, right there on the oak desk. *How curious.*

Upon closer inspection, she found a thick nail fastening it to the desk. Her cheeks burned with embarrassment. He knew her rages and had planned for this. She opened it and gave it a browse, her eyes widening with shock, then fresh tears.

Malotus a plan for everything.

CHAPTER TWO

It was a particularly chilly autumn morning. When Meleena left her family cottage, the ground was covered in multicolored leaves. Streaks of fog clung to the hills and blurred the sun, obscuring the sky into a bright white flurry.

A season had now passed since the summer of the Journey of Future Leaders and of her big adventure among the Warix. Meleena headed into the forest, passing yellow leaves clinging to trees like golden flakes, many of which littered the ground already, crusted in ice in the perpetual shade. Her blue ponytail bobbed behind her head, pulling lightly at her scalp as she hopped over quick-growth mushrooms as they popped through the amber leaf-covered ground. Everything smelled of fresh dampness, igniting her spirits. She needed to get away today and do something strenuous. She was too frustrated.

She took an unusual route, hoisting herself up with curling roots for support, up the hill towards a ridge on the mountainside. Her thickly wound kelpweave pant-stitching stretched uncomfortably, the semi-aquatic fabric was not made for climbing. She removed a knife from her bag and cut them off at the thigh there and then. She was already barefoot, so why not?

Despite the chilly air, her hands and feet remained comfortable. She'd come to know it was safe to be barefoot, and easier to maneuver than in the rudimentary Warix-made rope shoes Meruyan normally wore on land. Since shoes weren't natural to her kind; they had always been barefoot since the days underwater. Meruyan didn't store heat in their extremities, thus they stayed warm even when exposed like that.

From the canyon top, she took note of the vantage point and adjusted her thin-framed glasses as she spotted where to go next. There—loose soil was flinging through the air—a creature.

She crept closer to find it was coming from a hollow log: whiplike orange creatures with glass wings were digging out their winter dens. *First reward for the climb,* she thought, stretching them in her notebook.

A line of them came from all directions, holding tiny mushrooms in their claws to bring into finished parts of the burrows. Meleena pinched off a few small mushrooms to help their efforts along, tumbling them into the nest.

One of them made a rattling noise and she hopped back, dropping her journal to the floor with a soft plop, as her hands shot up to block the syrup that squirted from its long nose.

"Eww, thanks," she mused and wiped the sticky syrup into a cluster of wet leaves. "It's okay, no thank you needed."

At least it didn't hit my journal.

This one still bore the clay and shell cover that her mother had given her upon the start of the Journey of Future Leaders apprenticeship. It was a fond reminder that her mother understood her more than she ever realized. Since that journal had been mostly destroyed, she'd fastened the cover to a new stack of pages to create this fresh one. The pages had since been filled with new drawings, memories of every creature and plant she could recall from the journey, and time away from her home village, Pontai'Desa.

She trekked further into the white-gold autumn forest, stashing her journal in a satchel as she climbed up a steep slope her arms brushing between the silky-smooth tree barks, her mind slipping into the swimming, frustrated thoughts she was trying to avoid.

Word of her summer adventures on the Journey of Future Leaders had spread fast among the Meruyan villagers. They now wanted to learn about nature from her. How she'd broken out of a Warix prison with just seeds, survived the forest of moving trees, and ridden a cactus creature. All these things she had done with knowledge of the wild, which the other Meruyan had never known they had been missing out on. She had even grown a plant from a Legendary Pendant.

They'd asked her to teach a class in the local community space. It was better than the way they'd treated her before all her adventures, and certainly helped with her shyness in front of others. But it was not why she had stayed behind, certainly not what she'd turned down the council apprenticeship for. She had not expected to be stuck for so long in her village. By now...well, she'd expected to be with the Sen'Prin Warix.

At the very least, nobody bothered her about taking up any trade skill, yet suddenly, having as much time to journal as she wanted just seemed like far too much.

Thoughts of her friends, Deem and Talla, swam into her mind. They were also locals of her village of aquatic Meruyan people. She wondered how they were doing in the capital city, Dlawn'Edo, apprenticing for the Meruyan Council. They, who'd been on the journey with her, had *not* turned down the finest opportunity known to her kind.

Meleena stopped trudging a moment to give her legs a break and catch her breath, sloshing mud now under her feet, wet between her toes. She rested a hand on a black and white striped tree.

The thoughts returned. She had finally bothered to make some friends, and now they weren't even around. Though Deem, who she was closer to, returned occasionally on breaks and she would visit him at his family's farm underwater, which helped her practice speaking more fluently in the ancestral Meruyan tongue. Growing up on the shore, she had only recently realized she'd spent a lifetime speaking the Warix common tongue, brought by the original Warix colonizers.

Meleena glimpsed a flock of birds racing by, long legs bouncing under their soft bodies. She adjusted her fine-framed glasses for a better look, then took out her journal and turned to a blank page to half-heartedly began a new sketch, but it did not distract her as hoped.

Guilt twisted in her. She was happy for her friend's success, but she still felt utterly alone. It was not what she had signed up for when she turned down the apprenticeship of her own people for Governess Arenay. And yet, Meleena hadn't heard anything from the Sen'Prin leaders in weeks, despite waiting patiently on their word. They went up and vanished from her life, leaving her alone, increasingly unsure of herself and her future.

It was unnerving to say the least. She would have to answer for her decisions soon. Her parents were already complaining about it. Perhaps they were wondering if she'd made up most of, if not the whole, story.

Meleena peeked between ashen-purple leaved trees and glimpsed the top of the ridge. A view awaited, and she sat on the ledge and stared out the vast landscape, letting her feet dangle. She took a deep, full breath of the brisk air to quell her racing heart.

She thought of the other friend she'd met, Flax, a boy her age from a land race known as Warix, who could sense and control the wind through their horns. She had met Flax that past summer, briefly in the Meruyan capital, and then again in Sen'Drorn prison. He'd discovered his love of engineering and returned to his home city, Sen'Prin, after spying on Sen'Drorn. Meleena had helped him reunite with his long-lost father.

What was he up to now? She had lost touch with him after the summer.

Sen'Prin, which meant "loyal to the people," opposed the Sen'Drorn, meaning "loyal to the state", both nations of Warix. The Sen'Drorn had been exploiting her own people, The Meruyan, for cheap labor to produce resources, and together with Flax, she had escaped the Sen'Drorn prison, rescued his father, and helped her people start a revolution.

It was slow going. All that she knew about the Meruyan political situation came from Deem, who filled her in on his visits. What she knew was that the Hyish, a reptilian race, had built a tunnel which penetrated the mountain range, which separated the Meruyan from the Warix nations. This feat had never been accomplished before. And now, the Hyish were beginning to trade with the Meruyan, a historical first which was slowly improving the Meruyan livelihood. Pearls and shells were in high demand among the Hyish, who'd only newly discovered this arts and crafts commodity.

Meleena smiled to herself. *They really did love their shiny things.*

And it had saved her people. Not like the Sen'Drorn were taking it lying down, the gradual loss of willing Meruyan workers. They'd tried tightening their enforcers, but without workers, they had little power. Meleena was eager to hear any updates on the situation from Deem, and felt frustratingly behind all the time.

But here she was, locked out, trapped as a choice of her own devices. A bubbling panic over her purpose and future threatened from the pits of her stomach, churning from self-doubt into anger at herself.

Pontai'Desa, which always seemed too small for Meleena, was painfully suffocating now, after everything she'd learned of the world. Even journaling, which she used to enjoy, and now had all the time to spend on it, was now losing its spark.

A breeze swept through, pushing the pages of her journal onto a previous entry from some weeks back. She paused her drawing to read it. It was a picture of a kelpie horse, the typical Meruyan companion animal, sporting iridescent curving coral-like antlers.

The margins recorded a moment in time she'd had some weeks before: *Talla was in town and joined my lesson on Kelpies today.* The simple cartoon face of Talla sported a shocked expression and a speech bubble; *"Why won't Clover let me ride him!?"* The words 'mating season antlers' pointed with an arrow at his new growth. At the bottom: *Talla's not a natural, but she's come a long way.*

Meleena laughed at the sweet memory, one she'd never expected to have with Talla, her rival through the years at the schoolhouse.

She held her journal aloft as she read, when something outside its pages struck her attention. Purple wisps of smoke were rising around her, and she lowered the journal and looked around. The purple mist began to thicken, obscure her vision, burn as it came into her lungs, making her cough.

Spores!

Looking around, she found herself surrounded by a large hooded mushroom creature. It uttered a loud squeak as it released more purple dust from its pores and Meleena jumped up and staggered back. "Ouch!" something poked her in the back, and she realized she'd stumbled into some kind of wall of thorns. Or was it horns? Spines? It seemed to be held together by a scaly carapace.

"Is that a stalagmite?" she said aloud. She hadn't been this far up the mountain before but didn't recall any cave. She ran her fingers over the glossy red-grey surface. Steam escaped from the small cave.

Whatever it was, it was shifting. The living wall of thorns began to grow around her, sweeping her what were appeared to be pincers, opened wide, and Meleena froze, eight yellow eyes opening like gashes from the carapace, and they were transfixed on her. Her veins shot with adrenaline.

It was time to run. But she couldn't. Her body had frozen in fear.

She could only stare at the powerful jaws, the slathering teeth, skinny insect legs suspending it above the ground. She had never seen this creature before.

***

Yulah paced Malotus's former office, now her own. She had not yet forgiven him for leaving. But it was her prerogative to continue on and utilize anything in his things that could be helpful to her as new General.

She had discovered something of interest while going through his desk drawers. They were torn journal pages, a sketchbook. The pages were round and had been formerly contained in a clamshell cover. Clearly the work of a Meruyan.

Glancing at the scattered pages in front of her, they bore a theme. All were drawings and features of wild beasts and exotic plants, some an indistinguishable medley of both.

Malotus had confiscated the journal of a young Meruyan once. He'd found it in the Northern Hilly Villages, the biggest resources district for the city of Sen'Drorn. Her current problem. The sketchbook had belonged to one of the future Meruyan council apprentices, which would be the main reason someone would be traveling there. But why all the pictures of land animals? None of that made sense to her. General Malotus had in fact, officially given back what was left of the journal.

Evidently, he had kept some pages.

As General he was in charge of tactics, and he got to order and give direction for new supplies and elite forces. This included the design of new military technology.

He had most definitely seen value in these pages.

The elemental qualities of the creatures, guesses and explanations of their ecosystems. It could be a way to a new technology. She would need a skilled eye to look at these and make sense of how, exactly.

Most of the engineers had broken out of the Sen'Drorn work camp some months ago, and the military were currently stalled on tech, racing to train and find new Warix to fill the ranks from the city.

But Yulah, secretly knew an engineer, still of loyalty to her. It would remain her secret—Ryogrim could not know her secret recipe for success, bombing the Sen'Prin to keep them on their toes.

She dialed an identifier on her wristcom.

Her confidant picked up.

"Yes, I need you to...I have some pages for you. I can describe them best I can, but you may have to find a way to pick them up for yourself. I see. Yes, I have them right here...Excellent."

She described them to her confidant. "It says here that animals aren't born with plants on them, but acquired them from what's around. The creatures have special receptive cells in certain spots on their bodies depending on species, and thus accumulate them while young, and they live with the plants in a mutually beneficial way.

"So, the plants gain a home which helps with seed dispersal, and the animals gain protection, camouflage, and even sustenance from absorbing the plants. There're also some river creatures, who are sometimes in water and do both. Like neutolyth, kelpie. Small frogs. Some plants are rooted in the animal and also gain nutrients from them, while most are like moss, which sticks on but can be plucked off when desired and regrows. Some animals are general in their species acquisition, while some are specialized plant combos that are only found together, highly specialized species that co evolved. Some animals have a lot of space for plants, some few. Like just a mane and tail."

Like Malotus's pet falcon, thought Yulah.

"Yes, we could use this. This is where our domesticated breeds come from, you say? Ah, yes, like the Bramble sheep. So, our ancestors already have known some of this for a long time. Delicately spliced creatures to hold berries and fruit...but how can we weaponize this feature?

Though most of this made little practical sense to her, her engineering counterpart was a natural at turning this strange eco knowledge into tech. It had been difficult to trust and form this partnership, but this knowledge in their hands yielded amazing results. They'd created explosions, droughts, all to set back the progress of Sen'Prin. The sabotage of their small villages was working, and the Emperor was impressed and baffled by how Yulah was doing all of this.

"There's a Meruyan girl *there*? She must be the very same. You should collect any more information from her notes that you can, and I'll do my best on this end to acquire more. I would destroy what you find as well, we don't want her figuring out what we have been up to here. We don't need that info getting out. I shall help you from here how I can."

Yulah stood and stared out the window.

"…thanks for all you have done here. You will be greatly rewarded by Sen'Drorn. You are too kind."

In the meantime, she thought she'd found a way to use her elite agents, gear promised by her only other ally.

CHAPTER THREE

The insect held Meleena in its pinchers: a giant crab covered in prickly spines, which despite its large size, had blended right into the cliffs behind it.

Meleena scolded herself. *How could she lose her nerves like this?*

Then a chilly breeze made her shiver…The monster was unperturbed.

The wind blew, seemingly directed. The creature staggered back, its plethora of slit eyes closing tight against the wind. Suddenly, a spear sailed and wedged into the pincer, narrowly missing Meleena's body tight within its grasp.

"Wha—" Meleena let out a cry of disbelief.

The wind continued to thrash, dazing the beast. A pair of hands grabbed for the spear and pulled it from the wound, then began repeatedly whacking at the pincer that had trapped her. These were not the blue hue of Meruyan hands as she had known most of her life. They were light brown, that of a forest person, a Warix.

"Meleena!" came a shocked voice.

"Flax!?" she called out in confusion.

"I'll try get you out! Aren't you supposed to be the expert? How do you fight this thing?"

"What are you doing here?"

"Well apparently rescuing you from your own forest."

"I've never seen one of these before..." she grumbled, gazing at the creature. "Maybe try to spear at the eyes to scare it off?"

"Oh, good thinking," he called out. With all his strength he thrust the spear at the tender eye slits between the thick carapace. The creature let out a wailing moan and snapped open its pincer, just long enough for Meleena to jump to the floor and tumble a safe distance away from the beast.

"Let it go!" she scolded firmly, "Now!" and the beast recoiled its body to protect its watering eyes. Sure enough, as the image of Flax came into sight, the thing skittered away straight up the cliff wall behind it and out of sight.

Meleena worked to catch her breath. Flax reached out a hand and helped her up, velvety tan skin brushing against her. She didn't need the hand and resented taking it. "I would have gotten out myself," she murmured. "If you hadn't come along."

Flax was working to suppress a friendly grin. He lifted bulky copper goggles to his forehead, where they rested against the base of his horns.

It was then that she noticed Flax's gloved hand. He was wearing quite an ensemble in fact. Copper laced in intricate swirls like those found on a seashell, wrapping around gears ordaining the matching gloves and boots. He wore a vest of copper as well, with four copper spirals forming mirror images of each other on the front of his chest.

"It's nice to see you again," she said, looking him over, her lip forming a half smile.

"Likewise," he grinned, letting the shock of their reunion hang in the air. He smelled of leather, copper, and pine.

"What's with the fancy gear?" she indicated, subverting the subject.

"Oh this?" he asked, holding up his arm. "It's experimental new tech, best we have. I designed it with my father. The copper tubing amplifies my wind power with less effort. It was enough for me to fly here from Sen'Prin city within a day, fastest yet, and should be okay to carry a passenger as well."

Meleena nodded. The whole outfit was beautiful, clearly a masterwork. Borak, Flax's father, is an impressive artist and engineer after all.

The Warix Flax stood before her, a head taller than herself, with small horns skimming over his smooth dark brown hair, the color of...well, that deep brown space between distant, dense foliage. His large brown eyes showed concern, but also humor. She felt her cheeks go hot, embarrassed to be caught in such a situation.

"You sure were hard to find..." Flax started. "How do you decide where to go around here, anyway?" he asked, gazing perplexedly around at the bristling, white-bark golden leaf forest.

A warm wave of gratitude washed over Meleena. "I just *ask* the forest. When I uh, enter, I thank the trees for being there, for letting me into their space. I send them love, and surrender. I let a sort of *feeling* guide me," she said, teasingly.

He gave her an even more perplexed stare.

"I'm joking, I go wherever I feel like," she added with a shrug.

It didn't matter what he thought. She was in the habit of keeping these things secret from others, not that they ruin the magic with their disapproving or lack of understanding.

She shrugged. "I always find interesting things this way," she continued. Typical, but she was trying to make a habit of opening up these days. "I send my gratitude back when I leave. It makes my vision brighter and appreciate the little things more."

Flax looked around some more and Meleena patted the dirt from her clothes, now partly regretting opening up. "So, is this a social visit?" she asked.

"That is very cool, you will have to show me some time." He then said, triggering a wave of satisfaction washing over her. She simply nodded.

He crossed his arms, grinning. "I did come here on business actually."

Meleena's heart skipped a beat. Is this really happening now? After so long, waiting.

He was dressed in short sleeved linen tunic and slacks, and in all he blended in with the stark orange, golden, white, black, ashen dim purples and pouty puckered pinks of the autumn forest. She was always in awe of how much the Warix matched the forest. Another reminder that she, a blue Meruyan, was not native here. To land, at all, as a matter of fact. Though she lived and breathed to understand the mysteries of the forest and its creatures, she was always an outsider. Perhaps that was where the allure came from.

"You're looking healthier," Meleena noted letting her lip form a half smile. "Last time I saw you, you were limping, and couldn't even use wind with your horns cut off."

It was the first time, watching him stand there before her, that she started to notice that Flax was quite well-built: handsome, even. His bare arms showed muscle definition. Then there was his naturally serious resting expression and strong jaw. The sides of his eyes crinkling when he invited humor.

"Do you have any idea how hard you are to find?" he asked, now more sternly. "I've been looking all over town for you. Your mother told me to check the forest, as if that is an easy task. I trekked through here for ages, and was just about to give up, when I took to the air, and saw a small blue figure against the cliffs here."

"Apologies, I wasn't expecting any visitors," she said, starting to sound rather cross. "I haven't heard from the Sen'Prin at all in weeks." Anger rose in her to combat the predicament.

"Sketching, as always, huh?" he asked, and held up her journal and began to browse the pages. She had dropped it during the attack and had only now realized it had fallen to the ground. "You are a great artist, I'll give you that."

"Illustrator," she corrected.

"Huh?"

"An artist uses their imagination. I don't deserve that kind of credit. I merely sketch my surroundings," she said, her cheeks growing hot.

"Illustrator. Naturalist. Anyway," he bit his lip, nervously. "If you are still interested, I am here for that purpose. Arenay has an assignment in need of your skills and sent me to summon you as soon as possible."

"Summon me? To Sen'Prin?" The blood drained from her face. The moment she'd been waiting for. "Is it about finding more seeds, like the Pendant one? The beast with the seeds on its back that the wind spirit had mentioned when hers was destroyed…?"

"We have more urgent matters right now, I'm afraid," he said, and handed her a paper from his pocket. "I, uh, also wanted to say something personal- to thank you for your help this summer. I would never have gotten my father back or probably even escaped the Sen'Drorn prison without you."

Meleena was glad to have helped Flax reunite with his father. She was also fond of the old Warix and would ask about him when they had a free moment.

Now she stared at the paper. The image sent a shiver down her spine and tightened her windpipe. "How did it get like this? So burnt…and those poor Warix."

Flax sighed and scratched his left horn. "Yeah…we are in quite a predicament. This was a Sen'Prin village. We don't have many villages, as it's risky, but vital in order not to depend on Meruyan labor like the Sen'Drorn do."

Meleena had never thought of that before. How the Sen'Prin get resources and keep them, with Sen'Drorn threatening to destroy anything they built.

"This town grows a special fast-growing bamboo, which we use for all kinds of construction. We don't know how the explosion happened, which took out many crops, but we have seen some strange plant behavior around it. That's why we need you to come take a look. If you accept."

"Yeah, I mean, sure. Are we going there today?" She'd assumed he had come to deliver a message and perhaps they'd continue to check in on her from time to time with updates. Or something like that?

"Yes, though it will be a longer assignment. You will be working for us until we solve this. A few weeks perhaps."

"Okay, I accept," she nodded, slowly, tentatively. Her heart beat faster again. She didn't know what this meant exactly.

"I present you with this, too." He handed over a small object. It was the same as the ones she had seen many Warix wear, as well as her brothers working for the Meruyan capital. "Since you will work with our team, you will need your own wristcom. Standard issue among recruits. Now you can connect with the team."

"Thank you," she said, strapping it to her wrist and inspecting the whirring gears.

"You will need a Warix to help wind it up with fresh wind energy every few hours. Other than that, you can make calls to others with one, as well as record short voice notes," Flax said, indicating the dials.

Meleena was surprised by the necessity of Warix interaction for continued use. She thought of her brothers, who both had acquired wristcoms, and nobody to call but each other.

"Now, if you will take my hand, I will carry us out of here. We just need to find a flat clearing where I can take off," said Flax.

"Wait, we are going from here?" her head spun.

"Well, yeah," Flax said with a shrug. "I already stopped by your house. Your parents know the situation. We can go to the site directly."

Meleena gazed at the horizon beyond the peaks. "But..." she stuttered, not expecting any of this right now. "I'm not even wearing any foot-coverings! What about my stuff?"

"Err..." Flax looked at her feet, then made a face of concern. "I'll just have to order you some proper Warix boots... eh, custom, for Meruyan feet."

She noted, that as Warix walked on the balls of their feet, much like a canine, they had a differently shaped boot than her.

Meleena nodded. "Right then. I don't presume you have any sort of craft to get us there?"

Flax looked at the bush. "Oh well, right behind there! Eh, no I don't. I *did* once have a wind powered motorbike, which my father and I had altered, but it crashed into a swamp." He smiled in guilty-jest.

She flicked some hair away from her face to stare at him for any indication of a joke.

He shrugged. "...for a good cause. I have yet to rebuild it, thanks for the reminder."

"Okay, then, I guess if that's everything..." said Meleena, still not entirely convinced she was ready to ride in another Warix tornado.

Ah, Warix wind power. Meleena had mixed feelings about it. The residual memory of the Sen'Drorn, of the intimidating General Malotus, and how her first experiences being carried by their wind had been against her will. Since then she had gotten used to its productive uses by allied Warix but the notion still made her stomach flip with unease.

Flax spoke into his own wristcom to send out a message. "Kyra, I have found Meleena and we are on our way." Flax must have gotten a new one, since his original had been destroyed by the Sen'Drorn.

"Kyra?" Meleena asked.

"She works in the Sen'Prin crime division and Governess Arenay has assigned her as captain of the newly formed squad to investigate this unusual disaster. You will report to her and the others in the team. Anyway, this looks like a good spot to launch us. You will learn more when we arrive."

Flax fitted the goggles from his forehead, then palms outstretched, he gathered the air beneath him as it whipped around them. Meleena's wild blue tendrils of hair wavering in the wind.

"Here we go..." she grumbled uneasily. Another Warix wind tornado. She was not at ease with this form of travel, regardless of the efficient result.

Flax sank into a crouch and she held right against his torso as he launched them skyward in a puff of wind that carried them soon over the trees, a bushy quilt of deep purples, greens, oranges and away to unknown lands. The wind haze of the tornado made her skin shudder, from the chill and the thrill of such an unnatural viewpoint… that and Flax was the only entity keeping her from plunging to her death.

CHAPTER FOUR

Meleena watched the trees merge into a mass of entangled forest, hills leading to mountain slopes to the north. For a moment, she glimpsed Dlawn'Edo, the glorious Meruyan capital, with its cascading waterfall and mountain lake shrinking into a speck on the vast green landscape.

Carried along in the tornado, the horizon changed from lush forests to rolling hills as they headed eastward. They traveled southerly to avoid the Sen'Drorn territory, until at last the eastern mountain chain containing Sen'Prin city appeared on the horizon. To see how her village, for so long her whole world, connected to everywhere else, widened her whole perspective.

Of course, for the Warix it was natural to travel so far. The ability to manipulate the wind gave them so much power over the world on land. For a Meruyan, traveling across mountains, or far from any ocean, was just plain unheard of. It made her uneasy, how the Warix control over land compared to her own people.

As they headed eastward, they passed sprawling green hills, turning to sunlit plains, streaked with curling green bamboo crop, where they began to lower in altitude.

Meleena let out a gasp and the town came into view. Her body tensed, nervous at the landing. Flax held her in his arms, keeping her safe as they flew. She pressed against his soft yet strong torso to keep stable against the churning tornado winds. She'd never felt an attraction to someone's body before and pushed it away. She wasn't *into* him. But what if there was a chance *he* saw *her* that way? She wanted to be respected, as a friend and colleague. The idea of her body as feminine or a distraction made her uneasy. She took a deep breath, pushing away the discomfort to focus on the view.

They flew over dense bamboo which had grown into large groves. As they approached, she saw that a giant blackened smudge replaced a chunk of it, reducing it to a smoldering ruin. They were heading right for this dark patch.

They descended, revealing the outline of ruined buildings blown to their bases, which marked the center of a small town at the center of the blowout.

Meleena's feet finally touched the ground, and she breathed deeply in relief. Would she ever get used to traveling by air?

They were in the ruins of the Sen'Prin town— burnt and warped bamboo was lying everywhere in disarray. A Warix woman was awaiting them. With a shock of cropped pale purple hair and upward pointed copper-capped horns, she stood on the broad stairs of the largest ruined building. She smiled and gave a stern nod as they approached. "Chief officer Kyra, Sen'Prin crime. Nice to meet you, Meleena," she said. "Thank you for bringing her, Flax."

"And you," Meleena replied, and automatically rotated her hands in a swirling motion, as was the customary Meruyan greeting. Kyra knitted her brow, apparently confused.

Stupid, why did I do that? thought Meleena, realizing she was now among another culture. Meleena returned the nod, and Kyra smiled.

"Welcome to the team. I'm glad you have accepted our summons," Kyra said, making firm eye contact, head bowing in another nod.

Was this the Warix greeting? She'd have to ask Flax about their customs later. How had she not learned this last time? It struck her just how brief and distant her time among them had been.

"It's my pleasure," said Meleena. "I have been waiting for a call from Arenay." She adjusted her glasses and tucked her own hair behind her ear. "I heard she's not going to be joining us today."

"Correct," Kyra said. "She's busy leading the Sen'Prin in many matters. I am going to be doing my best as team captain, to figure out who burnt down our farms and village."

The place was deserted.

"Where are the people?" asked Meleena.

"We evacuated them, after survivors called in to report the attack," said Kyra. "They had been huddled curiously around the site," added Flax. "It was mayhem. Better to have missed it. They're now taken in by the next village until we figure out what to do."

Meleena looked around, confused. "But how is it, with the Sen'Drorn hunting your people, to have villages out in the open like that?"

"The Sen'Prin have been slowly taking over Sen'Drorn villages," explained Flax. "Converting them to our side, and we guard them. It weakens our enemy and gives us a better foothold, with more land, resources and people. They want to join us, if we can protect them. Usually, we do a good job of it, as the push and pull for territory goes. But this – it's almost like the Sen'Drorn have used some new technology, some new weapon, to destroy this village by fire..."

"Come," Kyra motioned, moving gracefully as she guided them up the stairs. Long and slim yet muscular limbs to be envied, and Meleena had an urge to draw her, like one of her rare forest creatures. Her skin a pale-purple, hair just a little darker, had been cut very short, which highlighted upward curving horns, tipped in copper fitted coverings. A glinting copper collar over her maroon uniform shirt indicated some kind of official rank. She wore a firm, confident expression, yet her eyes were kind. Multiple copper raindrop piercings garnished her pointed ears.

"As you can see, we grow quite a lot of bamboo here. It's integral to the Sen'Prin way of life. Fast growing, we make everything, from structures, to food, to furniture from it. We even eat the seeds, a staple crop in many of our dishes. We call it bristlenut."

"Oh yeah, you should try the noodles," added Flax.

"Oh, interesting," said Meleena. "I have not tried any Warix food, I suppose."

It came as a shock, but it hit her uncomfortably, how little she actually knew of their civilization.

"Please, let me show you around," Kyra said, gesturing to the ruined buildings around them. 'As you might have seen when you flew in, we have a very plentiful acreage. What happened here is a shocking disaster. We don't even know what technology they used to do this, which makes it particularly devastating."

Kyra turned to the building up the stairs. "This mill was the center of the explosion. We still don't know the cause of it but have noticed since the incident that there are some strange natural phenomenon here. You come with quite the accolades from Arenay."

At this, Meleena was quite shocked. How flattering, Arenay did remember her after all.

Meleena followed Kyra through the wreckage of a building. It was a processing mill, where the plants would have been taken for cleaning and rendering into materials. Large sawing instruments, oversized blades, now blackened, lay on their sides. There were crates ready for shipment, which had blasted open, spilling, now unusable, contents. Other Warix, about her age, were on the scene, already hard at work-some cleaning up and some organizing samples.

"You see," Kyra explained, "The Sen'Drorn has taken most of the good resources known around our part of the world. We have taken back some of their towns, defended them heavily, which is risky and costs much resources. Thus, the best way to obtain vital resources and expand has been to find places that are naturally well protected, often dangerous, and get creative with our crops. The bamboo, integral to our success, is for the first time threatened. We cannot withstand more attacks like this. We must find out how the Sen'Drorn have done this, and how to stop them. We have no leads yet, but the team I've assembled are working on that."

"Over there is Naia, field apprentice in engineering, and a tinkerer," Kyra said, indicating to a petite, dark-haired Warix girl with her back to them, crouched on the ground. She was bottling scraps and wielding an oversized backpack, which blocked much of her from view.

Another Warix, a male, large in frame with bright orange hair and a thick beard, was carrying something large, blackened, to the pile. Cloth covered large lumps. A sinking feeling ran through Meleena as she realized what it was: the crisp, charred remains of Warix citizens. "That's Riigs, doing the heavy lifting. He's also got a good head on his shoulders," indicated Kyra. "No better medic around."

There was a slim Warix guy, with bright yellow hair like piled leaves. He was looking around, eyes narrowed with his hand to his chin as he studied the scene.

"Young Zoltan is my promising apprentice from the crime division. Then there's Jessup over there, our data compiler and number cruncher." Kyra indicated to a long gossamer red haired Warix, who'd been taking notes on the scene in a ledger. "She's new to the team like you, having grown up in the villages. She also knows a thing about agriculture, which will prove useful."

Another Warix came out from behind a pillar, startling Meleena. He was covered in ash from head to toe. His fingers scratched at his messy mop of brown hair, releasing some of the ash in a cascade on the floor. Something about him seemed familiar.

"Kyra!" he moaned. "There were no clues in the air shafts."

"*Thian*," Kyra said flatly, to Meleena, hands moving instinctively her hips. "Hyish culture and communications specialist. He serves as coordinator with headquarters."

"Just a fancy term for 'errand boy'," Thian corrected with a lazy smirk, then his green eyes lit up at the sight of her. "Meleena!"

"Oh, I know you," she smiled. They'd been through quite a lot together. Turning to Kyra she said, "Thian rescued me once from Sen'Drorn City."

"Ah, you did the hard part first, busting out of prison with Flax," Thian said with a deep nod of respect. He had his arms folded, and a smirk, and shook more ash from his disheveled hair.

The group had noticed their interaction, but Kyra commanded them with a stern look, indicating to continue working. "Flax will mostly be in the tech lab, analyzing our samples. I'll give you all a proper introduction soon," she said to the team. Turning back to Meleena, "When we are back from our tour, they should be finishing up their work. Better they stay focused for now. I'll take you now to see the grove."

Flax joined them as Meleena followed Kyra out, walking through the burnt area to the fringes of bamboo grove.

Something was immediately unsettling. Her hair tingled, itched, as if its ability to draw energy from the sun were disturbed.

"What do you think?" asked Kyra, intense in her unwavering stare.

Something was floating in the air, glistening in the sun and catching her eye. What was that? Something smelled like burnt moss, it was painfully off-putting. Another shiver. Meleena caught it in her hands. It formed a sticky grey gunk she had trouble getting off her fingers.

"Yes, we don't know what that is, but we have seen it around here a lot since this happened."

They came to a spot where the bamboo grove and wild forest came together. The bamboo shoots grew in squiggly, elegant curls, like hair growing to the sky.

Meleena turned her attention on the forest. Kyra her gave a puzzled look.

Unfamiliar creatures clung to the trees, staring back at her from the safety of their perches. Their fur green like moss, was singed black. Worse, patches were missing, like it had fallen out in clumps.

Meleena's stomach clenched. That couldn't be good.

She moved closer, inspecting the trees, broad arms providing ample shade. The timid creatures fled at her approach, deeper into the forest, on silent limbs. The absence of sound from the forest in general was noticeable. Shouldn't there be insects chirping? Birds calling?

Something crunched under her feet, so she crouched down to get a better look. She recognized this type of tree, with the striped bark of purple and white.

"Strange..." she explained to Kyra. "All these seed pods have fallen to the ground at once. That shouldn't be. They are supposed to ripen and fall slowly over the whole season."

It was almost as if they were in a rush to drop everything, in critical condition, as if they would soon die. In a way, Meleena could sense the dryness of the area was affecting them harshly.

Kyra knitted her brow with concern. "We hadn't noticed that. I'll get the others to take note and collect some samples. Any ideas why?"

"Well, if they are stressed, or under some strange weather conditions."

"Like really windy?" asked Flax, a bad attempt at a joke.

"Uh, well not exactly," said Meleena, adjusting her glasses. "The burnt village...has there also been a drought or collapse in vegetation here?"

"But this happened overnight," countered Flax, thoughtfully.

"The forest and its creatures are clearly under stress. This would have been over a longer time frame than just one day."

"Fascinating," nodded Kyra, her horns raising and dipping with her head. "This could be a usable lead. How certain are you of this longer drought event leading up to the devastation?"

"Or could the explosion itself have been the only thing?" asked Flax, finishing the thought.

"The explosion was stressful to the forest and creatures, certainly in a dramatic way, but the effects of the disaster on the animals is clearly long-term, like drought," Meleena confirmed and collected a cluster of burnt mossy fur from the ground, shed from a creature.

Kyra put a hand on Flax's shoulder. "Flax works in the tech lab at headquarters, where we will send the samples for analysis."

"At your service. I will analyze the moss fur and gunk particles and see what we get," said Flax.

Kyra smiled for the first time.

They walked back to the main warehouse, where the others were just finishing, looking more casual now than earlier. Riigs had finished collecting the remains for burial and was sitting on the ground next to Naia, chatting.

Zoltan leaned against the last remaining wall, arms folded, with Thian and Jessup standing in a semi-circle around him.

"Here," laughed Thian, tossing a colorful garment at Jessup who held a notepad in her arms, pen poised to write. "This Hyish tunic would fit you nicely!"

"No, I'm not going to wear that!" Jessup giggled, arms outstretched to block it.

"Aww come on," said Thian. "At least write down how frilly they are. I'm telling you, it's going to be important later."

"How does documenting Hyish clothing matter?" Jessup asked in a skeptical, yet amused tone, her head at a tilt.

"I hate to agree with this clown, but he might actually be right," Zoltan said with a shrug, taking the garment. "This is a solid clue and may tell us what encampment it came from."

"Thanks, buddy," Thian laughed.

"Usually, you can safely ignore his suggestions," Zoltan mused, biting back a smile. "We grew up together, I can tell you that for certain."

Meleena felt her otherness for the first time among them. They didn't mean any harm, but it seemed insensitive towards the Hyish. Thian changed the subject as Meleena with Kyra and Flax approached. "Meleena, nice to see you again," Thian said with a grin.

Naia and Riigs got up and joined them as they all gathered around Meleena to see what she'd found.

"Wow a Meruyan!" exclaimed Jessup. Her delicate pale skin, like the bark of a birch tree, including dark gray swirling stripes running all along her skin. Amid her deep red hair the swirls continued as bronze inlaying her horns. A smile formed on her bright red lips. "It's nice to meet another newcomer to the team. It's a little intimidating being new," she admitted, and Meleena liked her at once.

"How do you do?" The petite one, Naia, said with a swish of short black hair, glistening blueish in the light, matching the slight hue of her dark skin. Standing close, Meleena came face to face with a bronze lug nut through her nose, and the tips of her small horns curling around to frame her face.

"It's nice to meet you, Meleena. I look forward to seeing your city and joining your team," said Riigs kindly, hulking at Naia's side. His voice came from a deep place in his chest, naturally booming, yet smooth and sweet of intonation.

"Yo," said Zoltan, his lips pinching as his head bounced lightly in a nod. Zoltan was thin and lanky, with pointed, fine features, horns in the shape of a z, and pale-yellow hair like brilliant fall leaves, long whips on top blowing around in the air. His chin and lips were delicate—there was something almost catlike about him.

Meleena knew the copper and bronze were not only ornamental, but conductive and enhanced the effectiveness of their wind powers by its presence, resonating with the wind, which they sensed through their horns. If a horn was cut, it set them off balance until it grew back days later. She had seen the effects firsthand. It was often cruelly used against prisoners, cutting their horns to prevent escape.

The Warix features, their skin, hair, eyes, and horns, it was like the colors of the forest. Birches of white, deep greens of oaks, bright yellows, more varieties of brown than Meleena knew existed; dark mud to bright reddish. She wondered if they knew how lovely they looked, it both inspired and ashamed her how fascinating she found it. Something so charming that seemingly didn't matter to anyone else. Wasn't that always her lot in life? Her alienating pride and curse.

They all welcomed Meleena in their own ways. Jessup whipped back her hair, Naia sniffled, arms akimbo. Riigs and Thian smiled broadly, though Thian's always crooked with a glint of jest.

"So, did the Meruyan girl find anything?" asked Zoltan, in a skeptical tone, addressing Kyra.

"Indeed," she replied. "I'll need a few spare jars."

"Now that won't be important," Zoltan said, pointing to the various tree nuts in Meleena's hand.

She blushed. "Why not?"

The others giggled and chuckled.

Zoltan shrugged, speaking matter-of-factly. "Because our markets are already full of them. Grown right here."

"Yes, well..." Meleena stood up straighter. "If you have a way to test *these* in particular, it could be helpful."

"I still don't see why—"

"Ah, quiet, Zoltan," Thian chimed in.

"What? We shouldn't waste time on dead ends and lose more time. It's nothing personal," he spoke genuinely, Meleena couldn't fault him for that.

Thian smacked the back of Zoltan's head playfully.

"What!"

"Have some tact man."

"It's alright," Meleena said, "I wouldn't believe me either, but the science will decide. If you are, objective like you say. Nothing personal." Meleena smirked and shrugged back, electricity tingling on her skin. She was actually enjoying this.

Eyes widened and gasps of approval emerged from the rest of the team.

"Ay," a smile crossed Zoltan's lips. He nodded with respect. "Well good luck with it then. And how are you planning to keep up with us without a tornado?"

"Oh, I..." Her victory deflated as her cheeks grew hot. Meleena tried not to let it get to her, struggling with a reply. When she had wanted to work for Arenay and the Sen'Drorn people, she hadn't considered how hard this might be. Was there really a place for her here?

"Ah enough messing with the new girl," argued Thian, then turned to Meleena. "Don't take it so seriously."

Meleena adjusted her glasses, the only one of the group who wore them. Like many Meruyan, she needed them for seeing outside the water clearly, since their eyes were not as well adapted to living on land.

She'd been a loner most of her life. She was different, but knew who she was, and so it had been easier to dismiss others and do things her own way. Only this past summer had she learned the importance of needing others, of accepting friendship and support from others. It was an adjustment. She didn't want to go back to her old ways, but the struggle was real.

Flax put a hand on her shoulder, and they smiled at each other. Meleena felt a warmth run through her, and took a deep relaxing breath, grateful to have him, someone familiar she could trust among the anxiety of so many fresh faces.

"I will carry you, we depart now for Sen'Prin in my tornado, and we will give you the tour of our city, help you settle in, show you where you will stay," said Flax.

"Oh, where am I living now, exactly?" Meleena asked.

"We've got a place for you in Sen'Prin, with the girls. You'll get the full tour of town," he said with a smile.

Kyra sent a questioning glance her way. If Meleena wanted to be on this team, this was the only chance. The others were getting dressed in their travel gear, more of the copper gloves and boots, chest plates, heavy but needed for the journey.

Meleena looked at the others. They seemed friendly enough. Plus, returning to her town would bore her to death if she didn't take the opportunity now. It was just very sudden. She hadn't realized she'd be moving in *today*.

"Of course I'm coming," Meleena declared, heart pounding with a mix of anticipations, slinging her pack over her shoulder.

Kyra handed her a pair of goggles, and said, “Welcome to the team. You’ll need these.”

CHAPTER FIVE

Yulah sat in the grand chair that was once War General Malotus's. His former office had not been delegated yet, though today's meeting would decide this.

She would no longer be a weak, pathetic, slave to her own emotions. How many times had she had been devastated by others? It made her question everything, all her relationships to anyone she'd ever encountered. She hated her uncle Malotus more for not teaching her this concept earlier. Who did he think he was, anyway?

Her thoughts spun as she left for the Emperor's throne room.

Malotus had been right about people, even if he was off questioning it now. She still needed him, but she would have to be her own advisor from now on. She had the capacity for strength, she would show them all.

She strolled the long hallway, scattered pillars casting dramatic contrast of light and dark striped lighting over the marble floors as she looked out over the city. Countless times, she had walked this path with Malotus, often hurrying to keep up with his long strides.

A shiver of longing ran through her. She missed him still. Their banter, his cleverness delivered with that cool kindness, a secret smile. Another emotion like a wave hit, a desire to be more like him. The realization that one could change themselves.

He had left her, but she had herself. She didn't have to hate herself, like she now hated him.

She took her place at the meeting, watching the top advisors take their seats around the semi-circular stone chamber below the black volcanic rock throne of Sen'Drorn. The room had been rebuilt since the fire; trailing streamers depicting the flower-maned lion, the symbol of Sen'Drorn dominance, adorning every corner once again.

His former position of War General would be decided here today. She would get a new direct superior, if they even kept her on as first assistant. For all she knew, she could be out of the fortress and on the streets before nightfall.

I am the victim here—no—I don't have to define myself by anyone else's actions. I can reinvent my own persona, be the person who I most want.

And why not?

She and the council stood as Emperor Ryogrim entered.

She stared at the ceiling, also freshly repaired since that loathsome night, when Flax had tricked her into fleeing with all of Sen'Drorn's top engineers. The memory of it almost sent her reeling again, but she fought to remain calm. Here, in the room with the others, she watched herself with a little smile for the anger had turned to a fire of self-love that burned in her heart.

The elder advisors bickered as a group. She had come to know many of them by their roles over the years. There were nine departments: Resource import; weapons development overseer; agriculture; city affairs including Meruyan migrant workers; financial; defense; Hyish relations; technology & innovation; and war logistics. The last of the roles now empty, without General Malotus, as denoted by the empty seat on Yulah's left. She had formerly been quite literally, his right-hand woman, and Malotus, right hand of The Emperor.

This meant her seat was within spitting distance to the Emperor, who now spoke.

They discussed the power vacuum left by Malotus. Yulah thought about the weight of this responsibility. These advisors were all begging for it. What she saw as burden, they desired. Always clamoring for more power. Why was it so attractive to them?

Then an idea struck her.

At a pause, Yulah raised a hand. She swallowed the shyness invoked by their eyes upon her.

"I know about a technology," she said, standing, "created by our engineers before they fled the fortress, that can expose and weaken the Sen'Prin. We will drain their resources by striking their villages." She twisted a curling moon shaped copper earring in her ear, the soft flesh against the warmed metal. The totem of power spurred her with confidence. "We can break through their protections like never before. Give me the role, and I will catch us up. We will weaken them, as they have us."

They blinked, bewildered, at this girl. A rush of energy, a powerful thrill, ran through her. She had done the unexpected.

The Emperor eyed her over, his clouded eyes hard to read after a lifetime of wind casting, overexerted in service of the military.

"I grant you this..." He groped the air for her name, one hand raised in a spinning motion.

"Yulah." She stated her name, still standing, and swept into a respectful bow to the Emperor.

"War General Yulah. You will take over for Malotus."

She beamed, her head swelling with pressure and the acknowledgement of her new title.

"That is all I ask," she said, still bent in the bow. "To serve you from his post."

"But emperor, she is but a youth! Far too young and brash to take over in Malotus's position!" cried one of the advisors.

Yulah gracefully swept to standing, making note of who he was.

"Hush," growled Ryogrim. "She has been training under Malotus directly for years. She's familiar with the intricacies of his work like no other."

The others looked from one to another, clearly nervous and testing the waters for argument.

"This is my decision!" The Emperor boomed, which sent them into a jolted silence, many suddenly shifting papers in front of them.

That shut them up, thought Yulah. *This is what everybody really wants. To be confident enough to ask, or to be dominated by the confident. It is the ultimate rush. The power to manipulate others: to have control of the room.*

And by me serving myself, I'm doing myself a favor. I'm showing others the way of truth by embracing myself.

It's about time I started playing this game right.

***

Meleena held onto Flax and he formed a spinning jet of wind. She tried to shake off the sense of unease. The surprise of moving to Sen'Prin, not getting saying goodbye to her parents. Perhaps it was for the best. She chose to focus on the bright side, the side that was eager to explore this new city, squashing the anxieties down and out of awareness.

She'd been to Sen'Prin before, technically, but only at the headquarters above the actual city.

The group flew together, which was exhilarating, especially now with the goggles, she could see much better without clinging as close. They fit snugly, encapsulating her glasses, while she watched the team alongside them in the airstream.

They lowered from the skies and pitched down into thick foliage, Meleena closed her eyes at the speed of the downward pitch. The others in front of them almost collided with the ground, at the last moment sliding back upwards and onto their feet, like a slide of wind. Meleena winced, and must has been holding Flax tighter, as he slowed further, and shouted over his ear, "Don't worry!" as they came to a much calmer landing.

"They love to show off," he said, she lowered off his back and onto firm ground. Their hands slid briefly through each other, which made her heart beat a little faster.

Meleena cleared her throat and looked at the foliage around her, not sure where they were. There was no sign of a city around them.

"Entry to Sen'Prin is kept secret, to prevent the Sen'Drorn from infiltrating," Kyra said, her ears perked up high, head pitched up, listening intently. "It is clear."

They continued down a winding path under leaves large enough to slide down a mountainside on.

"But Sen'Drorn wouldn't be like, snooping around here, would they?" asked Meleena. Surely, they could see them coming over the wide landscape from watch towers.

"Overall, no" explained Kyra. "But we must stay vigilant."

They came to a place in the path to Meleena's surprise, where two Hyish in leather guard stood before a bamboo fence, so tall it stretched through the landscape, its highest tendrils swaying in the wind above the canopy. The Hyish inspected the group, gripping tightly their moon hook glaives. Kyra nodded and everyone flashed wristcom badges with IDs, Meleena included. They lingered on her, golden eyes fixed. Then with a startling gesture, the glaive came up and Meleena jumped, the blade swiftly hooking and sliding open the bamboo gates.

Meleena breathed a quiet sigh of relief and outwardly pretended like nothing had happened.

Turning around as they went through, it was unclear there had even been a gate there once they ventured further into the jungle on the other side. *Very clever, using a natural gate,* she thought.

"There are Hyish working for Sen'Prin then?" Meleena inquired with Flax.

"The reptilian folk live in encampments everywhere in these forests. It is helpful to employ them for city defense, as they are more adept at crouching in trees, staying out in the forest all day, and it wouldn't be as obvious to Sen'Drorn where entrances are, with Hyish guards."

"Do any Hyish live in the city, then?"

"There are some who stay as citizens, but they are few. They are free to come and go as they like, but most visit for trade during market days. The Hyish tend to stick together and prefer to live with their own kind, and aren't much fans of the layout of a Warix city built for eh, wind-users."

Meleena recalled the few times she'd met a Hyish. Most weren't big fans of the Warix, and most had never met a Meruyan. She really didn't know much about their culture beyond what she'd seen today and on one previous occasion. She was feeling gracious to them now, as they had set up trade to help her people, as a direct result of her work with her friends, showing them Meruyan valuables for which the Hyish would pay a premium.

They followed the dark tunnels, on and on, toward a guiding light, until they popped out on the other side between ferns and revealed... something. It was structures that appeared to be built on bridges and platforms, all made of layers and layers of bamboo.

Similar to the Meruyan capital, the city had been built right into a mountain along the steep waterfall-river series of cliffs. There, it pooled into a large lake, ideal for water dwellers. This city was built into a steeper canyon along the flow of a narrow band of waterfalls with some small pools on multiple levels.

No wonder they grow so much of the stuff, Meleena thought with a laugh to herself.

Old growth trees with spiraling branches formed enormous reaching canopies with layers of cover, which gave the city a glow of dappled lighting. Flecks of sunlight sparkled between the radiant leaves shifting in the light breeze. The air smelled sweet of their pollen, tickling Meleena's nose.

The raised platform split to bridges that connected all the avenues of the city, alive with busy Warix going about their errands for the day. Buildings lined the platforms, made of the same material, with single and multi-story storefronts, cafes, and restaurants.

Once in the thick of the city, Kyra addressed the group. "Team, we will be having a meeting later today, at the Three Thistles Cafe. Enjoy some free time until then. I trust the rest of you will show Meleena and Jessup their quarters and help get them settled in."

Kyra went her separate way, her step light and bouncing, as she disappeared from sight around a bend up the clifflike street.

"See ya'll at the flat," said Zoltan, and with that he leapt into wind-aided quickstep as well, his feet taking on a trail of condensed air as he sped off.

"I think I'll follow his lead. "If that's not totally rude," Naia said apologetically, a yawn overtaking her.

"Later, then," smiled Riigs with a wave, and the two of them leapt off together.

***

That left Meleena with Flax, Thian, and Jessup, and the group headed towards their flat.

She peered down the exposed gorge to the water below, as they passed over rows of ripe fruit trees and low sprouting plants. *So, this was the way this hidden place sustains itself,* she thought.

"What happens in the rainy season? I imagine from all the bridges, this place floods." asked Meleena.

"Mmhmm. We grow most crops needed to feed the city internally down there. We don't have as many varieties like they do in Sen'Drorn City, you know, eh, they use Meruyan laborers, but we are self-sufficient."

"And the larger pools downriver are where we all hang out and cool off with a swim. It gets *dang* muggy around here," added Thian.

Jessup turned, finally looking interested. "Hey, a swimming hole, count me in!" She laughed.

They passed buildings on their left, two or three stories tall, stacked like little mismatched boxes. Warix sprang with light windsteps onto second or third story decks, coming and going with their business. A vertical city for flying people.

It was all…so much more vertical, than Meleena had anticipated. She rubbed her elbow nervously. "How am I going to get around?" she asked.

"What do you mean?" Flax's eyes widened as it dawned on him. "Oh…"

Meleena started out excited to see Sen'Prin…Sure, city was glorious, built into a gorge but were people staring at her?

She supposed a blue-skinned Meruyan, a good head shorter than a Warix, wasn't a common sight.

As the only Meruyan to live here, she supposed she was quite a sight. But being the center of attention gave her the urge to hide behind the nearest planter.

One Warix even stopped her, concerned, to ask *how "the Meruyan situation was going."*

People stopped to ask all kinds of questions.

"Can I see your fins?"

"Look at that fine hair, how it dances in the wind!"

Meleena's cheeks flamed. She was popular alright, but not in a way she was used to. Something poked her in the leg suddenly, and Meleena felt a panic rising up inside her, like she'd never felt before, and bolted like a Kelpie horse, leaving Thian, chatting with Jessup, to fall back into the crowds and Flax to run to catch up.

"Eh, she's with me," came Flax's urgent voice as he moved through the strangers, darting to her side.

"Can we just get to the lodgings, please?" Meleena said through bated breath. Her head spun, she'd never been more than ready for some alone time. To kick her shoes off and plop down on a bed.

Then something poked her in the ribs, causing her to jump and turn around growling, this time in anger, ready to lash out.

"Woah, sorry!" It was Thian, followed by Jessup, rushing to their side. "Don't worry yourself about the lot of 'em," he chided. "News travels fast around here. By next week you'll blend right in," he mused, bringing an arm around Flax's shoulder. "As for getting around this place, we will stick by you. And I'm sure Flax can tinker out a solution in his fancy new tech lab."

Thian pointed to the one familiar building in the city at the crown of the mountain: Sen'Prin military headquarters. It was barely visible at the clifftop, mostly obscured by the trees.

"New lab?" Meleena asked, trying to ignore the stares from passersby.

"Ah, just something they've given to the best engineers," Flax grinned. "My dad and I are working together again."

Meleena's heart swelled, happy for the two of them, and glad for the part she had played in making it happen.

They walked along the clanking smooth planks of the bridge-way and came to a spot where four buildings came together to form a plaza. The sweet smell of flowers and roasting meats wafted through the row of restaurants busy with citizens, many partying on overlooking balconies.

"So, what do you do for fun in the city?" Jessup asked.

"This is how we entertain ourselves,' Thian said, arms splayed. "It really gets better at night. We'll show you a good time, don't you worry," Thian assured, a flirtatious wink aimed at Jessup.

She lifted her eyebrows and beat back a coy smile. "Oh, do you need to show me how to have a good time?"

Meleena watched, envying Jessup's smooth, easy tone. Flirting didn't exactly come natural to her.

"That's the main street over there," said Flax, fluttering a hand lazily in each direction. "The place of social activities—the bars, the restaurants. And that over there." He pointed to crisscrossing streets among the bridges. "That's the start of the market quarter. It's nothing special, just a couple of streets. Nowhere near the scale of Sen'Drorn City."

Meleena still had occasional nightmares of running endlessly through Sen'Drorn's labyrinth of volcanic rocky corridors.

"We're almost at your lodging," stated Flax.

They slowed in front of a restaurant, a swinging sign held on by rope read, "Ma's Noodles."

"Are we stopping for lunch?" Meleena asked, suppressing a simmer of rising frustration. She really just wanted a quiet place to rest after all the overstimulation of the day. Why was meeting new people so exhausting?

Wisps of smoke danced from bubbling cauldrons of soup resting by open side panel windows.

"We stay in a sweet pad above the noodle house," explained Thian.

Warix were coming and going, and Thian held the door open for them to enter. They moved through the shop, passing chairs and a bar counter, bustling with hungry patrons, dodging the matron and waitresses. The smell of hot soup filled Meleena's lungs, and her stomach growled.

Whereas the wooden floors of the restaurant had been glazed and polished, it ended abruptly at the back, where a dusty bamboo continued. Being barefoot, it was somehow particularly noticeable. Through a back curtain, there was a narrow staircase that led to a barrel-shaped common room.

"I only moved in last night, actually," Jessup confided. "You, me, and Naia have bunkbeds upstairs, while the guys have a similar room down the hall."

Light streamed in from ample windows. Meleena looked around the common room: a simple kitchen, old stone sink, various reclaimed wooden bookshelves, and a scattering of wicker armchairs and hammocks. Excitement swelled in her solar plexus—wonderful reality of this new chapter of her life was sinking in.

Jessup reclaimed her attention, waving her to look at a chart on the wall. "These are the chores. We all pitch in, sweeping, cooking, that sort of thing." Meleena's name had already been written into 'clean the latrine' duty, she noticed, wondering if the worst job was saved for the new person, who'd had no say in the plan, but held her tongue. She tried to sound gracious in her reply, lest they think she was spoiled or a troublemaker.

Flax and Thian sat down in the armchairs as Jessup took over the tour, leading Meleena up the curving staircase to the loft rooms.

"This is our room," said Jessup, leading Meleena through a curtain on the upper balcony. The room held one stacked bed and one regular, and three desks. Naia was already there, relaxing on the single bed.

Right away Meleena noted that the room had one of those balcony landings for Warix to come and go on the wind. Through middle-opening doors, it also lit the room naturally.

Both of their things littered the ground, cramping the small room, and strings of clothing hung from every corner like exotic decor. Jessup's clothing littered the bottom bunk of the stacked bed.

"Careful where you step," warned Naia, not looking up from her book.

She wasn't referring to the clothing, but the fact that the ceiling beams in the room sloped downward, tapering off into a large gap in the floor. Air currents blew fresh air from the open terrace doors through the hole. Meleena had never seen anything like it before, but the ventilation probably had to do with using their wind indoors. At least the clothing lines made it harder to fall in, like an insect caught in a spider's web. That did seem exactly like where one would crawl out of. Meleena shuddered, remembering her morning in the forest.

"Eh, we'll make space," Jessup assured her, glancing at Meleena, who was eying the place with a mounting sense of unease.

"You also get a desk," said Jessup, indicating to the only clutter-free space in the room. Though an uneven smattering of dust on its surface revealed the haste at which they'd cleared their things from it. Meleena set her pack down under the desk. Still, a nice place for evening journaling. Jessup's desk was full of face paint and a pearl mirror. Naia's desk was a mess of oily tools.

"Eh, thanks." Meleena climbed the wobbly bamboo ladder to her new bed, brushing aside an insect net as it tickled her face. Finally, her own little dark corner.

She longed to blend in, to hide for the rest of the day here in the blankets. No, that was stupid. In this stifling hot climate, it'd be punishing. There was nowhere to hide here, she felt the strong presence of the other girls, worse than the heat.

Perhaps she could flee into the enclosed jungle at the edge of town. At least there she could breathe, away from the exhausting judgments of others. Too late. Tears welled in her eyes, and she cried silently, letting the overwhelm pour forth from her as her body began to shake uncontrollably. The lack of privacy slipped from relevance.

Being unable to use wind power was now a problem. A curse of fate. The Warix power had never bothered her in this way before. Now we were like one of them, but could never be.

She felt broken.

Was this it then? How things would be if she stayed here?

She turned around over the bedding, to face outward, and gasped.

Her eyes adjusted to the bright change in lighting out the double-doors. Centrally located indeed: views of winding boardwalks over the steep flowing gorge, fringed with jungle and cottages nestled in leaves so broad she could see them across the city. So green and lush.

The buildings along the winding golden paths with clay rooftop tiles sparkling like quartz.

"*Beautiful*," she whispered, her inhale catching the fresh breeze as it swept in. The shaking and silent crying resumed with a life of its own. *Damn that floor hole*, she thought. It provided an excellent cross-breeze, she'd have to give them that.

A profound tranquility rippled through her, as the tears and shaking ran out. *What a city to explore*, came the competing narrative in her mind. A swell of joy, and a new sense of purpose in such a place as this. She forgave the people, letting go of the feeling of being an invasive species here, stark, obvious, and blue.

“Meleena,” Flax called from downstairs, the sound of her own name startling her, sucking her breath back into her like a rodent racing into its den. “Any interest in checking out the lab now?”

The tiredness popped like a bubble and was gone.

“Yes, coming,” she called down to Flax, glancing at the backpack containing her journal, and deciding it was safe to leave it behind.

As she joined Flax, a thought crossed her mind of Deem and Talla, and she wondered of their new living arrangements and lives in Dlawn’Edo. Friends with relatable problems, fancy that. Her hand snapped to her wrist, over the metal of her new wristcom, and she resolved to check in on them before the days’ end.

CHAPTER SIX

Awareness came but Deem didn't open his eyes. He was in the Meruyan capital. Another day as junior council member. He shuddered, shoving the inevitable day ahead from his mind and nestling deeper into his soft, silty kelp bed, indulging in the pleasant weightlessness of dwelling underwater. The world up there was so heavy on his limbs in comparison. Why would anyone choose to live on land? It made little sense, long term.

Floating in the bed, there could be no better comfort, to sooth the anxiousness, the 'nothing is okay' feeling that often pervaded his being. He drifted, not ready for this bliss to end and face the workday ahead.

The others looked down on him for choosing to stay underwater. He'd known nothing else until the journey of future leaders, and was not about to give this up, even if society now saw it as old-fashioned and impoverished. The old traditions had value.

He saw Talla regularly, as they both worked for the council, but in different departments. He represented the underwater communities from Pontai'Desa, his home region, trying to better their lives without having to move to land. Talla worked on Northern Hilly Village relations, known by the council for short as, "the NHV." It was notorious these days as the epicenter of strife between the Meruyan and Sen'Drorn Warix. So, a lot more action than his department to say the least.

He considered Talla his friend, though they couldn't have been more different. She had been given, alongside her stipend, extra pearls from her parents, which afforded her a lovely flat on the central island. Unlike him, she liked nice, new things. And unlike him, she made lots of friends, and hosted parties with all the other junior apprentices. Not really his thing.

As he walked to work that morning, his chest tightened with the anxiety of the day. He was upset, bordering on exasperated, at his own department. He didn't mind the daily mundanity, running errands for more senior council members, which was nearly everybody. What he really couldn't stand was how ineffective his position was. He'd made propositions to improve life for his underwater brethren; done his research; put in requisitions. He even had to learn how to swallow his fears, quell his racing heart, to speak up at meetings to make such proposals.

He knew what would benefit his people, he had grown up in the underwater fishing village after all. Shark alarms for safety; resources like query stones for extra building materials; maybe some connections to other Meruyan regions for broader export of their haul.

Everything was rejected.

He took his seat at today's meeting, paperwork in his shaking hands. He practiced the breathing exercises that Talla had taught him. He had come prepared with the latest request he'd been working on.

The council took their seats in the meeting and things began. Deem was sweating under his tunic, but a wave of hope washed over him as he stared at the Meruyan national Flag on the wall: Azure blue and green swirling together in the coexistence of land and sea.

They called on someone else first, which bought Deem some time to get himself together to speak publicly. Every time for the first few weeks that he tried to speak up, his ears and cheeks would burn, his hands would go clammy, and he couldn't get the question out.

"Deem, speak."

So soon? Okay, he wasn't ready! His heart raced and a ringing in his ears replaced all good sense.

"Well, we are waiting. You had a proposal today?" asked the councilman.

"Err, ye-yes," he stuttered, stood up and cleared his throat. "I, uh…" he shuffled his papers. "It's about sharks."

"Sharks?"

"Not the bloody sharks again," groaned another councilmember.

That didn't help. His palms secreted too much sweat, such that he couldn't hold onto the papers anymore. He set them down and tried to wing it, through the pressure mounting in his temples.

"Yes, sharks! They're harmful, and we live underwater," he began as an outpouring of words released from his mouth against all control. "Did you know underwater sea Meruyan have to enter their caves by night, or else they are at risk of monstrous sharks and other beasts eating them? We hide our homes, our world, out of fear of these predators. I ask the council to install anti-shark safety lights, to ward them off and maybe a way to keep them out. High frequency sounds only they can hear."

His heart continued to race, he wanted to run from the room. His legs were poised, restless. The little metal thing that had held the pages together was crumbled into a knot in his fingers.

"Deem, that is a good idea."

The what now?

"Uh, thank you, sir." He tried to compose himself, taking a deep breath before adding, hopefully, "…you could even bring in new technology from Noyade, the underwater city has in their research areas. On the Journey of Future Leaders, I went to their Biodome, and I learned of how they're adapting Warix Tech. His mind raced with possibility. This could be the one. The thing that gets through. Finally, he was going to accomplish something of what he came here for.

"However, the council has no extra funds to allot to something like this right now," said the councilman.

It was like a pufferfish in his chest, spikes making sudden contact with his lungs, popping them.

It had been a couple of months since Deem had moved to the Meruyan capital, Dlawn'Edo, to start his apprenticeship. He was starting to think it was time to move back to his village. Farming life wasn't so bad. It was the pain of loss of hope in the system that was far worse. That his dreams of improving things were dumb, all a lie.

Back in the apprentice lounge, he slumped low on a cushion. He had hoped after his adventures in the apprenticeship traveling around, changing life for the Meruyan would be possible. He and Talla had opened channels for the Hyish to trade, which reduced the Warix grip over them. But even that had turned into chaos and retaliation, the details of which he didn't care to know. That was Talla's department and sounded even worse than his own mundane one.

Deem would have to read up if he'd be getting something done, clearly this wasn't enough. What would be the right ask, or tactic, to get through to them?

He continued feeling sorry for himself, down and out of ideas, when the doors flung open, making him jump and jerk his head up from the page. Talla's turquoise hair bounced in a flurry as she approached, her brow furrowed.

"You wouldn't believe what is going on!" she beseeched him.

Speak of the shark, he thought. Talla had an intense look in her eye, stomping over until she was directly in front of him.

"Hi, Talla," he grunted, bracing himself for what was likely going to be a whole lot about nothing.

"Trouble is going *down* in the NHV!"

"What's going on?" he asked, taking the bait.

Talla grinned like a wild beast about to snap on its prey.

***

"Alright, I'll bite. What's going on in the NHV?" asked Deem, to Talla who was standing over his slumped body in the council apprentice lounge. She was standing a bit too close, in his opinion. Yet her statement about trouble breaking out in the Northern Hilly Villages had him hooked. "Are the Hyish not accepting Meruyan trade goods anymore? Don't tell me they've gone back to working for the Sen'Drorn again?" he elaborated on his question while she held him enrapture.

It had been, after all, the joint idea of him and Talla, that had sort of started all these new events that changed everything between Warix, Hyish, and Meruyan civilizations.

"What, of course not!" Talla waved him off. "The Sen'Drorn are *pissed*! The shift has been rapid and they're seeing huge declines in productivity."

Since these populations lived divided by large mountain ranges, and neither could fly like the Warix, there was no natural way trade between the two groups would have occurred. Thus, the Warix moved between locations, at massive advantage to their people. They controlled trade.

"That's a good thing, right? It's what we wanted..." inquired Deem.

Since Deem and Talla had they'd traveled across the mountain range and met Hyish, had shown them pearls and shells. Nobody predicted that the Hyish had been determined to open direct trade routes after that. They had tunneled and blasted their way through the mountains in a way no Warix or Meruyan had ever seen, nor knew how the Hyish had even done it.

"Well," Talla stomped her foot. "Don't you get it? Sen'Drorn are not going to let this shift just *happen*. What did we think?"

This new trade was great for the Meruyan of the desperate Northern Hilly Villages region, who had plentiful things to trade.

"And since we are under contractual obligation, guess who's job it is to enforce this agreement?" Talla continued, sighing angrily. "The stone-brained Meruyan Council."

"Oh..." Deem cringed. The Sen'Drorn Warix had enough of the council's role in all this from the start, but trouble regaining their footing in the NHV without their help. The Sen'Drorn could no longer force the Meruyan to work harder, since the Meruyan were opting out of their positions entirely. This was unprecedented in the history of Warix-Meruyan contact.

"That's not great," he continued after his thoughts. "What side will the council take? This can't be easy..."

Historically the Meruyan could never survive on the land without Warix support, but now that the Hyish were involved, they had a new outlet and things there were rapidly changing.

"Yes, and—" urged Talla, face widening with a look of impatience, "The citizens of Dlawn'Edo, the Meruyan capital, are enriched by a percent of Sen'Drorn's gains from the NHV. This is actually hurting them." She nodded her head to the corner of the room. "Haven't you noticed the snack table is gone? It's the little things, I know, but hey."

"So, what will they do? You're not telling me they're siding with Sen'Drorn?"

"I'm saying, the Sen'Drorn are sending representatives *today*. To have a meeting about it. It's going to be wild. I am more than curious to see how it will go."

"*Oysters*! Let me know!" exclaimed Deem, now envious he couldn't have a little more going on in his department.

"Come with me! To the meeting!" declared Talla, topping his exclamation.

"What? I'm in another department," stammered Deem. This was certainly against the rules. "And I'm a junior council member, there's no way they would let me into that room."

"I can get you in, if you just say you're with me."

"It definitely doesn't work like that here," Deem said flatly.

"Ah," Talla waved off his words as if they were flies in the air, "They're going to be so distracted, nobody will notice one extra in there."

"I don't want to cause trouble or do something I'm not allowed to..." he trailed off, thinking, *then again, isn't that what I want? What does it matter to break the rules anymore?*

"Come on! You are my friend, I need you! You know you're curious about this!"

Deem made a nervous sound through his teeth. This was against his nature, even with recent disheartened thoughts.

Talla sensed his shift in mood. "*Goddess Noyade*, Deem! Ever since you got here, you've been trying to inhale the ocean! Trying to get so much done around here when you're still wet behind the gills."

"*Me?* I mean..." he stammered before retaliating properly. Maybe she did have a bit of a point, what with the constant proposals that felt like swimming against a tidal current all day long. However, she was doing it too! She'd always share stories, eyes shining, of speaking up during meetings, proposing grand ideas that never passed. He retorted with the old expression, "The turnip calls the carrot dirty!"

Talla scoffed and blinked rapidly as she responded. "I am trying to impress, not change. There's a massive difference. One gets you ahead, the other, exhausted." She flicked her multi-braided hair back in cocky confidence. "Also, how often do *Sen'Drorn Warix* come to council meetings? It's like watching a monster in a cage!"

"You know, that doesn't appeal to me in the way you think it does. I really, don't want to step on any toes..."

She gave him a face. A mix of anger and personal affront.

Like a bolt of lightning, it shot though him, the anger, it was just unbearable to see a friend like this.

"Okay, okay." He caved, again. How could he let this happen? This was the worst...Sneaking in was against his motto, but so was disappointing his friend. "As long as you can promise I won't get into trouble. You will take the rap for this."

"I'll say you were invited. I didn't know it was restricted!" she stood and crossed to the door.

Talla always had the answers; not always the right answers, but the ones he wanted to hear. "Come on, it's going to start soon!" she barked, heading for the door.

He stood from his chair, cracked his back, and followed her in a thick cloud of mixed emotions.

CHAPTER SEVEN

Once Flax and Meleena headed into town, Flax saw the city he'd grown up in with new eyes. While Flax could walk or use wind to speed him up, now he had to pause, confused, to ponder routes slowly and on foot. There had never been a Meruyan living here before in all the great wind city's history.

"Err...I'm not used to going the long way..." he said bashfully.

They passed the bustle of the city—folks about town, market street selling flowers and fresh produce.

"We just have a couple hot spots. This place has felt kind of small for me after living in Sen'Drorn. Cafes on every block. I used to go to one called The Quail Egg Cafe..." Flax started excited, then realized his mistake. With a half-smile to cover up his embarrassment, he paused uncomfortably. Since their products came from Meruyan labor, it was a sore subject to bring up now. Not to mention it reminded him of Yulah, his ex-girlfriend.

He pushed the painful thought of her from his mind.

Meleena gave him a confused look. "Ah well, to me it's quite a lot to take in, especially compared to my village," she said, staring around in awe, her blue hair swishing in the light wind.

He had to admit to himself, he was excited for Meleena coming to live here. Governess Arenay had arranged for him to watch over her, noting it might be rough for a Meruyan, adjusting to a new place.

At least she wasn't out of breath from all the uphill paths, probably from all the time she spent climbing through the mountainous jungle.

While he had to admit, she was a bit odd when they'd first met back in Sen'Drorn, she was growing on him.

There was something uniquely endearing about her. She was confident, but not imposing. A lover of knowledge. With that Inquisitive smile and deep searching eyes behind waning moons of glass. They tended to rest on things for a hint longer than normal, as if bating the recipient to gift her its secrets. Even as they moved through town, her attention was always appreciating the beauty of plant or animal. She'd see things nobody else did through careful study, all while sweeping her hair from her face. That strange silken Meruyan hair that dances in air.

"It's not that much further to headquarters and my lab," he said. This was the brain of Sen'Prin, at the top of the city, where Governess Arenay and her council met to deal with internal and external affairs; from defensive strategy against Sen'Drorn, to citizen wellbeing right down to the plumbing.

Meleena checked her wristcom. "I'm not sure how much time we've got before the team meeting," she said. "We need to find a better solution than walking everywhere."

Flax glanced up at the high mountain and steep slopes ahead of them. "It would seem so," he admitted. "If you don't mind, you can fly with me this time, until we can create an engineering solution for you at the top!" He was half joking of course, but why not? Why couldn't he and his father design something for her? It would be a unique challenge, but he'd be happy to help.

One of the famously huge shortcomings of Warix technology was the basis for the current political boondoggle. The promise of better technology had lured the starry eyed Meruyan to land nearly two centuries ago. Yet aside from simple farming practices and building structures on land, most of the Warix's promise to their kind was null.

Then and now, Warix tech was based upon the innate ability within all Warix to control the wind. It was one of their prime senses. All the gears, gadgets, and tubing they could rig up to motors and storage cells were based on the core energy from this sense. The funneling of large amounts of wind power, for that is what it was, funneling, through their sensitive horns into their body core, and out through their palms, breath, pads of feet.

Meruyan were not inferior, in Flax's opinion, for not possessing it, just built differently. Just as he could not breathe under water, nor sprout fins from his limbs as they could. The Meruyan had seen and built worlds in places he could never know, which stung deeply in his heart.

Meleena climbed on his back, his knees bracing for the weight of another as her legs around his hips, hands clasping his shoulders. He took a deep breath and let the wind course through and into him, clouding his peripheral vision and tingling in his every body cell as the energy redirected into his feet, and he bounded onwards until they reached the lower entrance.

When they landed, and the cloudiness abated, spiraling blue pervaded his peripheral vision, startling him. But it was only her hair, whipping from the wind. Never had he seen such a color, deep blue like the fathomless depths.

She slid from his back and he turned instinctively to see that she was alright. "What?" she smiled and lifted her eyebrows together in anticipated confusion.

"Eh, nothing. We are here," he said and cleared his throat. They'd landed in an enclosed courtyard which led to the Sen'Prin engineering technology lab, known as the "tech lab" for short.

Seeing it as if through her eyes, for the first time, Flax led her through the arched doorway into the lab and looked up at its high ceilings and broad breezy windows. The lab was indeed an enjoyable place to work, his best assignment yet.

The space was dense with worktables, and a plethora of shelving for tools, materials, experiments, and prototypes.

"There is a side room with devices set up," Flax explained. "We have been running tests on the samples from Kyra's project."

Light streamed in through tall windows, ribbed ceiling lined with drawers and hooks, with open roof sheets like the gills of a fish, for ventilation: bringing fresh air for stronger wind use.

"Arenay set us up with a great space of our own. Me, Borak, and many of the engineers we rescued from Sen'Drorn. The best engineer across both nations! Except Plymore, of course. Lost touch with him after he moved."

Borak, Flax's long-lost father and engineering master.

Meleena leaned forward over the counter. "Oh yeah, Plymore, the wise elderly Warix. My friends, Deem and Talla, work with him on the Meruyan council. Can you imagine? The only Warix ever invited to do so!"

Sen'Prin had quite a group of skilled engineers at their disposal. Many of whom they had rescued from the city and were more than glad to help fight against their enslavers. Although it was true that many still had ties to their home city when they defected, such as family members, being imprisoned was enough to turn them and hope to get their families out one day to live in Sen'Prin.

"We have all sorts of projects," he explained to Meleena. "I develop better engineering tech to defend ourselves against Sen'Drorn. Primarily with Borak, and one of the Sen'Drorn dungeon rescues, Phineas. He's the one with the crazy look in his eyes, but he's harmless, and quite talented."

Meleena gaped at Phineas, working with gloves in their workspace. He had a long face, and shocks of red hair so wild it curled up his vertical horns like vines. "He's brilliant!" breathed Meleena, to Flax's surprise that she would remember him at all. "The battle at Sen'Drorn fortress," she reminded him. "His thunder machine blew a hole in the side of the chamber! It's because of him we escaped."

"That's right," Flax recalled.

Perhaps Flax had only noticed Meleena's charms now that his mind was freer than ever before. He'd been too busy with all his plans and strife to rescue his father... as that all takes up space in the mind. Yulah was the only girl he'd been thinking about then. Still, sure, but he was working on that.

With all the trouble he'd caused for Yulah...

How could I have known she was the General's niece and top assistant? I never wanted to use her like that!

He'd never expected things to turn out that way. Never intended to run off like that and hurt her. It tormented him still, how things ended. If only he could show her that he was genuine, and okay, maybe still in love with her, if he was being honest with himself. Not that he'd ever breathe a word of that to anyone.

Still, his plate was full now. Having Meleena on his team was nice, he would surround himself with friends. It would keep him focused.

"So, what do we do with the samples?" asked Meleena, snapping him out of his daydream.

"Err, yeah, glad you asked. Check this out," he said, directing her attention. She followed him past counters full with materials, tubes, spacers, spanners and tracer papers, past the new and old tinkerers.

Borak was there, and immediately caught their eye, putting down his spanner, stripping his gloves. He came over and enwrapped Meleena in a hug.

"Lovely to see ye again, girl!" exclaimed Borak, beaming.

"You too!" Meleena replied, beaming back.

"Oh yeah, I'll need to draw you up a map of the city," Flax reminded her.

Borak turned to him, a tender smirk on his tan, wrinkling face pulled into a crinkled smile. "Eh, I could use one too. Mel's not the only one that's new here."

"Of course," said Flax. He apologetically sketched a quick map so she could get to the cafe where the team meeting would be held.

"If we don't want to be late, we should head out now." Flax said, noting the time. They were late, already, but he didn't want to alarm Meleena, or pull her away from her happy reunion with Borak.

"Yeah," said Meleena, "But you're not trying to fit in with a whole new team."

"How's that now?" asked Borak, head tilted to one side. He scratched his left horn in the same way Flax often did. Flax's heart soared, he couldn't help but love it.

"I am in Sen'Prin on an assignment with a group they assembled to investigate some attacks on outlying villages," explained Meleena, "It's my first time working with them, but I am nervous about fitting in, and the value I can provide to the team. It's hard, I feel alone, and for the first time like that's a bad thing. I'm still learning how to navigate in group dynamics." She rubbed her arm, her cheeks darkening into a blush.

"Well, you will have to earn their respect a little harder than most, I suspect. Being an outsider is hard for anyone, especially with creative, unusual talents such as yourself. I am new here, as you may recall, so dun' worry so much about it. You've got friends here."

Meleena took a deep breath and looked up from a wrench on the floor. Flax suspected she was fighting back tears. "Thanks, Borak. It's not exactly the same though, I'm also a Meruyan with physical trouble getting around this city."

Flax stayed silent and let them have their moment.

"Ah, ain't nothin' to feel bad about," growled Borak, waving off the worry in the air. "Perhaps I can do some tinkering with my son, and see what we can come up with, eh?" He turned to Flax, who felt a surge of excited anticipation.

"Yeah! We would love to support you however we can. I was going to bring that up as well," he agreed.

"Would be glad to!"

Flax felt an immense bond, a sense of warmth towards Meleena and Borak and he knew she felt the same. Borak didn't have a clue how much of a charmer he was. An old soul with a kind heart, too heavy with guilt and shame to notice it. It endeared him even more to his newly rediscovered father.

"Now, let's get on with testing those samples before today's meeting," Meleena announced, shuffling the energy in the room back to the task at hand.

"Oh yes—Dad, I brought the samples from the village explosion. Let's see, we have some tree seeds, clumps of animal hair, burnt scraps from different materials, those sorts of things."

"Let's see em'!"

Borak opened the rucksack and carefully removed the cloth bags full of each sample.

Meleena watched as Flax showed her how to remove small clusters from the samples and place them in small trays, where they could see them better under a microscope.

"Borak and I have recently been testing out a new theory, based on a discovery about the elements which make up our world," explained Flax, feeling the excitement well in his chest. "We wanted to locate the source of wind energy, the biological mechanism which allows us to feel and pull wind. We know there must be one, as Hyish can also breathe fire, and possess special glands in their throats which Warix and Meruyan don't have. And the Meruyan, you can sprout fins when you get wet."

Meleena nodded, listening intently, her large blue eyes fixed on him.

"So, we think there is something in your body or sensor in your arm in certain places, which only Meruyan have. We have been developing ways to see and handle these materials. That's why we handle this instead of the crime division. They have no idea what any of this stuff is."

"Let's pop it in the particles and see what we have...." Said Borak, looking into the table device.

"What makes this crime so scary, is that whoever did it, they created explosions like nobody has seen before. We don't have any combustion technology, in fact, it was a theory Borak and I had been kicking back and forth. It's looking like the Sen'Drorn had been developing a similar idea and got there first. That's our only lead. Borak and I think they are combining these elemental activating cells, those of wind and fire, but we have no idea how."

"Based on your samples, I'd confirm this," said Borak. "But what is this gunky gray residue..."

Meleena blinked at them. Flax thought maybe she didn't understand, or that he was crazy, and then she said, "That is fascinating! I would *love* to hear more!"

"Well, this is how it's done. We take a scraping from our horn, and have found these small crystal-like structures, only seen under our amplifying device here, the microscope. When we crush them up with mortar and pestle, they pop with stored energy. Watch this,"

He did a demonstration, crushing some from a dish. The crystals popped, releasing a whooshing sound and gushed open with thick, white smoke, curling into the air as if alive.

"Incredible," said Meleena. "This is like a whole new dimension to the natural world! I can't wait to see more. Do you have any fire or water samples?"

Flax rubbed his arm, "Eh, well not so much. I had wanted to get some fire samples, but it's not so easy. These cells would likely be inside the Hyish fire glands, which theoretically would require cutting it out from the inside. Err, and it's not like they turn up dead around here much."

"What about any other animals, who can use fire?"

"Oh yes, we have some fire-breathing lizards around here. I guess we could, but I felt bad to have to kill them and cut them open, even for a good cause."

"Also, you can scrape some from my arm," said Meleena, holding out her elbow. "Try to get some water crystals for your test and see what happens."

"Well, sure, why not." Flax carefully scraped some skin from her forearm and placed them in the sample tray. They took turns with the microscope, discovering a similar crystal, bluer in color.

They placed some into the mortar and pestle, and Flax braced himself for the result. The first time they'd crushed the wind crystals had been surprising and exciting indeed. He felt giddy all over again, like a child at play, for the new discovery to be made.

"I'll test the rest of burnt materials while you do that," said Borak. "Don't you kids have a meeting later?"

"Yes, thank you Borak," agreed Flax.

Flax and Meleena hovered over their little experiment. To the naked eye, the water crystals looked like glinting blue dust. With her fingertips, Meleena gently sprinkled them into the bowl he held aloft, and he prepared to crush them with the stone pestle.

Cautiously, he began to mix it, bracing himself and expecting a bang, only to find something even stranger. At first, nothing seemed to happen, so he mashed them harder, until floating water, bubbling water came out.

Flax stared, mesmerized, and Meleena sighed, also transfixed.

It was like thick, shimmering water, oozing upwards, almost buoyant in the air but held back by their bulk, dancing with a life force of their own.

"I got some interesting info for ye," came Borak's voice, the startle causing them to nearly jump out of their skin. "Sorry to spook you," he chuckled, raising a hand to his forehead.

"Exciting or scary?" Flax gasped in reply.

"Err, both," laughed Borak, tapering from genuine to distressed sounding.

"I tested the gunk, but still not sure what it is yet. But it's on all yer burnt samples. If it's all around the forest nearby, then I think it's safe to say it came from the explosion. Oh, and I also found Hyish scales among yer samples," Borak added. "That sounds like they were involved somehow. Could be the best lead ye got. If there's a village nearby, maybe they know a thing about it. That's all I got for ye for now."

"Since the Hyish ability to use fire, I am getting worried about what level of involvement they could have in this," said Flax.

"Hmm," Meleena said, looking at her wristcom. "Maybe it's better to continue this discussion with the team, before jumping to conclusions. Also, I think we're going to be late if we don't leave now."

Flax nodded. "You're right. We will need more areas of expertise to fully flesh out this theory. Thanks, Borak, this has been very helpful!"

"Always a pleasure," he smiled.

They hurried from the lab, excited to share their findings with the others. They didn't have time to process the meaning of those water crystals, but that would have to wait.

CHAPTER EIGHT

Meleena hopped on Flax's back, and they headed back down from headquarters into the city proper. The problem was, down was more nerve-wracking than up. Watching the ground flying at her, as Flax hopped from the path, flying down tight staircases between narrow buildings in the foothills, slick and wet from rushing water in between. Sen'Prin villagers meandered casually without use of wind power, between their residences and gardens. Some sat out on their terraces for late afternoon drinks, socializing with their friends.

It was all a strange mix of quaint curiosity and sped up terrifying downhill rush. Meleena grew dizzy as her eyes switched between trying to enjoy the sights and sounds of this new city, and hoping Flax was sheer footed enough not to fall on the stone paths.

Finally, she had enough, and cried out for him to stop. "Let's just go the rest of the way by foot, alight?" she asked with a nervous laugh.

"Yeah, no worries. Tonight is really more of an, eh, informal orientation more than anything."

"What? I was under the impression this was a serious meeting."

"I mean, yeah, but we still like to have a little fun," he said, winking.

That was all well and good, but her mind wandered, bristling with excitement at the thought of exploring the wilderness at the edges of the city. New friends were nice, but she still valued alone time and the feeling of freedom. She also wondered, curiously, if she'd ever get to see the inside of one of those little homes.

Flax saw her looking, and as if he could read her mind said, "Those cottages are adorable, right? My mother lives in that one, right up there." He pointed up the hillside. Meleena had trouble knowing which one he meant, but that was okay.

Questions flooded her mind and without thinking, she was halfway through speaking half of them. "Are you living with her? And speaking of your parents, how is ol' Borak? Is he living with you or your mother, like you'd hoped?"

"Oh, Borak er... He's cleared out a storage space in the lab and set up a hammock, at least for now." He gave her a knowing look. "But my parents are getting on well, so who knows. He might move in with my mother and I."

They crossed more bridges and storefronts. How would she ever find her way around this place only on foot? Her legs felt wobbly and exhausted from the thought alone. Impractical, if not impossible.

The sun was dimming through the trees, and darkness was soon upon them. In a place like this, a city under thick tree canopy in a gorge, there wasn't much of a sunset. It was striking, scary even—but just as the shadow of night threatened, the lights turned on. Thousands of tiny, glowing lights lined the bamboo walkways, and inside the domiciles.

Finally, they came to the place where four streets came together in the thickest part of town. It was loud and dense with nightlife, young Warix enjoying themselves. Rows of stalls formed night markets, selling seafood, meats, boiled roots on sticks, carved into delightful shapes. Some were hanging out in small clusters, enjoying their food, holding large flagons of drinks from the nearby bars. Many waited around for food, while more patrons jeered and cheered over beers from the four corner balconies that overlooked the central square.

"This is where we are having a meeting?" asked Meleena, nearly losing Flax in the confusion of it all. Tall bodies bumped up against each other, Meleena felt suffocated as the short Meruyan in the mix.

"Stay close," Flax said through the din, and took her hand, sending a wave of energy through her, a mix of excitement and safety. She held onto his hand tightly, following the flow of the crowd with the space his body plowed, though she could no longer see much.

They went through a doorway and things got tighter, as she let herself be led through the sound of clinking glass and up a winding staircase that wrapped around the huge trunk of a tree. It was stiflingly hot here, exacerbated by contact with so many bodies. Finally, Meleena recognized they were entering one of the balconies that overlooked the square. Glittering lights swirled among the vine-strangled walls, and Meleena realized with a thrill that they were all tiny critters responsible for lighting up most of the city.

Approaching the table, they came upon the familiar faces of the team. *Finally*!

Meleena had never been to a place like this before. There was nothing of this sort back in her village, or even on the road. She thought she'd seen everything, let alone what a city could offer, in her summer adventures. She now realized how much of her time had been spent in the wilderness. The Meruyan really didn't have a concept like this, even in the capital city, to her knowledge. She'd have to ask Deem and Talla about it to be sure, since she'd never lived there either. The point was, this place was nearly overwhelming— electrifying and terrifying at the same time, leaving her feeling frozen.

Thian, Zoltan, Naia, Riigs, Jessup, and Kyra were already sitting together, and at the sight of Flax and Meleena, they all waved and lifted their drinks to beckon them over, a range of big smiles and sarcastic grins on the varying faces.

"So, you order things and they bring food to the table," Flax said as they sat down.

"Welcome to the Three Thistles Bar," said Kyra, her half-shaved lilac hair hitting the light, her nose ring glinting. "Let's order you some fizzjuice."

They settled in, and the glowing faces of the group warmed Meleena's heart. Yes, it sounded silly, but it was in this moment that the reality of her new life came alive. The previous weeks droning by, uneventful and on edge, hoping and waiting for something like this. To be in service of Sen'Prin but to have a place to be useful in the world. This was better than she could have imagined.

"So, does anybody have any leads? We took a lot of samples today, should be *something*," asked Kyra.

"Yes, good idea, kicking off the so-called-productive portion of the evening," Riigs added with a belly laugh. "Naia and I found a footprint today, and then had a hell of a time with Zoltan in the detective's laboratory, trying to compare it to the existing records."

He held up a glass to his friend, Naia, the smallest Warix at the table with the dark purple hair and lug nut in her nose.

Kyra looked between them, lifting an eyebrow expectantly.

"Oh, yeah, we found some answers," Naia said, narrowing her eyes playfully at Zoltan before taking a swig of an amber colored drink. "It was a challenge. He's not good at playing with others."

"Ah, come on," Zoltan waved her off. "I was just trying to follow protocol. You don't want to mess up the evidence. Better to *have* evidence than theorize first and then mold all subsequent evidence to your biased theory."

"Whatever," Naia slapped his waving hand back several times in quick succession, playful yet annoyed. "Anyway, we found that it was a Hyish footprint. That's as far as we know. Likely from a clan who lives in the general area."

The group nodded in agreement amongst themselves. Meleena's drink came, and she took a sip. The cold, fizzy drink went down smooth, refreshing every cell in her after all the running around of that day. She realized how tired she was, and blinked her eyes heavily, fighting to stay awake.

"Well, that isn't bad then. Though not enough to go disturb their village about. Anyone else have more to back this up?"

Flax looked at Meleena, as if to ask which of them should speak up. She tried to nod for him to do it, it was easier. She was tired, and nervous in groups. The corner of his mouth crinkled, and he nodded back, insisting she do it. Probably for the best for her to learn to speak up.

He leaned over and whispered to her. "Remember, our fire gland cells theory is underdeveloped. Let's stick to the Hyish scale we found."

The others looked at them with curiosity, and Meleena explained how a lot of the evidence had Hyish scales in it.

"I knew it!" said Zoltan, flashing with anger.

"Those monsters, how could they!" echoed Jessup, crossing her arms. "I grew up in the Sen'Prin villages and they are always giving us trouble. Fighting us for land. They are unfriendly neighbors without obvious reason."

"But I don't think it was the Hyish," Meleena interjected. "The animals with the clusters of fur missing, all the stress to the forest. It's got to do with a drought, as in prolonged problems. The Hyish could never be responsible for it. I think they are a shared victim in this crime."

She wanted to say, it had something to do with technology, but didn't want to give away Flax's undeveloped theory. It was his to speak of and couldn't be of use now at this level anyway.

"Everybody knows the Hyish can breathe fire, I mean, not that well...in little bursts, sure. But that's a start. Maybe they have some secret methods of using it that we don't know about," said Thian, with a shrug. "I'm not saying they are out to get us, but I don't claim to understand their motives."

"Thian, what are you on about? You're our resident Hyish expert."

He chuckled. "Heh, I don't think so."

The group burst into laughter and took another swig of their drinks.

"They could be working *with* the Sen'Drorn. Maybe they are in cahoots?" offered Jessup.

Meleena's head was thick, she had drunk her chilled fizz juice too quickly. The room began to stir, lights and shapes, colors illuminated in strange ways, casting shadows and gemlike brilliant light on everything. She took a deep, grounding breath.

"Okay, then it is agreed," said Kyra cementing their plans. "We will investigate the Hyish villages tomorrow."

"To our first lead!" They cheered, lifting their drinks in solidarity. Meleena laughed, happy to be a part of things, though not so sure about the tone of their agreement. It made her uneasy how quickly they wanted to scapegoat the Hyish with so little proof of anything. But there was not much she could do about it at this point. She was only struggling to stay awake at this point and not embarrass herself by falling asleep on her first night.

Meleena didn't remember much after that point. There was a vague awareness of meandering through the crowds some more, in the later hours, and more drinks, more bars, a blur of heat and color, ending up in someone's muscular arms and a vague awareness of the common room before sleep swept her in like a tidal wave.

***

Yulah stood before Emperor Ryogrim in his private chambers. She had called a private meeting with him. Was this appropriate, or something Malotus had done as General of Tactics? He had not exactly left her with much protocol.

She waved away the budding feeling of insecurity. Better not to care. Things were working out in her favor as she had opened up to herself. Who knew confidence could be obtained by practice, opening a whole world to her.

If the Emperor wasn't happy, she could get in big trouble for this. He could have her stripped of her title, banished, imprisoned. Ryogrim was known to be volatile and impulsive.

"You can trust me with this power." She assured the Emperor in a calm voice. She was becoming more sure of herself by the day. "Our plan is going well. I have found a way to successfully bomb the Sen'Prin towns and get through their defenses where nobody else has thus far. The wreckage I've left behind for them is enough to keep them occupied and disrupt their resources. They are scrambling to sweep up the pieces and have no idea how we are doing it."

Ryogrim nodded, one beefy hand clasping his chin. "And? How are you doing it?" he asked in his rumbling voice.

"I admit I am no expert, my lord, in this technology. I have choreographed it only. I will tell you what I do know, however..."

She explained what she knew of the process while his eyebrows raised in rapt attention.

"You are a rare gem, girl," Ryogrim purred, its echo off the walls making her uneasy. "That traitor Malotus would have been proud."

"He was never truly loyal to you, Emperor," she admitted. "Not like me. I never condoned his disrespect for you..." She withheld her tongue before admitting the scratches upon his portrait, which Malotus had made a habit of inflicting on their way to the throne room each time.

The Emperor let out a low, disturbed growl. "I needed him, so I let his insolence go too far. But now I have you. I warn you, do not follow his footsteps."

"No, your grace, I shall always remain loyal," she said thoughtfully, with a bow. She felt it a nice touch.

What Malotus's issues with the Emperor had really entailed, if anything, she didn't know. It could have been simply because Ryogrim was a stubborn, self-righteous old war monger, who Malotus felt didn't deserve to rule.

These rumors about Ryogrim's character were certainly true, but why that meant he didn't deserve to rule, Yulah had not understood.

His way was law, his power absolute, and his desire to help his people, evident.

Sure, how he spoke was coarse and cruel, but in the end, she respected him. His policy on the Meruyan laborers was clever and created results which made his people prosperous. It was a win-win, really, the

Meruyan could live better on land in Warix territory than if they'd stayed under the sea. They prospered more than if they had not taken up with the Warix.

Thus, this Emperor is someone Yulah could get behind. His intentions are worth following.

Ryogrim raised his left hand and she bowed to kiss his right, glistening with assorted rings.

She left his chambers with glee, sweeping her hair away from her face and striding down the stone hallway of the fortress. A burst of satisfaction shot through her veins, rewarding her for the bold decision to call a private meeting.

Yes, the people of Sen'Drorn were simple, good, and hard working. They only wanted a good standard of living and did what they needed to take it. The Warix were more than generous to the Meruyan laborers.

Yulah stopped halfway down the halls in Sen'Drorn fortress. She had been walking the wrong way. She put a hand to her forehead and rubbed it, chuckling to herself. Her flat lay at the edge of the fortress, by a forest preserve. It had been her lovely home for two years now, ever since she had become apprentice to her uncle Malotus and moved out of her room in his flat at the age of sixteen. He had raised her like a father since she was very young.

Since becoming General Yulah, she had been granted the option to move up in the fortress as well, to the General's flat. She had spoken up and requested another suite, not to relive old memories. A fresh start, in a suite not too far from Malotus's office, now hers, with a spectacular view to boot.

Today was move-in day.

She changed directions and climbed the winding stairs towards her new place, finding the path blocked as Meruyan servants carried heavy furniture items into the bare space. She brushed past them for a better look.

Blue skinned gill breathers of the sea. They had it easy, working in the fortress. It was that Meleena girl's fault her people suddenly wanted more.

Then came a truth, resting on her shoulder like a bird. That even though her life had been a mess of inconvenience, here she was, doing better than ever. Her struggles were good for her, they made her tougher.

She felt invincible.

Yulah stretched out on her newly arranged daybed and watched them bring her things in. Yes, the Meruyan too needed to struggle for their long-term betterment. To start at the bottom, work hard. We will see in some generations from now if they want to be normal citizens. It was their turn to work hard, not shy away.

She recounted in her mind all the ways anxiety licked at her like ever-burning flames, and when she had sat with that discomfort, it began to fade. Even as it threatened to well up again in her in this moment, it was weaker. She took a heavy, calming breath and presence returned to her. Facing her fear of discomfort reduced its grip on her life, and in this moment, calmed her tense limbs.

She was practicing the fine art of overcoming anything.

CHAPTER NINE

There was no question where the Sen'Drorn meeting at the Meruyan Council would be held.

Deem and Talla peaked out the door and waited for a group of Meruyan to head towards the inner sanctum, the most prominent of rooms, reserved for the most important guests, such as Warix and Meruyan foreign diplomats.

Peering between the pillars of the balcony, they spotted the group below in the entry court. The vestibule halls echoed with the chatter of the council elders mingling with the Warix guests. Deem was looking down on wild leafy hair of reds, browns, and violets. They bore horns, gloved hands, and green cross-stitched military regalia. The Sen'drorn were unmistakable. Deem's flesh crawled.

He'd had enough contact with Sen'Drorn directly on the Journey of future leaders, having nearly died by their hand several times.

How could his own government entertain such deplorable types?

Things needed to change around here.

The Warix followed the elder Meruyan council members with curt, short steps.

Deem and Talla retreated until the group ascended the winding stairs and passed their part of the hallway. First, Meruyan councilman Ives, then the Warix, then the other elders. Talla grabbed Deem by the collar and pulled him behind a column before they passed. He was not expecting this.

"Act natural," she hissed under her breath, poking him in the ribs. She kept her posture straight and proud as she jumped out and joined at the tail of the group. "Sorry, but we needed to blend in," she said, as he joined beside her.

The train of attendees rounded a corner and entered the chamber room, where Deem glimpsed one of the nicest rooms he'd ever been in before. The walls were tall, with pillars of shells like scales, forming an archway of high peaks and intricate carvings of sea creatures. The pitched windows held a grand view of the waterfall at the highest level through colorfully stained Hyish glass.

These windows were a gift from the Sen'Drorn, no doubt, thought Deem.

Talla grabbed his arm as they filed into the room, so they were just before, but not, the last to enter.

"Talla..." prompted Deem as they took their seats. Something didn't sit right about this. A tightness in his chest, a wave of anxiety. "Talla? Were...Were you invited to this meeting?" he whispered urgently.

Talla looked him dead in the eyes and gave a wry smile.

Deem gulped, flooding with panic. "You did *not* just sneak us both in here..."

"*What?*" she moaned with indignant retaliation. "I *had* to. I told you I needed a friend. It'll be harder to get in trouble if it's both of us, rather than just me."

Unbelievable. Talla was just too much sometimes.

"You are the worst! How can you..." Deem didn't know where to begin, but they were stuck now, having followed the procession to the point where they could not leave without very clear, very uncomfortable notice. Deem gulped, body shaking with an impending panic.

There wasn't much he could do now.

***

The meeting started. The Sen'Drorn looked sharp, crisp green and black regalia glittering with copper jewelry. The councilmembers were clad in their usual blue robes. Elder Councilman Ives, as usual, leading the group. Elder Plymore was among them, a wise elderly Warix, the only one to ever have a seat on the Meruyan council.

Meleena had busted him out of the Sen'Drorn prison, among others, and he chose to move to the capital. He had been here decades earlier, as an explorer for their colonizing people, many years before, and he had discovered the historical monastery which preceded the city of Dlawn'Edo.

He had been mentoring Deem, one of his few allies, though they were in different departments. They had an outcasts' bond, newcomers from different places here. But Plymore was different than others. He didn't abide by the politics of the council, never pandering to Sen'Drorn. It was more than just the fact that he had been imprisoned for bringing his nation exactly what they wanted, just not what they expected.

They had sent him and others out seeking a weapon of legend, and he had found with it, discovered in this very city. However, it wasn't as expected. It brought only peace. Plymore was jaded with it all by now, and only turned his motives towards truth, honesty, greater values. He had no fear, only strong principles. He spoke his mind, rationally, and exuded a glowing, understanding energy. Truly an exceptional being. Deem idolized him, and he in turn coached Deem in what he knew. To face his fears, to reduce them, to breathe through trouble and it would reduce. Against his intuition, it worked.

There was someone familiar among the Warix as well. Deem recognized the violet-haired beauty, Yulah, who had been General Malotus's assistant. To his knowledge, she was decent and reasonable. Yulah had even saved his group's life once, when Malotus was out of control. Even stranger, the General Malotus was not among them today.

Deem gulped and glanced around nervously to see if anyone could tell they weren't supposed to be in there. Surely Yulah might recognize him, though as long as she didn't directly point him out to his own elders, he supposed it was okay. She was anyway turned away, whispering to one of her colleagues, while the more senior Meruyan councilmembers focused all their stares on their Warix visitors, keeping them comfortable, bringing them water flagons, helping them into their chairs.

Deem could swear he saw one councilman do a double take at them, but his attention quickly turned.

How Talla had guessed this would be fine, he had no way to guess. How did she always know the limits of what she could get away with? It was like an extra sense for the inner working of the mind. Deem couldn't help but be impressed, gulping in the mix of hopefulness to squelch the panic rising. His palms tingled with excess heat as the nervousness looked for a place to disperse.

Elder Councilman Ives, as usual, opened the floor to discussion.

"Let us get right to the point." The speaker, to Deem's surprise, was Yulah. An assistant like her, running this meeting? Now that was strange. "We cannot allow the Hyish to continue to trade with the Meruyan."

Her eyes glinted with a confident ferocity.

"What is going on here? Where is General Malotus?" Councilman Ives belted out.

Yulah cleared her throat, disgruntled. "Councilman Ives, your rudeness is unpalatable. You were told before our arrival— I am the General of Tactics now." She sat up straighter, chin upward, accentuating her delicate, foxlike face.

Deem and Talla exchanged disturbed glances. So much for her being pretty nice.

"Before we get into violence, General Yulah," cooed an older Warix of unhealthy frame with thick black sideburns. Yulah smiled respectfully and gave him the floor. "Speaking as Financial advisor to Sen'Drorn. You need to find a way to get the Meruyan in the Northern

Hilly Villages to get back to work for us. No more of this Hyish trade nonsense."

Another Warix spoke next. This one was youthful, with a strained voice that pushed too hard for dominance. "We have so few resources flowing in. We can't even stock our fruit markets, it's looking really bare. restaurants have had to cross everything off the menu and only serve local Sen'Drorn provincially grown food. How's this going to look if we can't keep it up?"

Councilman Ives spoke. "We do not wish for trouble with Emperor Ryogrim. Wouldn't it be better to incentivize the NHV Meruyan to come back and work for you, at a more competitive rate? To lure them away from the Hyish..."

Another Warix spoke, old and gray bearded, with clouded eyes. "Nobody wants a fight with the Hyish, they are too strong, it would be destruction for us all." he said in a flat tone. "No, no we need things to go back to how they were." Deem figured he must be their advisor of Hyish relations.

"Well, the Meruyan have been suffering for much longer! This is insanity!" Talla burst out, to Deem's horror.

A shockwave ran through him. *What was she thinking!* "What are you doing, you said not to make a scene. We can't expect backup." He whispered fiercely to her. Her face was downright enrapt. He kicked her under the table.

His temples feeling hot, throbbing, he knew he had to keep her calm.

The Meruyan faces tightened, foreheads beaded with sweat. They said nothing to back her up.

Yulah turned to them. "Such disrespect from such low-ranking youths. Who invited them to this meeting?"

"Deem, Talla? What's the meaning of this?" Councilman Ives said. "I'm so sorry, they must have snuck in. I will reprimand them accordingly. They aren't supposed to be here." He hissed.

Steam was rising from every pore to the point where Deem's arms became wet and the nubs of fins began to form from his own self-created moisture. They were beginning to itch under his shirt.

How much more of this could he take?

Then Plymore put his hand on Deem's shoulder. He gave him a sweet, knowing look, making him feel much more at ease.

"It's okay kids, I got this."

Then Elder Plymore stood up, the only Warix on the Meruyan council. His long, rust-colored hair sweeping over his long twitching ears. "Why is it always about the bottom line with you?" he asked the Warix, scathingly. "This is unconscionable. I'm not afraid of you, Sen'Drorn. Your time has come. This is what happens when you exploit and gain power in an unfair advantage. Did you think it would last forever? This is the process of fairness naturally restoring balance. The Hyish beat your deal, that's only fair. The Meruyan era is changing, they are finding freedom."

"You would dare, Warix traitor!" the Yulah exclaimed, leaning across the table. "I'll have you locked up again!"

"Yes, how laughable—the Meruyan put a prisoner on their council. What a disgrace!" echoed the Financial advisor.

A fight broke out across the table.

Plymore's lips curled into a soft grin. "It will be worse for you, than for the Meruyan, if you get involved in this. There is no reason we should."

"Wind Goddess smite you! You are a traitor to your people!"

"ENOUGH!" shouted Yulah. "We're not here to lock up this old man. They're not worth our time. You need to do something, Meruyan, before we do something much worse to the NHV. And I'm sure you don't want that. This was a curtesy visit, to try the diplomatic way and give you a chance to solve without violence."

Ives nearly groveled. "Yes, thank you, indeed we are grateful!"

Deem thought it was pathetic.

Yulah swept her hair aside. "In the meantime, we will start stripping resources from the Meruyan council coffers. You live lavishly enough, we need to make up our deficits."

"Please, I implore you, give us a chance. We promise you!" Councilman Ives cut in. Pathetic groveling, Deem thought. "Give us a chance to make this right. The council promises the Sen'Drorn normalcy."

"I believe that is what I am doing here, gracing you with my presence now!" Yulah slammed her palms on the table, shaking the glasses. She kicked her chair away so hard that the soft wood smashed into the wall and unhinged with a bang into a mass of wooden sticks, giving Deem a fresh startle.

"We are done here." Yulah and her accompanying Warix stood and marched from the room, leaving the rest of them stiff.

"Yes, good idea, General Yulah," said the Financial advisor.

Almost immediately, the Meruyan council began stammering and chatter bloomed among them. "This is some bad dung we've stepped in. We need things to go back to how they were. It's got to be settled." Plymore held an expression of disdain and pity.

The sound of breaking things, stealing, looting, and yelling in the background as they took what they wanted.

Ives put his hands in his face, beard hair plucked from stress. "It will be a whole lot worse for all Meruyan if their trade with the Hyish continues. Let's face it, as long as there's a Sen'Drorn, we have to concede to their will. It really is best for everyone."

"This council has no backbone!" Plymore roared, standing. "You have given away your dignity. What is wrong with you all? You must not let them push you around. Have principle, regardless of their threats. They are empty."

The group looked from one to the other, appalled and in stunned silence.

Their voices low, they murmured against him.

"You yourself have been trapped in their prison for what was it, decades? How can you even say this?"

"Clearly this old man is mad." Declared one councilman.

"And what of the Hyish?" asked another.

"Yes, certainly it won't be easy to get them to uproot their settlement. We will have to spread rumors to undermine them. To make the Meruyan turn against the Hyish, mistrust them enough to want to return to work."

"This is absurd!" Plymore objected. His ear began to twitch.

"Shut up old man, the senior members have decided," said a council member who Deem didn't recognize.

"If that is all you can see, I cannot convince you, but this is my official stance on the matter," Plymore warned, and returned to silence.

Deem wasn't happy with the way any of that had gone. He nudged Talla under the table, and they took the opportunity to slip out and process this in the apprentice lounge.

What would happen now? Were Deem and Talla going to be booted from the Council?

Isn't that what I wanted?

Soon, footsteps and clanking were heard in the hall outside. Deem ducked behind a chair, heart pounding.

"It's okay it's just me," came the soft voice of Plymore. "I told them you were my invited guests. Nobody can be kicked off. I'll fight tooth and nail."

He bolted the door.

"We need to make our own plans to counteract whatever they are doing. Are you in?"

Plymore tipped his head and urged them to follow. Wordlessly, he slipped into a small conference room and opened the tall stained-glass windows. The sound of rushing water filled the room and fresh humidity sweetened the air.

"Get in close," he said. "Listen, the council are trying, but they don't know everything," said Plymore. It was hard to hear him above the din of the roaring waterfall and Deem had to lean in. They drew in close, Plymore's face was grave, his eyes shining under his bushy auburn hair. "You two know it. I've seen you. Tell me it is so?"

"Yes," confessed Deem, drawing out a large calming breath. "I admit it. It was us who came up with the idea for the Meruyan and Hyish to work together. It made sense at the time, showing the pearls and shells to them to buy the valuable Wind Goddess Pendant from the traders, and then as a general solution it seemed brilliant for the Northern Hilly Villagers. I just didn't realize what kind of trouble it would cause!" he let it all out, panting, tears stinging the sides of his eyes.

"It is okay, boy, relax," assured Plymore in a low voice, laying a hand on his shoulder. "I think we can count on each other."

"How are you not afraid of the council? Wont they kick us off for this?" asked Deem.

Plymore waved him off with a shine in his green eyes. "Oh please, they're just old children who've taken themselves too seriously. When I was here many, many years ago, before the council and city, it was a much humbler Meruyan settlement. Before they hid behind elaborate establishments, these caves were but cracks in the walls, with curtains. Everyone ate together in the open courtyard, bringing food for one another. Not the place I know today. Trust was part of life without second thought. Sad I too must use locks now, to keep out our associates. The Meruyan government have nothing left of value to lose. They just don't realize what they've already lost.

He looked from Deem to Talla, and they nodded.

"We just want to help the Meruyan people, even if our own council will not," Talla said in agreement.

"I'll see what I can do to bring you onto my department. You will work under me now."

Deem worked hard not to let his emotions out.

"Boy, you deserve a good cry. It's healthy. You will be stronger for the next meeting. I'm proud you faced your fears. I know that couldn't have been easy. Good job, lad."

And with that, Deem felt he couldn't hold any longer, angry at himself for the deep welling up of tears about to burst forth from him. Then Talla did something very unexpected which changed the winds on it entirety.

"Yes, let the darkness in, let it swirl around you!" Talla burst out, moving into a sort of freeform version Meruyan dance. "Let it storm, let it rage, let it conjure up its worst—and then just smile as it washes over you..." Deem blinked blankly at this strange side of Talla.

"You will feel so much better afterward." Talla added with a smile.

The energy that was about to become crying transformed into full-blown laughter. It burst from him like a wellspring, and he was cry-laughing hysterically.

"What was *that*?" he gasped through the breaths.

"I was part of our village traditional dance and poetry, it's how I got my emotions out. Mostly by fighting against being forced to be there and making up my own things. Rebellious phase, you know?" She shrugged, then she and Plymore burst out in uncontrollable laughter as well.

His body shook from the core, shivering with laughter like he had never felt before, sad, happy, he didn't know anymore. He felt stronger, clearer, less afraid.

He had made a plan to call Meleena, but she didn't pick up. He had to catch her up on everything and to tell her that Yulah had become the new General, that Malotus had gone missing.

CHAPTER TEN

Meleena woke to the sound of birds calling. Upon opening her eyes, broad green leaves dangled above her head and a sense of confusion and vertigo overtook her. She stirred, her body in motion with the swaying of a hammock. She must have fallen asleep in the common room. They'd had a first-night get-together and she'd only vaguely remembered being too tired to climb the stairs to her new room.

The sun was barely over the horizon, the sky streaked with red and orange. She squinted against the bright light streaming in from the long windows. Not feeling very rested, head thick, she shuffled a multicolored blanket aside, its tassels bobbing as the hammock tilted and deposit her feet onto the floor. The bamboo cool and refreshing under her bare feet in the already sweltering morning.

It was eerily quiet. She gazed to the second story, wondering if they were still asleep. She didn't have the energy to climb the stairs and check, deciding instead to get a head start on breakfast in the noodle shop. She went to the wash basin and splashed her face, put on her glasses, and made her way downstairs.

Still half asleep, she was surprised to find the others, all there! The group were just getting out of their chairs, six empty noodle bowls in front of them. They were about ready to leave, dressed with lots of shoulder straps for gear, binoculars, and the like. All of them were here, except Kyra and Flax, who weren't bunking here and would be meeting them at headquarters. Flax was working at the tech lab and would not join them to visit the Hyish today.

"Are we going already?" Meleena grunted, not sure what else to say. *How could they get up so early after the night they'd had?* she thought. *And I was the first to sleep!*

This all was going to take some getting used to, clearly.

"Oh, still in bed? I thought you were downstairs," said Zoltan, standing and slinging his pack over his shoulder. The others had smug grins or showed little interest about her lateness. What were they planning to do, just leave her behind?

She fumed inside but tried not to let on that she was upset. How could he think she was downstairs? Or not even think to check. She was the only blue person in this group!

Meleena hurried back upstairs, put on clothes and threw some things in her pack, including the journal, head swimming, her stomach growling all the while. There would be no time for breakfast.

A feeling like heavy clay in her chest, regret, made her wish she'd never come here or perhaps picked an easier course. Maybe the Meruyan capital wasn't so bad. Was it too late to join the council? She was in over her head here.

Making friends wasn't something that came easily to her. She had worked so hard to make some friends already, only for them to now live in another city! What was the point, all this making friends business.

She raced back down the stairs, hoping they hadn't left without her. Glancing around the patrons, her heart skipped a beat, not to see any of them, and she pushed her way through, making a beeline for the door to the street.

The group were standing out front, making her stop in a frenzy and regain her bearings.

"Don't worry little one, we wouldn't leave you behind," said Riigs, smiling, tree trunk arms crossed over his chest. Naia laughed in a patronizing way.

Thian and Jessup gave welcoming smiles, Zoltan a half vague nod.

"Yeah, Kyra would never let us," Naia muttered, as a very unnecessary adage.

"What's your problem with me, anyway?" Meleena snapped, the remaining stressful energy forking from her like lightning, surprising her. She was appalled at it came out. That she didn't have more self-control. She needed these people to like her! To be on a team! The pressure was too much.

"Not me. You're too sensitive." Naia said with narrowing eyes and crinkling nose. She stood close, her lugnut nose ring in Meleena's face. She was about the same height as Meleena.

Meleena glared back in challenge. Naia's dark hair was so sleek, it shone in a way that reminded Meleena of the sea, making her homesick for her Meruyan friends. Naia was small and of vaguely 'ocean-like' complexion, thus she'd hoped a strange kinship could blossom between them, or at least that she'd be somehow more understanding of a Meruyan among them. Stupid.

"If you wanna fight, I will gladly duel you," Naia said.

"I could fight you under water."

Naia's glare vanished. Was that a hint of fear?

What did any of that matter? It's almost like she was trying to distance herself from, not to cramp her own individuality. *I'm the small, blue one of this group.*

"Now, now," said Riigs, putting an arm around Naia, in a teasing fashion, as if soothing a savage beast. "Let's all be nice!"

"Meleena is new, she deserves to feel welcome," said Thian.

Jessup hummed in agreement. She was also new, but she seemed to be having no trouble fitting in, to nobody's surprise.

They headed out on foot to a place described as "the speedway" which would take them to the top of the city, to headquarters faster than going through the city. Meleena had no idea what this meant.

At the edge of the boardwalk, there was a sort of copper cross-crossing partially open tube. It was actually a pair of tubes. One had a jettison of wind moving upstream, the other down.

Naia, still angry, was first to power into the jet of air.

"She has trouble making new friends, sometimes," Riigs whispered to Meleena as soon as Naia had gone. "Don't let her get to you. She's had it rough all her life."

Why is that an excuse to take her frustrations out on me? Meleena thought, angrier than before.

Thian—either out of kindness, pity, possibly both—carried her on his back as they soared through the swirling copper tube. They traversed a new route, closer to the cheeks of the gorge, away from the city proper, in an efficient jet stream towards the military headquarters. There were entry points at each platform height. It was another amazing Warix invention, designed by and for Warix. Another feature she could not use.

Her mind wandered to Talla and Deem as they went. She bet they were fitting in better than this in Dlawn'Edo.

Loneliness stung her. Missing Talla was the last thing she ever thought she'd feel, how funny life was sometimes. Once she regained her bearings, she remembered to check her wristcom for the first time, finding a missed call from Deem, during the blur of last night. She'd have to call him back at the next chance.

The copper speedway shot them out onto a platform at the lower entrance of Sen'Prin Headquarters. They entered the round entry chamber from beneath. Looking up at the domed skylight, and the large Sen'Prin flag along the main wall, a purple nectar sprig on a white background. A nectar sprig was a sort of tiny dragon, known for its dangerous, and symbolically courageous work of pollinating the flower-maned lion's central flower. As this lion was the symbol of Sen'Drorn, it was sort of response; the white background as a fresh start.

While the lower half of the walls were stone, upper half was glass, and from the center, they could see into conference rooms, work chambers, and up until recently, the engineering facilities. The new engineering space, where she'd visited yesterday, she calculated, would be below this level, tucked deeper into the mountain.

Kyra paced in one of the conference rooms, and Meleena lit up when she caught sight of the *amber mohawk, like flames in an autumn forest*—Governess Arenay, the leader of Sen'Prin. She sat in one of the chairs, staring sternly at Kyra. They appeared to be in heated conversation.

Arenay was the founder of the Sen'Prin nation, after daring to stand against the Sen'Drorn government as a young member of its military, nearly eighteen years ago. She shined with poise, even as her face displayed such concern.

Catching sight of them, she turned, eyes flashing bright silver momentarily as she jumped to her feet. Then a look of relief and she came out to greet them.

Arenay was not in the bright mood Meleena had previously known.

"Welcome. I was just telling Kyra about this very delicate situation. I would rather not send a group of you to the Hyish. We have a very delicate relationship…" she gritted her teeth. "Kyra is insisting it is necessary. I warn, be the utmost cautious. We do not wish to upset the Hyish."

They nodded, none daring to utter a word.

Meleena had wanted to greet her more personally but thought better of it. She'd first encountered the Governess in the Meruyan city, Dlawn'Edo, the previous year, and at that meeting had inspired Meleena to forge her own unique path. In a way, Arenay had shaped Meleena's year, perhaps her entire future.

She looked tense, uneasy. She glared at Kyra something fierce before shaking it off and trying to sound calm.

"Meleena, it is so good to see you," Arenay said with a bow. "How are you enjoying Sen'Prin city?"

Zoltan's jaw actually dropped, and Naia scoffed at the familiarity.

"You have a beautiful city," replied Meleena, mimicking her bow out of respect.

"Wonderful. And hopefully making new friends already," she smiled.

"Heh, yeah."

"Extraordinary," Arenay sighed, then excused herself. "I am burdened with too many projects at the moment, but we are so grateful for the work you're doing." She gestured in gratitude to the group, then bounded off.

That was strange, thought Meleena, wondering what she and Kyra had discussed. Wishing Kyra would be more open and honest with this group, for all their sakes.

CHAPTER ELEVEN

Today, the group would borrow an airship for speed. Other groups had already checked out the gloves and top flying gear for use at the headquarters. Unlike Sen'Drorn, they had limited availability for supplies.

The team arranged themselves, Kyra steering at the rudder, the others by copper tubes for wind propulsion. Their eyes glowed silver and the ship launched from the platform, Meleena gripped the railing for support as the wind burst forth from the propellers.

Meleena looked around. The view from up here was actually quite spectacular. A Steep cliff above a bend in a river. They could see the forest. Birds and reptiles with algae fur flew by, close enough to see details.

They sped over the forests and landed on the side of a creek. No city was visible. "This seemed like the best place. Arenay's intel gave us a map, they said the Hyish encampment is just in the forest beyond."

Meleena and the others followed Kyra's lead, as they went into the forest, which was so tall Meleena couldn't fathom it. Spindly trees, higher than she'd ever seen before, but with ample space between them, and strangler vines traversing every which-way.

There was no clear Hyish village here. But something was odd. A shiver ran down from her neck.

It was the sound which caught her attention first. Rows and rows of insect nests, swarming up and down the tree trunks. Meleena wasn't afraid of bugs, but this was...a lot. It was primal, the urge to hide from it. Too many flying, winged, swarming creatures.

"Are you sure this is the right place?" Meleena asked, shuddering.

"Yep, looks like it," said Thian, holding the map, squinting at it.

"Why is their village so close to all these hives?" asked Jessup, beating Meleena to it.

Zoltan made a face of disgust. Naia and Riigs seemed unfazed, and were looking at Thian, skeptically amused. "I hope you didn't lead us to the wrong place," he said.

Thian raised his eyebrows. "Food source o' course!"

"Look up," Kyra said, one finger nervously twisting her earring, as her head pitched upward in the direction of the canopy. "Looks like we will have to climb."

Meleena followed her gaze, realizing that the vines were more than natural. There were innumerable masses, from braided and preserved vines, forming webbings which crisscrossed and formed pathways. The skittering of reptilian feet rose above them, of claws hooking into this world high above the forest floor.

Kyra said, too casually, as if this was obviously just like any other place. "We will split into three groups. Thian, as a veteran of Hyish culture, you will come with me. Zoltan and Jessup, find the town center and interview who you can. Naia and Riigs, talk to anyone you can on the ground, or outskirts of town. Talk to locals, get a sense of the mood. Find out any leads, attitudes towards Warix, motives. Remember they may not know the difference between Warix factions. They think were all the same. Try to keep them from disliking us in any regard."

"I have to go with *him*?" Jessup huffed.

Zoltan folded his arms and snarled. "I could say the same."

"Yes, report on anything strange. In their behavior or if they've seen any possible leads."

They scowled at one another but nodded and wandered off. Meleena wondered what that was about. Perhaps she'd missed some drama the night before.

"You never gave me an assignment," stated Meleena, unsure about where to go. Kyra looked her up and down, also unsure. "I have experience with Hyish, as well." Meleena added, a little dejected.

"Alright, the three of us will go together and split up in the center. Time to climb."

Kyra took the lead as she went, one boot first, then hand, boot, hand, and repeat—Onto the vine web which formed the—Meleena supposed there was no other way to call it than a '*village tapestry*.'

It was quite confusing. Meleena followed behind Thian. She gripped the vine ropes and found them to be surprisingly springy, and thus not that hard to keep up with.

For the Hyish who passed, it was clear they were quite interested in this band of outsiders trying to move through it. Hyish carried baskets by their tails, smaller items were strapped over their simple clothing via netlike clothing on hooks. Hooks that were talons gleaned from varying bird species. Woven structures interwove much like a bird's nests. Elongated burrows provided storage for insects and food.

The sounds of their smooth bodies and hissing language formed a soft whisper through the air. The smell was of ripe fruit and a bit of reptilian musk, though the gentle breeze that shook the trees also brought fresh air.

Thian pointed. "There, see those rows of bones bound with twine? That's a symbol of power, rank. The higher ranking, the more bones in the string. We will follow the bones to find their chieftains."

Meleena nodded. She was already trying to take in the scene, even if they were lost, and it was thrilling. Meleena had seen a Hyish encampment before, but this is totally different. The Hyish she had seen were of a desert variety, and they lived in tent villages in the sand dunes, sunning themselves on desert rocks and doing glassblowing for trade. Nomadic riders living out of caravans also passed through, and she recalled the leaders of those wealthier tribes having strong influence over Warix politics. Hyish trading had spread rare resources around the nations, including the Warix's coveted Pendant of Nushen'yu.

As the crowds became denser, it became obvious they were reaching the center of town. They reached a spot where Kyra stopped and looked up the closest vine way. "We are going to have to do some climbing if we are to get any further."

Meleena had been wondering this as well. The city was spread up there, and just like her problems in the Warix city, this place was not designed for non-Hyish. Meleena wondered out loud, "what, if any, negative effects might a Warix's wind power have here?"

"Even if I can without warping or tearing the vines, I have to land somewhere, and it's not going to be so accurate without any flat, open landing points."

"It will be safer, and more diplomatic, if we do it their way." Agreed Thian. "Trust me, back in the day, Flax and I had quite the time figuring out the jungle Hyish."

They took to the wall, grabbing, and it was surprisingly springy, helping to propel their legs, with slight bend and jump. They began to make high progress without tiring out. They passed the structures previously seen from below and saw their amazing intricate webbing.

They passed lots of rodents in cages. Near the cages were open fire grills, filled with rodents on spits, juices dripping in the fire causing a spike of flame and a popping sound. Looking into entry holes, the inside was surprisingly flat. There was indeed a floor, of wood or filled in soil, often green with soft moss covering. It likely depended on wealth. Furniture was wood logs or flat stones, with Hyish sprawled and lounging like lizards.

They took periodic breaks to look around. Meleena soon lost track of the bones, noticing them only occasionally, letting Thian take the lead there. She felt it best to focus on hers, searching for clues that may link these Hyish to a motive for blowing up a Sen'Prin city.

They had stopped climbing. Webbed paths giving rise to nodes, woven, and more nest-like living structures.

She touched the webbing, feeling its smooth surface, but when she removed her finger, her blue skin had a strange grayish residue.

What is that? Some kind of slick substance, like gunk. Unpleasant, cool to the touch. This could be important.

"There," said Thian. He pointed to a larger, more intricate bundling in a convergence in the web of vine ways. "That's where the royals meet. See the four bone structures? And there is the fifth at the top of it, where the chieftain lives."

They found two Hyish men blocking the entry hole, already eyeing them as they approached. They puffed their uniformed chests.

"Gentlemen." Thian said.

"This strange. Warix? And this Blue Warix?"

"She's a Meruyan, but whatever," Thian said with a shrug. "We are here to visit your chieftains. To know if anything strange has been going on."

One stayed at the door, blocking it with his large body, while the other slipped inside. They waited for a moment, and Thian said, "he's alerting their butler, who will speak to the leader, but you should have no more issues getting inside." He bowed.

Sure enough, the guard returned a moment later. "Chieftain A'dandali will see you. He is expecting Warix."

He escorted them inside, where A'dandali sat on what looked like a nest. Hyish came by with platters of fried insects and strange fruit. Some Meleena recognized from coming from as far away as the Northern Meruyan farming regions.

They must be on the trade route, which means Warix must be visiting here, Meleena thought. The chieftain was clearly intrigued at her presence, and likely never saw a Meruyan in the flesh before. Meleena suppressed a feeling of annoyance. This wasn't the time or place to fret about disparities.

Chieftain A'dandali stopped eating and bid them to approach, staring all the while with those large yellow slit eyes. Eyes which grew wider, buggier, as they came close. "Warixxx. Please, sit down. You will be needing refreshments. I was starting to wonder if you would ever show your faces here. To pay us a curtesy visit."

Pillows on smooth stones, surprisingly comfortable, to sit on.

Kyra began, "I am the leader of the investigative division of Sen'Prin, and we recently had a disaster."

"Yes, yes, we know."

"A Sen'Prin villages has been attacked, destroyed in fact, by fire… We have come to ask, kindly, if your people have seen other Warix approach from here."

"Approach? What means this? We cannot distinguish the Warix. Any more than you know us by one tribe to the nessst." His tongue flickered at the last elongated syllable.

"We have *let you* visit usss. Hoping for an apology in fact."

"An apology? I mean, um, sorry, for what?"

Meleena could already tell this wasn't going so great.

"A little resssspect, is all the Hyish ask. Especially after so much difficulty in these times."

"Difficulty, in what?"

His long neck shot out, striking like a snake. They couldn't help it. Flinching back, not great. Not respectful enough, that much was evident.

"Don't play dead mouse with us! Our insects, which we rely on for food source, have been depleted by your spray! They die in record numbers. We get sick. This is very bad. And it is more than this! We have seen drought, last months, gunk, clogging up rivers, tainting our drinking water. It doesn't help that the weather has been so dry for the entire wet season."

"Is that why your people blew up our village?"

Wrong move. What was she thinking, letting that slip? Meleena felt her cheeks grow hot. She suddenly felt a newfound kinship alongside it, finding herself on the side of the Hyish. Their gravitas towards nature, both respect and synchronic lifestyle.

A'dandali went rigid with displeasure.

"Animals of the forest, sick! Hair coming out in patches! Whole forest unhappy! And you accuse *us* of making *harm* on your village? This is outrageous, coming here and accusing us of this crime?"

"We are the victims of all of this! Our community keeps to itself, peacefully living nearby your Warix settlement without previous problems. Now, your fire rained a terrible plague upon us. This gray ooze is everywhere. It has tried up our vines, causing Hyish to fall through and the need for repairs. It has harmed our crops. We have had much smaller food yields. If the crops continue to fail like this, they will have no choice soon but to pack up and settle elsewhere." He bellowed. "This is unheard of. Warix depravity knowing no boundaries..."

His eyes enlarged, he tilted his head back, and from his throat a bolt of fire shot out at them. They threw their arms up, flinching in self-defense. But the fire didn't reach them.

A'dandali laughed. The smell of smoke hung in the air, and Meleena opened her eyes to see it had burnt out before arriving at them.

More evidence as far as she was concerned that it couldn't have been them.

"Did you recently perform, perhaps some kind of event, like a fire festival?" Meleena asked, coming up with possible ideas. "Hyish scales were found at the scene of our town's bombing."

A'dandali's tongue slipped from his wide mouth and whipped back in.

"Even if we have a festival, the people's fire breath is not to destroy. We empower with self-control." He spat out the words as the guards stared down at them. *When did they slither in here on silent feet?* "It is time for you all to leave."

Meleena looked from Kyra to the chieftain. She wasn't a trained integrator, but showing this level of outright suspicion towards their Hyish hosts didn't seem like the best way to go about this.

Kyra was trying to act calm but was clearly fuming. "Thank you for your time," she started. "We will be returning if we have more questions."

They left promptly. The guards bearing long curled blades on spikes were intimating enough.

To their surprise, Jessup and Zoltan were grasping at the edge of the webbing, waiting for them.

They waited expectantly for Kyra's reply.

She merely shook her head in embarrassed dismay. Meleena was flat out angry at Kyra. She hadn't listened at all, nor kept herself under control.

"Do you think the dryness has to do with our village catching fire like that? It's got to have something to do with it," Kyra grasped for backup from the others. "Somehow, it was unusually dry, enough where the explosion had a greater impact. If it had been heavy rainfall, like normally in this time, a large fire like that could not have happened.

"But the Hyish don't know how to create explosions!" argued Meleena. She'd had enough of this. "They shoot tiny fires. It's not clear how they are related. Except that their scales were found at the scene maybe because they were also victims of the same type of problems.

"Thought you might want to know," cut in Zoltan.

"What!?" shouted Meleena.

Zoltan held up a finger. "In fact, the Hyish we spoke to agree. They said their crops were failing, from a drought." He explained as they climbed down to the ropes again, heading towards the ground floor.

Between breathy gaps, Jessup added more to the story. "Worse than that! Their citizens have been killed. There are Reports of a monster, a wild beast, seen in the area, scaring them. This whole village is pretty unhappy."

Kyra went even paler at this news.

Meleena's eyes narrowed. "There is something you're not telling us, Kyra.

"Yes...I'm afraid so. There is more at stake here," Kyra admitted. "I really messed up. There is more going on you don't know about...There's been some issues with the Hyish in our city as well. The Hyish guards of Sen'Prin want more money, claim there's a beast or something unnatural out there, terrorizing them. Killing and dragging into the forest by the neck. Never seen. Something out there scares them."

"So, that's bad," Thian said, just about summing it up.

"Well then we have to go back there!" said Meleena. "I would like another chance to talk to the chieftain." She was so angry, heat rose in the palms of her hands, making them hot and slippery on the vine meshing. "Also, *now* do you believe me, that there's another cause? Something larger that is messing with the earth beneath our…feet."

The point wasn't lost even though they dangled so far off their 'precious ground'.

Meleena was fed up with them and their distrust, she wanted nothing more than to wash her hands of the Warix. Nothing but trouble, is what they are. She found herself agreeing with the chieftain, whose hospitality had run dry with them so quickly this same hour.

Meleena grappled with the vines, but down turned out to be much harder than up. After a mere few minutes, her legs were starting to feel wobbly.

"…but lived in peace with the Warix town nearby. thankful it wasn't them in the explosion." Thian continued.

"Well, we can't assume it's Sen'Drorn yet. There simply isn't enough evidence," Kyra said defensively.

"Nothing about this is obvious!" argued Thian back.

"How are we going to find the others at the edge of town?" Meleena asked.

"Wristcoms, remember?" chided Thian.

"Oh right."

"It was a good job, badly done, but we did our best," said Thian.

"Yeah, we got our horns caught so many times in these nets!" laughed Jessup.

"What are you talking ab—" Meleena began to protest, and then, Meleena's hand gave way and she fell…down, down…her body filled with claylike fears at the fear of the impending fall as the ground rushed closer.

CHAPTER TWELVE

Someone grabbed Meleena's wrist like an angry parent and pulled her onto their back as the tornado formed. Meleena braced herself against the thrust of heavy winds.

They broke through the trees' layers until Meleena could look down, a sinking feeling taking hold, her feet dangling. A half terrified, half exhilarated rush flushed her. Then a steep cliff carved from the riverside. She and her rescuer seemed to be flying right into it. She winced, bracing herself for the end, when the tornado halted, and they fell into a breezy downward spiral that led them safely on an earthen ledge. Meleena collapsed onto the hard surface. Noodley legs not willing to stand. She fought to catch her breath.

"What the blowhole was *that*?" Meleena shouted, angry at the way in which she'd been handled.

Kyra looked down at her, the usual stern look on her face.

Thian's tornado came spiraling down by their side, which had her crouching. He was less graceful at landing than Kyra had been.

"Why so frazzled, Meruyan?" Thian asked.

"I saved your life, that's what," said Kyra.

"Ah, yeah, Kyra's a real talent. Showin' off her delicate wind slice skills." Thian held up his hands, "Don't look at me, I can't do that."

"Then perhaps better I ride with you next time. If you don't mind," said Meleena, still not loving the idea of having to be carried around everywhere.

Jessup was giggling, and even Zoltan cracked a half-smile.

It was like being caught in a riptide. If only she could control the wind like them, anticipating where to go. She suspected they didn't enjoy bringing her around everywhere, but oh well. She wasn't going to apologize for being a Meruyan.

"Time to call the others and see where they're at," said Kyra.

Riigs didn't pick up, but Naia's muffled voice came in.

"Naia—Naia?" Kyra sounded concerned, as if Naia was picnicked. "Don't worry. We are at the southern border of the town, on a ledge. Come find us! We won't move!"

'Well, that was one way of getting to the outskirts of this town without climbing," said Thian, beaming.

The loud slapping of feet on the ground made them turn, defensive at the perpetrator rushing towards them.

It was no Hyish, but a smallish Warix girl—Naia. Her hair was chaotic purple-black and her eyes fiery with fear.

"Help! It's Riigs! They have him!" she shouted before even coming close. "I wasn't far, but my wristcom was smashed!" She hurried over to them, holding it up in her hand. "They thought it was evil technology and I had to take it off, or my arm would have been cut off!" she gasped, clutching her wrist.

"Now who is the villain, here, eh?" scowled Zoltan.

They followed Naia on foot, and ran over to find a large web structure, with a squirming Riigs upside-down at the center. The Hyish farmers had imprisoned him.

Thian scratched his head. "Hah, poor Riigs," he mused. "Better get him out of there."

"What is this all about?" Demanded Kyra, approaching the farmers. Meleena liked how Kyra got right down to business. Sure, she didn't have much of well, any, sense of humor, but it was nice to see someone taking action.

Naia acted tough with her hands on her hips but stayed a safe distance behind Kyra.

"They think he's some kind of monster!" Naia hollered.

"We saw the beast, it killed our people! It's known all around!" spat the Hyish farmer in broken common, through gritted teeth. He pointed at the hulking, upside-down figure that was Riigs.

"Let him out!" shouted Naia, angrily, stomping her thick black boot.

"Is okay, I'm alright!" Riigs' muffled voice came through the webbing.

"*We need to be delicate here. Arenay warned us*," hissed Meleena, looking at Kyra. "No need to make an enemy."

"So, you *did* see a Warix here?" Kyra asked the Hyish local.

"Yes," said Naia, desperately. "And he had some kind of machine with him. They didn't know much else about it."

"Well, we did learn something then. The Sen'Drorn are behind this. It is some form of new weapon they are attacking with."

Riigs laughed and wriggled in his ropes. "If someone can cut me loose..."

Thian negotiated his release, half-speaking the hissing tongue with lots of miming.

The Hyish stated again that there was a large beast on the loose and could not let Riigs loose.

"Sounds like Meleena's department," shrugged Zoltan. "Care to explain the origin of these mysterious forest animals, coming to attack?"

"Do you know of any creatures like that?" echoed Kyra. "Who would be ripping the throats but not eating their victims."

Meleena thought for a moment. Vangrots stole from you, if you were loud, and had food, but they'd never main someone too badly...nor were they so large as to be confused with a Warix.

"It had large wings," muttered the Hyish.

"And claws, and feathered tail! And green fur," said another.

"No, it has shiny brown short coat, metallic shine, red eyes!" shivered the other Hyish, hugging her arms to her chest.

"Well, does he look like he's got any of those?" beseeched Naia.

Meleena never knew of any creature like that, nor who would only eat the throat. "I haven't heard of any. But the destruction of their crops and this gunk stuff on everything, that is concerning..." Meleena said.

She suspected it came from the destroyed or transmuted tissues of plants and animals, but it was too soon to tell.

Kyra looked at her in bewilderment.

"Ehh. Flax and I were waiting to tell you later about it, when we had more information. But, there is a new theory about nature which none of us understand yet, which may be involved."

"This isn't the place to speak of the case," said Kyra, annoyed.

Meleena turned to the Hyish, "We need to work together to find out. Eyes and ears. That's why we really came. We both are victims, you are right. There's clearly a third party behind this."

The two Hyish nodded in approval, as Kyra shook hers in disapproval. But it had worked well enough to get them to cut the bindings and release Riigs.

"I knew the Meruyan were good people..." he said, and pulled out a necklace, string of pearls. "From the new trade routes, all open now." He smiled with his tongue whipping outward. "You may go now in peace," said the Hyish.

The team bid farewell to the Hyish farmers and regrouped in a more private location in the forest.

"Many farmers we spoke to said their crops have been failing. Smaller fruit. Gunk inside of them. All around drought," said Riigs.

"Dry and cracked earth," added Naia, after giving a big hug to her friend, now free.

"What about the insects they eat?" asked Meleena. "Hard to feed them when there's no food chain."

"Yes, fewer water, fewer bugs," confirmed Jessup. "Nobody saw Warix coming and going strangely. Maybe it was someone who blended in and snuck into the facility. I suspect it was sabotage to the agricultural system."

"Why is that?" asked Kyra, turning to her.

"Because maybe there's a way to harness it for use? See I have this theory. What is it that makes my fins form and spring up when my arms and legs hit water? Or breathing water? There's something to this that we have. Maybe it can be harnessed outward as well. Now that I realize it, the lizards I saw in Sen'Prin city were often dead, with missing fire glands. Maybe that's because someone is stealing it. Maybe someone on the inside of Sen'Prin."

"Careful with an accusation like that."

"It's probably just a hawk or something," said Zoltan. "Just because Meleena's never heard of it doesn't mean anything."

"Oh yeah, what did it look like?" Meleena asked, getting defensive. She couldn't admit she was wrong now. She needed them to respect her. She knew enough about most animals, certainly more than them.

"If it's metallic, then it doesn't sound like an animal…more like a machine. Or copper like you all wear which enhances your wind energy," Meleena pointed out.

"It was just a small bird. It was flying in small wind gusts, as if it controlled them."

"Okay, they can agree on something at least," said Thian.

Meleena thought for a moment. ""Like…like a Warix?"

The others looked at her.

"I really have never heard of any creature that can do that. I know of other creatures that function like the Meruyan. Crossing between land and sea. I would even say the green fur plant blends in some animals are earth's touch. But I wouldn't say I know of air. It seems like animals come in clusters, even. Somehow elemental connection."

"That's ridiculous!" said Kyra.

"Again, just because you haven't heard of it doesn't make it not real." argued Zoltan.

Meleena smirked. She was starting to like this strange Zoltan. He was rude, tough with his praise, but doled out logic and stated his mind, equally on everyone regardless of rank.

"Look, maybe," Meleena countered. "But I'm just saying, nobody else has thought to study this stuff. Make connections here. I'm new, but if they had maybe we would have more to work with. I'm trying to document the connections between plants, animals, and their connections to the elements in my journal with Flax."

"Yeah, okay. If it was important we would have had it by now."

"That's ridiculous logic."

"Prove me wrong."

"I will."

"Okay then." He crossed his arms.

Zoltan may indeed argue this forever.

"They saw magical copper monsters," Meleena explained, a laugh caught in her throat at his gal. "That could use wind power! That has Warix written all over it. When were back at the lab we can do more work to check it out."

Kyra agreed, finally backing her up. "Indeed. We shall see how it will work."

"See, not all our technology is the same," urged Naia, pouting at her broken wristcom.

"We'll get you a new one when we return to headquarters," assured Kyra, putting a hand on her shoulder.

"So, we know there's a drought, a machine, not many Warix involved. That's a few things." The group surmised.

And with that, they gathered themselves up, and they headed off in the airship over the hills towards Sen'Prin. Over the ruined village of Sen'Prin, over the forest which she now knew contained the Hyish, though couldn't tell from above.

They returned exhausted, Meleena ready to crash and finally try her bed out. The group had other plans. As soon as they had returned to the safe comfort of Sen'Prin City, they were off, to the social square for some drinks and escapades into the late night. Meleena felt the tug to join them, just for the bonding, not to miss out, but was so exhausted, she couldn't will herself to keep up.

What was one night, missing out, worth in the grand scheme? She had to take it easy if she was to keep up in the morning. She remained unsure how they managed to pull all that off and have energy for the day.

CHAPTER THIRTEEN

Yulah spent her first night in her new apartment, in the highest tower of Sen'Drorn Fortress. It was naturally reserved only for the top guards. The fineries of their power were now at her disposal.

And yet, she was restless, waking through the night in cold sweat, tormented by forgotten dreams. Positive memories of Malotus, popped by the pain of finding the stars shining through the balcony, her heart pounding, her eyes wet with tears.

She wiped her face and thrust the covers from herself.

I need to cool off, get some fresh air maybe. She moved to the balcony, unlatching the intricate carved wooden panels, and letting the night wind burst in, causing them to clatter.

Sen'Drorn City was built on a natural geographic wind-tunnel, between two steep valleys, atop a volcanic peak in its center, which provided the perfect place for maximal wind energy. Being at the top of the Fortress was to live, exposed to the best wind anywhere in the known world. Thus, she felt stimulated by it, like batteries supercharged. The wind flowing was euphoric, energizing, like nothing she'd ever known. They lived well here, the Sen'Drorn elites.

Lightning often struck the top of the fortress, and it was frequently rebuilt, but the risk was worth it to be so close to such elemental majesty.

Yulah caressed the curling vines which bloomed with fragrant purple flowers. They twisted around the columned edges of the balcony, softening her mind.

She reminded herself of her new mental strategy, to quell her anxiety by sitting with it, breathing deeply, and accepting it until it drained from her like so much polluted air.

She stroked her soft hair, always calming, and keenly her horns picked up the strength of the wind, sending a tingling ripple through her body.

There was the urge to fly, to move.

She looked out over the dark city, twinkling with tiny lights. The city was mirrored basin, reflecting the sky. Stars above, stars below.

But flying all alone at night? She had never done something like that before. But then, this was a time of change and experiments. Another strong breeze brushed over her, and she inhaled the chill, crisp air which bristled over her skin with keen wonderment.

Barefoot, she stepped over the ledge of the balcony, wearing just her night gown as she plunged off the balcony, perfectly catching a breeze stream, trusting—following its path through the night wherever it would lead.

Her eyes misted at the periphery with silver light, dampening her vision. The tips of her sleek horns, sensitive to every vibration, her shoulders, rudders, guided her through the Windstream like a slide.

Drifting images of Malotus haunted her and she let them go, like fall leaves from a tree. She sailed over the rooftops of the upper city, where the upper class dwelled nearest to the fortress. The founders, the merchants, the stewards to the emperor, those who suckled near the throne and enjoyed its decadence. This was where she'd lived with Uncle Malotus when she first came to live with him at the age of six. She didn't want to live there, and the finer things gave her no pleasure. She had only wanted her parents back…

After two years, Malotus was promoted from high military rank to General and they moved into the fortress proper.

The current carried her over the middle bulk of the city, where most citizens dwelled in more than reasonable prosperity. The twisting black volcanic stone walkways absorbed light, so that only occasional lanterns lit nodes, bathing an eerie, warm light on the alleyways and stairs, narrow passageways between tall, jagged buildings. Every so often the light would bounce off the copper piping which ran up the sides of buildings, causing shimmers of warmer light.

Every so often, a glimpse of blue skin flickered in the lamplight as Meruyan night workers cleaned the city.

Flieg street was down there somewhere, though she could not locate it. The place where most of her memories of the main city were forged. Running errands for Malotus there, even as a child. She had loved it, flying through the streets, bouncing off balconies in jets of concentrated wind. Even her time with her first love, Flax, had been there.

She drifted closer to the city's outer walls. This is where her earliest memories were, where she'd grown up with her parents in the lower, transitional part of the city. She and Malotus, their family tree, they had all been here, historically.

Malotus and his older brother, Yulah's father, had grown up on the streets here. A pair of orphans, fed by the kindness of strangers. She knew some of the history, but not much. Only that when her father came of age, he had apprenticed as a furniture carver, which finally gave them a decent bed. Eventually marrying her mother, they managed their own little shop.

Then the Great Split happened. That delinquent and military dissenter Arenay, gained a following and she with her band of rioters broke through the city walls, they left a wake of looting and chaos which destroyed Yulah's parent's shop.

Yulah was only three then, but remembered the fires, and the screaming, and the smashing. Uncle Malotus had protected her, as she shrank into his arms. She had thought of him like an older brother. He was still a teenager himself, on break from the mandatory Sen'Drorn military duty.

Over the next three years, Malotus had gone away for military duties, and she didn't see him, while her parents struggled to survive on Sen'Drorn government assistance but fell ill and passed away before Malotus returned.

Yulah was just six, then, when Malotus returned from leave to claim her as guardian. He gave up whatever he was doing far away, to stay in the city and raise her. He must have been important even then, as they moved into that house on the upper rung.

Uncle Malotus had told her that he'd known Arenay personally, which earned him the ear of the emperor. Thus, the promotion to General only two years after.

As the wind tunnel rushed her onwards from the lower district, she entered the neighborhoods directly up against the walls. The buildings became tighter, denser. Growing up by the edge of this neighborhood, she had spent much time walking here around as a young child. The shopfronts were squashed, and the beautiful scent of seafood cooking from open steaming barrels. This is where the Meruyan foreign workers lived.

Behold the generosity of Sen'Drorn. Letting them live in our walls and share in our prosperity, she thought, sliding over the rooftop terraces, dipping to avoid entanglement herself in strings of hanging clothing blowing in the wind.

She didn't know any Meruyan personally and had always kept her distance from the strange aquatic beings.

Of course! How could she have forgotten!? The Warix guards worked tirelessly to forge the great wind wall that circled the city from atop the outer walls. She had let her mind and body drift, now too far. She was being sucked in.

She struggled against the pull, but it was like a magnet, with a gravity of its own. Panic threatened to set in, her heart jumping with the action at hand, and she turned upright, her horns trying to grasp at any thread of wind elsewhere, a direction to go in. She was unable to harness any, the guards were soaking it all up with the momentum from their wind. She would be smashed into the walls or worse, suffocated, if she didn't get out now.

She was without any of her copper jewelry or other gear to enhance the potency of her powers like an electrical current. She was to be absorbed by the thrashing gray winds.

She struggled again, as hard as she could, feeling the wind flow from her horns, through her being, into her chest, setting a great ball of energy, grasping what she could from the outer edges at fresh air, pumping the air out her hands and feet, trying to unstuck her and pull her from the whirlpool. She would certainly suffocate in the storm, should she lose all control. How could she have been so unawares, caught reminiscing in the daydreams of her youth.

An undercurrent pulled her in, choking her. She screamed but no sound emerged, muffled by the whipping which engulfed her ears. She worked to keep herself calm, her heart thrumming, her hand and feet tingling with horror. She fought, directing herself in a zigzag, diagonal line away, head forward, swimming through the air, head butting at the riptide, her horns seeking fresh streams like sheets of cloth piled in layers. At last, she found one sweeping downwards to grasp and carry herself further down, like rope, and struggled further until she caught ahold of a copper pipe on the side of a building, and pulled herself tight to it, conducting the crude copper, not designed for personal use, but to carry wind from outside into buildings for internal use. Like a glow around her, she concentrated to push all wind off her, repelling, rather than pulling, like an egg of light, shielding her, she dropped suddenly, and fell with a clank onto the rooftop.

She sighed hard, panting and catching her breath. This was exactly why the Meruyan lived here, close to the wind wall. They had no wind power, they couldn't fly and get caught in it. This area is perfectly unlivable for a Warix. The accidents would be too much. She had never tried to fly around here, a natural no-go zone.

It only made sense.

With wobbly feet, she stood up and dusted herself off. She needed place to climb down and began her walk through the dark streets back up to the fortress, utterly exhausted. It had been worth the trip down memory lane, and she would soon be able to use wind powered quick-steps to get home. Now she only had to work out which was *her* balcony on those dark fortress windows high above…

CHAPTER FOURTEEN

As the airship landed on the platform in Sen'Prin headquarters, Meleena was surprised to see a small figure outside awaiting them.

It was Governess Arenay. She was eager for the news on how things had gone with the Hyish.

"So?" she said, coming close to Kyra.

"It's not my fault…"

This was not a good look for her.

"You did exactly what I told you not to!" Arenay seethed. "This is not a good look for us. I told you, laying low…"

The team cringed and looked at each other, many ears flattened into their head, a Warix sign of muffled subservience.

"Maybe this team was a mistake. This has led nowhere. I'm sorry I asked you to lead it."

Kyra's cheeks bloomed deep red on her pale pink face. Arenay walked off without another word, and Kyra ran after her. They watched as the two argued out of earshot, visible through the glass, and Arenay left Kyra standing, tense with frustration.

"I've never seen Arenay like this before," said Meleena to nobody in particular, like a bubble coming from deep in a swamp that wanted release.

Riigs nudged her and she looked up. The giant Warix bent low and said quietly, "They have a history. School rivals or something. I'm not sure of the details."

"I heard they grew up together and used to be friends, but had a falling out over a guy," added Naia.

"Who cares about any of this? If it's not relevant to the case, it doesn't matter. Arenay is being fair. Kyra messed up. Sounds like she should have been more professional in there," he said, turning to Thian and Meleena inquisitively.

"Yes, Zoltan is right, I mean, she kinda did," said Thian, shrugging with a crumbled face.

"Ouch," said Jessup. "I admire her for trying to keep it together but look at them."

Arenay was waving her hands above her head now, and Kyra folded her arms, then let her hands loose, quickly changing stances, as if unsure what posture would suffice— strength or an apology.

"I mean, she could have been a lot less assuming of the Hyish," argued Meleena.

"Well then, there you have it. For our next mission, we will need to be much more careful," said Zoltan flatly.

Kyra slunk back to the team, straightening up as she came through the doorway, and cleared her throat.

They all stared expectantly at her for the next step of the mission. What would they be investigating next?

"I'm sad to report that another village has blown up..." Kyra said stiffly. "And we are not allowed to investigate any Hyish things anymore after our mess-up. Arenay said the politics are too delicate now. I have to send you all back to your own departments, to investigate and brainstorm new ideas that don't involve them. For now, team efforts are frozen until we can find a useful lead to stop more of this from happening. We need to be quick about it though. The longer we are out of commission, and out of ideas, the harder this is going to be to solve, and the more lives will be lost. Sen'Prin is counting on us."

The group looked from one to the other, baffled and saddened by the news.

"Since all we know so far is that in some vague way, Sen'Drorn are involved, with very few on the ground required to use some kind of strange new technology," Kyra continued. "So, assignments. Jessup, research agriculture for locations of other instances of droughts among Sen'Prin villages. Zoltan, take all the evidence so far and stare deeply at it, the way you do, and look for any patterns. Riigs, Thian, and Naia, you are both going to help with the newest post-explosion clean-up. You are not there to investigate but take mental notes on anything strange. I'm sorry we can't all go together for now, but we will all meet again in three days' time, to see if anyone has a new direction for this to go in. It is unfortunate, but it is Arenay's order."

She bowed low to them, then promptly took off in quickstep to the closest copper pipeline back to the city center.

Meleena was left, realizing she'd been entirely forgotten. It stung her, feeling left out and of less value than the others. But her head swam with tiredness. It had been a long day, and an intense first few days.

She was almost willing to admit she was ready for a break, if perhaps only to herself.

Everyone was looking a bit disgruntled.

Then, someone broke the silence.

"But they can't, like, pull the water from the sky, that would be nuts," said Jessup, as the group prepared to disband.

They all looked at her, and she shrugged. "I mean, isn't that what they were implying? That some kind of machine was sucking the water from the sky?"

They blinked.

"What? Am I the only one who drew that conclusion?"

"Actually, that's pretty brilliant." Blinked Zoltan, surprising even himself at the admission. They all stared at him now, tense, "I'd have said it's an impossibility," he continued, running a hand through his hair, "but, come on. After what all we've seen."

The tension rippled in the air and turned over its belly, unleashing a burst of laughter from the group.

"And didn't Meleena say they were looking at a technology that could harness elemental energy? I mean if copper enhances wind, why not enhance fire, or water? Am I wrong?" Thian added ponderously.

Meleena perked up at her name. "Oh, yeah. Flax and I have some work ahead of us there. We need to figure out a lot more of that."

Several of them patted her on the back. "Great job!"

She beamed, it was amazing to be needed. What a turn-around. Only Naia folded her arms.

"Yeah, well, it's not like much of a lead yet. Still pretty random stuff," said Meleena, rubbing her arm and then recalling the experiment they did with taking cells from her skin in that spot. She was looking forward to the time spent with Flax, though. He was a locus of familiarity in this sea of new experiences.

Thian was nice and brought her back through the copper tubing, to the main part of the city, though they all came as a group, happily chatting all together. For the first time Meleena felt like part of a team, ironically as they were temporarily disbanded.

Meleena buzzed Deem on the wristcom in a spare moment and they finally touched base on their now very different lives. She was so happy to hear from him that she got a little disturbed with the urge to talk and tell him everything about the last days.

He hadn't after all even known she was living in Sen'Prin. After a lengthy catchup and feeding her own urge to know about like in the city she hadn't chosen—with some guilty pleasure at hearing of his escapades and even failures with the Meruyan government— she learned of his new team and their secret agenda. They would visit and infiltrate the Northern Hilly Villages, to learn of and sabotage whatever plans the Meruyan Council had to block the newfound comradery between the Hyish and Meruyan.

He did, however, tell her one detail of utter importance.

"Yulah was there. General Malotus is history, wherever he is. Nobody knows, he up and left."

"Maybe he resigned to the countryside? You know, in some lavish estate granted him by the emperor?"

"No, I think it was more in disgrace. Nobody knows, but Yulah is General now, and her blood boiled at the mention of him. You know they were close. Related or something..."

"Yeah, that is strange. General Yulah, I wonder what she'll do now."

"Who knows, but she seems ambitious. One to worry about."

"Thanks. Our team is out of commission now anyway for the time being."

CHAPTER FIFTEEN

Deem was in the council intern's lounge, reading up on shark behavior for an upcoming meeting. Another long shot, but if only he could just prove how much coin they would save in the long run with safety…then maybe he'd get some funding for this project.

He knew Plymore had put in for a transfer, but that could be a while, or denied entirely. He wanted to give his best efforts while he could.

Just then, Talla burst in, jolting his eyes up to watch her blue-green hair float around her—a large distracting bobble.

"You will never believe what happened! There is a team going to visit the Hyish to convince them to destroy their trade route and pack up! In order to keep the peace and bend over to the Sen'Drorn, boo!" she said, plopping into the armchair next to him.

Deem "Why didn't you buzz me on the wristcom first?"

"Oh, never-mind," she waved him off. "We need to do something. I'm going with the team, and secretly going to try and sabotage it, according to our plan with Plymore. To try to prevent them sinking the tunnel so they can't trade anymore. But it's going to be tough, in front of our own people. I'm going to have to be playing both sides, it will not be easy to pull this off!"

Deem nodded. "Righty, good luck with it!" he said, beaming at his friend and turning back to shuffle through his book.

"What are you doing?" she shifted over the arm to look at him closely.

"Reading?"

"Well, stop it. I actually came here to get you. Suprise!" she clapped her hands together in mock joy.

"Wait, what?" he stuttered. "I already snuck into a different department...and now I am drafting up a proposal for underwater safety to stop sharks from eating citizens!"

"Well stop doing it, because congratulations, you have been transferred to my team!"

"What?!"

"Yes! I need a friend alongside me. Someone I can trust. I'm not bold enough to do this alone. And we make a good team! We need the Hyish to resist the Sen'Drorn pressure. We need to fight this thing from the inside!"

"I thought the transfer would take weeks; I mean I just wasn't expecting this. I just...wasn't quite ready to commit to this department yet." He started to argue, dumbfounded, that the transfer could possibly have been this quick. Nothing was ever fast around here! "There are still some more things I have to do here."

"Come on—there's no downside to it. We make a more effective team than either of us failing in council meetings all day anyway."

He growled at her.

"Face it."

"Err..."

"Come on, aren't you my friend? Going to the Northern Hilly Villages during a strike like this, it's historical! How could you not! This effects our people much more than whatever you were doing, I can promise that." Her eyes shone with a bright hope and a 'don't test me' at the same time, and he recoiled from it.

Ruining this friendship wasn't worth it.

He shut the book on his lap to give her his full attention, as clearly continuing wasn't going to happen.

He took a deep breath. His palms were sweaty. Yes, he probably would have chosen this, but he just didn't like the feeling of being pushed into this. The thought of arguing about it was worse.

"Ugh, alright!" he conceded.

"Yesss."

Flattered, yet a little shattered. That's how it was. A heaviness in his chest, guilt, weighing him down for all the Meruyans of his home town he was walking away from.

"I knew you'd say yes, cuz you're a pushover just like my baby brother," she added. That one was too far.

"Aren't I older than you?"

She shrugged and headed towards the door, holding it open for him with a look of urgency, eyes bulging, "We gotta go!"

Why do I have to be such a pushover? Because fighting is unbearable... Like being stung by an electric eel, he thought.

"First, we need to visit the stables. I will be riding Clover, my kelpie. Since Meleena's training course back home, he finally lets me ride him. Can you believe it? I suggest you take Pinchy."

Any excuse for more time with his beloved lobster was a welcome retreat. He followed her out the door and got mentally prepared to face one of the biggest controversies of his lifetime head-on.

How would this play out? Hyish and Meruyan.

***

Deem was surprised when they ended up on a Sen'Drorn airship.

He guessed it was the least they could do, to provide quick transport to the Hyish site. They wanted this issue resolved as hastily as possible.

He joined Talla beside others from the council, with whom he wasn't familiar, and tall Sen'Drorn pilots, dressed in green and black military garb.

It was unsettling, standing so close to them like this. He suspected they were more than pilots but guarding and witnessing their endeavors.

Deem wondered how Talla planned to pull off some secret sabotage. With him around, or otherwise, she didn't exactly seem to have a plan.

His eyes moved from the guards to Talla, her face exorbitantly bright.

He fought the tightening feeling in his chest.

The airship brought them over Dlawn'Edo's roaring waterfall and rising slopes of the mountains and headed northerly toward the contested villages.

The change was not obvious at first, the village centers and their rolling hills dusted with crops expanding throughout the landscape. Deem had never witnessed it from the air before, but squinting down at it he had a pretty good idea. Having spent most of his life swimming and being in the sea, he often knew villages from a multitude of angles and thus had developed a strong sense of direction.

When they skimmed the mountainside, and came to a large, gaping mouth of a tunnel, swarming with blue hued citizens, it became obvious things were quite different.

They dismounted and discovered a marketplace, alive and thriving, with bartering Meruyan, who had set up carts strapped to giant neutolyths, shelled beasts of burden of land and sea.

Piled high with undersea treasures, pearls, oysters, brittle stars, shell of all shapes sizes and cuts, raw and rendered as one might find underwater-- into household things like buttons, boxes, combs. Though what a Hyish would do with a comb, he did not know. The image of them attempting to run it through webby waddles or bumps made him both shudder and giggle.

And the Hyish were scrambling for every last bit of it. They were going mad for it all.

Something Plymore had said earlier—they have fallen so far, they know not what they have lost—echoed in his mind. It was such a mess. No matter what side you looked at desperation and clamoring to escape their fears of being left behind. The Meruyan didn't need all this. A big part of him didn't like it at all. That he had accepted life on land as a fact, sure, but you couldn't stop instinct.

Meruyan thrived underwater, and suffered for their seeking of novelty at the total loss of their homes. Their traditions were nothing more than a commodity to sell to the Hyish. When did prosperity become just feeding greed?

Still, how could he blame them for wanting to get out from Sen'Drorn rule? He just wasn't convinced the best course would be rushing into the clawed hands of the Hyish.

The markets transitioned right into the Hyish caves, which were slates of hard rock, blown out by unknown forces. Deem ran his fingers along the darkened edges of the rock—scorch marks as if by fire. He had no idea what the extent of Hyish firepower was, but it made his flesh crawl with unease.

If they turned on the Meruyan, well...

A party of Hyish joined them, led by their liaison, who introduced herself as Skoakya, daughter to the chieftain. "My father is busy, and I am effectively in charge around the markets."

Deem marveled at the pink frills, forming a crest on her head, and how she often cocked her head, causing them to bob around as she mused at their points.

"Ever since you helped us start a regular trade route here, we have found the Meruyan quite agreeable," Skoakya explained to the group of Meruyan council visitors. "You Meruyan are trading us pearls and shells of many colors and shapes. It's become quite a trend here, see," she showed off her bejeweled, scaled body. Pearls lined her cloak, and on her finger, twisting coral rings. Like many Hyish around here, but to a much bolder degree, she was adorned with Meruyan treasures—pearls, shark teeth, piercing nubs in her hide and in layers of necklaces.

"And the Meruyan?" asked a councilman who Deem did not know. This was, after all, not his normal department.

"We have, as you said, started to supply them with shaped glass to wear on their faces," Skoakya said proudly. A passing smile glinted over her lipless, toothy mouth.

"We implore you, Skoakya, you must listen. Shut down the trade, or there will be a lot of trouble!" The councilman was getting upset now.

Skoakya turned and stared deep into his eyes. With a hiss she replied, "*My* tribe were nobody, until we built the tunnel under the mountain to conjoin our two nations. *We* collect good coin from the Hyish nomads on the other side, because of the rare sea treasures from our trade with the Meruyan. Whoever told you we would agree to destroy the tunnel?"

"But the Sen'Drorn won't let this stand, they will shut it down, by force. We are here as a warning."

"It. Will. NEVER. *Happen*!" she hissed, raising her arms. "By the *Sess'ke'l'skelesses*!"

Deem did not catch that last part, assuming it was in her native tongue, and not meant for them. It rang out, through the tunnels many of her kinship began looking their way, piercing eyes that would not look away.

Even Talla was silent for all of this, eyes wide with surprise and lack of direction. Echoing whispers behind them made Deem uneasy.

"Who would try to destroy *our* busssinessss?" Skoakya asked one more time, before a group of Hyish crept from the tunnel walls, surrounding them.

"Okay, we don't want to cause you any trouble..." said the head Sen'Drorn guard, showing his empty hands. "We came here in a good-faith negotiation."

In a flash of lanky scaled limbs, they were upon them. With sharp teeth and swiping claws, and a lot of vine-netting, Deem's head hit the floor with a sharp thwack. His head throbbing, he searched around from his position on the floor, finding Talla by his side, the rest of the group equally subdued.

The Sen'Drorn guards had proven ineffective, now under too much rope, their hands bound first to prevent any focused wind action. They struggled beside him, plastered to the floor by so many Hyish and even a few Meruyan. Deem never thought he'd find himself on the same side as these scowling Warix in their notable green and black regalia, symbol to their faith in Emperor Ryogrim's nation of Meruyan servitude.

After much yelling and ineffective struggling, the group were hauled onto a cart. "Where are you taking us?" shouted the Meruyan councilmen. "I know of a Meruyan," Skoakya's voice rippled off the cave walls behind them, "Who would pay a pretty pearl to meet with you, essspecilaly in a position sssuch as thisss," her Hyish accent grew more pronounced as her excitement grew. She couldn't hold it together any longer.

Then the world went dark and began to shake. Someone must have thrown a covering over them, and the cart began its forward momentum towards the *mysterious Meruyan who would meet them,* thought Deem in a huff.

***

Squinting against the early morning sun, Yulah strode to the old bakery on Fleeg Street. She'd decided to pay her former favorite place a visit, finding herself growing increasingly nostalgic for the trade districts after so much time in the upper rungs of the Fortress.

She was disappointed to see that a line had already formed.

A customer, sitting with his friend, leaned over his pasty at one of the outdoor tables.

"Blugh, what is in this?" he croaked.

"Some kind of preserves, from *waaay* in the back, I bet. They haven't had fresh stuff for a while."

"Here, too? My family's weekly rations of bread and produce from the city have been reduced."

"Their saying ever since the Meruyan workers ate that poison fruit, they have refused to work. No fresh fruit and vegetables for Sen'Drorn City."

"What a disaster," said the friend, shaking his head. "Well, isn't the Emperor going to do anything to fix this? Send someone down there?"

"I heard they are sending some peacekeepers down there, but the Meruyan are out of control! Totally irrational. What are they going to do, move back to the sea?"

His friend leaned back and shrugged. "Entitled, that's what they are! This is their thanks? After we brought them out of the *ocean*!"

Yulah listened to it all from the comfort of the line. She congratulated herself for coming on her day off, despite the long line. She'd come wearing a sundress, whereas any other day she might have been wearing her Sen'Drorn official's uniform.

When she came to the front, she noted they were out of almost everything, this early, including her favorite rose scones. She spoke with the baker over more than just her usual order.

He wiped his hands on his smock. "Eh?" the squat Warix squinted. "The flour ration has been cut. We ain't got enough to bake 'em all anymore. And it's true, we have been burning through the preserves. Nothing new comin' in here a while now. Emperor Ryogrim not fulfilling the promises to the people of Sen'Drorn, that much for certain."

Yulah blinked, thoroughly taken aback.

It struck her for the first time, how the common folk spoke of those on top. What was the real issue here? These citizens would never know, she'd not divulge.

Their Emperor is weak, she thought. *He doesn't have what it takes to fix things, to maintain order.*

She left the bakery without breakfast, yet the pull of her raised eyebrows and tug of a smile pervaded, her heart in twisted anticipation.

What if she were in charge around here? Well, something that outlandish would be impossible. Was it? It would take the support of nearly all of the elder advisors.

As many as possible, far more than half.

Was she really calculating this?

How, how, could she go about doing something like that?

Clearly, there was much work to be done.

***

Deem and Talla embraced in a friend-hug. It was great to be together again. They were unbound, lifted by the arms, still reeling from the ride, but happy to see and be in a stable place once again. Though Deem had no notion of where that was, aside from a cave-like chamber.

A group of Meruyan stood around them, one prominently in front. Deem and the group of Meruyan councilmen were at the center, at Hyish spearpoint. The Sen'Drorn Guards were still bound, struggling against the vines, and on their knees.

"Welcome, Council. I am Iringbon. I will be succinct, as not to waste any of our time. I speak for the Meruyan of the NHV. We are angry, and we are organized in our efforts to keep the Warix out, for the prosperity of Meruyan living in this region. You have met Skoakya, leader of our new local Hyish clan. She does not fight, but is loyal to our shared interest." He paused, "We will. If you condone the Warix coming here with weapons, to force us to work for them, it is in an act of violence against us, and we will retaliate. We are prepared. Think of us as a council of our own. The NHV council, whose interests sadly seem to diverge from those of the Capital...I give you this warning, to tell you, take our side in this fight, or face no more loyalty from your brethren. That is why I am sending you back home, this time."

"What...has happened to Triz, the capital councilman assigned to this post?" asked the elder Meruyan councilman, shaking.

"My people raided his manor this morning. All dead."

"...and Sen'Drorn Warix guards in this area?"

"We have driven off most of the Sen'Drorn guards." And with that, they all turned to the Warix guards at their knees in front of them. Iringbon gave a nod, and several Meruyan crowded around them. One held up a knife, and grabbed hold of the Warix's horns, slicing them from their heads. They fell to the floor with a clank as the military men howled with displeasure. Deem didn't know if it was painful, his fingernails tingling as he imagined if it felt anything similar to that.

"Please, let them return with us," The councilmen begged for their release. "The Sen'Drorn will have our heads if we return without their men...No!"

The Warix soldiers were dragged from the chamber rather unceremoniously.

Iringbon put a finger to his chin. "Then you better have a really good story for them. And don't say you need them to carry you back, the airship has already been...decommissioned for parts." He shrugged. "We need what we can to defend ourselves."

While the Warix had to stay, the council Meruyan were sent back on Kelpies. They doubled up and Deem and Talla held onto the backs of the more senior members as they rode at full speed through the steep, lush mountainside towards Dlawn'Edo.

CHAPTER SIXTEEN

Meleena prepared to meet Flax for her first trip to the jungle, to look for clues and help the mission in any way they could. Hopefully to get a better understanding of these elemental cells using all the forest creatures as samples.

She wondered if she'd ever get to see the inside of one of those little cottages. She remembered that Flax's mother lives in one but asking to visit her cottage might be construed as something else.

She set the journal in her pack, slug it like a sash, and set off to meet up with Flax outside the noodle house.

They traversed the winding rope bridges of Sen'Prin on foot, and Meleena observed from above the hills flanking the cliff's edge, where the barrel-shaped cottages lay, their tops green tree canopies. For the first time, she realized they were built *around* a living tree trunk.

They crossed more bridges and storefronts. How would she ever find her way around this place only on foot? Her legs felt wobbly and exhausted already, and they weren't even to the jungle yet.

She had heard from the others that there were trails leading onto the steep mountain forest.

She glimpsed a lizard, sitting on a barrel as they passed, like the ones she'd seen around town, and on her windowsill. It blinked at her, then burped a fireball, which shot out and fizzled.

Meleena's eyes widened. A small fire-breathing lizard. She wondered what secrets he held, but the thought of hurting one for the answers was out of the question. She hoped they could find more ways to get samples in the forest, which didn't involve killing anything. She pointed it out to Flax.

As soon as they crossed over from town to forest, the large leaves greeted them as they entered—it was another world. It was not the city world of bamboo paths, structures, and wagons, but a dense greenery, chirping, sweet floral smelling jungle. It was somehow even denser than the one Meleena had grown up with on the mountainside behind her village, Pontai'Desa.

There were flowers the size of her, glowing purple and blue, with large spouts. Her feet crackled on the mossy soft ground. She blinked for a moment when something glittered by her, and it stopped to land on one of the giant pod flowers, a long proboscis nose/mouth. It used that to slurp up the pollen in the flower. "A nectar sprig!" she gasped, nudging Flax who turned.

"Yes, the symbol of Sen'Prin. Lucky you saw it your first day out," Flax said, "they aren't that common around here."

A droplet of water landed square on the top of her head. "Ah!" Squinting upward she saw giant sloping leaves with crystalline droplets decorating the tips, one of which had sent it spout-like onto her head.

As Meleena whipped out her sketchbook, Flax called out to her, "Hey, looks like there's more of those lizards!"

She turned on her heels to find the round pudgy bodies swaying as they moved in a line over roots and undergrowth.

They decided to follow the trail for clues. Possibly, dead lizards who could be harvested as samples, morbid though that was.

The lizards led them through the ferns and bushes and between thick vine-strangled trees, clambering over rough rocks, and under thick foliage. A bright light impeded their path, until it became clear this was the nest. And it was on fire. A burrow dug out from the soil, and smoldering.

"Fire lizard den!" Meleena said with a gasp. She bent down to inspect the trail they'd left behind.

The lizards' maws expanded as they shot tiny flames into the air, their fast tongues flicking to catch falling, charred insect bodies. They stepped through the bursts of each other's flames to steal prey.

Above her head, a crunching noise made her freeze and look up. The creature's purple-blue wings unfolded and bloomed magnificently around it. Its pinprick silver eyes gazed lazily around, and Meleena knew something was about to happen. She kept still.

In a graceful unfurling, it leapt from its tree perch with a single swift flap of its wings, revealing a dark-furred feline body which launched at the lizards, snuffing out part of the flames of its nest in the process. Meleena followed it with her eyes as it continued in one swift glide to another tree to chomp its prey. The lustrous feathers and furry coat contrasted around the head and neck.

Meleena watched the creature hunch its shoulders and prepare for another launch. It was so agile, almost unreal in a forest of such close settings, turning on a dime, stopping almost in midair for a moment, as its wings beat and small thunderclaps appeared in its vicinity. When it was near, the fire from the lizards exploded into little fire claps. The mixing of air and fire had created a localized explosion.

A thrill shot through Meleena from cheek to fingertip at the sight of it all. That moment, an idea struck her. A theory…

"Perhaps these creatures have wind powers." She posed the question to Flax.

"It certainly would explain such precision flying in a forest, such a tight setting. And the interaction between fire and wind…what was that?" he asked.

Perhaps whoever was blowing up Sen'Prin cities had some idea of this as well, mixing fire with wind. Upon further observation, Meleena noticed the neck feathers on the back of the Featherpaw's head were glowing. Its eyes didn't light up like a Warix, but something was. The shining feathers flew off its head behind it like a trail. Meleena caught one out of the air, holding up the silvery glowing arrowhead-shaped head feather. The silver glow faded and its fine architecture crumbled to dust in her hand.

"In Warix, the concentration of wind energy is in their eyes," she said slowly, thinking. "They cloud silver when taking the extra energy in. This creature has head feathers which take it, then fall out and re-grow."

Something swooshed in front of her eyes, causing her to jump back. There were two talons and a large feline head. She rolled out of the way just in time as the lizard in front of her face was snatched up in the sharp talons. As it flew away, Meleena saw a flurry of blue and purple feathers landing on a tree trunk nearby perch. It licked its talons and gulped down the lizard with its panther head.

"So, what do you call that thing?" asked Meleena.

"That's a Featherpaw," said Flax. "There's all kinds here. I bet they have wind powers same as me. They dive and move in tight forest spaces, leveraging their wings with their horns. If I had wings, I know I'd be way more precise a flyer out here. Even the Warix can't fly in dense space like this. These are known to be stealthy hunters, I've never seen one in person like that."

It stared at her with big yellow cat eyes, and as it finished chomping down its prey it stared at Meleena, catching her staring at it. Her heart raced and she jumped back. The panther leapt from its branch towards them.

Meleena and Flax huddled to avoid the talons. It stopped at the borrow in front of them for another lizard. However, Meleena's jumping motion startled the lizards and they all screeched in alarm. It scurried into the burrow and out of sight, quicker than the beasts' talons.

The featherpaw glared at Meleena, emanating a low growl, as if to say, *you got in my way.*

"We should get out of here," said Flax.

Meleena blinked. "Wait, let me try something."

"It's not worth risking our lives for this," Flax said.

Meleena waved off his concerns. "It's alright, I have been around predators in my own forest," she said. Then she reached out and grabbed the lizard, freshly dead but uncollected, from the ground. "hold still and be quiet," Meleena said, blinking slowly into the feather paw's yellow slit eyes—a way to say, *I am not here to threaten you.* It blinked heavily in reply, then sniffed the air, curving horns crested around its fury head.

Still weary, Meleena tossed the lizard to the creature, who caught it and gobbled it down, then in a burst of wind, flew back up into the tree with a beating of its aquamarine wings.

Meleena smiled, and Flax made a small cheer behind her.

"But can we get out of here, now?" he asked with caution. "We don't have to go back to town, but I would feel more comfortable if we went back to the path. I am accountable for our safety here."

"Alright," agreed Meleena, though already in her mind, plotting her return alone.

"You know, when it comes to the fire glands missing, I had this idea. Maybe there was power to round up the material," Flax said as they returned through the thick trees back to the path.

"But I thought fire was only made by Hyish?" asked Meleena.

"Some creatures can as well. These lizards were just pests in town."

"That makes sense. Lots of creatures have particular elemental traits in common. I think they are following evolutionary lines," answered Meleena.

"I had the same idea when I lived in Sen'Drorn, but never tried it out. Killing them just seemed upsetting. Maybe another engineer thought of it too?" speculated Flax.

Just then, two figures appeared from the other direction. It was Borak and the new engineer, Phineas.

"Just out for a stroll," said Borak cheerily. "Helps clear the head after so long inside the lab."

"Meleena was just showing me some fascinating things about the local flora and fauna," explained Flax.

"Do tell," said Phineas. "Just like Borak here."

Meleena opened her journal and showed him some pages.

"From what we know so far, the creatures evolved from one or more of the elementals. Some have mossy fur that gives them sun energy, like plants. They survive in difficult places and never feel too hungry, as long as there is sunlight, that is. That's why you see it more in flying and climbing creatures. They can get to the canopy better. Whereas fire creatures often live on the bottom, creating their own fire. That occurs in wet places, so they can't burn much."

"There's both algae and moss, and more," agreed Borak.

"Well, the layout of it depends on the Ecosystem and environment," Meleena clarified. "So, creatures that hang out in or near water like ponds would have more algae on them, and they go through their life cycles too so you would get flowers and seeds and such."

Phineas had on a look of fascination, nodding slowly as Meleena spoke. Strange fellow, thought Meleena, though it was nice feeling important.

"We have also the wind creatures here." Said Flax.

"Yes, nectar sprig," said Borak. "They are also found by Sen'Drorn forest. Four legs, cute green, long face."

Meleena nodded. "Didn't get a chance to see it up close, sadly."

"Well, you need to stand real quiet by their favorite spots," explained Borak, and happiness bloomed in Meleena at having someone who loved this stuff as much as she. "If you see another, you may notice it moves erratically, in a flurry. The wings are like rudders, to help it guide as it goes. It has tiny horns behind the neck to sense the wind. And it sheds feathers regularly, lucky bastard, as they refill after they fall out. With Warix, it's in our eyes. They become silver when we harness wind, but also are poor of vision, especially at the periphery. We go blind eventually, if we do it often enough. Only those with military careers really have to worry about that, though."

Meleena took notes, enjoying her time spent learning with Borak.

Then Meleena and Flax parted ways with Borak and Phineas and headed back through the rainforest on foot.

Out of the corner of her eye, something stirred that made her head turn. Through the trees, a rustling, like a black bushy shadow, a predatory presence. As if there was a creature there, but soon gone. A cold shiver ran up her spine.

"Did you see that?" Meleena asked, nudging Flax.

"What-now?" he asked, lifting an eyebrow and scratching his left horn.

"There was something out there." She pointed in the direction.

"Probably just another prowling feather paw. They are stealthy. Nothing to worry about."

"Yeah, your right." It was strange, as most beasts didn't give her fear, where in fact she felt compassion and love towards them all. This was a worrisome presence, completely out of harmony. It reminded her of Malotus, who had been such a thorn in her side and source of fear for her. Even though he had inexplicably aided her and Flax, the dark impression of his otherwise pervasively cruel nature remained. It couldn't be him of course, she told herself.

That would be utterly preposterous. What would that fiend even be doing in a place like this? Ridiculous, she decided, and put it out of her head. It was just some top predator, surprisingly, that she wouldn't like to meet.

CHAPTER SEVENTEEN

A week had passed since the run-in with Iringbon and his, so called "troublemakers" as they were officially being called now by the Meruyan council.

The meetings had been rough, and The Sen'Drorn were seething. As predicted, the Meruyan Council losing their Warix guards went over extremely poorly. They were about ready to send troops into the NHV.

The Council's best effort was to come up with a plan to spread lies about the Hyish among the local Meruyan, hoping to dissuade their trade. Deem had thought this would never work, they were in too deep, and the Sen'Drorn seemed to share the sentiment.

The very existence of the Meruyan Council was at risk here. Their perks had been cut, as the Sen'Drorn commanded, and Deem knew this was partly to do with their own loss of resources. But the Sen'Drorn were a nation in power long enough to have accumulated enough copper and metals useful to their technology to have an ever-strong military.

Wasn't that the iron fist of irony? Deem chuckled to himself at the clever thought. *More like copper, to speak literally.*

He sat with the elder Plymore and Talla in his office. The only Warix on their team, and the only one loyal to the true cause, the plight of the NHV Meruyan.

So, what can we do about it? was on all their minds.

“I think you should ride into the NHV and join them,” said Plymore.

“Sounds like treason to me,” mused Deem.

“Someone has to warn the people about the Sen’Drorn invasion,” Talla said, bargaining that he’d be open to the idea. And risk everything? This was a little much. He wasn’t sure how far he would go to risk his entire future on this.

“What future? Everything is messed up!” Talla argued. “Aren’t you disenchanted with the Council?”

“Well, yes, but…”

Deem let out a heavy sigh. It was all very jarring.

“If the Meruyan don’t want to work for Sen’Drorn for their crap wages, they should either give the Meruyan a better deal—you know, incentivize them to come back to work, or accept that the Meruyan don’t want to. The Sen'Drorn have been spoiled with this bad deal for generations. Let them live with lower standards in their fancy city!”

“The aim isn’t to make the Sen’Drorn suffer,” Plymore interjected. “It is to, eventually, find a better balance for the prosperity of all. That said, I agree with Talla, in that you should go warn their militia so they can defend themselves…from this…” he rubbed his face, “impending slaughter.”

Deem felt his cheeks grow hot. Was he really going to do this? What choice did he have? He felt like he was up hiding in an underwater volcanic tube, with sharks on either side circling the only ways out, ready to rip him to shreds whichever direction he went.

Another thought occurred to him. “How could we even get there without transport?”

“We break into the stables and get our pets, Clover and Pinchy,” said Talla with a shrug, thinking fast.

Deem made an uneasy sound. He didn’t like the idea of that.

“Come on, what can we do, watch history be made? Let’s go and help. This is the only way.”

“But break into the stables?”

"What? We have every right to get our mounts. They're ours."

Deem was out of arguments. The ride at normal pace would be a couple of hours, easier than the time they went on foot around the mountain during the Journey of future leaders.

"We don't know exactly when the Sen'Drorn 'peacekeepers' will roll in, but we need to beat them."

One trip to the stables later and they were on their way, pounding the stone pavement down the steep mountain paths off towards the Northern Villages.

***

Pinchy hummed under Deem as his hands clasped the base of his massive antenna.

They broke through the forest path onto the grounds at the far end of a small village which could only be part of the Northern hilly Villages. Though Deem didn't recognize it and had no strong sense of direction. His heart pounded. How could they be doing something like this? His veins burned with the push to go home and forget about this, but his sense of duty, it threatened to tear him asunder.

They rode through the central valley to the main village. Some Meruyan still worked in the hillsides, but very few.

There were no Warix strapping containers to airships, carts of fruit and vegetables always on the move. Things were quieter, less of a functional production line feel.

Meruyan and their children played in the streets. Life was happening...like normal? There hadn't been a normal here before. life was blooming. There had never been community here before. There was a surprising amount of new construction, the Meruyan had an energy about them.

You wouldn't think this would happen amid such bubbling strife. This was the eye of the storm.

Talla atop Clover strode beside them, his new growth horns bright curling orange coral florets crowning his head. He patted Pinchy.

Deem felt sick to his stomach about everything.

He longed to be transferred back to his original underwater department. Nothing going on there, it was nice and safe. And there was hope. He was going to voice this thought aloud, but thought better of it.

He drew in a breath to reinvigorate his shaking body as Pinchy stopped scuttling for him to survey the area. "Where do we go from here? We even don't know where to find Iringbon and his militia."

It turned out easier than they thought. Iringbon apparently had eyes everywhere. A Meruyan rode up to them on a kelpie to confront them for wearing Council uniforms. Deem laughed despite himself. *Wrong side around here, but sure got us noticed.*

"We want to pledge ourselves to his cause," Talla explained, while Deem was a bit shy, struggling for the proper words. "And we have an important message for Iringbon from the Meruyan Council."

"Yes, I can lead you him," he replied sternly.

Deem wished for the old days, underwater. Simpler times. When everyone was joking around, when his first impression of a Meruyan wouldn't be described as 'stern.'

He led them to the east, the mountain range side, to where Deem knew from his last time here contained a lot of the Meruyan worker dwellings among the ribbonlike valleys between the steep mountain spires. They dismounted outside a burrow hole and entered to find the familiar chamber of their earlier capture. Iringbon was not there, in fact the space was currently empty.

"If you want to see Iringbon, as an ambassador of your people and not a prisoner, you must join us in our true place, under water."

Deem's heart swelled. So, the Meruyan were going back to their roots after all? He had learned about the generations living on land, the loss of culture living the only life they'd known.

"We agree," said Deem.

Talla was less sure. "I am wearing some nice non-waterproof accessories...This belt is plant-skin! And the shoes..."

Deem noted that none of the other Meruyan were wearing shoes, and thinking bad, had not been then either. It was a relatively recent phenomenon to wear shoes as a Meruyan, same with glasses. He happily removed his presently and stowed them in his clipping shirt-pocket designed for this very purpose. It was a minor wonder that the Meruyan council still made their uniforms from Kelpweave. Though he suspected otherwise of some senior members, what with silk all the rage now.

Talla grumbled at the loss of her confiscated trinkets, and they followed their guide into gaps at the edges of the cave, diving steadfast into crystal clear water, down, deep. Deem kicked his legs and felt the tingle of his forearms and legs as the fins bloomed.

Deep in the wedges of the underwater cavern, the rock split into smaller chamber pockets, lit by goopy nodes in various scattered positions among the walls. Upon further inspection, they revealed themselves to be some kind of invertebrate that lived down here.

Iringbon's chambers was the last one at the end, full of thick algae soft for wedging and lounging among.

He floated upright to greet them, in the cool blue-green aura of light, speaking using the Meruyan clicking language, the only communication possible down here.

"I am happy to meet with you," he clicked, to which Deem had to reply, as Talla merely shook her head.

"My talking...so-so," she clicked.

Iringbon shook his head, disappointed. "The Meruyan rarely do anymore," he replied.

"I am fluent," said Deem. "I grew up underwater."

"I don't know that I've met anyone who has these days." His eyes were wide. "Maybe you can teach some of us. In the meantime, what is your purpose here?"

"We are from the council, here to warn you that the Sen'Drorn aren't going to stand around and let you change things so easily around here. They are sending troops to fight and force you all back to work."

"I'd like to see them try. But thank you for the warning." His brows knitted. "Why would you warn me about this, if you are from the council?"

Deem did a flip, a non-verbal indicator well-intent. Iringbon floated backwards, his brow ridge deepened, and he looked disturbed.

Talla nudged Deem in the ribs.

"What I mean to say is," Deem hurriedly clicked, "That they aren't, er, the council isn't great, but we are descending from being loyal to them, and we came here to assist you."

Iringbon said nothing, still floated there looked ever more concerned.

Talla turned to Deem. "What, you say? I thought—you fluent."

"Really? You would want to help us?"

"In any way we can," Deem confided.

Talla looked from one to the other, still appearing confused.

"You would have to fully commit to our cause. Leave the council."

"Or better yet, spy on the council, for you," Deem pointed out.

"You would have to prove your loyalty to me."

"Yes, whatever you need."

He nodded. Deem resisted the urge to pull another flip, realizing non-verbal signals had been lost to them.

"Some Meruyan are still working in the fields," Iringbon explained. "Some might be there out of fear and lack of support, or perhaps of their own accord. Go speak with them, free those you can, convince those you must, and return to us with as many as possible."

Deem agreed, they were dismissed back to the main chamber, and once above the water, Talla pulled at Deem's wet shirtsleeve. "You need to fill me in, remember. What's the plan?"

***

They rode back into the hills surrounding town, trying to find some action.

"Maybe we should start over there," said Talla with a nod to the distant hills, where Deem could make out the image of Warix and Meruyan in an orchard.

And distant shouting?

They rode closer, trying to blend in among the thick, stumpy orchard trees, until they could overhear more.

"I refuse to pick fruit in your orchard another day!" shouted the Meruyan.

"What else will you do to put food on your plate?" hissed the Warix. He was short for a Warix, plump with a broad forehead.

Deem recognized him. Overseer Thowler. He shuddered, thinking he would never have to interact with that claim-brain again.

"Well, they are sending backup and we will see who gets to do what around here!" Overseer Thowler spat.

The Meruyan reached a hand to his head, and crunched up the hat he was wearing, throwing it forcefully to the floor at Thowler's feet.

Thowler's eyes widened and then his face contorted into a scowl, but the Meruyan was already stomping off. Thowler yowled like a wounded predator at the act of disrespect, and sent wind energy from his extended hands to shove the Meruyan, knocking him to the floor.

A squabble ensued, rendering the Meruyan helpless on the floor, but also unable to work. He was not hurt, but simply and quite literally refusing to move. He crossed his arms while Thowler stomped his feet.

Deem's fingers were contorting in pain from trying to hold on as Pinchy scuttled onward in their direction. Deem hop-slid from Pinchy's back, as Pinchy to run out of sight.

"Quite an entrance," barked Thowler. "When did you entitled brats return to the NHV? Shouldn't our show-and-tell be a one-time thing?"

"You...uh, remember me?" gaped Deem, struggling to his feet as Talla rode up on her kelpie.

"Why did you dismount!" she griped.

Thowler laughed deeply. "Your council outfits, youthfulness, and clueless expressions gave you away. Do you think I'm dumb? You Meruyan youth's causing trouble, I would not forget a face. And I know that there's no way you're supposed to be here."

"And how is that?" stammered Deem. "There can't be a good reason you are here either."

"Deem, get on, what are you standing around for?" She reached out an outstretched hand for him.

"NO KELPIES HERE!" Thowler roared. "They are banned from the Northern Villages! I am confiscating him!"

"Excuse me!?" Talla burst back.

"He will make a nice meal for the capital. Dismount immediately, girl!"

"I don't think so," she all but chuckled in disbelief.

Thowler grabbed the reins and threatened to pull Talla off, so she nudged his side and he reared up, claw-like hoofs flailing in the air, slashing at Thowler's face, a horrible yell and ripping sound confirming the damage was done, as his hands dropped the harness and sprang to his face, now bleeding profusely. "Arrgg!!!"

Deem's heart beat wildly as though his throat sunk into his stomach.

This was really bad.

The wounded Meruyan who he'd been struggling with got up, and Talla helped him aboard.

"GET ON!" boomed Talla. "FOR FISH-SAKE!" and Deem jolted back and leapt with all his might onto the back of Clover, who galloped off as he held tight with the momentum, leaving Thowler to gripe about on the pavement.

"This is BAD, Talla. He not only recognized us, but now we've injured a ranking member of Sen'Drorn."

"Yeah, it's bad." Talla's voice came out flustered, surprisingly straightforward.

Deem shook his head. How could this be happening? Ugh!

"Won't worry so much. We need to go back to Iringbon and tell him everything, plus we have recruited this new guy, so boom, loyalty proven."

Deem let out a heavy sigh, his veins feeling thick. He whistled for Pinchy, who came scuttling up alongside them as they fled the fields.

Talla whipped the vine reins that connected her to Clover and he made a gleeful bubble-like rumbling sound and ran faster.

The breeze blew as they brushed past the townsfolk, Meruyan of the Northern Hilly Villages looking more animated and livelier than he'd ever seen them. They weren't in the stooping postures he'd known the first time they'd visited.

Many still worked on the hillsides, laboring for the Sen'Drorn, but the airships were clearly taking longer to fill, with far fewer willing to work. Only the most desperate would bother now.

"How are there still Meruyan in the fields?" asked Talla, baffled.

"Perhaps they didn't feel like part of a strong community who could help raise them up. In the underwater district of Pontai'Desa where I grew up, everyone worked together at the times of harvest and if a crop didn't come in, we always helped each other out."

From what he'd seen, he guessed their culture had deteriorated here, with the Warix, ingrained further from in the time living so far from the natural world underwater. He had never realized how deeply the Meruyan roots could run.

He wondered how his host mother, Saru, was doing in all the changes here, and hoped she and her family were okay. He'd have to make a note to visit her or at least ask around.

They delivered the Meruyan man safely to Iringbon's team. Another active opposer to the Warix for the militia, and just in time, as the group prepared for the first battle with Sen'Drorn.

Deem and Talla decided to stick around to witness it. Deem was hesitant, as always, but Talla assured him, as usual, that returning to the council would be pointless now. They were allowed to stay at the lair, and sleep underwater in an empty moss pod cavern. Deem had to admit that was a perk for him, though uncomfortable for Talla. At least they were safe here, underwater where no Warix could take them by surprise. Deem liked to think he wouldn't have agreed to this if not for this fact.

Talla merely waved him off and told him to stop being so afraid of everything.

It hardly mattered. Deem could hardly sleep as he rolled around in anticipation of what kind of nightmare tomorrow would bring.

CHAPTER EIGHTEEN

Meleena and Flax had collected enough samples from the jungle beasts to have something to work with in the lab. Feathers from the feather paw, some dead lizards, and a couple of swampy plant samples.

In the lab, they tested it all by gently crushing them with the mortar and pestle. First on their own, and sure enough, the featherpaw's feather samples had the same effect as the Warix horns. Lots of wispy light floated from it, as the bulk of the material compressed, leaving but a shell, the gray gunk, behind in the dish.

What they weren't expecting, however, was what would happen when they put the two together. As per Meleena's field idea, when the feather paw produced thunderclaps when its wings gusted on the lizard's fire mound, they found it reproducible.

Flax crushed wind and fire samples together, and the pair of them jumped back when they found it exploded in their face.

"Wow, this could do some serious damage in larger amounts!" Flax said, excitedly.

"This is our own private theory, but we need to share it with the others," said Meleena. "It is working. Imagine if there was a device someone built, that scaled this up."

"They'd need a lot of fire, but if they mixed it with their wind powers, maybe it could produce the same effect?" he speculated.

"And if the fallout creates that gunk, then there we have it. The gunk in large numbers gets into the water supply and causes it to jam up and infect the Hyish insect crops."

The team came to meet them towards the end of the testing, for a purely speculative meeting. They had agreed to meet up at the lab.

They were laughing amongst themselves. Meleena and Flax had apparently missed a night of bar hopping and entertainment which had brought the others together.

"I wasn't invited," Zoltan said, rolling his eyes and shaking it off by changing the subject abruptly. "This explains everything we've seen," he confirmed, sparking Meleena's pride.

"But it still doesn't explain the drought," added Meleena. "Still, not bad!" applauded Riigs.

Naia folded her arms and added to the list of unknowns. "...Or what kind of tech he used to accomplish it and the explosions. And of course, who put this together, and how we might go about finding and stopping them."

Thian and Jessup were excited to share their own findings. They had gone together on a scouting mission, looking for places where drought had been occurring in Sen'Prin villages.

Meleena knew that talking to the Hyish would have been a useful sentiment, as they tended to stick to one another, and dwelled in more lands than the sparse Sen'Prin secured outposts.

However, as they all were painfully aware, with such security around Hyish in these times, their team wouldn't have been not trusted to ask. Real shame.

Why can't we just communicate better? It would be beneficial to us all, we are all on the same side here, thought Meleena, frustrated, powerless to speak up.

Nonetheless, they did manage to discover one Sen'Prin outpost which reported several weeks of no rain. "This is certainly a lead!" Jessup said.

"Now we need to convince Kyra to let us go there for a stakeout," said Naia. "Maybe we can stay there and camp around the town periphery, until they strike. Catch him in the act with whatever kind of gadget he's built. Subdue him, then destroy the machine!"

The others looked at her and nodded in agreement.

"...Or use it to our own ends," Naia continued. "See how they like it!"

"I would certainly be interested in that, seeing how it functions," Flax added.

"Obviously, so would I," Naia added, rolling her eyes and tapping a wrench on the table casually.

"Let's go talk to Kyra, or Arenay, about it." They agreed and began to leave the lab.

Meleena lagged behind, noting Flax was finishing cleaning up after all the samples they'd tested.

"Great job, Flax!" she said, catching a smile.

"Oh yeah, I'm happy about it," he said, not looking up from cleaning the device.

He seemed distracted. Strange, and distant. It stung like rejection, after such a great time she thought they'd had out there in the forest.

She didn't prod him further, and turned to go, drifting between the benches wondering what, if anything, she'd done wrong.

She nearly tripped over Borak, as he came out from a back room, removing a pair of thick gloves as he came over to greet them.

"Meleena! Good to see ye. I heard all of you out here and wanted to stop you before heading out. I finished building that jetpack! Thought maybe Flax could show you how to use it," he said cheerily.

"Ah," Meleena hung her head. "That's very kind of you, I would like that. Just," she looked back at Flax. "I don't think he's so much in that mood. He seemed kind of reserved just now.'

"Ah, naw, he's just lost in thought. He gets that way a lot these days, don't think about it. It ain't personal. He's lost in his head, swimming around, I dunno. Maybe something to do with Yulah. Not entirely over what he did to her, holds onto a lot of guilt."

Shock coursed through her. "He's… not over her?" asked Meleena. And here she was, thinking she might have some kind of chance with him.

"He's upset because they ain't had no closure. Gets stuck in looping thoughts, is all. It's only natural. He'll get over it." Borak sighed. "His mother, Odella, and I have been seeing each other in secret, and it's been like a dream. I think it doesn't help him, you know, not think about his own love life. Anyway, ask him about testing the jetpack. That will be good to clear his mind. He really likes you, it just takes a while to notice." The corners of his eyes crinkled with softness.

"Flax, to notice me?" Meleena stammered, blushing. "It's not like that, were just friends."

Borak gave her a wink and left it at that.

***

The next morning, Meleena woke late. Naia and Jessup were already up and out, her bed made, as Meleena climbed down from her bunk to check. She dressed in her blouse and trousers, then headed to the common room. She knew they would be meeting officially downstairs at the noodle house for an early lunch, but this seemed like a lot.

She found the group was gathered around Kyra at a table outside the noodle house. She didn't know if they hadn't woken her on purpose or what, but it stung.

Meleena didn't know if she had any right to feel bad about it, which made it somehow worse.

Flax was there today. He had a strange large, clunky contraption like a large backpack of copper coils and bronze circuits sitting by his feet. At least there was no food in front of them yet. Meleena sat down, nodding politely at the others. Of the six places, the only seat open was between Zoltan and Kyra, which left Flax and Thian on the other side of the table, in an odd position to talk to.

A Warix came over to take her order, and she ordered a large bowl.

"Did I miss anything?" asked Meleena, as the low conversation ended.

"Naw, we were just sharing memories of our days back in school," explained Thian.

Meleena nodded, trying to look casual.

"Now that we're all here," said Kyra, matter-of-factly. "I would like to turn the subject to important matters. I'm proud of all of you, and because of your efforts, Arenay is allowing us to return to our search, as long as we stay away from the Hyish. We need to scout the villages and find one with a drought going on. Everyone except Meleena can do the legwork, and report back. You will spend your day scouting, I have assignments for which direction you will go in and notes you will take."

She passed out their assignments, sliding folders across the table to Thian, Flax, Jessup, and Zoltan.

"Because of agriculture, Jessup, do you have any suggestions?"

"I suggest looking at crop health, wilted or yellowing plants. You can see it from above in your tornados."

Kyra nodded, impressed.

Meleena timidly decided to speak up. "Should I be doing anything?" she asked quietly to Kyra.

"You have the day off, Meleena," she said.

"I did learn something in the forest the other day actually," she said eagerly. They looked at her rather judgmentally. "Flax was there with me. We followed these fire Lizards to their nest. We saw that they spit fire, and this large creature ate some of them. It uses wind magic—"

"Sorry I'm going to stop you there. How is this relevant to the case?" asked Zoltan, as the others stared, the words on their tongues. So much for yesterday. Now they were all turning on her, the moment Kyra was here.

Meleena looked awkwardly from Naia's nose ring to Kyra's mohawk. A waitress came over balancing fix bowls of noodles and placed them around the table. The steam from her bowl rose up in front of her, and her stomach gurgled. "It's..." she tried to defend. "I don't know yet. I just suspect however they are doing the drought, it might have to do with new technology. And maybe with the lizards...it might be that someone was using them for their experiments, that it has to do with how they cause the droughts..." She trailed off. "Never mind, I'll just take a day off," she grumbled. She wasn't sure how it fit in, exactly. She would have to keep it to herself until she had a better idea.

She picked up her spoon and took a mouthful of hot noodles, letting the steam fill her glasses. She would not look up from the delicious meal to give input again. She'd just pretend like it was fine. She really had no reason to be upset. She was here on business, not to make friends. Maybe she was the only one with other expectations that had to be dialed down.

The group continued to discuss logistics, how low they would fly, what the best way to tell what city would be. To take accurate notes on levels of drought.

Meleena didn't speak the rest of the meeting. With Flax on the other side of the table, she was socially isolated.

Once the soup bowls were empty, Kyra gave the waitress coins to pay as she took the bowls away and the meeting ended.

As the group got up to prepare for their scouting mission flight, Flax approached Meleena with the big clunky contraption which had been at his feet during the meeting.

"Here is the prototype jetpack from Borak," he said grinning excitedly. "He was sorry not to be able to give it to you himself. He wanted to see your face when I gave it to you, but also wanted to make sure you got it as soon as possible, since you weren't stopping by the lab soon. That way you can get around the city better."

"Thanks Flax!" she said. "But why didn't you say anything about the flying mission today?"

"Ah, I still wouldn't trust it on missions just yet. In the open skies. It's pretty much untested, except by me and Borak. I was actually hoping you had time today, so we can go somewhere to test it out."

"Oh, okay sure," she agreed, heart beating rapidly as a nectarsprig's. She rubbed her arm. This whole place and its people confused her.

"You know, to make sure you are safe and feel comfortable in it and can get around. It'll need some calibration and stuff."

CHAPTER NINETEEN

Deem was awoken in a delirious haze before the next morning. Though he and Talla had slept underwater in Ironbon's lair, safe from the Warix, all was not well. Meruyan swam in to wake them, and they swam to the surface, Talla particularly confused and upset. She was always one for sleeping in.

The main chamber was hazy, and busy with the sounds of Warix footsteps echoing. Deem dripped on something round and fell to the floor, his jaw smacking against the stone, and his eyes meeting the small, round culprit. It was a smoke bomb, designed to look natural, acorn-like in shape, with many openings releasing a gray smoke which stank like salty metal.

He and Talla and the other Meruyan around them ran from the caverns. There was nowhere else to go, the coughing was intense, filling his lungs and burning. They took to the streets, in search of any kind of order. Meruyan ran, Warix marched. They had the upper hand, striking earlier than anyone had expected.

Deem felt sheepish. How could the Meruyan not have prepared better?

Ugh!

The mouth of the stronghold lay on the mountain's foothills. Iringbon and his dissenters had done well choosing this spot, Deem could see the main NHV village and other smaller valleys of the region.

On the hillsides, Warix were rounding up Meruyan with whips and ordering them to harvest the fruit trees. More Warix with heavily laden airships even helped the process along, apparently desperate to recoup some of their crops.

Meruyan were entering the mines for the first time as well. How had the Warix mobilized all of this so quickly? The words of Plymore entered his mind. Clearly this was a short-term solution. It would never last.

It was all ridiculous, he saw now with fresh eyes. The Sen'Drorn and their brute-force strategy would never get Meruyan workers to want to stay; they were now effectively convincing all their last loyal workers not to abide—they had shown their true colors for the last time.

They were only feeding more rebellion this way. If only they'd listened to Plymore and created better compensation and living situation for the Meruyan. It would have been a win-win.

All of this, Deem thought as he watched the scene in horror from the vantage point above.

Meruyan, though less organized, were starting to band together, clustering in places and around the mouth of the lair.

Talla shouted, "Who's in charge here?!"

"Follow us for reinforcements!" someone shouted. Talla's shouting attracted results. They followed other Meruyan to the makeshift stables, where they had been keeping illegal kelpies.

Deem gaped at her. Iringbon was nowhere to be found in these moments. Perhaps he was among the Hyish, wondered Deem.

A Meruyan worker, a bit older than them, already astride came up to them. He carried a crude weapon of steel and wood, hooked at the end. A scythe for cutting the harvest. His kelpie had a pack, from which he drew a long-reach picking instrument. "We have found these useful for attacking the Warix and driving them back."

He tossed it and Talla caught it. "Very nice."

"What are you doing...?" Deem murmured. "We can't fight!"

Talla gave him a heavy look. "Deem, sometimes drastic actions are called for. And right now, we need to help them drive out the Warix. It's our civic duty. Also, let's go get our mounts."

"What? Are you crazy? We didn't come here to join the rioters! We are just warning them and going home or else, if the council finds we are involved in this, we will lose our apprenticeships! Besides, we aren't fighting, I thought we were going to have the groups talk, I don't know, negotiate!"

"You're joking, right?"

"We need to find whoever is in charge and reach some agreement between the Meruyan and the Sen'Drorn."

Deem was amazed at her optimism. There was no way this would work. Her brains were more scrambled than a breakfast sea urchin.

However, once mounted, it seems much safer to stay with the group, who moved as a school of fish atop their kelpies. Clearly, they had a plan pre-set for such an instance, and was not dependent on any leader present.

They hurried to a crag at the edge of the Hyish cave, to a leg of the stalled Meruyan markets. Here, stockpiles of Meruyan marine items were more than just trinkets. These seashells were large, spiny, durable.

One type of seashell fanned out like a boney hand and made for an easy fist weapon. Meruyan were free to take them.

It was there they found Iringbon, already in the middle of a pre-battle prep speech. "Now that the Hyish glass has given us sight, we have enough of what we need to do as we wish. We can drive the Warix out and return to our heritage, but in a new era on land."

The group cheered, some on kelpies and some on huge, shelled beasts of burden, the neutolyth, which resembled a giant land squid. Both beasts pounded the dirt pavement, ready to charge.

"We refuse to let the Meruyan Council tell us to work again for the same awful treatment on Warix soil. We want to live on land like they do!" finished Iringbon.

"Well someone needs to farm the land then." Talla said under her breath. "I mean, yeah we should drive those Warix away! If the Warix and council deserve a more posh life, why not them?" she said in earnest. Deem looked at her, realizing she had only now realized the hypocrisy. "And why not drive them off? More space for the Meruyan to prosper without them. You'll still provide to the Meruyan council, right? I mean, we are here in full support of your cause."

Deem shook his head.

"It's about damn time," Iringbon asserted. "Take up arms with me."

Deem continued to protest, but Talla's mind was made up.

Iringbon glared at him. "You with us or are you dead to us?"

"Let's ride!" Talla called, and they bounded off on the clomps of kelpie hooves towards the central base of Warix operations, joining others in the momentum, brandishing their makeshift weapons.

Deem felt a flood of mixed emotions. Fear and anger, disappointment, disapproval in himself for whatever direction he went in. He could not so easily just turn off his brain.

He followed Talla as she charged.

***

Deem flooded with unease as they followed like leaves caught in a rushing stream.

As the Meruyan charged into the village, the Warix soldiers could see them coming, assembling over the hill, taking defensive stance to fend off attacks. Their eyes glowed as they rose in torrents of wind, but the Meruyan were ready.

Deem ducked low on Pinchy, who swerved form the wind bursts, too heavy to lift into the air, as the group shot slingshots of mud right into the Warix's eyes, or caking their bodies, confusing and knocking them off course, and finally weighing them down.

Meruyan calls in the echolocating clicking language called upon the heavy neutolyths, controlling them, and pinned many of the offending Warix down to the ground.

Pinchy bolted at the sound and Deem launched backwards, grasping his thorax just before a fall, and trailing behind his mount, gasping for breath. "Pinchy, stop!" He shouted tactlessly, forehead releasing sweat as his faithful pet uncontrollably fled the scene. Deem hung on with all his might, his muscles burning.

"Hey, wait for me!" shouted Talla behind him. "What happened to tact!"

It was too late, they had entered the fray in the center of the village. Deem climbed back into Pinchy with an exasperated sigh as he paused at the chaos of the scene he'd run into.

Warix blasted wind, some Meruyan were blown off their mounts, beaten and subdued on the ground, but enough of them brandished farming equipment and shell blades, and managed to help their downed comrades, beating the Warix further back, and into submission, powerless to knock back heavy animals, who often bit and snapped at the Warix with tendril mouths. The Warix were afraid of these animals on an instinctual level, which was likely why they banned them from being ridden in the first place. Deem guessed all these kelpies were smuggled in from the underwater city of Noyade, the largest and closest offshore Meruyan city.

Beaten to submission, The Warix limbs were tied with rope and dragged with the help of the animals into storage basements.

The head production supervisor, a Warix who Deem could appreciate had a good sense of leadership, tried to control the situation.

He shouted desperately, calling out the direction of attacks, imploring his people forward with confidence. He held out, faring well against the onslaught, but the group lost ground and were pushed from the orchards.

When hope for the Warix overseers was lost, at the far side of the orchards, out of their control, he called out, pulling the Warix back.

Deem followed his group atop Kelpies as the Warix retreated towards the factory districts. From the hill, they could see the remaining soldiers fleeing into the factories. Deem kicked off and urged Pinchy forward, where they found the Warix slamming the doors and locking themselves inside.

Some popped their heads from the higher-level rooftops, the head Warix watching, his frame silhouetted against the bright, cloudy skies.

Deem squinted, his eyes burning; the Warix had his wrist raised to his face, likely reporting the situation to Sen'Drorn headquarters. A shudder passed over Deem, a fear of this hopeless endeavor to make any real difference. This violence was only going to cause a bigger backlash. More Warix would come, their city had more to provide. He turned his kelpie, they strode off to rejoin his group. Talla would not share his fear, so he kept it to himself, where it would live inside him in the form of a low, distasteful thrumming in his veins.

***

A horde of Meruyan crowded around Yulah.

She had ordered a little pampering, getting her horns done. With flat tree-bark paddles, they ground and filed. This guided their growth and sharpened her focus. A fine glaze finish made them shine in her mirrored reflection.

Life was good.

Except that it wasn't, really, outside the Fortress walls. She found herself, despite all this, nostalgic for her time in the normal city.

That day, she resolved to walk among the normal folk, strolling down Fleeg Street. She walked by Borak's old shop, the windows boarded shut. It sent a shiver down her spine.

The sign was still here, swinging, announcing only a lie now.

Sadness washed through her.

The Quail egg cafe was open, but she could not bring herself to stop and eat there. Too many memories, once sublime, turned foul.

She couldn't help herself from glimpsing their daily specials, however, only to see many of their menu items had been crossed out. Typical these days. Meruyan delicacies were on serious backorder.

Only in the fortress could she get such delicacies, like exotic fruit pies, made from what could still be brought from the NVH crop. The Emperor probably kept most of it for himself, sharing a trickle with her and the other top advisors on special days only.

It bothered her, deeply. Those pompous Meruyan. Something had to be done. The time to strike back with a firm hand of fury was now.

"Yulah, how good to see you! It has been forever!" a shrill voice called out in front of the cafe. It was the shop owner of the Quail Egg Cafe. "It seems life in the fortress is treating you well."

Yulah put on an agreeable face and cheery disposition, though didn't feel it inside. She made an unnatural smile, and agreed politely. "Oh yes, lovely."

"I miss having you around here. And that boy you were seeing…anyway, sorry about the food shortages. You wouldn't happen to know of anything coming in, any time soon?"

She gave Yulah large, expectant eyes, as if Yulah had a say in this. In a way she did, as the new General of tactics. This Warix woman was not wrong to cozy up to her.

"Please, have a free pastry!" her voice went low. "I'm sure I have a secret stash in the back. Just for someone special, like yourself."

Yulah nodded, but felt bad, admittedly, taking this from the mid-level city. It only confirmed her theory that the average members of society wanted to be ruled. They did what they could to maintain the order, the status quo. Yulah was at the top, her feelings of being undeserving resolved at this notion. The woman was insisting, after all.

Muffin basket in hand, she hurried away from the shop, and made it to the end of the long, busy merchant center of Fleeg street, into the dark alleys. She was about to take her first bite, when she spotted some children playing in the courtyard. Their aproned mother stood at the front steps to a small home, open to the courtyard, warm light aglow inside behind her.

The children ran in circles, their mother watching with worry.

In a moment of generosity, Yulah turned to her, and handed over the basket of muffins, lifting the cloth to show her. "They are Mozenberry, from the Meruyan lands. Hard to come by, but please, I insist you take them."

The woman's eyes widened, and she nodded graciously, still slightly bewildered. "Thank you, dear! This is a real treat." Yulah noticed her eyes went to the royal seal on her jacket coat. "You are from the Emperor's council?" she asked, amazed.

"Do share them with the neighbors," Yulah said, returning the nod. "I wouldn't want the fine people of Sen'Drorn to forget the wondrous taste of Meruyan crops. Could you imagine if your children grew up without knowing?"

"It would be a real shame," the woman agreed, her eyes lowering.

Yulah's heart lifted as she continued her stroll through the labyrinthine city. She'd done well, she was proud.

It was more than that. She believed in them. A better future for her people, they deserved it. A new determination glowed in her, at the thought of those children.

I need to fight for a better world for them, she resolved on her way back to the fortress. It was time to get more hands-on in the going on in the NHV.

CHAPTER TWENTY

"Those Meruyan are destroying us out there!" Yulah declared, pacing the room.

She had called for a private meeting with Ryogrim to discuss the state of the Meruyan uprising in the Northern Hilly Villages.

It was a total disaster. And as Yulah had assumed responsibility for supervising all of Malotus's old duties, this mess was included in the slack he'd left behind!

General Yulah, that is.

What a time Malotus had chosen to leave.

"What would you say I do, General Yulah?" Emperor Ryogrim paced his domicile, his heavy steps trembling the wooden floor. Her heart soared at the sound of her title, and she breathed deeply, drinking up the joyful feeling.

Her left hand formed a fist, her right covering it, the long nails clasping and pulling at her velvet flesh. "They have a fervor we lack. We need to pump up the men. Give them someone to lose, who can become a martyr. To show off the value of our cause, give our people the bloodlust to fight back," Yulah suggested. "Your man, head production supervisor Raalin. He is very popular with the Warix on the ground in the N.H.V.... If he is killed in the line of duty, it will change the game."

The emperor stopped pacing and stared at Yulah. His bloodshot eyes with faded pupils, blind at the edges. Just like his policy.

"I shall never!" he growled, eyes flashing. "He's a good, loyal man. I would never sacrifice him!" he rubbed his temples, pitching his curling horns downward.

"That's precisely why it must be him," she implored. "I don't see another way if we are to keep this city from sinking into chaos. We must keep the good people of Sen'Drorn satisfied. If their bread fails to come, if they run out of copper, we aren't doing to bode well this winter."

What was his game? Could he not have the foresight to keep his people happy? This was important! The Meruyan were entitled and could not be allowed to get away with their short-sighted uprising.

This would have to be settled with blood. With a hard and fast approach. It surprised her that the emperor, a tyrant of his own right, and a lover of his people, would not go for this. Perhaps he had been too long in this game. He had grown soft.

Yulah needed to drive her imperative. She shot an arm out and stirred her inner wind energy, launching it like a blast towards the door, which stood ajar, the torrent of wind blast slamming it shut.

The old ruler pulsed with a startled shock, though quickly recovered with a jolt of angry ferocity. His eyes became a cloudy mass and he stomped the ground, regaining command and attention.

"Girl, I warn you!" he snarled. "You cannot intimidate me. I will have your neck broken and your body never found. I will rip you to shreds. If your precious uncle Malotus ever returns, I swear he will never know what happened to you."

Her heart pounded in her chest, an anger threatening to take charge, demanded the room back. But she was not the emperor, she indeed had no right to cross him.

She would not forget herself, but rest assured, she would not forget his decision either.

"I will send more soldiers, what are they doing anyway, it's not like were ready to attack the Sen'Prin. We trained them, they wait around. This will be good for them—they will shatter and scatter those

Meruyan who dared to turn themselves loose on us and scoff at their duties."

"It will not work..." she mumbled but trailed off seeing his challenging expression. She could not argue it further. She turned on her heel, threw open the door, and left, trying to appear calm while her pounding heart protested in her chest.

Within two days, the Meruyan had retaken the NHV. The Warix troops had failed, maybe were taken captive, some dead, unprecedented among the once peaceful Meruyan race. To Yulah's dismay, when things got this bad, Ryogrim had pulled his man, Raalin the head production supervisor, from the field, thereby relinquishing his chances of martyrdom. Had the emperor done this to spite Yulah? She suspected so, but this only proved his weakness.

For the first time, she questioned the command of the emperor.

Her loyalty faltering, she couldn't help but think of Malotus. He'd been right again... she had to respect her old mentor for that. He was always the sharpest among the Sen'Drorn commanding personnel. If she was to get her way, she'd have to go behind the Emperor's back.

***

Flax helped Meleena try on the newly designed jetpack, slipping her arms through the holes, it fit snugly, though as he let go to let the thing's full weight down, her feet sunk, knees buckling.

"It is kind of heavy," she grunted.

"Sorry, we may have to remove some parts. That will reduce power though," he warned, rubbing his arm, feeling bad about all this hassle she had to go through just to keep up around her. "Ready to give it a whirl?" he said cheerily.

"Yeah," she agreed with a sigh. "It is certainly a great distraction from the letdown of the group."

"Maybe it was better, skipping the stakeout," Flax said, trying to cheer her up. "It's going to be really dull for them, sitting around, looking for the next probable location."

"Yeah, but I feel like I'm already at the fringes of the group."

Flax furrowed his brow, uneasy at her discomfort, but not sure what she meant.

"You know, not well liked. Everything they do without me feels like some great bonding experience I'm not a part of. It's so frustrating."

Flax felt his ears droop. He wished he could do more. "I've spent most of my life with about half that group, and they aren't all that interesting. Don't worry about being great friends. It takes time to build up mutual trust."

Meleena made a sound of hesitant agreement, then followed him, lugging the jetpack yet refusing to complain, as they walked over the bridges of Sen'Prin city. He was leading them to a location where they could descend to the riverbank below the walkways.

"This area is mainly for recreation, but it's pretty deserted today," Flax explained. "Let's try to stay by the water, just in case we need it to break your fall," he added, indicating to the small pools and waterfalls between them which formed the canyon river.

He helped her down the hill and they settled at a spot by the riverbank.

Flax came up close to her and rested his hands on the backpack-like structure strapped to her back. "I'll start it up, and you attempt to fly along the river."

His body tingled electrically from their nearness. "I suggest taking off now," he said. "Let's see how you feel. Get ready…And, Liftoff!" he called, pulling the ripcord.

"Okay, here goes!" Meleena cried, and bent her knees, then a low rattle emanated through the clunky pack, and she kicked off, launching off the ground. Flax kicked upward to stay on her this time, heavy energy emanating through his core and into his padded feet.

The world sank away. The tops of trees came dangerously near, he cringed as she skidded headfirst through the highest branches.

"Try to steer!" shouted Flax from below, trying to keep his distance. With his eyes cloudy silver at the peripheries, his vision impaired while casting wind energy. He launched himself towards her in the air.

She grabbed for the straps for stability, clearly not at ease up there. Her body tipped and she lost purchase, plummeting towards the ground. Flax's stomach flipped into a falling sensation as he watched, and tried to catch her, missing, but she rode it out into a slide, regaining control just before crashing into a pool.

"This is madness!" she shouted. "I feel like I'm continuously falling! I don't know if I like it!"

Flax landed on a rock and nervously pushed back strands of his messy brown hair.

"Try to follow me!" he said jovially, testing her.

Meleena let out a groan of uncertainty as she whipped around in dizzying aerial circles in an attempt to head towards him.

He whizzed away, bouncing off a tree trunk as she came after him.

"Goggles would have been nice," she shouted, starting to sound a bit frustrated.

Wind-spirit be damned, why hadn't he thought of that? He scolded himself.

He looked back at her as he zoomed up the canyon. Her jaw was clenched tight, and her hands gripped hard on the straps. Her knuckles and cheeks were pale as the pressure pulsed from his clunky prototype.

Then, to his shock and horror, her fly-like motions became too tight, and she began to nose dive again. Flax's heart beat wildly as he dashed to save her, but it was too late, she crashed heavily into a deep pond, to his horror.

"Mel, are you okay!?" he shouted, diving towards her, and finding her swimming below the surface, jetpack like a turtle shell, four fins streaming behind her elegantly rippling in the water.

Her head popped to the surface, long blue hair heavy and dripping. Her eyes sparkled.

"Good thing you are a Meruyan, strong swimming skills upon landing are a must," he joked, rubbing his elbow. "How did it feel?"

"Like perpetual falling, and the fear of crashing constantly tearing at my insights," she laughed out loud like a thrill escaping her. She was genuinely beaming though, so wide as he'd never seen on her face before. "Not to sound ungrateful—because I am, really, it is better than walking everywhere."

The thrill of it had shocked her out of her protective, semi-gruff shell. Flax felt warm inside knowing she was finally letting loose, enjoying herself. She was like a feline, sleek and small, timid of movement, and gracefully assessing with keen eyes whether or not they like you. A being whose trust and admiration you had to earn.

They took a break for a while to rest, then composed themselves to try another round of flying.

Flax whisked across her path, following the updrafts. Meleena tried not to veer off course as she followed him, swept up in the stirring winds. She chased him up the river, up the waterfalls, the city raised bamboo platforms and buildings streaming by on the sides of the river.

"This is a perfect space for practice," Flax shouted back over the wind. Most townsfolk stayed within the paths, on foot, only flying to get to particular buildings or as shortcuts to higher paths.

He whizzed up the waterfall, feeling the fresh water spray on his cheeks, then up to the dazzling sight of the next story up in the forest. The steam of the hot day poured over the river sent a surge of excitement through him, granting a boon to his wind energy.

"Now let's try a little tougher!" called Flax with a sneaky grin.

She cried out nervously.

"I'll be here to catch you if anything happens," he assured her, flying by.

He dipped between columns in the parklands below a building, and Meleena followed. But the angle proved difficult, and she swerved, miscalculating and spiraling out of control. Flax's heart pounded in a panic and she closed her eyes and shouted, "ahhrg!" before plummeting down and splashing right into the water all over again.

She stood up from the water. "I'm okay...again." she said, laughing and standing up again. Her legs shook, and he offered to help release her from the jetpack. They both agreed that was enough for one day.

All her fins reactivated, long and shimmering in the dappled light. Meleena doubled over and took a lot of deep gulps of air as she caught her breath. She splashed the water from the fresh stream into her face.

They sat on the stoop together, by the encircled pond with its crisp, clear water. It was quite a private spot near the top of the city.

They hung out, dangling their feet in the pools. Meleena's skin matched the color of the water, each somehow shining off the other, making her glow. The long fins steaming from her forearms were like the finest silk gown, adding elegance to her. Her hair trailed freely around her, lighter than air, and braided in places to keep it heavy.

And why am I noticing all this now? He scolded himself, as part of his mind drifted to Yulah, and a strange desire to remain virtuous to her. It wasn't like they were back together, far from it, but some part of him still had something to prove. It was childish. Like that his feelings and loyalty towards his first girlfriend had been real, that he hadn't been using her, and thus could not fall so quickly for someone else.

He shook it all from his head as the confused thoughts fought a small battle in his mind.

He took a deep breath and eased, letting his shoulder slouch, a lazy smile forming on his lips. "It's been a nice day with you, Meleena," he said, confirming it for himself as much as her.

"Flax, can I ask you something strange?" Meleena said suddenly.

"Uh, sure," he said, heart, skipping a beat. He had no idea where this was going.

"You are sure of yourself, patient with others," she started. "I wish I could be more like that. Carefree, nice, liked. Not care so much what they think. How can I be more like that?" her hands balled into determined fists and a sparkling tear trickled from her eye.

"Huh, never thought of myself that way. I see the opposite in you. I like that you always speak your mind. You're always questioning, and don't let others tell you what to think."

"But nobody likes me, because I do that..." she mumbled.

"Maybe, but don't feel bad about it."

"It's fine, I can take a little criticism. Let me have it!" she grinned at him.

"Err, I..." His cheeks grew hot. If she insisted. His palms grew hot, and he pressed his fingertips into his palms as he spoke. "The only advice I could give is, maybe to give others' intentions the benefit of the doubt more, and you will naturally come off as more welcoming, friendly, while also questioning like you already do. You will shine only brighter."

She considered for a moment, eyes on the water, and took a deep breath. "I know, I need to learn to lighten up. It's hard. Thank you for being honest, though. You're a good friend."

He too took a deep heavy breath, and his respect for her grew at that moment. She was always putting learning first, even if that meant how to navigate socially. It was like she saw others like a puzzle as mysterious yet study worthy as the forest, and herself as tech, which could always be refined.

He made a mental note to do the same for himself.

"Just trust yourself," he said finally. "You have more amazing instincts for this world than you know."

Meleena gave him a long, ponderous look.

"I am so sleepy," was all she said, yawning and closing her eyes. To his shock, she rested her head softly on his shoulder. He leaned into it, and they held each other in a dreary pause, as the shadows of the trees danced on the pond surfaces.

***

Yulah rubbed her weary, burning eyes. She had poured through paperwork all night. There were nine advisors in total, including herself, corresponding to the heads of various departments.

Financial—spending and all things currency; Agricultural—mainly outlying Warix territories; City planning—including Meruyan migrant workers; Defense—including wind wall upkeep, city and villages; Resource Import—all lands; Hyish relations—including trade routes; technology—investing in research of new inventions; Engineering technology—development of weapons, gear, works closely with: Military—War tactics including enforcing Meruyan productivity. General Malotus' former job, now Yulah's.

General Yulah, head of military. What good it did her. Ryogrim did not respect her enough to listen to her ideas.

Now, if she were to go about such a treasonous act, as to overthrow the Emperor, she would have to do it subtly…in a way that wouldn't get her into trouble in the planning stages, if she weren't successful.

In fact, her actions would have to appear as if they were towards the Emperor's wishes. Things that wouldn't be suspicious. She just had to win the allegiance of *most* of the advisors. This would be no small task, and serve her well regardless of a coup.

It would require learning the needs of the individuals involved.

She spent the rest of the evening going through documents. Something would come up. They were mainly old coots, though there was a youngster on the team, his grandfather, one such, had recently died. Young, desperate for acceptance. That could work. She'd put a pin in that.

All that aside, one advisor she knew she could earn an easy ally with was the advisor of Engineering Technology.

He was a middle-aged Warix, more of a brow-beaten donkey of a man, and a manager, not an actual tech guy. He had worked closely with General Malotus, and thus Yulah knew him quite well.

He was also the overseer of engineering when everything under his jurisdiction was ransacked, his entire workforce of engineers lost.

Yulah didn't particularly like him, he was a cruel Warix whose idea of managing a team was locking them in a basement. Yet he now hated Ryogrim more, who threatened him openly in front of the other advisors, and very nearly threw him in prison after the debacle.

But they were desperate to rebuild as well, and needed him around—to train new engineers, identify talent in the city, and start a team for this vital project of war as soon as possible. They had no time for the spectacle of locking their advisor, one of the last Engineers on staff, in the dungeons. He got a beating and thirty lashes, and *wind goddess* did he hate Ryogrim after that.

The Engineering Advisor was just looking for an excuse to go behind his back, Yulah could assume. Not that any of the advisors had the will or motivation, the foresight to do so on their own.

Only General Yulah, unbeknownst to them all, would dare. And that kind of leadership would be something they could get behind, or rather, hide behind in secret, she bet.

She decided it was time to start. Time to approach the advisor of Engineering Technology. That'd be easy. With one down, the momentum could make this real.

She strode through the Fortress, in a cruel twist of fate his quarters were reduced to the basement of the fortress.

She knocked, and he called back cautiously, inquisitively.

"General Yulah."

"You may enter."

She pulled the heavy latched wooden door and it swung open, revealing the small Warix in his laboratory and light green coat, holding a flask.

"The Emperor does not know I am here," she said as he lifted his bronze goggles to meet her gaze, squinting slightly.

"I need someone to fight for me. I have a wild idea," Yulah said, sitting on one corner of the long table.

She told him of her plan to take over.

A grim face, between a smile and a scowl crossed over his weary face. "I would be honored to help you. What would you like me to do?"

She leaned over and whispered in his ear. "Regardless, if I successfully overthrow him, it will look good for both of us if we pull this off."

"You want me to go where? I can provide some of our advanced tech for your squadron. With copper shortages these days, you will need me to meet your wind power needs for something like that."

She knew she theoretically could not send her men without consulting the Emperor first, but that was a risk she'd have to take. This would be her first time going behind his back.

"I will call upon you for the use of your gear when I need the favor," Yulah said. "For now, I am only here for your pledge. I am glad we are on the same page as regards to our dear Emperor."

She smiled at him, happy to have her first ally. There was no room to back down now. She didn't yet know what she would use his services for, but it would come in handy.

"In any case, it will take you some time to build up my order. I will need a stockpile of your finest copper wind-enhancement gauntlets and boots, whatever you have to give in these lean times. Divert resources away from Ryogrim as needed."

"Yes, General, as you wish."

Yulah liked the sound of that.

CHAPTER TWENTY-ONE

Yulah was exhausted. She had spent too many days awake, going through old documents in Malotus's files. Yes, she had trouble sleeping in her new bed, the fancy flat atop Sen'Drorn Fortress, with all its wonderful tapestries, fine silks and personal Meruyan service. It wasn't that she *couldn't* sleep, mainly, that she had more important things to do. Yes, that was it.

She had found nothing usable towards her vague idea of overthrowing the Emperor. This would never work. See, just a hypothetical. Gaining the *guaranteed* loyalty of those slimy elder advisors? It was farfetched.

Still, she poured through the papers littering every part of Malotus's former desk. Was she losing her mind, this far into the night, or did the numbers not add up anymore? She thought for sure the advisor of financial affairs would be stealing for his own benefit. Especially in tough times like these. But that would have been too easy. Nope, somehow his record was clean.

She pounded her fist on the desk and shouted in frustration. "Ugh!"

No, it's time to get some rest. This is all blurring together.

She stood, closing the last file on the finances department, and pinched the bridge of her nose to rest her eyes. She traversed the corridors, holding up a torch for light, her feet the only sound in the dead of night.

Numbers swirled in her mind, dizzying her. She collapsed onto her bed, still unable to sleep. She paced the room. The minutes droned by. Heavy, so heavy, yet unable to rest. The demons in her dreams, the pain of it. She pushed away the thought.

No, she was awake out of love for her people. The heavy air she expelled from her lungs and out her palms was energy for good. That's what she told herself. She tried to focus on her mind, noticing her thoughts and feelings, letting the tremulous energy seep from her as she rested on the daybed. A drop at first, like metal from the veins, escalating, oozing from every pore. It was like the inane wind energy in her was combining with something she'd been holding in a long time, and cleansing from her body like a release vent. Her cheeks, her armpits, the elbow joints, wrists, her palms, a steaming caldera of energy seeping out.

It felt good, euphoric and yet exhausting. She wasn't sure what time she had passed out. But the sun pounded something powerful upon her eyelids when they flickered open. The day was nearly over, the late afternoon sun dipping snugly into the mountainside when she peeled her face from the daybed and went to wash up.

She gulped down water, and found to her surprise, her head felt lighter and clearer now than she had in... such a long time. Sharp, clarity. And just like that, in a spark of inspiration, she resumed her work in Malotus's office, this time looking into the background of the Elder Advisor of Resource Import for all Warix lands.

"Ah ha... Siphoning extra resources for yourself, naughty," she said out loud to herself.

She wasted no time in confronting him.

"I need to! Long-term resource planning is security, you never know in this unstable world."

"So, it's been going back years. I hadn't checked that far...I just assumed, you know, with how things are now...but this!" she laughed, looking the poor old fellow up and down. "This is treason against the Emperor. Double—for if you are accused publicly, you are admitting to the people of Sen'Drorn that you think the market is unstable with little hope for improvement. You will be outing our current situation, when Emperor Ryogrim has worked so hard to keep things under wraps here, assuring the people we'll be back on track shortly. This is a minor hiccup and all. When we both know the Meruyan problem is not a quick fix. They will not be going back to work without a fight, and then some. That is worse than the stealing itself."

He gulped.

"You will be beheaded when the Emperor finds out."

"Please! You can't! What do you want, anything! Don't tell Emperor Ryogrim or anyone about this... I must provide and protect my family, I don't care about myself."

Yulah scoffed at that notion.

"I won't tell another soul. But, in return, I need you to swear your loyalty to me. If anything were to happen, if Ryogrim decided to turn against me, I'm on your side and you are on mine."

He hung his head in shame, and bowed deeply to her. "Alright. You have my word."

"Look me in the eye when you say it," she said softly.

And as he struggled and finally met her gaze, nodding again, her heart soared. She had her second ally.

***

Meleena was ready to go back to the jungle. Exhausting though that was, exhilarating even, she needed some time alone to journal. Flax had other things to attend to, and though she would have liked his company, the thought of going into the forest alone was tantalizing. She could take her time to study and sketch without someone over her shoulder.

He started the jetpack for her, so she could fly it back to her flat. She hid how she felt about it all. He was just a friend, nothing more. How she thought he could be more was silly. Her stomach was in knots, but she brushed it off. It was nothing, never anything. Of course, she couldn't match up to Yulah, who was gorgeous. Of course, he wasn't over her. But enough of these thoughts.

She stopped by her room to grab her journal, flying the jetpack up to her balcony window herself for the first time. That was a very nice feeling—to take a step and land there, just like any Warix. It was closer to fitting in, though by now she doubted it would help her lack of friendships.

She lowered herself to plunk it down behind her on the ground, and released herself from the straps. Newly released of the heavy burden, she stretched her back.

Putting it on again, alone, required squatting low to the ground, and snuggling back up into it.

Only after she did so, did the realization occur to her that she couldn't start it again without a Warix. She grumbled and wriggled out of it again.

The trip to the trail would have to be on foot. She picked up a satchel, stashed the journal, and headed for the winding stairs. She would have to pass through the noodle house as well. No wonder Warix preferred aerial landings.

She passed the Warix walking up and down the lane, until finally she climbed the sloping track out of town where the bamboo path met natural rock. She stepped onto the earthen trail and ducked through the broad leaves, marking the entrance to the forest. She took a right up the hill, off path, over the logs and ferns, to where she'd discovered the lizard nest. She was certain there was more to learn there, to understand their behavior, and to know how they use fire.

She came upon the bonfire-like lizard nest, where they came and went, and skittered around their burrow.

Up in the tree, behind some ferns, she spotted the great featherpaw, who was resting in the tree licking one paw, the other dangling casually off the thick branch. Its dark iridescent black-purple glossy fur blended into the shadows.

This must be his regular spot.

Just then, something rustled in the leaves. The featherpaw? Meleena turned, and a bright shiver spread up her spine, burning bloomed in her cheeks.

It was three Warix. Their right hands encased in copper- threaded military gloves, their uniforms dark green blending with the surrounding forest. Meleena knew at once they were Sen'Drorn, and they were here for her.

She bolted into the undergrowth, and they darted after her, swift and fierce-faced, grinning condescendingly at her. They wouldn't catch her so quickly. Her heart beat in her ears, whole body engulfed in heat. They were gaining on her, thrashing at the leaves, tearing a path, but Meleena had agility. She ran, ducked in the undergrowth, slid under a huge root, slipped around a tree. Her countless experience escaping predators in the wild never included Warix, they would be harder to outsmart. However, this was an unfamiliar forest. She didn't know what creatures or obstacles could help her here.

Meleena tried, but one of them seized her by the shirtsleeve and pulled her up. "This is the girl. We here to kill her?" He snarled at his comrade. Meleena struggled and kicked him in the shins, making him yowl and drop her, but the other caught her immediately.

"Yes, I believe that would be better than dragging her all the way back to headquarters."

"Don't you listen!" another shouted.

She squirmed but couldn't loosen herself. She gulped. How could she get out of this?

She blinked. A dark shape emerged from behind her from the shadows. It moved like an animal, stalking, jumping from a tree. perhaps the feather mane?

Its wings were a bit small on its back as it shrieked and leapt downward onto the assailants. It had a long, ferocious beak that shimmered white like a skull, and large vacant eyes, and sweep of black fur but kept its face low.

She couldn't get a great look at it as it swept a blast of wind at the assailants, knocking them off their feet. Meleena sprung up a coiling tree to get away.

The great black-maned beast drew up on two legs and attacked, claws and teeth in a flurry. They used their gloves and slashed the air, channeled wind energy pinning the great beast to a tree in a loud huff. Meleena gave a kick and *snap!* a branch fell and landed on one of their heads, giving the beast a moment of freedom to regain leverage. It growled, a low resonating purr. He crouched on clawed heels and flew upward, kicked them midair, knocking them backwards. It was enough time for Meleena to turn and run through the tangle of spiral trees, with no time to look back. She heard them continue to battle as trees crashed around her, slowly growing more distant.

Jumping from one type to the ground, panting and sticky wet from the fuss, she didn't stop until she got to the clearing in the trees, where the lights of Sen'Prin were visible.

Whatever that beast was, she was in its debt. It was too dark to be the feather paw. And why had it come to her aid like that? Very strange, but perhaps it could perceive she was in danger, or trouble to its own nest? It had green wings, but she never got a good look, but mane and claws. And a wind user. She felt a surge of love and gratefulness that the forest was there for her, keeping her safe.

CHAPTER TWENTY-TWO

The fighting continued on in the Northern Hilly Villages, as the Sen'Drorn sent a never-ending wave of enforcers. It had devolved from an attempt at civility to daily skirmishes to beat the other into submission.

Each night, Deem and Talla huddled in the underwater dwellings of the Iringbon caves, safely in the lakes system where the Warix could not strike them. It was the one solace of this awful place and time. Deem had no intention of ever being a part of any of this, and now here he was, stuck in it.

"I still say the Meruyan need to own their own land," griped Talla. "And why not in the northern villages?"

"Well it is Warix land..." reasoned Deem.

They spoke in the native clicks of Meruyan, from their kelpweave bedding underwater.

"Who says it's Warix land? Everything is Warix land! They claimed it all before we had any chance. I don't see how that's fair. So, we are going to take it back."

"It's not exactly what I signed up for when he said he wanted to help our people," said Deem.

He was always expecting to join the council and help with the political aspect. Gaining better rights for them, learning of the intricacies of their world had proved difficult, emotionally and for the future of the underwater dwellers. He hadn't expected them to full-on protest to stay on the Warix land. He personally didn't think any of this was a great idea.

"This is our duty now," said Talla matter-of-factly as she brushed her turquoise hair, its long tendrils streaming like a halo around her head.

"Isn't there a way to, I dunno, get along?" Deem reasoned, one hand picking at a bump on his face. "To talk this out, to have rational Meruyan meet with Warix and find a solution?"

Talla tilted her head, granting a view of cheeky disapproval.

He knew in his heart that everyone's motives came from a place of good intention. Doing what was best for "them and theirs" was from a place of caring, of love, like he had for his own family and community. His lifelong belief had only been confirmed when he ate of the legendary fruit. He had felt it, deep in his core, that this connection linking all living things together was important, that it meant we were meant to love one another. Everyone was so caught up in their own particular interests, they lost sight of this greater truth.

There had to be a way to fix this through understanding.

Although Deem didn't know then the extent of Warix bias, and how far they would go to maintain their current living standards, to which they'd become accustomed.

Talla pinched the glowing orb sea creature which lit up the room, causing it to swim up through a hole in the natural shell ceiling hole, dimming the room to utter darkness.

Deem soon heard her peaceful snoring breath, and knew she was out.

His skin sweated into the watery surroundings, exchanging fresh nutrients from the water, calming him slightly. Lying in the inverted shell bed, he remained awake wondering, nervously, what tomorrow would bring.

And all too quickly, he awoke with a startle, bubbles bursting from his lips. He had drifted to sleep and now it was dawn. The light refracting off the water particles, brightening everything at once. In these shallow lakes, morning tended to come earlier than the underwater village of Pontai'Desa where he'd grown up.

Talla was ahead of him, saying only, "Good, you're up! Let's get to it then!" excitedly swimming in a spiral, filling the room with a swarm of bubbles to prod him out of sleepiness.

"Why are you so energetic this morning?" he grumbled, lightly nudging himself from the kelpweave nest of bedding. "You're usually the tired one!"

"Yeah, but I get excited sometimes!" Talla said impatiently.

Deem only ever saw Talla like this when she was nervous. He knew this must be something serious. He dressed in a fresh tunic and pants, tight fitting for battle, and stretched his arms to follow her out their cave room.

They headed to the stables, where Clover and Pinchy awaited. Pinchy was nervously pacing in the stall. Deem petted his chittering friend, calming him with clicking coos, and they swam together to the surface, Deem's pulse quickening as he anticipated the scene on land, and what kind of day they would have ahead of them. Another day outside the safety of underwater. Why couldn't they just stay there, beyond the Warix grasp? How hard could it be, living this way? Oh well, he was in too deep to turn back at this point.

It wasn't long before the group was back out there, Deem riding atop Pinchy, prowling the streets and hills for Warix to chase away, and further overtaking more of the territory.

Pinchy clamored up the hill, his many legs swift and even, as if he was rolling on wheels. Deem enjoyed the sensation and power, comradely, safety, of having his best friend by his side. Pinchy, but also Talla. A turquoise shadow blossomed at the corner of his vision, as Talla galloped at his side atop Clover, his coral horns now prominent and beautiful in the morning mist, smoke from their collective breath visibly forming a vale around them. Other Meruyan rode alongside them atop Kelpies and even the occasional Neutolyth.

A group of Warix came directly to confront the group, striding with wind at their heels. They stood no chance against the Meruyan, who swiftly used produce collection polearms to knock the Warix off their feet and slam them back.

Overseer Thowler, the Warix who took charge of the main district of the Northern Hilly Villages, came out from his barn offices, face contorted in utter rage. He clearly was caught off-guard by all of this strange and un-Meruyan-like behavior.

"Kelpies!" He shouted, running forward to confront the rebellious group. "You can't ride these! You know the rules!" His grey face had turned bright purple, his fists quivered with rage. He did not hold back, ordering the Warix management to fight back, using full wind force.

Eyes glowing silver as they summoned the wind to their aid, tens of Warix kept into the air, and sending a forceful wind in unison at the group. This sent Meruyan on foot spinning back. Kelpies let out high pitched, otherworldly shrieks which Deem had never heard before, as they reared on two legs in a panic. Some Meruyan lost their balance and fell from their mounts, only to be struck by more wind bursts and subdued by the imposing Warix.

But the Meruyan held their ground, as they pushed back best they could. Meruyan and Warix were locked in hand-to-hand combat. As surprised as the Warix were, they had the manpower to keep their word on enforcement of labor. The Meruyan were not equipped. Many Warix held hooked glaives of their own, chain ropes to bind those on the ground and drag them away.

Deem's heart pounded in his chest as Pinchy charged into a group. He shut is eyes tight as a Warix slammed down wind on him, but he flattened onto Pinchy's body and held tight. He could feel movement, as his faithful friend skittered in some direction. All around him, cries and clanking, crashing of bodies, filled his ears. Shivering all over, Deem felt like he was going to throw up.

Iringbon's voice cut through the battle sounds, shouting, "Retreat! Hang back!" and there was more movement of legs and storming of hoofs, as the group lost ground and those still mounted attempted to escape.

When Deem opened his eyes, he saw that they had managed to knock back several Warix pursuers, as they slipped between buildings and up the hillside, into the cover of the orchards, where aerial attack by the Warix would be harder to aim. Crouching close to Pinchy, sweating like mad, Deem scanned for enemies between the trees, his hair in his eyes as the herd galloped back to the base. Some Meruyan had bows and arrows, and shot down some of the pursuers, who made their hit known by loud screams and a calming of the winds which whipped from all sides.

The panting group hurried into their caves, protected now. The Warix surely knew where their base was at this point. At least one must have seen it. The existence of the rebel group was known. All elements of surprise were now spent.

This lack of success would not bode well, Deem feared.

Once they regrouped, dismounted, and established who was still here, Iringbon addressed them with words of condolence and hope. "You all fought valiantly. Yes, we lost ground. We didn't expect such a prepared recourse, but we must formulate a new plan of action."

Deem found Talla, and they broke into weeps in each other's arms. The release of all the stress felt good. He never thought he'd share a moment of vulnerability with her like this, but things had gotten so escalated. And why not? They were close.

"Perhaps it is time to ask the Hyish for aid," Iringbon announced to the group. "They have helped us to find our freedom through our recent trade. Perhaps they would assist in holding stable this arrangement by providing us some reinforcements—brothers and sisters in arms. Let's break for lunch, gain our strength, and then we'll need a team of volunteers to go persuade them."

Deem and Talla looked at one another, a smirk forming across her lips, his to match. They agreed to join the group to speak to the Hyish.

It was better than charging into a pack of Warix any day, but also diplomacy was their specialty. Deem shivered at the thought that he'd joined a full-scale rebellion in the first place, abandoned his desk job and the safety of the capital for this. Life could still surprise him.

That turned out to be the straightforward part… the series of events and his own convictions that had led him to this point. Surviving it all with his sanity intact, harder still. But he hadn't thought dealing with the Hyish would be the hardest yet.

When he and Talla, and others had come to their encampment, they were directed to the village Welch. This was a small group of ancient Hyish, lizard folk with skin tight on their bones, and piercings upon every bump and ridge.

Talla took the lead in their request, sitting amongst them on hot rocks surrounded by a central warming fire. "Please, we need reinforcement if we are to continue trading with you. The Warix are trying to keep us tethered to their work by force, producing crops for their cities."

The lead Welch watched them intently, fire reflection glistening off his large eyes. His forked tongue shot in and out as he hissed in barely audible, broken common tongue. "The Warix don't know unity. They fight forevvver, climbing to top of hill made from their own bonnnesss." His tongue flicked at the word. "Meruyan shall not follow in bloody footsteps."

"Yes, but, please help us. If things are to continue—"

"The Hyish contribute not to the bloodshed."

"But we have heard rumors!" Deem blurted out. "Warix are afraid of provoking you. The Hyish are rumored to be fierce warriors who can keep even them in check."

"Only for our survival or last possible form of justice. You see, Warix do not bother us because they know better. No more war is needed."

"But…The Meruyan need your help."

"Trade is only trade. Your people can adhere to both professions, as has gone on for a century. This can continue as such without battle. No, you get greedy. This is the problem. Do not poke the beast. Leave your people to their labors."

Talla jumped to her feet, getting angry now. "This is unfair! Why should you be able to enjoy your freedom and even prosper with us, and we can't even choose our direction in any of this?"

Deem eyed her fearfully.

The Welch coughed out what seemed to be a laugh. "Hyish are where we are, for we give thanks. We know the universe is aware, and we work with it. Meruyan have lost their way, their connection with greater Meruyan-kind. It pains us to see, you small Meruyan, alone and wandering, struggle to get what is yours in the world. But you forgot your origins, and your connection to the Mother. Follow footsteps of Hyish, not Warix path of greed."

"What do you mean? Small Meruyan?" Deem asked, blinking in confusion. Did they mean for leaving the water, or were there more Meruyan somewhere? He wasn't even sure these Hyish knew what they were talking about. From where he sat, it was them who had lost touch with this world.

"Must understand with the heart, not the mind. Must teach yourself to shift."

"Fish guts! Here you sit, adorned in lavish things, and speak to us about greed?" Talla spat, face contorted. "How dare you speak to us like we are undeserving of fighting for our own fate!"

"This is just business to you," the Welch sighed. "These are simply vectors of my joy, a reminder of appreciation of what is greater. Shells and stones from Mother Bhumiya. We trade for the joy of interaction, novelty, the cycle of movement in all things. Unattached to the material possession beyond what keeps us alive. We honor Mother Bhumiya, and she grants us happy and connected life. I will say no more of your greed and attachment to wrong values. You will not understand."

Deem thought of the Nushen'yu seed, and the connectivity of all. Perhaps this was only a start of something bigger, which the Hyish were more connected with. It dawned on him, the possibility of unknown depths of their knowledge. Like looking into a murky lake, bottom unseen. Their culture was a mystery to all other peoples. It's not like the Meruyan knew much, and what they knew of Hyish was through the Warix, who, now that he thought of it, were not exactly sensitive in this way to understanding wisdom of other peoples. No, the Warix had their perspective and that was what they exported.

The group left the meeting distraught from the bad news, of the lack of physical support. But Deem was disturbed beyond the facts in front of him.

Had Deem been unknowingly buying into some perspective, his upbringing tainted by Warix values, cut off from the true depths of Meruyan culture, and thus the secret reality of their planet? The Hyish knew something which they weren't telling.

***

Deem grumbled to himself as they rode on back to the rebel camp. He couldn't stop the thoughts that bubbled up. It felt like an itching under his skin. Something was not right with the world. Why had he agreed to all of this in the first place? Everything seemed to be futile, falling apart.

He looked to Talla. She was cursing about the lack of support from the Hyish, seemingly having dismissed all of the cryptic messages he had eluded to. Deem couldn't help the lurching feeling in the pit of his stomach, that the Hyish were right somehow. But craving more information, where could he even go to find out more? Part of him wished this door hadn't been opened.

"Deem, will you help me wash Clover after this? He's getting a bit smelly."

Deem agreed. He liked to help, but hated to disappoint. He just wanted some time alone after all of this. The unnerving sensation was thrashing at his insides. *Ah,* he reasoned, *I can take on another thing. Why not. I can handle this, just one more thing.*

The undulating sensation of riding atop Pinchy kept him present as he held himself together. He felt a starling shove, knocking him aware, as a jet current hit him square in the back, pitching him forward and flat onto the top of Pinchy's carapace. He stayed down, turning Pinchy in a whip-like motion in an attempt to trip whoever was behind them, but missed as something copper flung right at his neck, pulling him off his mount by a chain and down into the mud.

"Deem!" shouted Talla, as Clover reared up.

The culprit dragged him as Deem attempted to struggle, failing and choking with a gloved hand on his mouth. A high-pitched scream emanated from Pinchy, the last thing Deem heard before a dizziness overtook him and everything went dark.

CHAPTER TWENTY-THREE

After her incident in the forest, the run-in with Sen'Drorn assassins and the mysterious beast who came to her aid, Meleena ran to tell Flax, and he had urged her to tell the group at the meeting the following day.

In the morning, Meleena, after a poor night's sleep, still shaken up, hurried down to Ma's noodle house for breakfast and to see what the group had discovered without her on yesterday's mission. Everyone in the team aside from her had done the legwork of the previous day, and meeting down in the noodle house was quite fruitful.

Meleena sat nervously, wondering when would be a good time, if any, to bring up the attack she'd encountered in the forest.

When she sat down, the others were all laughing as though there was some joke she missed and quieted down at her arrival. Her ears felt hot and her chest tight.

"So much gunk," sighed Naia after the meeting began.

Riigs handed over the jar containing the gray goop to Flax, who made an uneasy face.

"Don't you worry, there's barrels more of it already being delivered to your lab," said Thian with a merry wink.

"Oh, great, thanks," Flax murmured back. "I'll test it out, but we already know that it's the byproduct of the elemental cells breaking apart inside the tech's mechanism."

"It's all been confirmed and then some," added Jessup. "Mass droughts across our lands—but it's not been happening in Sen'Drorn's villages in the same valley. Suspicious!"

Zoltan counted on his fingers, frowning. "Drought, stressed animals, gunk and more gunk. Crop failure. The theory checks out, as well as that it's been done at by Sen'Drorn hands. Whatever new tech they've got, it's blowing us away."

Thian guffawed. "Zoltan! Did you just say something in jest?" He looked baffled and looked to the others, wide-eyed, in support.

Riigs sat back and crossed his arms with a smirk, while Naia let out a little hick-up laugh then closed her hand over her mouth.

A melodic laugh escaped Jessup's lips, and even Meleena couldn't help but relax a bit into her chair.

Kyra toughened her jaw. "This is quite serious," she scolded. "The picture is coming into focus, and it looks very bad for us. Farmers across Sen'Prin are reporting crop failure. We may have to restrict resources soon. Arenay will likely call a state of emergency ration. The Sen'Drorn plan to weaken us. To starve us out. If they succeed, and send even a small army could force us to surrender to Sen'Drorn rule. We may be safe geographically, but we won't last long without enough food. It is something we've never faced before."

She let out a steady breath, and the group sat in pressured silence.

Meleena made a fist under the table, hiding her annoyance. Never mind that this theory was hers from early on, and none had believed her. When the evidence lined up, they just said, that's the natural way it points. Meleena attempted no argument. She didn't want to cause trouble, but certainly felt frustratingly undervalued.

Not that I even need the praise...but it would be nice to feel seen, she grumbled to herself.

She was nervous and distracted still by the soldiers in the forest. If she told the others, they may think she'd been making it up...and how she'd escaped it, even more so, what with a mysterious beast rescuing her. Maybe she shouldn't say anything at all. But what if she was in real danger?

"Now, what we need is to follow our next lead," Kyra said, ready to explain the next mission. "We will join the Sen'Prin under-cover agents, as they attempt to take over more Sen'Drorn outpost villages for our allegiance. By claiming them, we gain access to wider resources, and reduce theirs."

Meleena caught Flax's eye by mistake. She quickly looked away, wondering if he ever begrudged the non-use of Meruyan products in Sen'Prin. He had tasted luxury, in his time as a spy in Sen'Drorn.

For the Sen'Prin offshoot nation, getting by without the supplementary resources must be hard to keep up. No wonder Sen'Prin, scraping by on food and defense minerals, never directly came to the aid of the Meruyan. She let go of any last grudges she held against them for their lack of support all her life.

Meleena wouldn't blame Flax either, if part of him longed to return to the more stable and prosperous nation of Sen'Drorn. The enemy, but living better than anyone else, that was certain. How could she think that? Ugh, she was so dazed and confused these days. She didn't fully feel like a Meruyan anymore, somehow. Being the only one here was both stark and forgettable, in differing moments.

What else could Flax burn for there?

Or, *who* else.

A prickle of jealousy made her jaw tighten and shoulders curl inward, just slightly. She straightened, releasing the tension with a silent breath. It was none of her concern what or whom Flax thought about.

Kyra explained more of the mission. "You will do a stakeout in newly held Sen'Prin villages, and camp out by the edges of orchard and forest, looking for evidence of a Sen'Drorn drought machine. You will have guards, as this is your most dangerous mission yet. I wouldn't normally send you there, but this is the only way to be at the forefront of where it will likely be now. Maybe we can catch someone behind it, or the machine itself."

"And why here, exactly?" asked Zoltan wearily.

"This area was recently captured by Sen'Prin, like I said. They've reported drought and—I guess we are officially calling it, '*gunk*'—as have all other villages, but only after capture. Previously lush areas are suddenly seeing crop failure with gunk and drought. Sen'Drorn are certainly behind this, destroying their previously held resources rather than recapturing the villages. Possibly because we capture them using diplomacy, and those are the sort they would have to win back by force. This would indicate that their fighting resources are spread thin, but the tech is making up for it in other ways." She rubbed her eyes. "It's not looking good for anyone. Now go get your things and prepare to head out. We have equipment waiting in headquarters."

Meleena was bubbling, looking for the right opportunity to mention her own issue, and theirs. Sen'Drorn soldiers, so close to Sen'Prin. She knew it was about her, and likely not going to affect them. But if she went on this mission, they could kidnap her, or worse. If they were after her, this could be even more dangerous than for the others. She could be walking right into their hands.

As the group got up, Meleena resolved to speak to Kyra alone.

"Also," Flax cut in with a raised finger unexpectedly, stopping them as the group began to stir. "I've been experimenting myself," he said. "Borak and I designed some sparking gloves for use on the mission, which should also be fire-resistant. They have an open tube at the base of the wrist, lined with fire cells, and when you focus wind from the hands and snap your finger, it will ignite a small fire. It may be a small-scale version, along the same lines, as the tech they used to blow up the villages."

He opened his rucksack, revealing it was full of several pairs.

The group was quite impressed as he pulled out the copper threaded thick pairs of gloves. Meleena felt a pang of jealousy that she was not included, yet again, on a perk of the team. They looked very fun to use.

"Wow Flax, way to use their tools against them," said Meleena in surprise. She'd had no idea he had been working on this.

"Heh, you wild man," said Thian, clapping Flax on the back.

"That is high-tech at its finest!" Riigs complimented, taking the extra-large pair for his pack.

Meleena made eye contact and signaled to Kyra, to speak to her alone before they left. It was the only worthy opportunity to bring up her incident. "The Sen'Drorn sent some soldiers to the jungle here and tried to kidnap me. I can't go walking into this."

Kyra was startled, concerned. "I believe you," she said, putting a hand on Meleena's shoulder. "They know you are especially valuable for your tracking skills. It is alarming, to say the least, and I will alert Arenay so we can send patrols out there. I do believe you will be safe though, surrounded by soldiers and your friends..." She gave her a more stern look, furrowed brow and all. "You also know, you cannot go into the jungle un-escorted anymore after this."

Meleena felt sick to her stomach. She agreed, reluctantly, and yet the idea of losing her place of freedom and sanity was more alarming perhaps than even the covert attack. She turned to go, and Kyra added one last word. "And, Meleena, thank you for being here. I know it can't be easy. This horror truly shows your value to this group."

"If we're going camping, I'll bring my lute," said Riigs, specifically looking at Meleena. "It's a Meruyan thing. I got it on a trip to the Arctic city ages ago!"

Thian helped her retrieve her jetpack from her room, so that she wouldn't be late, and helped her start it. They made a quick stop by the engineering lab to check some of the issues she'd had during yesterday's testing. "You love it right?" beamed Borak when she entered.

"Yeah," she chuckled in awkward agreement. "Thank you for building it for me, Borak, really," she added earnestly. "I am grateful."

Then she attempted to fly the jetpack out of there. Following Thian, they flew upwards to the capital, where the launching area was. Meleena had seen this before via airship and it was quick nerve-racking to be jumping off with nothing but a glorified backpack, into the wind below. Her stomach lurched and could swear Zoltan had pushed her, the others giggling, as she launched herself off. The others followed and sped past her soon after.

Over the hills and horizon, the view of the rainforest waterfall of Sen'Prin City.

It wasn't that easy to control the jetpack. She flew in wide circles, like a fly, not straight paths like them. Her arms had to pull her for stability, it was an exhausting mess. Her arms burned from the constant work.

The wind blew in her face, and she wore special goggles instead of glasses for the flight over there.

He sailed over and could see little houses surrounded by fields, flanked by woods in the surrounding area. it was tall, steep Rolling hills, creating long valley corridors, as they descended into the valley.

Meleena landed after the other's tornadoes dispersed, taking a lap in the air to avoid getting caught in their drafts.

There was a dry hot discomfort in her skin. A drought was certainly in the air. The forest trees looked tired, their tops dipping. Much of the underbrush was dead. A nearby river was so jammed with gunk, there was no more discernible water. Half-decomposed corpses of reptiles, fish, and shriveled plants stank up the riverbanks. More signs that the explosive technology was harming the wilderness.

Sen'Prin guards met up with them, and the group headed from the village to the outskirts. They hiked the rest of the way to the dense forest edge. Kyra kept the map out and directed them. The path was narrow and unclear, as the locals knew better than to leave an easy trail for the Sen'Drorn.

They spread out to talk to the locals, then met back at the meeting point an hour later.

"The locals I spoke to report having seen a Warix, over the past weeks, by the side of the forest at night with some strange, large tank. Like a globe on wheels. He was apparently using it with an attached hose," reported Jessup on behalf of her group.

"And get this," added Thian. "He was using it, aiming it at the sky. We think he was sucking up clouds. Sounds crazy, but what else? We need to go find this thing to know for sure though."

They all frowned and looked at each other.

This meant they would be spending the next few nights camping outside the village safety zone. "Out there!? Where the beasties are?" gulped Zoltan.

"Yes. Get over it. We will have to sleep in shifts and protect each other," said Kyra.

They gathered some supplies in town that they'd need for a more rugged stay. She returned after a while carrying supplies and they set up camp.

It wasn't even as comfortable as Meleena had recalled her nights in the wild with Deem and Talla on her first mission.

The sky cracked with Thunder, an aggregate of clouds came in, which made the humidity choking. Meleena couldn't wait to leave this place. It was eerie and uncomfortable.

Before nightfall, they searched the area, scouring for the machine described, but found nothing.

Meleena fell asleep by the fire, until a loud bang made her jump, like a boom-crack, and she looked up in time to see a cloud, red and thick with flame, billow upwards over the mill, shattering the bamboo structure, shards and broken sticks blasting every which way.

The team jumped from their hammocks and mats. Meleena instantly thought of the fire cloud she'd seen in the forest. It was a gigantic version of the one the predator had spawned when it launched itself at the lizards. The interaction of flame and wind.

Meleena followed the others, aimed her jetpack and kicked off, flying with the others as they approached the ruins in a frenzy.

"Did you see anyone try to leave?!" shouted Kyra above the din as the group spread out on wind jets.

Meanwhile, thunderstorms collected overhead. Whereas the sky had been so clear all day, now the clouds descended, condensing. A chill ran through Meleena, the wind was encroaching with the amassing clouds.

"I didn't see anyone!" shouted Zoltan.

Jessup ran out from the pile, kicking bamboo out of her way, her face all scratched up. "He went that way!" she shouted. "I saw someone! A Warix!"

They turned and followed her, but she was slow from her injuries. The clouds and thunder darkened the sky so suddenly, and lightning even began to crack, thunder roaring above them.

How was this possible? So quickly? No Warix had a power like that.

The Warix flew into the storm and slipped out of sight before they could catch him.

It was too dark and grim. Then, something even more remarkable happened. Something quite disgusting.

Meleena felt a droplet on her head. One landed on her forehead, and another blocked her vision, making her remove her glasses and wipe them down. She scooped up a bit in her hand, rubbing it in her fingers. "Eww!" she gasped. "It's the gunk...that grey stuff."

It was raining from the sky. Now that they'd not seen it before.

"We should take samples," said Kyra, in a shaken, letdown tone. "Let's get to the town!"

They packed up the campsite in a disturbing silence and flew back to Sen'Prin crestfallen. Nobody wanted to speak of their failed attempt to stop the destruction of the village.

When they made it to the platforms of Sen'Prin, Kyra stopped them.

"Thian, go straight to Arenay and report we have seen. And to get the word out about if there are others like this in the area, who have seen any of these globe vehicles or dents like that. The rest of us, straight to the lab," said Kyra. "We need to solve this drought problem as soon as we can. Or the Sen'Prin nation is ruined, in many ways. Also, the copper mines are going to need reinforcements to help reopen."

***

Yulah lay sighing and sweaty in her new domicile.

"So, Ranfaf the *Fifth*, eh?" She turned her head to face her lover.

The boy lying next to her—that's what he was, older than her though he may be—was the youngest advisor to ever join the council. "Well, you may have known my grandfather, Ranfaf the third…Nushen'yu rest his soul. My father, Ranfaf the fourth," he explained, wiping the sweat from his long brow, "…didn't want the responsibility. So, I was more than eager!"

"Fantastic opportunity for you."

"Oh yes! I just, wow, you're so pretty. I can't believe you are here with me right now."

"You're pretty cute yourself."

He blushed. "You really think so? I never thought of myself as attractive, I mean."

Sure, it was true. He was bug-eyed and scraggly, lanky like others of his family lineage, though no nobler lineage existed—Ranfaf the Second had been the Emperor before Ryogrim. Yulah had passed his picture every day on the way to the throne room. Looking like the previous emperor was an attractive quality of its own.

"Of course," she mused. She kissed his forehead and began to rise. He stared after her, a goofy awe about him.

"Well, I gotta go…" she said, pulling her slip over her shoulder, then tying the laces up the front.

That had been entertaining enough.

"Wh—where are you going?" he asked, still panting slightly, bug eyes fixed on her, blinking rapidly.

Yulah pulled her boots on. "I have plans. But I'll see you again shortly, darling."

He blushed again and nodded deeply.

And with that, she left without the bother of another look back. One more advisor whose allegiance she could count on.

***

"Storm and thunder! I'm so sick of all these Ranfafs," she muttered to herself. The wind whipped around her, just as the edges of her vision were dulled by the silver haze of wind magic coursing through her. Yulah flew over the mountains in her tornado, swirling around her like a cocoon, as she retraced a path she had been on only once before, about a last year before.

Only this time she was in charge, with several Warix soldiers under her command flying in her wake. There was no Malotus to watch, to keep calm. At first, she had planned it alone, to slip in by stealth at night. She had figured Malotus's way was too destructive and obvious, creating a storm to cause the whole Meruyan village to flee underwater. But then she realized why he'd done it. For one thing, he wanted to make it less obvious exactly *what* was stolen, and two, since storms sometimes happened, it wouldn't be clear something was stolen at all. It could hide the Sen'Drorn motive, at least long enough to grant the perpetrator a head start. And that could not be done alone. She'd need a group to carry out a strong enough storm.

She indicated for her group to land as they flew over the last mountain range, which tapered off into foothills which eventually met the seaside village. It would be a last meeting point to plan the details of their attack.

Once on solid ground, the air was brisk and windy. She wrapped her arms around her, pulling up her long-collared coat for warmth. She and the group had some of Borak's last batch of wind-enhancing armor, gloves of intricate, artisan copper wiring. "We will need everyone, in groups, three on each side, maybe three high above, to cast their energy downward," she directed. "It's hard, you will need to shoot outward and float freely, trust your body in the air."

The group nodded and the plan was forged. Then they continued onward towards their goal. Her heart beat wildly with the excitement of it.

CHAPTER TWENTY-FOUR

After their big stakeout, Meleena was happy to have an afternoon off to visit the jungle on her own. A good break from the team would do her good. So, what if Kyra told her not to go out there alone. Yulah wouldn't keep her men out there, waiting, would she?

Meleena resolved to go. She felt burdened by everything, and maybe a part of her wanted to risk safety. More the reason to go. Should anything happen to her, they would really feel bad. Why not show off how well she could manage on her own.

She first needed to stop by her flat to go grab her journal. She ran through the noodle house, tripping over a weightless, and up the stairs to her room. Jessup and was already there, relaxing in her bed, while Naia and the boys, Riigs, Thian, and Zoltan chatted in the common area.

Meleena opened the drawer in the bamboo desk where she kept her journal. But something was not quite right. She turned the pages, looking at pages.

Upon closer look she realized a drawing was missing. It had been torn carefully out. What a strange thing, how could that be? Who would want that drawing? Was it a prank by her cohorts? She hadn't thought they even cared about her work. They sure didn't take her seriously.

Who was touching her things? Perhaps it was a prank. Her stomach tightened.

Maybe they wanted to keep her down so she would get out of here? Hmm. Was she going nuts?

She shut the journal and stared out the window.

"Did you see anyone touch my journal?" she asked Jessup.

Jessup looked up from her book and shrugged.

"I think someone is going through my things. Took the files. But if it's not any of them, which I don't think, then something is up."

"Don't be so paranoid."

Meleena kept it to herself, trying to let it go. She was being paranoid about her village journals being taken. She tried to put it out of her mind.

The impulse to blow off steam and get away from them urged her to explore deeper into the forest today. If she found inspiration for the team, all the better.

She ran up the boardwalk, not even bothering with the jetpack, ignoring the passersby and their wayward glances at her as she retraced the steps to the jungle path. She pushed away large green fronds wrapping along thick tree trunks, some moving at alarming rates, growing new leaves and shedding before her eyes. Large insects crawled along vines making her imagine a tiny model of Sen'Prin. The wet floor mushed under her feet and bright white mushrooms grew in crevices behind decrepit logs.

Going nowhere in particular, looking for nothing except what the jungle offered, and tracking deep in the wilderness, she didn't stop until a sound made her look up. The crunching of beaks eating something? There was a flock of creatures, kind of hard to see, munching in the large tree above. They were messily eating seeds, dropping much onto the ground like heavy rain.

Meleena climbed off path again towards the trees where she could make out their shape between branches as they chattered, squawked, and socialized across various nearby broad trees.

A group of young ones whizzed by, flapping dazzling red, green, and purple wings. No, blue, yellow, and black? They were feather paws, smaller than the one she'd seen earlier with Flax, with long ears and colorful bodies. They seemed to be changing colors, signaling to each other. A slower one was failing to keep up with the others, landing for a break silently on a gnarled branch, watching them go. It had different coloration and appeared to be another breed entirely.

"Yeah, I know the feeling," Meleena spoke aloud to herself, a prickle of sorrow in her heart.

It stared silently after the others, then nervously licked one of its paws.

The branch was low enough for Meleena to offer it some of the fallen seed pod snacks. The creature turned towards her with a cautious yet curious disposition and Meleena got a good look at it.

She reached out a hand and the creature took the snacks in its mouth, crunching them with trouble, without a beak like the others.

This beast was in fact more similar to the great feline beast which had been hunting the fire salamanders, with black fur and silver crescent moon spots on its body. Overlapping rings along the feathery tail and neck resembled waves on a midnight ocean shore. It wore the same crest of feathers and small horns on the back of its head like the other feather paw.

It let out a mournful whimper, but dodged her attempt to stroke its neck feathers.

She pulled off her heavy bag, letting it drop to the ground as she retrieved a nut cookie, a snack she'd brought for herself, and offered it. It was probably healthy enough.

The creature's bright yellow eyes stared, nose sniffing, but it stretched and took the cookie daintily in its mouth.

"Alright you're cute," she said out loud.

She reached out and gave the head a pat. Then it flapped its wings and stirred, rubbing its body against her, so she could feel its soft fur and feathers. She suspected this exchange was easier than it ought to be, because the creature was both young, lost among these others, and desperate for social interaction. Meleena sighed, wondering if she herself was really just like this creature trying to live in Sen'Prin. Desperate, silly, and failing to keep up.

The beast showed interest in her bag and rolled around, getting wrapped up in the straps as it snuffled and exploring it playfully.

Any attempt to touch her or free the bag only led to a swipe from the clawed paw. Thus, without anywhere to go, Meleena sat down and sketched the creature.

It was a lovely way to spend an afternoon, relaxing with this beautiful featherpaw. However, at some point, she felt antsy to go. The sun was low, it was getting late. She pulled the bag back from under the lounging creature, now calmer, and leaving her there as Meleena headed back along the path towards home.

Before arriving into town, she came upon a place with broad bowl-like flowers, with large pools of water inside, which made her think of the team's earlier stakeout. Inside the pools sat plump creatures with long trunks pointed upwards, seemingly draining air from the clouds. Misty, heavy clouds hung low. This could be a useful clue not to be passed up. She stopped at a pond to sketch the creatures. They drank the clouds, absorbing the clouds into their full bodies.

Huh. She wondered if the tech that had created the drought might work by some kind of similar mechanism. Clearly, there was a way, already utilized by these creatures, of pulling and exchanging water from the sky.

As she walked back along the path into town, she thought more of her discoveries. She thought of the neutolyths and kelpies, of similar nature. Were they of a water-based lineage? While all these wind, fire, and earthen creatures had their own paths. Meruyan were confusing, in that they had traits of both earth and water. Malotus's falcon had green fur. It never occurred to her whether or not it flew using wind powers or not. Likely not, as it was light and different somehow to these beasts. It's flying could be of a convergent nature.

Once she left the jungle, she took another deep breath at the relief of making it back to town, tired after a long successful day.

She passed Sen'Prin Warix unloading crates for their shops, when suddenly, a gasping whiz startled her and she turned, and nearly jumped out of her skin. There was a silver flash, and a passing wagon stopped short, its fruit toppling out and the Warix at the helm screaming in fright. Meleena stopped dead, then had the idea to crouch low under the cart to see the trouble. There was the young midnight-ocean featherpaw, cowering under the cart, upside down, claws clinging to the bottom.

Meleena had nearly forgotten about her after her relevant discovery, and was struck with guilt that the creature had somehow stalked her all this way.

It growled low and stared with wide fearful full moon eyes.

"Come here, you," Meleena said softly, urging it out. The creature crawled tentatively from the cart.

Meleena felt stuck, confused, unsure what to do now. This was very strange. Nothing like this had ever happened before on her interactions in the wild.

"Get your pet out of here!" the cart driver called out, irritated. "I got goods to deliver!"

"Sorry!" Meleena called back, and moved away, towards a ramp to the river that flowed below town. The feather paw followed her, desperate for a point of reference, as Meleena had counted on.

At the river, the creature stretched its wings. Meleena was tempted to try and ride it, peevishly thinking, this will either be really fun or cause her to scratch me and return right to the wild. Either way.

She came closer and it bent its head, revealing sharp shoulder blades on its strong body. Meleena started to climb on and took hold of one of the curved horns protruding close to its head. It took off before Meleena could fully climb on, perhaps of fright or excitement, it all happened so quick. She clutched its torso with her legs and kept a tight grasp on the neck, as it gained height and bounded towards the rooftops.

It let out an excited howl from deep in its core as Meleena fought to catch her own breath.

"Well, this is something else," Meleena panted loudly to the both of them. At the top of its head, the feathers flickered silver as its wings beat. Terrified they would crash, as it clearly had no clue where it was going, Meleena decided to give some guidance by moving her hands to the horns, and gently directing its head. Exhilaration filled her, her lungs taking in the fresh air, her cheeks hot from flight. Glancing backward, the long-feathered tail swished behind her, moving like a rudder.

The feather paw leopard landed at the fruit market, of which they randomly had found themselves higher up the mountain.

The beast sniffed about the fruit, and Meleena apologized to the vendor and purchased the ones her newfound friend had already decided to eat. At least she knew what to feed her.

Was she really going to keep this wild animal as a pet?

Ugh. She sighed heavily.

Though it enjoyed the fruit, it was overjoyed by the cart of nut cookies, favoring the crunchy snacks. Meleena was able to purchase some to lead her away from the markets before disaster struck.

"Okay, I guess you can come home with me, if you've really made up your mind about leaving your pack…I can hardly say I blame you. I had the same idea myself until now…" she murmured, a new sense of hope rekindling in her. "Anyway, you are going to need a name. I think I'll call you, Upala."

The great black and silver beast cocked its head sideways at her, then nudged for another cookie.

"Yeah, I guess the food is quite good here," Meleena agreed, tossing her one to crunch on.

Meleena climbed atop Upala who chattered and sprang upward, catching a windy updraft. The wind swirled around them, as if its wings were gathering and pulling the wind, bending to its control. This affirmed her theory of wind powers, especially the glowing silver feathers. The horns must be a vector of sensing the wind, as Flax had once said of the Warix. Now it was Meleena who sensed the wind, alongside her friend. They flew over the heads of the Warix who could only use wind step here in the city. Meleena directed them down the mountain, towards her flat.

Except, it didn't work. Upala returned to the forest, and there was nothing Meleena could do about it. They soared over the little drum-like homes swirling up the cliff's edge, and back over the tree canopy. Meleena's heartbeat quickened in panic. This was all too good to be true, it could not last. Meleena was too quick to imagine Upala would be staying with her—perhaps the featherpaw thought it more the other way around.

What if she got lost in the jungle and could not return before dark? A wave of panic rose in her.

And yet, against all sense, she wanted to trust this animal. Upala's heartbeat matched her own, as if in response. The palms of Meleena's hands, holding contact with the horns, were hot and sweating, releasing heat as if she were a Warix emitting wind energy. It was like Upala's wind sensing was getting jumbled up with Meleena's emotional body.

Nectar sprigs whizzed by and she felt their counter-wind. They passed over a river with slippery beasts of fins and shells, passing between water and land like a Meruyan might; and mossy-furred beasts blended into their surroundings.

When they passed under a waterfall, and Meleena's fins sprouted, she had an epiphany. They could be used as rudders! Sticking her elbows out, she directed the wind around them, slicing the air and making them turn around. Both of their desired actions could be known by the other now. Not that it could last.

Meleena managed to direct them back to town, navigating overhead and lowering, until they fell on her flat balcony window.

The shimmering silver feathers fell out and new ones began to grow in their place. Meleena dismounted, thanked the creature, expecting it to fly away now. At least she made it home in one piece.

Upala soared off, and that was that. Certainly, this was better than the heavy jetpack the engineers had designed, however thoughtfully, but not to last. Naia and Jessup were in the room, and barely looked up from their tools and book.

Meleena tossed her bag down, opened and closed her mouth expecting to explain herself, but shockingly didn't have to. She went off to shower and cry her excitement out in some solitude, then went downstairs for dinner as if nothing out of the ordinary had happened.

In the morning she'd have a busy day with Flax at the lab and could tell him all about her adventure. Whatever of it he would believe.

She slept well, dreaming of the wild adventures with her pet. In a half-awake state, she planned to take the jetpack to the lab, grumbling at its heaviness, as she awoke to realize it was already in her bed with her... *Wait, what?*

How could that be?

Jessup let out a scream and Meleena shot upright, head smacking the low ceiling.

"Ouch! What is it?"

"Meleena! There's a wild animal in your bed!" Jessup screamed. "Don't move!"

Meleena rubbed her eyes and even without her glasses on could see what was going on. A cold shiver ran down her spine.

Upala was there. Meleena had no clue how, but somehow, she'd snuck in and curled up on the end of her bed sometime in the night.

"It looks dangerous!" cried Jessup, as Naia climbed from her bed to take a look as well. She emitted a muffled gasp, her voice caught in her throat.

"Uh, I can, sort of explain..." Meleena started. "I didn't mean to. But, it seems she wants to come live with me...eh."

Jessup fainted and Naia's face crinkled into utter disbelief.

CHAPTER TWENTY-FIVE

It had been a crazy morning to say the least. Meleena had awoken with her new pet, Upala, sleeping at the end of her feet, and Jessup and Naia freaking out about it.

Upala's eyes flittered open as she tossed off the covers and began to climb out, looking at her with intrigue. Its facial range was quite expressive, with a brow ridge which lifted like eyebrows.

Once the initial shock wore off, and the others were sure Upala was not going to eat any of them or destroy the place, they could move on with the day. In fact, she was quite light of step, not disturbing them in the night nor chewing any of their stuff.

They were meeting back at the lab that morning, to see the samples Flax had tested, and if they had discovered anything new.

Meleena rode on Upala, grasping the horns and flying out the double door landing after the Warix.

When Upala soared, her black and silver streaked wings spread wide, Meleena's heart soared in unison. This a majestic creature she would never be tired of watching, sleek and agile body that could weave between the woven buildings of Sen'Prin.

They landed outside the lab and Meleena urged her to wait by the river, where she could play in the river. Upala's eyes blinked heavily and it seemed to understand. She was off, without any hint she'd ever come back. Meleena simply had to trust and stay unattached.

In the lab, Borak was just coming downstairs wearing a robe, with a heavy cup of seed and nut blend in his hand. "Ah, g'mornin' all. Bright and early, I see."

Kyra arrived, and Thian and the boys followed soon after.

Nothing new had been found, concretely. Sightings here and there, but that was it. Meleena had something to share from her journal, regarding yesterday's jungle findings. She explained about the water creature she had seen, who'd absorbed and released clouds of water vapor, offering it as a clue perhaps. "This could be the mechanism which they are using to steal water from the air," she posed.

Flax, Borak, and Phineas, the other engineer nodded in contemplation. But it seemed to go over the heads of the other members of the team.

"You really think they would copy some jungle animal? That is silly," said Jessup. "I'm sure it's more like an agricultural anomaly."

Zoltan agreed that it could be how the machine worked, from what they'd seen at the previous stakeout, though he figured it would have to be working on such a big level. Naia simply shrugged, agreeing it was plausible, but so what? Knowing the mechanism was helpful, but not going to get them any closer to actually catching the perpetrator.

Kyra said they'd put a pin in it.

The group left for an early lunch, as the weather was nice and there were sports to be played in this unusual down time.

Meleena stayed back, sitting on a stood and folding her head in her arms on the long laboratory desk, feeling dejected.

It was like nothing she did mattered. Never had self-doubt crept in at this level. The last she could remember brought flashes of memory back, of when she started the Meruyan Council Journey earlier that year. Falling and slipping at the river crossing, unsure of herself.

"Why do you care what they think?" asked Flax in earnest. He came over to try and cheer her up. Meleena didn't lift her head. "Don't try to impress them, it will only backfire. Just report your findings, that's it."

Here it had a mildly more bitter flavor now. "I'm always being undervalued," she moaned. "I thought I'd already proved myself."

It was as if the world under her feet were shifted. That her ability to discern reality was called into doubt. How could she know truth if it was always shifting?

Maybe they were right, to question her findings. A small, twinkling part in her said otherwise—that her natural observations had a story to tell. This was the last chance she'd give.

"Perhaps I should stop trying and admit that I don't fit in here," she said finally. "The others are nice enough…" she trailed off. Though who knows what they said behind her back. They couldn't really be trusted.

Flax reminded her of their conversation during their jetpack training session. What he'd said about opening her heart and trusting more… "I want to be more like that, but it's hard."

She could only move at her own pace. Maybe part of her felt like they were always looking for a way to laugh at her, to prove she was a failure the moment she let her guard down.

"So, what? They have their own insecurities too. They laugh because you take it too seriously. It's okay to be silly."

"Thanks."

"Ah, lighten up," he said, and gave her a peck on the cheek. She lit up at this, heart racing, cheeks hot, and looked at him.

He smiled, searched her eyes, and she smiled back, looking around to see that Borak and Phineas where not there. They'd left out of respect for her mood, that was sweet. And Flax had stayed.

She stood and faced him, blinking away the tears, and their lips met.

It was like innumerable explosions of tiny fire through her veins, filling her, as they embraced. A feeling she had never known nor knew could exist in the body. They continued to kiss, as if it was lifeblood keeping her from falling to pieces. Such awe and wonder.

It seemed to wipe everything else clean from her mind. Feeling overtaking her overabundant thoughts, like the antidote to a poison long sapping her energy, finally washed away.

***

Yulah marched into the office of the next advisor on her list: The Advisor of City Planning and Migrant Meruyan Affairs.

An older Warix of lumpy physique, he sat at his desk, going through papers. "Yes, who—oh, General Yulah. What brings me the honor?" he asked, looking up.

"Advisor of Migrant Meruyan Affairs..." she said in a low voice. "Word has it, you have taken that last part of your title a little too literally," she purred, leaning an elbow on his desk and throwing a wink in there for good measure. She knew it was over the top, but she liked to toy with them, have a little fun.

"What...What are you implying?" e stammered, eyes widening as he scanned her eyes.

Her heart pounded with delight. She'd caught him. "I think you know what," she started again.

He stuttered, drawing back. "How did you...find out about us?"

Yulah shook her head. "I never would have guessed. You did, didn't you...It was all just a nasty rumor until now."

"I..." he gasped, hands instinctively going to his throat.

"Such a shame, you were respected by your peers. But you're having an affair with one of your Meruyan servants. Just, yikes."

"Please, I'll do you a favor, what do you want? Gold, silver, rare gemstones? I can't have anyone spreading rumors like that around. Even if they are true." He looked down, ashamed, shivering slightly.

"Well..." Yulah said pensively, drawing herself up, her elbow moving to her waist as she put a fist under her chin in thought.

Her thoughts danced. *Yes, play it coy and cheeky.*

It was good, how fast he was cracking. But it wouldn't be enough to win his full allegiance. There was a stronger card to be played.

"I heard it was worse than just the affair. I heard from one of my own servants, that there was an illegitimate child born."

The blood drained form his face. So, the rumors were true.

"A Meruyan-Warix hybrid, now that is unheard of. What happened to them? Probably not safe to have a child like that running around the fortress, it would be *quite* obvious..."

His eyes narrowed. "What are you implying?" he hissed defensively.

"I suppose, if you got rid of it, well now that is an even bigger scandal," she said with a chuckle.

"What. Do. You. Want?" he said, seething with angry fear and sweating all over.

"Simple. Your support, darling. In the event I attempt take power from The Emperor."

He broke what was left of his composure, barking out a laugh. "Ha! You are insane if you think you'd stand a chance against the iron fist of Emperor Ryogrim."

"Which is why I need you...Bring the others to my aid, whose respect you still have. The advisors, the rest of them! Don't look at me like that."

"Sure, they would follow me, so long as you keep my secret. If you staged a takeover, many would look to me to decide whether or not to support you. But I don't have *all* their ears. Not nearly enough for success on their own."

She winked coyly, "Ah, don't think the others don't have weaknesses to exploit as well. I have already begun my campaign. I only need you to seal the deal."

He nodded, red in the face.

She turned and strode out of his office.

Next, Yulah paid a visit to the office of the Advisor of Hyish Affairs. He was an ancient Warix with a long gray beard and one cracked horn.

She leaned over his desk. He was blind and couldn't see her anyway. With fully clouded eyes, blind from a lifetime of too much wind use, serving Sen'Drorn somehow. That was a rare feat indeed, as it took quite a lot to wear out one's eyes like that, though he was quite old. Probably some kind of war hero or criminal, she cared to wager.

"Advisor of Hyish Affairs, it is General Yulah."

The advisor grumbled. "A woman in charge of War Operations, feh!" he spat. "What's this nonsense?"

She ignored this remark. He was one to win over. "We want the same thing, sir. I know you don't like The Emperor," she said politely. "Why is that?"

"Feh!" He spat on the stony ground again. Yulah cringed, glad that he couldn't see it. "My granddaughter just married! I bade The Emperor to grant the happy couple a home in the upper ring. You know, as a gift. A fair gift for everything I've done to serve this great nation! But Ryogrim is being stingy, the windbag! Maybe thinks I will die soon and he can save that house for his mistress. Nonsense!"

Yulah cringed again.

"You know, you should get married and leave this post to a real man who can handle it! Malotus! Now that was a great General."

Again, Yulah ignored this, clenching her jaw and taking a deep, silent breath. This old fool was beginning to make her blood boil. She had to get to her point and get out of here.

"Well, good news for you, sir. I have a little side project going on. Side with me, do my bidding on this project. What if I told you, I would vacate as General soon, and there would be a new Emperor? Would you support a takeover? You would be greatly rewarded if you did."

"Eh? A takeover of Emperor? Who dares?"

Yulah held her tongue. There wasn't much more of this she could take. "It is right now secret, for their safety. But let's say it were to happen. Would you support it? I am but a messenger, but will make sure your granddaughter gets a beautiful new home afterwards."

"I never liked Ryogrim. Real piece of work."

Look who's talking, Yulah thought.

"Sure, I would support any of the advisors, should they decide to stand up to the ol' windbag. Stage a takeover, or whatnot. Especially if it gets my granddaughter a new house."

"Wonderful news. For the record, I respect a grandfather who cares. That is very sweet."

The advisor nodded his ancient head. "Ah, well, you're a sweet girl. You should keep your nose out of trouble. But I will support your cause—in secret. If you can get enough other advisors to tip the scales, I will remain in the backdrop until its clear."

"Agreed."

Yulah smiled to herself, thrilled. This had gone better than expected.

She was about to leave, when she realized she actually had business with him. Being the advisor for Hyish affairs was actually relevant to the situation in the NHV, which she had plenty on her plate about lately.

"By the way, did you know about the uprisings going on in the NHV?" she asked.

The blind old Warix stroked his long gray beard. "Yes, quite a pity. Resources have been slow coming into Sen'Drorn City, so I hear. But there is nothing we have been able to do about it in my department. The Hyish are crazy for Meruyan goods right now. Things are going very well for them. The Meruyan are even buying eye glasses directly from the Hyish glass-weavers. They've cut us out as middle-man for the first time in a century."

Yulah held back a laugh. He'd probably been advisor for half of that century. She thought for a moment.

"Glasses? What a strange and specific thing."

"Oh yes, our monopoly on glasses has kept us in power, in many ways. Meruyan need them, the majority cannot see on land without them, thus the need for continued trade with us. The Hyish always made them, with their fire breath and glass craftsmanship, but the two peoples never made direct contact until now. I suppose it was inevitable."

"Perhaps...We go in another direction..." Yulah said thoughtfully after some time. "We need something to make the Hyish relationship obsolete. If they've got glass, we could invent something better."

Yulah played with a crack on his desk with the tip of her claw, lost in thought, chipping off some of the sheen protecting the wood. It broke off into her fingers like a film.

He cringed at the sound. "What are you doing? Please don't touch that!"

An idea struck her.

"What is this made of?"

"If you are referring to my desk, I believe it's a type of tree sap, coagulated and hardened to protect the wood. I don't know," he waved a veiny hand. "Ask the Advisor of Research & Technology. Maybe those inventors can cook something up for you."

"Yes, I think I will," Yulah agreed. She thanked him and made her way out of his office.

She headed down the hall to pay the Advisor of Research & Technology a visit. He was a younger adult, mid-thirties, who probably got to this point through connections to the higher nobles. He was the right Warix for the job, amazingly. Passionate, with lots of big ideas, he enjoyed puzzling out.

"Imagine if we can invent a sap that stays in their eyes, but melts away by evening, making them forever dependent on us again," he said after they exchanged ideas.

"We need to do this. To make them choose dependency again," Yulah agreed.

"A little positive incentive to return to working for us, love it!" He combed his long red hair with his fingers, alongside silver horns that shaped his face. He was quite attractive.

He lifted the copper goggles from his eyes onto his forehead. "I'd move forward with it today, but Emperor Ryogrim hasn't approved it. We need to run it by him at the next meeting before we can proceed."

"Right…Ryogrim…" Echoed Yulah, crestfallen.

She drew closer to his long, pointed ear, the tips of which were pierced with copper lug nuts.

"I'll let you in on a secret," Yulah whispered. "I don't plan on doing any of that. There may be a regime change coming soon. It would be best if you kept this our secret, and did some tinkering for now. I'll take the blame if you get caught."

He looked into her eyes, searching, deciding if she could be trusted.

She gave a wry smile and a wink.

He blushed and turned away.

Boys were so easy.

"Let's see…I already have a few advisors on my side. Hyish Relations, Agriculture, Resource Import, City planning. That's four on my side—plus anyone Hyish relations brings in," she said in earnest. Then with a sigh, added, "You know how Defense and Financial will follow wherever he goes. Me and Engineering Tech go way back, but you knew that."

He continued to study her face, as though wondering if she were bluffing. Emerald-green eyes tense, and lips pursed, he said finally, "You really are planning this…That's, insane, I mean—brilliant—but insane…"

Yulah smiled. "If you do this for me now, I'll make sure you have a seat in the new government."

He sighed and bent his head. "I can hide it among the other projects, I suppose. Ryogrim will never know."

"Good boy," she said, and patted his head. He blushed, and she felt the urge to kiss him, out of a sense of pure excitement. Things were going her way, and she could use a moment to share her passion with someone.

She looked him up and down, and he got the hint. "I want to see your workshop," was all she had to say. He began to lead her by the hand to the back room.

Then her wristcom buzzed, causing her to pull away and check her wrist. "Sorry, hold on, I have to take this."

Yulah left his chambers and spoke into her wristcom.

"Hey you," she said sweetly. She leaned with her back to the lab desk and curled her hair around her finger. "I'm paying a visit to the lab in the fortress right now, reminded me of you. Yes, I will handle Meleena's other journals, don't worry about it...you take care of the one with her now. Do whatever it takes, yeah, invent whatever you need to. Sounds great. You have done a fine job, and you will be rewarded with a glorious return to the Sen'Drorn Nation. Whether that be under Ryogrim, or my rule."

She winked at the advisor, returning to check on her.

"I fully support you, my mistress," came the voice in her wristcom. "For all you have done, giving me another chance and generously forgiving me for everything I've done."

She hung up, smiling to herself.

He was good, this one, Yulah thought to herself.

A part of me still hates him for what he did to me. He is nuts, but I gotta respect his work ethic. He's proven himself, and we do work very well together. I certainly couldn't have come this far without him. I think I will keep my word, make him head engineer when I am in charge around here. There will certainly be a way to extract him from Sen'Prin. He really doesn't belong there.

"Mistress, are you coming?" came the voice of the Advisor of Research & Tech from the doorway. It was time to celebrate: treat herself.

She approached and took hold of his horn, leading him by the face into the back room.

***

At dawn, Meleena stirred awake. Her head was for once without thought, swimming with the wonder of the previous day. Kissing Flax. Her breath was lighter, as though breathing underwater from the freshest of brooks.

She'd spent the rest of the day with him by the river, showing off Upala and relaxing. It had been her best day in Sen'Prin yet.

Then her eyes snapped open to a sudden sound: her window appeared to be open, flapping and bobbing in ambient wind, hitting the walls with a slam.

Something silver…It was a clunky, round, with luminous scales, and—digging in her drawer? She sat up, Upala stirred by her feet, whipped her head to the intruder, neck feathers standing on end. She jumped off the bed and leapt at it, growling fiercely.

It was some kind of metallic creature. It straightened on the desk, and to Meleena's horror, held her journal in its tiny claws. It swiftly dodged as Upala landed on the desk, unfolding her winds and growling menacingly.

It launched upwards, and Meleena, still in a sleeping gown, hurried down from her bunkbed and gave chase, trying to head it off, grabbing at the latches to shut the open window to and prevent its escape.

The slamming door woke Naia, who shook Jessup awake. "What's this about?" she cried out.

Meleena didn't have time to answer as the creature turned to her, eyes glowing bright, when she noticed its head had copper inserts and mechanical arms. It hugged her journal tight to its paneled chest, then something knocked her off her feet. It must have been hiding under the table, another metallic critter, with external bronze gears spinning. They resembled a mechanically built nectar sprig, with little arms, rapid-fire beating wings, and a long snout.

"Kooky!" Naia shouted.

Jessup rubbed their eyes sleepily.

"Help me stop them!" shouted Meleena.

One of them pooped a grey gunk. "Eww!" Jessup called, and jumped back.

They smashed through the closed doors, shattering the light wood. A third one buzzed in, similar to the first two.

Naia and Jessup struggled to catch them, dancing about the room with Meleena and Upala heading outside after the first one.

Meleena's heart skipped a beat as she launched herself onto Upala before she bounded skyward after the critters.

Luckily, the city was still asleep. Unluckily, it was still pretty dark out, as the sun had barely risen.

Upala pounced on one the edge of a roof, smacking it from the air and crashing to the ground in a broken heap.

A quick glance revealed there was no journal in its hand.

Meleena and the other girls continued to give chase. They bobbed and weaved as they split up following the other two. They chased them as they spun through a small farmland, into a herd of bramble sheep.

One of the mechanical beasts crashed through the brambles, but lifted off, body only slightly askew. Naia tackled it like a ball, but it slipped away and she fell, barely able to slow herself from fall damage as the mechanical nectar sprigs buzzed out of sight, journal still in hand.

And that was it. Meleena couldn't believe it.

They slunk back to the house, entering through the balcony.

Holding up the destroyed one, Meleena was at least able to collect it for evidence. Naia collected the gunk excretion in a glass vial, the group already suspecting what it could be.

"I would bet it's the same gunk created in the explosions," Meleena asserted.

"We need to wake the others," Jessup said in alarm.

It took a while to wake up the boys, and summon Kyra from her flat, still in bright magenta sleeping robes.

They all stood around the common room, rattled.

Naia filled them in on what had happened.

"It busted in just to steal Meleena's journal?" Riigs asked in baffled disbelief, arms folded over his large chest.

"Yeah, and I've never seen anything like them. Like, machine automata," said Naia. "In my lab practice, we tinkered with wind-up creations like that, but nothing so complex or able to move on its own. Do you think they were wind-powered?"

"Like my jetpack, but more complicated?" asked Meleena.

They shook their heads. It was not normal.

Meleena wasn't sure, as she was new to all this Warix technology. She wasn't sure where the common limits were, as even an airship had been new to her until quite recently.

"So, some kind of engineer had to design this. They could have flown into our city from Sen'Drorn, or what?" she asked, groping for more clarity.

"Who's to say?" asked Thian, shrugging and lifting the wing up like it was a dead bird. "Impressive little beasts, though. I bet Flax and the engineers would find them very interesting."

Naia spun a spanner in one hand, and stared at the thing.

"So Sen'Drorn created a whole new tech, and tested it to steal Meleena's *journal*?" concluded Zoltan, baffled.

"Well, this is bad," concluded Thian.

"This means it's definitely someone on the inside," said Naia. The others nodded. This was the first real evidence to back up any claim like this. Everyone shivered, upset by the news.

Kyra stood and declared the meeting over. There was nothing more to be done. "We still need to track down more evidence of the machine, check for droughts, track the strange thunderstorms."

Meleena felt crummy. *Now* they believed her, under such poor circumstances.

The others stirred, making a move towards their rooms.

They all shuffled off to get ready for the scouting mission of the day.

CHAPTER TWENTY-SIX

Deem awoke in confusion, his vision coming in as bubbles of vivid colors. He was home again, in the lovely mud cave he grew up in. That was nice. His mother was gathering up a basket of sea creatures and undersea mushrooms for dinner, as his father came bustling into the one-room home.

"Why isn't dinner ready yet? And Deem! Why aren't you helping your mother? What an ungrateful urchin!" His dad roared, smacking down a sack of clams with a reverberating crash that made Deem's shoulders rise to his pulsing ears.

"Yes, it will be ready soon," his mother stammered, groping for words. They were more like hissing clicks, as resounded in their underwater dialect. She hurried to cut up the mushrooms as Deem gutted the fish, wincing as he cut himself. Blue blood streamed like ink into the salty water.

"This family can hardly keep it together," groaned his father, slithering into an outcropping for sitting in the rocks. He looked ragged and tired from a day of digging up the clams. Deem couldn't really blame him for his annoyance and short temper. He knew how hard he worked to feed them, Deem and his sisters.

His mother tried to keep a straight face, but the ruffle between her eyes betrayed her anxiety. She was a pleaser, like Deem. How had he not noticed this before.

"And where are your sisters?" asked his father shortly. "Aren't they hungry? I swear, it's too much sometimes!"

He swam outside and called for them. Shortly after, Deem's younger sisters entered the cave, swimming inside to gather around the food mound with quiet politeness. They all sat cross-legged to anchor and wedge themselves around the mound.

One of his sisters asked a question about the distinct lack of seasoning, which triggered their mom to explode and leave in a rage-filled huff.

His father and the kids sat around, baffled, then he broke the silence with, "How dare you kids stress out your mother! She's burdened enough by all of our needs!"

"They didn't mean to—" Deem started, but his father cut him off with a beastly expression on his face.

His father swam angrily outside to follow her, while tears welled in Deem's eyes. He was afraid to move. His sisters sobbed. They all wanted to hide, to be invisible. None of them understood. He embraced his sisters, as they swam together into his arms, all cowering, appetites lost.

They sat frozen there until his parents returned, swimming back to finish eating, even conversing, as if nothing had happened, while the children sat in confusion and shock.

It was like this, from time to time. Seldom yet cyclical.

Deem had pushed these memories deep down, yet only now realized that they had embedded themselves like a poisonous thorn in the heart all his life.

The scene faded into abstract, swirling colors. He cowered, so unsettled from the pain and helplessness. The ground swept out from under him. Was this why he avoided conflict like a plague?

The swirling of thoughts and colors opened as he became aware of his actual surroundings beyond the memory. He became aware of a weight around his neck and some sort of covering over his head, blocking his vision. He struggled to move his hands, which were tied behind his back. He sighed. It was useless to try and move. Surrendering to it felt good, calming somehow. At least the Warix couldn't attack him in battle, he was already here. In some ways, his body relaxed into the safety of it.

The smell of moldy wood and earthy excretions told him he was in some kind of Warix dungeon, possibly under a barn, and thus somewhere in the NHV. They wouldn't have taken him far.

He hoped the others were coming to rescue him soon. For now, he had ample time to sit with himself. Not that he liked what he saw. Insecurity, fear of standing up for himself. Well, maybe this was the time for things to change.

Unlucky for him, there were more immediate problems. He was a prisoner of the Warix. Though nobody came to speak to him, they did work together to keep the wind strong all night to scare and annoy. Sounds of snapping trees, flopping in the wind, doors opening and slamming in their frames kept him awake and on edge for hours. He sat in anticipation, as if something worse was about to happen. The winds howled like a whispering beast through the hills. His throat was so dry, his eyes burning. He tried to sleep, wondering if they'd ever bring him water or food. He wondered if he'd been forgotten, if he'd die here. He was too tired to panic, and his head throbbed from the hit that brought him here.

He was so sick of being the butt of jokes. Of being embarrassed. Weak. Going along with everyone else's whims. Now he sat, captured. It all made him sick to his stomach. He had long since stopped saying no, and it was driving him crazy. It made him weaker. He was afraid of anger...in himself and others. He wanted to be nice to everyone, and expected it back, but it had gotten him stepped on. Enough was enough. Somebody needed to stand up for him one way or another and it wasn't going to be any of them, clearly.

Something bubbled in his gut. Fast moving energy like hyperventilation, desperate, animalistic. A sleeping cave shark was awakening.

***

Deem was surprised to awaken again to the sound of Talla's voice echoing off stone. Overseer Thowler was alongside her, by the sound of the second low grumbling voice.

What the barnacle was going on? Could they be working together in this mess? Maybe this was another one of his visions.

The bag flew from his head in a bright flurry and he gaped at Talla's face. Sure enough, Thowler grinned behind her.

"Talla! What is going on here?" Deem reiterated aloud. He felt anger fuming up inside him, a rare thing he hadn't felt since those days when it was suppressed with his parents. But now, something had snapped inside him. He had sat alone on the ground, cold and without control. It was enough.

He stood before she could remove his arm bindings.

She gave her usual knowing smirk, and that was it. Deem had had it. From deep in his gut erupted a fire, an anger so sincere, like a long-lost comrade come to his aid. His face contorted bitterly, tears flowing down his face, and he pushed passed her with his shoulder, jumping to bring his bound hands to the front of his chest. He charged at Overseer Thowler, using his hands like a club to strike at his ugly, confused face.

Thowler's mouth hung agape as Deem's fist met his face with a heavy blow to his nose and lip.

"Deem!" screamed Talla in utter shock, which only made Deem shiver with encouragement.

"Wait, I'll explain everything, Deem, stop!" She continued, hands in the air, then turned and spoke to Thowler in a softer tone. "I swear I've never seen him like this. This is all a big misunderstanding!"

"How did you get the key?" growled Deem, turning on Talla. He had awakened. He felt a blaze in his eyes.

"We are on the council, or have you forgotten?" answered Talla in stammering shock, yet the condescension streak remained. How had he not realized she spoke down to him always? Or was this just the way she was? "We have special privileges. They will free you, as long as we *leave* the Northern Hilly Villages and don't return. We have to report on the goings-on here to the capital."

He snorted with incredulity.

"You have made it easy for me to change my mind, and keep you here for more punishment, boy," grunted Thowler, holding his bulging lip and bloodied nose. "It would not be hard to change my mind."

Thowler growl-smiled, showing his teeth in an attempt to intimidate, but Deem didn't fall for it. He knew Thowler was afraid of the consequences of going against this order, which probably came from Sen'Drorn headquarters. Thowler was a by-the-book lacky of the Sen'Drorn.

Deem's heart thudded with pride and power, and long unfelt emotions. So, this was what it was like to have others be afraid of you. He spat on the ground, and said only, "let's get out of here."

"Good call, bud." Talla cut his hands loose with a small knife, and walked Deem by the shoulders towards the dungeon exit, her face contorted in nervous laughter as Thowler watched them go. One hand wiped across his face, flicking blood from the tips of his fingers and onto the stone floor.

They climbed the steps and out the dungeon which sure enough was actually a cellar. Double wooden doors gave way to bright sunlight and Deem closed his burning eyes against it.

It hardly seemed fair that they could be freed so easily, while so many other Meruyan were likely still rotting in Warix cells all over this place.

They found Clover and Pinchy tied up outside, ready to ride.

"We're really going back to Dlawn'Edo?" Deem asked in surprise, coming down from all the riled-up emotions, into a dull confusion.

"Back home. Come on, we need to inform headquarters about the rebellion. Get back to our posts," Talla said flatly, without looking at him.

"How are we just giving up?!" argued Deem, anger ready and willing to come to his aid now. "After all you've put me through!"

"Me?! How can you blame me! We both *agreed* to this." He had her there, and only himself to scorch with this newfound anger. It burned, but he didn't flinch.

"So that's it then? We're giving up helping the Meruyan in the NHV? Back to paperwork?"

"What do you want from me, Deem?" She barked back. "We did what we could! But we are of no use to anyone dead! I was so worried when you were taken!"

"You were?" he stammered in confusion.

"Yes! Of course! You matter to me! I had to argue big time to get us back. Played the whole game with them like, 'we are here against our will, just send us back, we'll be good'!" She waved her arms in silly miming, then snorted in mixed nervous amusement.

They both burst into laughing-crying heaves—rapid pulses of breath. The release they both needed after such an ordeal.

"So that's it?" squeaked Deem through the breaths. "Just ride back to the capital now, like nothing happened? Like we didn't just commit high treason or something?"

"Yep, that's it!" laughed Talla in disbelief of her own words. It was all so ridiculous. "Iringbon and the others are still fighting, best they can, with what they have, but are hanging back for now. Without the Hyish forces, they can't really stop the Warix from forcing some Meruyan to work. We'll follow from afar for now, how it will progress. Meanwhile, I heard there's a fair in Sen'Prin coming up. We can go visit Meleena."

"Alright then..." said Deem with a big sigh. His head was spinning.

They tapped their mounts and dashed onwards through the village, wind in their hair, the smell of freedom and pain tingling their senses as they charged towards the forest which would lead them back to Dlawn'Edo, the Meruyan capital, and whatever remained for them there.

CHAPTER TWENTY-SEVEN

Meleena paced the small loft bedroom. It had been days since her journal was stolen. The group had followed through on missions, and she had been at least cheered by having her new pet, Upala, who was currently out somewhere, hunting, she presumed.

Though it was hard to know when and if Upala would return, so far, she always did. Whether by riding or jetpack as backup, Meleena could now visit at the lab whenever she wanted. They were having fun together, and things were starting to look up, despite the journal and impending terrors of what it implied.

She was shocked that her journal had been stolen at all! The fact that it had any value to anyone but her was almost more amazing than anything else. She took a heavy deep sigh, releasing a knot in her stomach.

She stopped pacing and stood by the balcony doors to look out over the view of Sen'Prin City.

It was all for them.

Her own team didn't seem to care about her work or take her seriously, but the culprit of all these crimes very much did. After all the struggles she'd gone through to be heard, her ideas had been scaring someone. Enough to design creatures to take all of her work away. At this thought, a feeling tickled her, as if caught in her throat, and she gasped to free it.

It emerged as a baffled laugh from deep inside, uncontrollable and pulsing throughout her being. Anger and irony. The silliness of her own self-doubt, regrets for being so dower, and even a little taste of pride.

So, what if her journal was gone? Now she could relax and let them deal with the consequences of this mess.

Today was better than just the mission, even.

The Hyish trader nomads had come to town, and built a large fairground at the edge of town. Even Deem and Talla had gotten away from their work in Dlawn'Edo to help them out.

The Hyish seasonal markets were set up in the foothills just outside of Sen'Prin City, but under its presumed protection and local hired Hyish guards. It was under the grand tree cover, and therefore not a particularly easy place to disturb.

Meleena hoped this meant Yulah's soldiers wouldn't be coming to give her any trouble. The worry panged at the back of her neck, but she waved it off as silly. She'd be on Flax's arm and with the rest of the team, Deem, and Talla, as a large group.

The idea of Yulah burned her from the inside out. More than from the very real sense of danger she posed, illogically, from the lingering jealousy. The unfinished business between her and Flax...but to what extent? If Flax still had feelings for her was not clear, and knowing they could still communicate via wristcom was troubling to say the least.

Meleena waited with the team at the fairground airship platforms below Sen'Prin, as they watched the arriving airship in anticipation, bringing Deem and Talla.

Hopping off the ship and hugging was followed by laughter as the three Meruyans twirled their hands in their traditional greeting. It was nice to have someone to share it with again. Meleena felt genuinely happy for some familiarity—to see her friends was like a breath of fresh air on this fine day.

She gave them the introduction. "You know Flax and Thian," she said, as they smiled and waved. "The tall blonde is Zoltan. The redhead is Jessup. The cheery big guy and gruff diminutive girl over there are

Riigs and Naia. They're always together, longtime friends or something. Jessup is from the villages. Zoltan's local, and a bit of a salty know-it-all, but you'll come to like him."

The group engaged in some light banter, getting to know one another, all excited for the adventure ahead.

"Oh yeah, she's always been SO strange," said Talla to the Warix. "I mean, we're friends now, but she's always been different, even for a Meruyan. It's not just you guys."

Meleena froze, horrified. A wave of embarrassment washed over her.

Flax put a hand on her shoulder. "Ah, it's okay. Remember, don't let it bother you, and just laugh at yourself, it loses its power and they can even respect you more for that."

She trembled with anger. She knew he was right, but it wasn't helping in this moment.

They hung back from the group as they entered the fair, letting the others get lost in the crowd.

"Hey, Meleena, I'm sorry. I was just trying to be supportive. What do you really want? What can I do to help you relax and have a good time tonight?"

She sighed, cheeks still burning. She hadn't realized she was being so grumpy.

"Really. You can trust me," Flax assured her again.

He took her hands in his and looked into her eyes. Her jaw trembled and it became clear how stiff she was standing. How awkward this all felt. "I guess what I really want, is to feel safe. To not feel on my guard all the time. To..." the tears were coming, she didn't like this. She didn't want to show him this weakness.

"It's okay, cry with me," he said, and pulled her closer. She surrendered to the wonderful feeling of their embrace. This was what she wanted. Someone she could cry with, without fear of judgement. She let herself relax, safe in his grip, and the tears flowed. She couldn't have stopped them if she'd wanted to. She'd been feeling so wound up for so long, since she'd been here perhaps. It was even annoying to admit to herself that she was so full of pent up, unexpressed aggravation.

She lost control, crying into his shoulder for what felt endless, wave after wave like fiery currents smashing upon the rocks, who took it firmly without a word. Only acceptance, and holding her.

She sniffled, wiping away the ugliness from her face. "It's okay, you don't have to look presentable, you are beautiful as you are," he said, coming to kiss her cheeks. She caused another surge of tears and lurching of her shoulders, now a strange salty mix indistinguishable between sorrow and ecstasy. It flipped brightly into laughter.

"You're so corny," was all she managed to say. "But I love it so much."

"Feeling better?"

"Yeah, much."

She laughed nervously.

He chuckled as they rejoined in a perfectly protective hug in reply. She could get used to this. Flax was so intuitive, and she was grateful that he saw what she didn't. She could trust him to show her when she needed help releasing some of that pent-up energy.

They laughed and when Meleena had calmed down, it was like she was reborn, fresh and excited to enjoy the fair. Her blood tingled with the renewal, her breath coming lighter.

Down by the fair, booths lined the avenue, selling all sorts of woven linens, and spun, fired glass and pottery. The smell of exotic spices and foods cooking, the humming melody of unknown Hyish instruments colored the atmosphere. Hyish gathered in clusters around game boards atop rounded stones and gambled. Strange games with tiny carved pieces of which Meleena couldn't care to guess at.

It was a place of wonder.

"Where did you learn to be so intuitive with your feelings, anyway?" Meleena asked Flax as they wandered the booths. "I knew you were the sensitive type but this is like a whole other level."

"Ah," Flax waved it off. "Hangin' out with ol' Borak."

She laughed at how well he mimicked his father's mannerisms in that moment.

"He says stuff like that now. It tested him, finding out I was his son, and being willing to leave his shop and life's work in Sen'Drorn to find my mother. Ever since returning to Sen'Prin City, he's been more in-tune with his feelings. After a lifetime of pouring himself into work and nobody else, he's new to emotions but he knows how to line up his passions. He approaches it like an engineer, a mechanism to be studied and observed, recorded, repeated. Our emotions are a bit of tech built into all of us."

"Huh, I never thought of it like that."

"See, nothing to be embarrassed about. Whatever you feel, just sit with it, like locating an overworked air sack in our tech, ready to be drained of gas. See, Borak uses what he's passionate about to approach new problems the same way."

"Borak is very wise."

"That's because he knows how to enjoy, experiment, be creative. Like you. When you are in the forest."

"Ah, naw, it's not the same."

"Question, but don't doubt yourself. You really are amazing, Meleena, you don't need to prove it. It's like you said yourself, when a creature intakes so much water vapor, it bloats, until it processes and releases it. Simple biology." He spoke in a soothing blend of truth-in-humor which made Meleena want to kiss him again.

They wandered the fair, not long after that they found the others snacking on food skewers, and they drifted as a group to watch a band of minstrels play.

One Hyish in particular with golden scales and a perpetual smirk sat on a stool, playing. His clawed feet shimmered in the light as they waggled to the beat of the long string instrument in his hands. His playing was soft, light, as his fingers gently plucked at the strings. Meleena had never heard something so radiant.

Next to him, another Hyish of green and black scales played a long wind instrument of versatile notes. His fingers skillfully moved over the holes, while a female in a flowing dress sang a soft hissing melody.

Meleena put her head on Flax's shoulder and closed her eyes to listen. It was truly the best day she'd had in Sen'Prin yet.

The group split off naturally after that, wandering off in pairs as the attractions pulled them. There were so many stalls and lanes to explore. Crafted clothing, glass blowing, entertainment, ever more food and games.

The day went on, hours of fun were had, as Meleena and Flax were sometimes alone, and sometimes with Thian, Deem and Talla, and sporadically others from the team.

They played games and tasted Hyish specialties. They sipped sweet, pulpy fruit concoctions and munched spongey cakes with tangy creme fillings.

As the sky purpled and brilliant clouds hung low overhead on this warm night, lights twinkled in the darkening ambiance. Lanterns were lit in trees, and fireflies danced in the air above. They walked from stall areas marked by their smells: the saccharine of toasting sugar, onward to the smoky savory meats.

At some point, while Meleena and Flax were alone, they spotted the others at a distance by a game stand. It was odd to see a Meruyan among them, Deem and Talla's blue-green skin among their varying earthen shades.

Zoltan and Thian were competitively shooting jets of water at giant paper insects while Jessup, Deem, Talla, Naia, and Riigs watched and cheered. Then Naia must have said something to offend Zoltan, probably that he was a terrible shot, and he turned and sprayed her all over. She shouted and stormed off in anger before Flax and Meleena got close enough to rejoin the group.

"What's up with her?" asked Talla.

"She's always been shy about the water," said Riigs.

"Doesn't go in the river with us either," shrugged Zoltan. "I don't get it."

Talla and Deem looked at Meleena.

"What?"

"She's got an arm condition on her skin."

"Like, fins."

"What, that's—there's no way. She's a Warix. It's just a skin condition."

"Do you think it's possible that she's part Meruyan?"

Riigs folded his arms and looked away.

"No way!" squealed Talla.

"She's very sensitive. Doesn't know who her real parents are. Don't ask her about it."

Meleena wondered if a Meruyan-Warix hybrid was possible, and looking at Naia, it was certainly a possibility. Her size and complexion were hued more to the Meruyan. Perhaps she had come from Sen'Drorn, and been abandoned, as Meleena knew there were many Meruyan working there in servitude. She'd been found and taken in like so many others to Sen'Prin.

Far, far off, someone was shrieking. A Hyish, hissing tone.

Meleena glanced at Flax, and he nodded. They ran in the direction of the horrible screams.

Several Hyish were gathered around one of their own, behind a tent, who lay on the ground unmoving.

"It's a terrible thing!" cried one of them, grabbing Flax by the collar.

"What happened?" he demanded, soft and calm, dutifully.

"I'm checking his heartbeat," she said so they'd let her pass. Meleena bent to see through the knobby knees in the crowd.

She gasped- his throat had been slit, and the wide gash revealed more than streaming blood. She winced and dug her fingers there, opening it up to reveal her fears: the fire gland was cleanly and plainly missing. Whoever did this had removed skillfully, so finely, it in a way that wasn't obvious.

Sen'Prin peacekeepers rushed through to clear the crowd. The body was wrapped in silk and given to the Hyish kin for burial. The fair was shut down. Lights flickered and shut off, and the crowds were shooed back to the city. The stalls shut, their owners packed the linen flaps and sticks, dismantling them into their caravan homes, and retreated to a silent night in the forest.

"We know how it was done. This is a misuse of nature! It shouldn't be! But who did it?" pondered Meleena aloud as she and Flax found the others in the stream of guests being funneled back to town. She shook with the horror. Whoever did this had moved up from experimenting on fire salamanders. It was one thing with the small critters, and she hadn't spoken up. But now it really was looking serious, and like someone on the inside was not to be trusted.

"I don't know, but we'd better get home. We can call a meeting and discuss tomorrow with the group."

Such a dreadful end to such a delightful day, thought Meleena, fidgeting with her mass of heavy blue hair.

Meleena almost lost Flax in the crowd. Finding the others would be impossible.

"Our only hope is to get to Arenay and tell her what happened."

She agreed to let Flax carry her from the fairgrounds to headquarters, they propelled upward through the canopy and over to the round, nearly hidden structure.

Arenay stood at the balcony, which overlooked the grounds. She looked concerned at their approach. They were the first to arrive.

"What's going on?" she probed. "I saw there is a commotion down there. Is the fair ending early?"

"There was an accident, someone is dead. A Hyish."

Arenay raised her eyebrows in alarm.

They explained what had happened, and soon the others were arriving, including Deem and Talla on their backs. But they were not the only ones.

At the bottom of the platform ramparts, a small crowd was gathering in the clearing. Wild tails thrashed. They were Hyish.

They pitched rocks at the wall and held flaming branches, lit by their own fire breath.

At least a voice among them distinguished itself from the group. "Sen'Prin leader Arenay. I speak on behalf of the Hyish tribes present. We demand justice for our fallen brother."

Arenay addressed the crowd. "What am I do to? This is public land, and we are not to blame. We use this space at our own discretion."

"But it is your trade grounds."

"My reports tell me it was an accident. What am I do to?"

"He was killed purposely! By one of yours, that is certain. You mussst pay with the blood of your citizens. Turn over whoever did it so we may strip their flesh from them."

Meleena gaped at Arenay. She'd not known her to be so…well, firm. She supposed this was not out of character for her after all.

Though she and the society were pretty enlightened, they were not about to hand someone over. There had to be a better way.

"What are we to do?" Arenay queried the crowd further. "We don't know who did it."

Arenay looked concerned at those standing around her. "We have no idea who did this?"

Meleena spoke up. "I think it was whoever has been doing all of this."

"So, we have no idea," Zoltan confirmed, finger pinching the bridge of his nose.

"Yeah…" added Naia.

Arenay addressed the leader in the crowd again, "We don't know who is responsible. Give us a day to discover this. Grant us the time to weed them out. They are an enemy to us both."

The Hyish leaders' shining yellow eyes stared, its tail whipped behind the draping folds of clothing. "Very well…we will grant you this, but we are not leaving this spot. The tribes will not reopen the fair, and trade with select traders at an inflated higher price until this is resolved. Until you deliver the perpetrator into our hands."

The group looked nervously around at each other.

"Well, we better get on it then," Arenay urged. She'd begun pacing again, her nervous habit.

Kyra finally arrived, panting and in disheveled distress. She combed her hands through her purplish crest of hair.

"Kyra, more than ever we need to find out who's responsible. Send your group out to look for clues around the fair, in case any Sen'Drorn has infiltrated the fair somehow. If it's not them, then it confirms the worst...We may be looking at someone on the inside. I'll call an airship for Deem and Talla to return to Dlawn'Edo tonight."

The group looked around at each other. The fear had brought them together. Many moaned their displeasure, their outfits not equipped for this night off.

Someone on the inside? Arenay's words rang true with her.

"Whoever did this harvested the fire glands, and is using them for their technology. Whatever they are doing to explode, they are tinkering. Working on it, making it worse. I've seen dead lizards around here without their fire glands for a while now." Meleena explained.

"Ah, here we go again, with the lizards," huffed Zoltan.

The others waved her off.

"It's nothing important. You're seeing patterns that aren't there," said Naia.

Meleena bit her tongue.

"All right, settle down," Kyra asserted to regain focus. "It will be determined in time. Regardless, we have a breach, someone on the inside cannot be trusted," Kyra asserted.

They looked around at each other. Naia and Riigs, Zoltan, Jessup, Thian, Flax, and Meleena.

CHAPTER TWENTY-EIGHT

Deem and Talla sat in the lounge at the Meruyan council library, working on a plan for the NHV with Plymore.

Though they couldn't return there, for now, they could still postulate solutions.

Deem had enjoyed the weekend off at the Sen'Prin Hyish fair, dire conclusion aside. He had certainly enjoyed seeing Thian again.

That boy was fun and funny. He could light up a room with that smile—wait what—focus Deem!

He slapped himself back to the present. It wasn't nearly as nice as the daydream. Back in the capital, all he could do was bask in the monotony of paperwork. But in a way, it was nice to have some calm after all their adventures in the NHV, regardless of how guilty he felt by the thought.

The Warix had retaken the land, and many Meruyan were back to work, with only small covert disruptions here and there by Iringbon and his group. It seemed they had lost their steam, without backup. The Sen'Drorn Warix simply had better weapons, tech, and more trained soldiers to throw at the problem. Not to mention wind powers, that was certainly a distinct advantage.

Councilman Ives had said at their last meeting, "We must provide them with even more workers to keep their way of life going to their liking. It's now our top priority." The council had agreed.

Deem leaned forward in the oversized lounge chair. "How can the Meruyan council still abide by what the Sen'Drorn wants? They're so infuriating. I wish the Sen'Drorn would just drop dead and get out of our hair!"

Plymore rubbed his face. "We can't lose track of the point. They aren't bad people. Thinking like that doesn't help. We need to work to understand their side and work with their underlying needs."

"Soo...Is it too late to move back to the sea? Maybe it's not worth it after all." He joked. Something else had been bothering him since that meeting when they had asked the Hyish for aid and been turned away. "They mentioned the Meruyan focus on stuff. About being disconnected with our true culture, our roots. Even about how we are such a small population compared to the Warix. I feel like there's so much they know that we could learn. But nobody will teach us. It's so frustrating."

"Indeed. Now you feel how I do, every day here. I don't know much myself, having spent most of my time in the Sen'Drorn dungeons, but in the days of my youthful travels for the Pendant seed, the Meruyan were different. Back when this governing cave was but a humble monastery. There is so much more to this life than trade and politics, amazing truth to be felt by connecting with our planet. But this cannot be shown or forced, it must be experienced directly to be understood. The mother seed was just a hint at something greater."

He looked tired, close to giving up on all of this. His eyes were sunken. Deem felt a sinking feeling in his chest, like there was no way forward. They just had to walk away from what they couldn't control, be grateful to be safe now, and perhaps not put so much mental effort into this frustration. It was going nowhere.

"We are not so unlike the animals. We seek like they do, but on another level. They seek food, shelter, it is a survival built on love of the self. It's easy for us to control them when we know how they function. Consistently provide their basic needs, feeding, sheltering, being kind to, and they will stick around and be truly devoted to us. We are akin to a god to them, and our world is infinitely complex to them. But on our level, we are searching for all kinds of things, which can be distilled down to love without judgment. To a being who understands this, we are akin to animals and their gods. Their love comes not externally but from inside. They are therefore immune to judgments. And they can control those of us who still demand love. Yulah understands this."

Plymore took a break to sip his tea. "She has found an internal source of love through serving herself. Others choose to get that source from loving others, understanding others. They also understand that there is no good or bad among us, only those seeking to live and belong. They create judgments to push each other into love-deserving schemas. But we all seek love and to be understood. And so, if we are to stop Sen'Drorn, we must have compassion for them, and realize like children, they are misguided. Their biases, seeing 'the other' in each other, only creates more 'others', an infinite cycle of hate, anger, suffering."

"How do we fix it then?" asked Talla, not entirely sure and able to process this. Deem felt right there with her.

"Diplomacy. Somehow." Plymore said, leaning over a wisp of piping hot tea in his lopsided clay mug. "I'm not saying it won't be difficult. I'm saying I'm not afraid of the challenge. Should we make the world a worse place, because the lives of some are easier? No, we aim to improve for more."

Deem and Talla thought eagerly.

"Speaking of well-off. What if we get the Arctic City to contribute supplies to the NHV cause?" asked Talla in earnest.

"Yeah, that could work!" exclaimed Deem. "That's brilliant, Talla! Diplomatic as always."

"That could work," said Plymore flatly.

There was a knock at the door. Deem jerked his head up to see Councilman Ives's long beard as he poked his head in. "Sorry to bother you," he said. "Deem and Talla, there's been another 'flee to the sea' and storm, which as you know by now means the Warix have paid us an unofficial visit. You should go, visit with your families, and assess the damages. You will go with Council Historian Loroh and his caravan, leaving before dusk."

***

Riding through the forest's edge and back into town, Deem and Talla could see a few caved-in roofs, but the damage wasn't too extensive.

They stayed a couple of days to visit their families and help take assessments of the town. Loroh, who was Meleena's father, invited Deem and Talla to their home for dinner and to catch up on how Meleena was doing in Sen'Prin, as Deem and Talla had seen her much more recently.

The ceiling in Meleena's room had been one of the rooms attacked. Deem remembered Meleena telling him, months ago, about the last 'flee to the sea' warning, in which her father's study had been destroyed, while Malotus had searched for the Legendary Pendant. How when they had come for it, the Sen'Drorn had made it look like an accident. But that couldn't be the case now, right?

Ives seemed to think it was no random storm. He had implied some kind of Warix intervention.

"We reported the damages to the council, already," explained Vivia, Meleena's mother, when he asked. "You can look around if you like."

"I've never been inside Meleena's room before," Talla said, staring at the bookshelves and her bed.

Deem inspected the damage to the ceiling, broken through as if by a tree. It was like the Sen'Drorn Warix weren't even trying to hide their clear assaults.

"But what could they want from Meleena?" asked Talla, bemused.

Her mother looked concerned and utterly bewildered at the idea. "Do you think she's safe there, in Sen'Prin?" she asked doubtfully.

"Perhaps this is because she's mixed up with all of their drama. Maybe this was all a bad idea, letting her go off and join them."

A thought hit Deem when he looked at the bookshelf. "Was there anything out of place here after the storm?" he asked Vivia.

"Oh, well, the usual sort you'd expect. Books were all over the floor, scattered. I cleaned it all up and put things back the best I could."

"I don't suppose her nature journals are missing?" Deem asked.

Vivian gasped and sifted through the spines. "Oh no! Where could those have gone!"

Deem took a deep breath. Her journals were missing? How could that be?

"Maybe she took them with her?" Talla offered.

"No, she left them," Vivia said shaking her head. "They were too precious to her. I sent her clothing but she specifically didn't want me to take the journals. She told me to look after them, that they were too important..."

She put her hands over her face. "What am I going to do! This is terrible!"

Deem gulped. This was bad. What would the Sen'Drorn want with her journals, was beyond him? He'd have to be the one to tell Meleena about this. He wasn't even sure if that should go in the official report.

***

Meleena had been invited to hang out with Borak and Flax at Odella's house for the first time. She figured it was their way to comfort her after the events at the fair, her new closeness with Flax, and all.

In the aftermath of the fair, she was certainly shaken. If someone on the inside was doing this, and they stole her journals to create their new technology, then how could she even trust Flax and Borak? It dawned on her that perhaps the culprit had been looking through her journal since she'd arrived in Sen'Prin. Maybe their best tech ideas were inspired by the animals and systems documented in her notebook? She often suspected someone had been, when she left it out in the lab, but never thought it was something to hide before.

Meleena rode on Upala over the rooftops and tree-covered hillside by the forest where Odella's cottage was nestled among the hills that flanked the river and forest. residence lay in the center of town, higher up for theoretical ease of access to headquarters.

Odella was already outside, stooping over a patch of flowers under her window, and gave a frightful cry of surprise when she arrived on the large, winged panther.

"Well, she is gorgeous," Odella said. "Gave me quite a fright, sneaking up like that!"

Odella stood, slipping her gloves off and casually tossing them into her apron pouch.

"Oh yeah, she's a bit of a silent hunter," Meleena joked.

"Can I get her some food?"

Upala pounced at a butterfly then flew off in the direction of the forest.

"Eh, she's good."

"It's good to see you. I know we have met before."

"Ah yes, I remember," Meleena said politely. She had met Odella only once before, at Sen'Prin headquarters that summer. It was the day they'd escaped Sen'Drorn fortress and brought all engineers home.

She embraced Meleena in a warm, motherly hug. Meleena had been missing this kind of connection, having now been away from her parents so long. It was nice to be at a home with a loving atmosphere.

"Well, come in," said Odella. "I will make us some tea."

The cottage had a surprisingly spacious interior. The curved walls formed a combined cozy kitchen and living room.

Flax came out from a side room, presumably his bedroom and Odella fixed them tea in thick clay mugs.

"My mom makes sculptures from the clay," he explained. "Anyway, dinner will be a while. Want to hang out in my room?"

She nodded and they went down the hall.

"Sorry it's messy," he apologized in advance of her seeing it.

He motioned for her to sit in the armchair, while he pulled a footrest out from under it and sat on it as a stool.

Looking around Flax's room, she could see how his new-found passion for engineering affected him in many ways.

"Borak has been staying at the lab in headquarters, but sometimes here. my mom's getting used to the idea. They're getting on well. Meanwhile, I'm looking to move out soon. Maybe Thian and I will find a place after this whole ordeal is over."

She watched the steam rise from her tea. "Are you planning to keep working for the war effort in the Sen'Prin military lab?" she asked, hoping he may reveal more information to quell her suspicions.

"Who knows, maybe I'll start a new engineering shop with Borak if the conflict is ever over." Smooth as always.

Then something that caught her eye. It was a paper amongst the stacks on his shelf, with sketches hypothesizing the use of fire glands in copper tubing technology. It had a compartment drawn out and everything.

"What's this?" she asked casually.

"Oh, it's just actually a thing I came up with some time ago with Borak. While coming up with stuff, theoretical though."

"Well, not anymore."

They heard a loud scream from outside that made them jump, followed by a laugh.

"Sounds like Borak has arrived," said Flax, chuckling.

Meleena laughed along with him, and carefully tucked the paper into her pockets. Perhaps this evidence would be useful later. Not that she suspected him, but...well, who knows?

Dinner that evening was lovely, but Meleena couldn't help wondering...They were engineers, and they knew all about the fire gland technology. Who's to say it wasn't one of them?

But she couldn't let them know her suspicions, it was too soon to tell. She hated the idea of even suspecting them, they were her closest friends here and had always been kind to her.

But the evidence was starting to point to them, how could this even be?

"Ah, remember the good old times?" Flax reminisced, nudging Borak. "When we had access to all the materials we wanted?"

"Ye," grunted Borak, "I miss my shop 'n' all, with all the copper we wanted. Here it's all mixed in with the bronze. Ah well, I wouldn't trade it for my life now. You and Odella!"

Flax laughed and shook his head. Then he got serious and stared into the distance, exuded himself, and went into his room.

Nothing to be suspicious about, Meleena consoled herself, but she felt queasy. She could barely finish her beans.

"What's with Flax?" she asked.

"Ah, he still thinks of Yulah from time to time, guilt ya'know," Odella said.

It felt like the floor had come out from under her. Her heart pounded in her chest.

"What?" Meleena squeaked out.

"Ah, don't worry about it. Nothin' to be jealous of. They had, you know, a painful history."

She sighed. The knot in her stomach hadn't left. Could Flax still have feelings for her? And if so, what could he be capable of?

The world swirled like getting caught in a riptide.

The Hyish who had turned up dead at the fair was killed by someone on the inside, she knew it. But was Flax really capable of that? It was disturbing.

She wanted to excuse herself, but Borak put a gentle hand on her shoulder. "It'll be alrigh'."

"I just…" she started, letting the stream of problems bubble up. "It's not just Flax. It's also that the information my journal is being used to create technology which is destroying everything! What if I never had written all that down? I didn't know!"

Though it was a digression from her main worries, it was still a point of pain she hadn't even begun to explore yet.

"It's alright," Borak comforted. "I know how ye feel. My tech has been designed with love, out of my own creative hands, an' yet it has been taken for use in war efforts. Ye think this makes me happy? Designing war tools…? Technology is about growth. You can't control how people are going to use it. Great ideas can always be used for good and evil."

"Any ideas about who the person on the inside could be?" Meleena asked outright. Why not give them a chance to speculate?

Flax had been with her the whole time during the murder. She shuddered to think he'd be the most likely suspect. And of Borak?

Are they both in on it? No that's silly. It's got to be just Flax or neither. What am I thinking.

He had come from Sen'Drorn. Could he be capable of being a double agent? Could the two of them be in on it together? No, surely, they'd always been genuine with her. It was Flax who had to make the tough choice to rejoin Sen'Prin already. Certainly, he was honest…

"I don't care to speculate," said Borak. Wouldn't feel right, speaking ill of our colleagues. I haven't got much of an idea myself. We have had so many lab assistants and interns coming and going. The place isn't exactly safety kept. I think Arenay believes it is, as we are so far from Sen'Drorn and what with all the defenses outside, that the city is therefore impenetrable. It's all quite shocking."

"Personally, I've never been a fan of Zoltan. Guy gives me the creeps. Or maybe Jessup. She's from the villages. Who says a nice girl like that can't be involved with Sen'Drorn. I mean, nobody vetted me that hard when I was a spy in their city. My town had been taken over by Sen'Prin and they didn't even know it. Who's to say it didn't happen in reverse?" speculated Flax. "Don't tell anyone any of this, by the way," he added.

But even as she left that night, she couldn't curb the strange, sickening feeling bubbling inside.

Upala had not returned from her hunt, so Meleena walked along the bridges back to her flat.

She missed home, her parents, the safety of knowing who one could trust.

CHAPTER TWENTY-NINE

"Ah that beast!" cried Jessup, waking Meleena at dawn. "Scratching at the door!"

Meleena opened the balcony door and Upala slunk in. Her fur was covered in sharp thorns. Meleena sighed. Perhaps she'd messed with the bramble sheep. It took a while to brush the thorns out, get her cleaned up, while the others got ready for the morning team meeting.

In truth, she was moving slowly, partly because of the ordeal with Flax. She had no idea really, no matter how suspicious he and Borak looked, but needed to put it aside and focus on the mission ahead of them.

When she finally got downstairs, the noodle house was empty. A wave of panic washed over her.

"They must be at headquarters. But for a morning meeting? Ah, fish brains!" Meleena cursed aloud to Upala, then led her back upstairs and they took off out the balcony and soared over the city.

She could see through the glass windows inside that the group was gathered around the table in one of the larger meeting rooms. Meleena apologized for being late, confused as to why they were meeting there in the first place.

"Ehem..." Kyra cleared her throat and glowered at the interruption. "We have tightened security. We cannot trust the general public with our meetings after the knowledge about the insider."

"There was a note in the common room about it," teased Zoltan.

This was their idea of security? Ugh. Meleena plopped down in a chair.

Upala had followed her in and sat beside her to receive a neck scratch.

"Now then," Kyra spoke solemnly, elbows on the table, her hands clasped. "As I was saying, our thunderstorm searching has to lead us to a new destination for a stakeout. There's been a sighting of the strange bubble-shaped vehicle."

Meleena smirked. "You mean like I postulated from the animal I saw in the forest..." she started. She couldn't help herself.

"Indeed. Good job, Meleena. This could be our chance to find it and destroy it this time *before* it destroys another village."

"Maybe even catch whoever is behind it, wouldn't that be nice?" joked Thian half-heartedly. The group was becoming exhausted from all these failures. First to stop the explosion and the close call on their last outing, and now the murder at the Hyish fair—too close to home.

Meleena wondered who among them suspected each other.

"In the mountains behind us," Kyra went on, "among the high peaks, Sen'Prin has a small operation set up. There are large high-tech bronze nets set up to collect the wind. It's very cold and wet up there, so check out any necessary gear from headquarters. Although we thought the Sen'Drorn did not know of our presence in the high mountains, we have gotten word of the wet forest amongst the ravines is facing unusually dry skies. When we inquired further, the workers at the village there have reported seeing this 'bubble vehicle' as well, the same which we have also glimpsed."

The group looked from one to the other, excited for the lead. "Are you ready to find and apprehend those responsible for this?" Kyra tried to sound enthusiastic through her stern style.

The team was pumped.

"We will take a gondola and then an airship through the treacherous way to this remote, frozen place," she concluded.

As they left the meeting, Meleena saw through the glass that Arenay was in another meeting with several Hyish in the conference room.

She stepped out to greet them when she saw the team arrive in the central hall.

"What was that about?" asked Kyra.

Arenay gave an exasperated sigh. "I don't know what to tell them. They want justice for the murdered Hyish at the fair, but we don't know who did it. I don't know why they blame us. It happened on our grounds sure but what can we do?"

The Hyish trio followed her into the hall. "I am not pleasseddd, with you Sen'Prin. This is a most dishonorable behavior. We do business here, expect safety. What will I tell my people?"

"I am sorry this happened on our land, but I have no leads on why," said Arenay, pleading for understanding.

"If justice is not met, we will take action on our own," he hissed in menacing warning.

"I'm sorry, but we can't promise anything," she said with the slightest hint of desperation in her tone.

The Hyish stormed away, upset, climbing and then disappearing over the wall of the rampart on foot, down the sheer cliffs, and into the forest.

"Nothing to worry about," said Arenay. "I'm sure our diplomatic efforts will win them over soon."

Meleena gazed up at a series of copper chutes and pulleys, holding together a thick rope that disappeared into the foggy oblivion above. The gondola was of glass and metal, windows bearing a view as it shot upwards. The momentum was thrilling...too much so. The gondola climbed the peaks higher than she had ever been. Meleena held the sides firmly, standing and trying to stop herself from giving in to vertigo as her stomach flipped. She clung to Upala's soft fur.

Then suddenly from bedrock, darkness to light as they charged up the mountain, and the view before them emerged. They ascended the mountain above the tree line. A fresh chill ran through the air. They landed on a dry, brown exposed earth, between wild low brush and small curling trees.

Stepping out of the gondola, she had expected to be in a village of some sort. Yet the ground was not visible to them.

They were at the edge of a long valley carved from the huge horizontal mountainside, crusting upward to form wall basins from which these thick sturdy fungi grew. Glistening snowy peaks above the tree line. Deep, dark woods creaked far below, and the natural wind tunnel created by the shape of the ravine howled with terrifying, rapid winds. Meleena shivered from the chilly air.

How could anyone live here?

Meleena was baffled at what lengths the Warix would go to for resources.

A representative met them from the town, a Warix dressed in a parka, and provided similar coats to the team, before they took two airships to the strange town.

The village atop the enormous mushrooms was some distance away, small buildings built into the cliffside, thus shielded from the winds. Paths carved into the mountainside connected the mushrooms to one another.

That was when the representative pointed out the invaluable reason they live here. Across the span of the ravine in several places, stretched fractals of metallic webbing, waving in the wind and shining with synaptic energy.

"These are the resources we farm," the representative pointed out. "As the wind passes through the webbed tubing of bronze and copper, wind energy flows to the core, which contains a storage cell. Sen'Prin city functions would not have the energy to run without them." Meleena wondered if they were combustible, as they appeared a perfect target for a Sen'Drorn explosive attack.

"But I called you here because we have a problem," he explained. Meleena surmised he was the head operations manager. "We've seen this gray gunk fall from the sky like rain, which Arenay has told us to watch out for, as well as a lack of rain lately. We thought nothing of this at first until these strange, silver flying creatures started showing up and buzzing around the wind webs. They approach the core cell, and sometimes fly directly into it, and crash. We've never seen anything like it. We've had extra operators shooing them away all week."

Automata, like the ones that had stolen Meleena's journal. This was direct evidence they were in the right place. This delicate network of energy would be a perfect target to disrupt Sen'Prin on a massive scale.

"Then, the other day, someone reported seeing a round, bulbous machine you mentioned, somewhere in one of the ravines." The operations manager put his hands on his hips and shook his head. "It didn't last though, whoever had it, clearly left before I arrived."

"Don't worry, we will get on it," said Kyra on behalf of the group, who nodded in excited agreement. This could be their chance to finally apprehend whoever was responsible, catch them in the act, and take out their machinery.

"I suggest you stay at the lodge and search the area by day," the manager concluded. "It gets freezing here at night."

Meleena shivered in her borrowed parka, not wanting to know how much colder it could get.

The days that followed turned out quite inopportune. Fog rolled in, making visibility poor, grounding them and wasting valuable searching time. Finally, when it was clear skies, the group huddled in a specialized, reinforced airship dome, as the heavy winds in the ravine made it too dangerous for anyone to use wind energy on their own most of the time. Those operators who collected the energy cells had specialized suits, created to counteract and redirect the wind, absorbing and redirecting it. These were expensive and few.

Meleena felt useless in this place, and preferred to avoid missions entirely, feeling torn. She didn't want to miss out if they found something, but was growing tired of the tiresome hunts, getting geared up for the cold, riding around in the dizzying heights all day, standing cooped up with the group for long hours. And yet, after days of searching in shifts, stalking up and down the ravines and their various forest crags, dodging the webbing as they peered into crevices, something came to fruition.

Kyra, Thian, Zoltan, and Jessup had been out on an airship run, and buzzed in via wristcom. A large, round globe-like machine held up by copper had been found. Meleena, Riigs, and Naia had been playing cards in the lodge, and hurriedly rushed to find a way over there. The two of them were granted anti-wind suits, and carried Meleena in a parka atop Riig's back, much to her discomfort.

They battled the freezing winds and finally landed in a tornado to lay eyes on the machine that had eluded them for so long.

"There, through the trees," announced Thian excitedly at their arrival. They had stalked it from a far-off vantage point: a Warix wearing a black robe that covered his head was standing by a large glass globe full of water, held in a sort of, copper-clawed holder on wheels. The Warix held a hose attached to a sucking instrument, pointed at the sky. Sure enough, it was sucking away moisture from the clouds, with amazing speed.

"It's like he's got wind power channeled backward, to suck in the water from the clouds," said Kyra.

Meleena was reminded of the bulbous creatures by the ponds, sucking moisture from the foggy air for sustenance. This would be a modified version, with wind added to the machine to incorporate the strength of Warix wind power. It would have been documented right there on the pages of her stolen journal. But this machine existed long before her sketches. This Warix thought in the same vein as her, developed ideas by watching nature and animals, learned from them as she did. Like Borak or Flax, she thought with a chill. Whoever it was, that was why they destroyed her work. Her notebooks were evidence of how his devices worked, his sacred, unique technology.

They blasted down and descended quickly on the machine, surrounding it. As they approached, they saw he was hooked into the device with his hand, and he turned, seeing them approach, quickly flipping a switch on the machine. Pressurized water blasted out in a torrent and slammed each of them back, casting the team in all directions into trees and bushes. Meleena stayed back to watch, as without wind power she had no defenses.

When the group regained their footing, and Riigs pounced from behind on the machine, Thian fanning out his arms to tackle him, the perpetrator realized he was outnumbered, and dropped the hose, pulling his arm free from the device. Thick protective goggles and gloves made it impossible to make out his form his form. He fled on wind power so quickly between the leaves, Meleena guessed he had some kind of spring boots.

She watched as Kyra and Jessup gave chase into the jungle, but he grew ever more distant and soon was out of sight.

They returned, crestfallen, sometime later, as Meleena, Thian, Zoltan, Riigs, and Naia began to inspect and prod at the machine. Thian pried opened a panel on the side, and Naia all but crawled in. "It's been stealing water alight, but it's running on some kind of green liquid," echoed her voice from inside.

"It's not running on it, it's mixing wind energy with the bile from glands!" expressed Meleena. "As I've said, he's utilizing the fire and water elements from the glands of animals to mix the elements with the wind in new combinations."

"I get why fire and wind would create a dry explosion, but not a large-scale drought," said Zoltan.

"Maybe it's water cell bile...? Like what is in your arms to make your fins grow?" Thian pointed out.

Wait, he had actually been listening to me? thought Meleena, starting to laugh.

"Yes!" Meleena continued, pinching her nose under her glasses. "That could be it. If he's extracting moisture from the clouds, to create drought, it could likely be a mix of air and water cells in this machine."

Her heart pounded with excitement and worry. She felt a horrible sinking feeling. Whoever had been making these had been using her ideas about the elemental aspects of creatures. Her own ideas had been turned into an extreme and awful technology. She was sure they had used her journal to build this machine. They had broken into her home, stolen the journals, and now this. She wouldn't allow herself to say it aloud.

Thian pulled apart the machine. "There's copper wiring all intertwined in here. The work of an engineer no doubt. The water element cells are right here, in these chambers. Looks like the wind energy from a Warix would pass through these chambers and that would affect the outcome."

"Confirmed," said Naia, nosing around in the open compartment. "Now we know how it's built."

They opened another compartment and the gray sludge oozed out in waves onto the ground.

"...And there's that byproduct," Thian pointed out.

Kyra's wristcom buzzed. "It's a message from the operator. He says we should get back to town right away. Something is going on. Those automata were seen again, the ones that stole Meleena's journal. They were seen at the bases of the wind netting structures. That can't be good. We need to go, now. This could be real trouble."

They squeezed into the domed airship and rushed back to the village. The day had become unusually bright and calm, probably the reason those little beasts could fly in to attack the wind nets in the first place. They imagined it would have been a great idea, bringing small remote-controlled automata to attack wind turbines, until the engineer responsible discovered how sharp the wind was here. They likely lost more than a few to the surprising weather up here before figuring out that they had to fly under perfect conditions if they were going to destroy anything. Perhaps that's what he was doing out there with the machine today, Meleena surmised. Clearing a hole in the clouds so his destructive mechanized beasts could have a clear shot.

That fishhead probably fled the bubble device and went right to the second part of his plan.

Meleena borrowed a pair of thick goggles to fit over her glasses and found she was able to fly on Upala.

The light bounced off their metallic coats as the small creatures buzzed and flew around the netting all throughout the ravine. The group took wing, diving from the mushrooms towards the fluttering in the air, splitting up to give chase.

Riigs tackled one midair, while Zoltan broke the wings off of one, as it fell in a spiral into the depths below. Jessup swatted one, sending it crashing into the wall in a fiery explosion.

Meleena darted between the others on the back of Upala, guiding her gently in flight by her horns. She grabbed a tree branch and used it to prod at a flying wind-up rat, smashing it until the gears flew apart. Then Upala nailed one through the heart with a buck of her horns and shook it loose. It imploded, bursting into flames in midair.

As the shocking ripple of an explosion rang out, Meleena looked up, a large hole had been blown in one of the wind nets. Jessup clung to the netting in an attempt to stop it, her red hair flying behind her. She had to bail as the remaining strands came apart, throwing herself off into the gorge to avoid the shards of self-detonated automata, recovering after nearly hitting the cliff wall.

Meleena landed on one of the enormous, uninhabited wood mushrooms looking around. She could see no more automata buzzing around. The team flew around, some landing to look around for a better view. Then they regrouped, returning to the mushroom bearing the lodge, hugging and congratulating one another.

Most of the turbines were saved, only one was fully destroyed, and there had been mild damage to about three from the critters flying attacks. They could project small firebolts, and claw attacks, but not do serious damage without destroying themselves. It could have been much worse.

"What a rush! Did you see me pummel them!" cheered Naia.

"I'd count this as a win...for once," said Riigs. He embraced the group, his large body towering over them in a warm hug.

"All's well that ends well," said Thian. Meleena agreed, sliding her goggles up to her forehead.

"Not really," said Zoltan. "I mean, the damage is something and we still didn't catch the operative responsible."

"But we blasted his little pets to cogs!" Naia argued.

"Well, it's good we saved the turbines," said Kyra, looking around. "But what about that mess?" she indicated to the junk metal scraps that were once beasts, littering the landscape. She punched her brow. "I guess collect the samples, though I'm unconvinced of what good it will do us. The Warix in charge got away."

"We'll get him..." Riigs said comfortingly.

CHAPTER THIRTY

After their victory, Meleena and the team boarded two domed airships to take them to the gondola back to Sen'Prin City. As they headed down through the mist on this particularly frosty, foggy morning, it was as if the sun had failed to rise.

Airships just weren't built for this kind of thing, even those with specialized, protected tops. As a way to balance out their weight, Meleena rode with Zoltan, Jessup, and Upala, while Kyra went with Riigs, Naia, and Thian.

They descended cautiously into the canyon, through the darkness, the fog, into the deep green bristly tree line.

Kyra may have misjudged the distance to the wall.

The sides slapped something from under, a horrid bumping sound, and the ship pitched everyone lurching forward. Many lost their balance and cried out as the dome cracked the side of a tree and split open.

Upala, who had been lying on the ground at Meleena's feet, jumped up and Meleena grabbed onto her, mounting up and grasping her horns as they separated from the airship.

It hovered below, as a spin, and Meleena could only watch in horror as they thumped and bounced, ricocheted off a giant leaf, with no ground in sight, and toppled over. The Warix team flew and pitched forward, screaming, arms outstretched, as they tumbled out. Many blasted air, trying to break their falls, but it was such chaos that they impeded each other's intake.

Upala lurched back, to avoid getting caught in the tumultuous pulling. Thian and Naia grabbed at large leaves, catching themselves to it, while Jessup landed on a petal and Zoltan was sucked into a flower and out of sight. Kyra held onto the airship as it lost momentum and spiraled down and out of sight. Meleena clenched her jaw. Fear shot through her.

Meleena cried out, heart pounding, she was slipping off. She pulled at Upala's horns so she recalibrated, tilting upwards, but she slipped off her side and screamed as the floor dropped beneath her and she tumbled down, into fathomless depths. Upala's cries were as painful as the anticipation of the fall as the two separated amongst the fog until her forlorn cries could not be heard.

Meleena fell, groping about in the air, until her hand made slicing contact with something bouncy. The long tendrils of a tree slowed her falling speed enough for her body to roll into the bushes in a heap.

"Upala!" she called upward, before even attempting to get up. She squinted, glasses long gone. The sky was invisible above the dense tree cover. Strange animal sounds clicked and hummer as they called out to one another in this unknown place.

She grabbed a sturdy branch to arm herself as her boots crunched along the sodden ground.

She was alone. Her wristcom didn't work down here in the ravine. How was she going to survive overnight? She shivered, perhaps from more than cold. Love of nature aside, she wasn't prepared for this. She huddled in her parka, happy at least for that. First things first, avoid panicking. She'd have to make a camp. There was always a way to survive. What did the animals around here do?

She could find dry materials to start a fire for herself, and maybe find something to eat or drink. She kept her ears open, listening for any signs of water running.

Feeling lightheaded, she inspected some berries, tasting one and letting it pop between her teeth. It was sweet and tangy, with no hint of bitterness. To her experience, this meant edible. She had to keep moving, and chances of finding a patch like this again were slim, so she picked a handful and continued on.

But soon they were melting in her warm hand, so she had no choice but to stuff them all at once into her mouth, caressing each round globule trying hard to savor them, but soon she was thirsty and worried again.

Stepping over a white branch, she walked along with it as it forked and connected to a base. She realized with horror that it was the spinal column of some huge dead beast. Something about it made her think back on that 'Navanax' beast that the wind spirit had mentioned, even though she had not described it. Or perhaps that was a coincidence?

First signs of losing my mind, fantastic.

The sun was setting already, the dense chilly forest darkened fast in the depths of the ravine. She continued on, her hands paddling through leaves until the distant babble of a river had her heart quickening, and she ran towards the fresh stream.

Scooping the water fervently into her mouth, the surprise of its warmth tingled in her hands. If she got too wet, she'd freeze in the open air. She sipped warm water, squinting at the muddy embankment. The river seemed to be dropping away, disappearing from sight, into a sinkhole of some kind.

She investigated downstream, nearly falling over in the mud, climbing into a steeper canyon, until she lowered into a cave, shadows all around, until it was pitch black. The mud under her hands was warm. Her body shivered from the cold again, loving the warm mud and wanting to follow. The risk was worth it.

She crawled further, following the warmth, towards a light ahead, something of a bright blue glow. A thought crossed her mind and she hoped she wasn't inside the mouth of some giant monster.

Then, through the darkness, blue lights erupted like thousands of stars falling. Hot bubbling water and a waterfall! Meleena's heart pounded with longing, taking in the small space, stone carved by millennia of water.

She removed her clothing, then reached a hand into the dazzling waterfall. To avoid freezing further, she dove headlong into the hot shining blue water, huddling into the warm, glowing water pouring forth from the cave wall to sponge the chill from her bones. It was like life energy itself. Her cold feet protested the burning of the contrasting water, and she danced around, hands clasped and pressed to her chest as the sprig of water fell there. She lifted it to her face, letting the warmth permeate her shuddering body.

Falling asleep after this was quite easy. She'd sacrificed one layer and let it dry overnight, and she huddled in the parka inside the warm, steamy, shelter.

She found herself lying among the warm rocks in the morning light. The blue lights of the waterfall were dimmer now, unable to compete with the sun.

It wasn't long before, to her utter shock and horror, a figure appeared through the trees, heading to the mouth of the cave.

A Warix! *Wait, this is good right?*

Her heart leapt with mixed shock, and wonder for how she'd been found, and by whom, though part of that was answered as the figure was staring down at the ground, apparently following a line.

Her tracks in the mud…yep that would do it, she thought.

She slid around a corner of the mouth of the cave to peer out. *That clothing. That bright violet hair…Yulah?!*

Meleena could hardly believe it. What was she doing here? How did she find her deep in this jungle?

Unless…*someone* must have told her about the team's visit to this place…

"Come out, girl…" Yulah's voice came, crisp and clear over the bubbling water.

Her armor was neat and shining. Meleena stepped out, head held high.

"Yulah, I know it was you who attacked Sen'Prin," she stated, finding no better way to announce herself than with this accusation.

"How did you know; your little buddy Flax tell you?" she said mock-sweetly. "You have been quite the terror yourself. I have been using your ideas though, it's been quite helpful, thanks. But you are a liability, and this is the perfect place to get rid of you. Lost out here, never seen again. I'm almost sorry to do it, but taking down your airship was remarkably easy. I was surprised you hadn't died in the wreckage, personally. I had to come looking for you to be sure."

"What happened to the others?" Meleena questioned, staring her down.

"Oh, a little banged up, but they mostly got away. I got a couple of the slower ones, however. They'll make great additions for my tech experiments in the dungeons of Sen'Drorn."

"Come off it, Yulah! Malotus is gone, now what, you want to be worse than him, carry on his legacy? You used to be so kind, reasonable. We have a history!"

Yulah made a face as if Meleena had thrown sand into her eyes. "We don't talk about the previous general around Sen'Drorn anymore. I've moved up in his stead, so I can't afford to be kind."

"What? You chose this path, Yulah. I'm sorry to see you become this way. You must have been hurt a lot," Meleena started to say, chest tightening.

Yulah gave a momentary pause. A flash of something honest across her face: true pain, that's what it was. But she quickly recomposed herself back to the hardened stare, cheekbones high, jaw stiffening.

Meleena had never given much thought previously to how Yulah had been a victim in all of this, betrayed and left by all those she knew and loved.

"Now come with me, so you can revisit the inside of a jail cell in Sen'Drorn," Yulah said flatly.

Meleena gave a little laugh. "Oh, see, isn't that better? I knew you didn't really want to kill me."

Yulah sneered. "Perhaps working as a slave for Sen'Drorn is better, with your talents. Where else could I get my new tech ideas? We'll take you on little walks in the forest, you will be my pet. Yes, I like that idea."

Meleena sighed and followed Yulah out of the cave. Pretending to be taken prisoner was better than dying out here. She had no choice at this stage, really.

As soon as they reached any sort of civilization, they'd eventually have to stop. Meleena could find a way to run.

"Fair enough, Yulah. So how have you been doing it, then?"

"What?"

"Blowing up Sen'Prin villages, you know." She waved a hand.

"Why would I tell you any of that?" Yulah griped.

"Thought I'd ask. And what would you do after that? Blow up all of Sen'Prin's resources? Starve them out?"

"I can still kill you if you don't shut up."

"Fine, fine." Meleena was enjoying this. Yulah was so easily annoyed.

They walked in silence for some time, the ground crunching under their feet as they trudged in the dense jungle. Meleena was scared, sure, but a little disoriented after all this, really just wanting to get out of this jungle.

Huh, first time for everything, she thought.

Her mind had turned to humor as a surprising coping mechanism amongst the uncertainty. Things were bad, how much worse could they get? At least nobody from her team was dead. That was a start.

Her head was spinning, she felt almost goofy. They passed a large fronded plant—*huh, that would have been better than my shirt after my dip in the waterfall last night.*

"Of course," grumbled Yulah, breaking her train of thought, "I have a greater plan. I don't plan to stay a General forever."

Was she bragging?

"Sure, sure. I bet," said Meleena. *Keep her talking.*

"What? You think I'm some low-level nothing, that I can't be promoted to a higher rank? I am in the same position as Malotus ever got to!"

"Well, I mean, he was there a long time, sure, but he was more experienced than you, and got there because of his personal ties to Arenay. Sen'Drorn enemy number one. Malotus was a master strategist, well respected. No offense but, factually speaking you were like, his assistant until he left your Emperor desperate…"

Yulah stopped walking and turned around abruptly. "Well for your information, that pompous knob is about to get what's coming. I don't enjoy working for him any more than Malotus did—but he's overjoyed with my work. I'm moving up, and I'm going to do what's in Sen'Drorn's citizen's best interest. They're good people and they who deserve to prosper."

Meleena only made a sound, something in sarcastic agreement. It was enough to put Yulah over the edge.

"What do you know?" her eyes were aglow with frightful anger.

"Are you saying you are doing it for the people? Not really just for yourself?"

Yulah flew into a rage. Because it was all true, and hit too close to her heart. An open-handed smack made Meleena see stars. Perhaps she'd pushed the girl too far.

Yulah, at least a head taller than Meleena, as most Warix were, had the advantage. She shoved and Meleena to the ground, the painful hardness coming to meet her back. Yulah flung herself atop Meleena, hands around her neck, as Meleena struggled, in total shock. Meleena didn't know what she had been thinking. Angering Yulah had given her a sort of rise, power of the situation, but things had certainly taken a turn for the worse. She wished she could have just kept quiet, but it was too late for that now.

She kicked, which was enough to pry Yulah off, break her grasp, but stayed on her back as kicking would be her best defense mechanism.

Yulah broke the stalemate by one pulling an arm over her shoulder and releasing a pole-arm weapon.

Well dang, of course she'd come more prepared to fight.

Yulah directed the pointed end at Meleena's forehead, keeping her pinned her to the ground. "You must want to die today..."

Just then, a creature emerged from the shadows from behind Yulah. Meleena kept still. At first, she thought it was Upala, large wings outstretched as it stalked Yulah.

It thrust forward in a flying leap, claws long and razor-sharp as it slashed into Yulah's back, causing her to lunge forward as Meleena rolled out of the way.

As it turned around, elegant green wings splayed each feather out wide. An onyx and green mass of wild fur held a fleshless boney head with gaping holes for eyes and a long-pointed beak.

What the hell was going on here...?!

Yulah fought back, cast an arm outward, gripping her gloves and swirling copper staff, stopping the creature and locking them in a struggle, each trying to push the other to gain ground.

"Aargg!!" Yulah cried out, muffled under the weight. The beast was far larger than her, towering at least a head above her. It kept its head low and growled, a low resonating almost purr. Yulah, losing ground, turned her whole body, and plunged headlong into the ground. The beast stood between her and Meleena.

Meleena watched in horror, as Yulah sent a burst of wind, back on her feet now with catlike grace, as the beast changed course, pumping its wings and gaining ground between them just enough to strike with wind, in a change of tactics.

Yulah kicked with her strong boots, wind enhancements granting her fine actions. They both took to the air in a flurry of wind, a dance of tackling and dodging. Yulah got some narrow hits in with her pole-arm, the great bipedal beast amazingly agile as it dodged, and strong as it endured her hits, arms up, slashing them away through the air with both clawed arms. It dispelled her wind, shot it back in her face, and finally knocked her back to the ground before looming over her. Meleena could only watch, mesmerized, and having some idea now of what was really happening.

"You…you aren't going to really hurt me…" Yulah gasped. She roared and raced towards it, the beast deflecting her and shoving her headlong to the ground again.

"Well you have to do better than that," she shouted to it, "I won't stop. This girl is mine."

The beast grabbed Yulah in reply, shoved her against a tree trunk, growled low in her face, a threat. But she was right. It was not going to do more to actually hurt her.

Yulah breathed heavily at it and then did something even stranger. She reached forward with the part of her hand only partly able to maneuver under the grip, and to Meleena's horror, ripped the skeletal bird's face clean off! Meleena's skin crawled as it plopped to the ground in one swath, almost like a mask. But instead of blood, or whatever Meleena was expecting—she didn't exactly know—there was…

Her stomach did a flip…another face appeared.

It was a humanoid.

"You…!" gaped Yulah, falling limp against the tree. "So, that's why…" she trailed off. She was in utter shock, her mouth dangling open and closed. "I…I can't believe you would be here."

Just like he'd appeared to her once before in the forests of Sen'Prin, Malotus had again tracked her down against the threat of Yulah.

Finally, it spoke in the gravelly voice of someone who had not done so in a long time. "Yulah, do not become a killer. I cannot let you. It is important that you turn her over to me."

"I have been doing fine without you, thanks for asking. I am going further than you ever did! Could imagine, even!" She sounded maniacal.

His grip softened as Yulah struggled. He backed away, his dark emerald wings closing. With his back directly to her in the light, Meleena finally understood what he was. This was the huge falcon, Grimley, nestled in his back, its claws gripped fight into the fur, which was not his own, but something he was wearing. A mix of black and green moss hide pelts, blending seamlessly with his body and even longer black mane, which he always had, now so much longer and wilder. He had let his claws grow long, all Warix had clawed hands, but they usually filed them down in society. Meleena stared in contrast at her own hand, semi-aquatic, and soft-tipped, with no claws.

"You ask me what I'm doing here?" Malotus laughed, smooth and calm. "I do not belong to society…but this is not your place Yulah."

"This is what I have to do, if I am to get things done." She huffed. She sounded more like his child than any leader at that moment. "The average Warix doesn't know what they want! I need to show the people how things ought to be. My leadership will improve the Sen'Drorn civilization for everyone in ways they could not have known before! They will be grateful for my work when I become their Empress."

"Yulah, I am sorry," Malotus said slowly, green eyes cast down. "I was wrong. Others are not all bad. We all have our own problems to sort out, and we cannot blame one another, for we try our best with what we know."

Yulah pouted. "If you believe that, then you have become weak. Just like Ryogrim, our unfit Emperor. At least you were right about one thing when you warned me of that. Now, I should kill you where you stand."

Malotus removed the hair from his face, to look at her clearly. "I wish you had not taken my cynical lessons so seriously, Yulah. I was wrong, as the Meruyan says. I lived as a wounded shell all my life, letting in the pain," Malotus admitted. "Kill me if you must. The horrors I've committed as General—I don't deserve better."

Yulah snarled. "Indeed. It would do me great honor." She raised her weapon.

Meleena's jaw dropped. What had become of this soldier, this treacherous war General? It was ungraspable. Malotus and Yulah, two

Warix who had both had tried to kill her, standing before her, carrying on like children. "No!" she found herself interjecting.

They stared at her blankly. "Don't you see?" Meleena continued breathlessly. "Both of you are stuck in an entangled web. Yulah obviously loves you, Malotus. You are like a father to her, and she felt abandoned. I mean, you did well, leaving that horrible place and quitting your monstrous role there. It's good you left! And, I guess, went to go find yourself, sure. But Yulah, he loves you, you can't even see it because you're hurt. I think you just need to apologize to one another and make up. You are being very silly."

She had her hands on her hips and was surprised by how easy this felt to belt out. She'd done enough of this in her own life, trying to be alone, not needing friends, taking her frustration at not having any out on others. It was all just smoke and mirrors for the fact that she was lonely and wanted to be accepted.

"Telling yourself he's weak or that you don't care about Malotus is just a guise," she finished off her point aloud.

Yulah stared at Meleena, taken aback, then to Meleena's surprise, Malotus started to laugh, and their gazes turned to him.

"Ah, darling Yulah. I raised you like my daughter. Of course, she is right. And my poor manners. It would be better to prove it to you, to redeem myself, by returning the favor. You once saved this girl from my cruelty, when she trespassed with her friends in restricted Sen'Dorn's lands. Now you have brought her to this place against her will, for her meddling once again. If I let you kill me, I would deserve it by the very fact that I did nothing to protect her against you know. Better to fight you off, and bring her to safety. Perhaps it makes me less irredeemable."

He ended on a laugh, which echoed through the trees. Maybe he had lost his mind, but the logic that kept her alive was welcome.

"Go ahead and try to stop me," Yulah growled, coming at him now.

Malotus leapt upwards to counter her. They met in midair, wind whistling at their feet, creating a swirl of leaves beneath. Malotus's falcon dislodged from his back and came at Yulah from behind as his claws sank into her pole-arm and his knee came up, snapping it in two.

Yulah rolled over him in a tumble, landing on the ground behind him, two halves of her weapon still in hand. The falcon flew in a circle around them, and at a low whistle from Malotus, the bird dove, striking Yulah on the back of her head.

"Ouch, hey!" she protested, flinging the pole-arm halves at the falcon, who dodged and backed off. She ran again, gloved arms outstretched, to launch more wind at Malotus, who dodged sideways, then came at her with a sliding leg, tripping her off her feet. He lunged like a great beast, and pinned her down, pulling the gloves off her hands, where the falcon swiped them in his talons and carried them out far over the trees.

"You have been bested, child." Malotus spoke in a low growl. "Surrender, let us leave in peace."

Yulah's eyes twinkled, her face contorted into a wild rage. "Get off me! I'll keep fighting, if you lack the will to stop me!"

"Oh, Yulah. I am sorry for how you've turned out. I partly blame myself."

"Don't take so much credit, I've become myself without you." She struggled against him, angrier than before. Her ego was bruised.

Malotus put an arm to her throat, and she began to choke. "Yield, or you will pass out," he said simply.

She struggled, harder, then weaker, growling all the way. It was horrible to watch. Meleena almost for sorry for Yulah, yet feared the madness and cruelty that she had embraced. If she came out of here, she may really become Empress. That would certainly be worse for her people than the way things were now. Meleena had met Ryogrim. While he wasn't a sympathetic Emperor by any stretch, he was far mellower and had his priorities clear, and a far less convoluted sense of idealism than this.

Yulah struggled, weakening, and a tear hit her forehead, and Meleena realized Malotus was silently crying. A depth of emotion Meleena wouldn't have guessed him capable of.

He stood, flipping her around so her hands were bound. He could not kill her.

"Meleena," said Malotus, uttering her name for the first time. "There is a hunting knife strapped to my leg. Can you retrieve it, and remove her horns?"

Meleena gasped. She knew this task, the cutting of a Warix's horns, was an act of public disgrace not often done, and would also weaken their wind power. Their species sensed the wind through their horns and took some time to grow back.

Yulah's head was bowed in front of Malotus's broad chest, her neck limp, but she uttered ungraspable words. Her horns traced her head, in the feminine manner, partly hidden by her silken purple hair. They were not easy to get at, unlike Malotus's masculine, outward-growing horns.

Meleena found the knife and removed it from his leg sheath. It helped that Yulah was weakened, though she still had the wherewithal to move her head about, and Meleena had to hold her by the horns, to pull the knife blade under. They sliced slowly, with a painful grinding and gnawing action, like cutting a small tree; not so easily removed.

Yet when it was done, Yulah's precious wind powers were disarmed, and the horns lay on the ground beside the helpless Warix woman. She spat at them, sat there, staring with so much hate, but knowing she was beaten for now.

Malotus gave her one more look of shame and sorrow, then told Meleena to get on his back, and he plodded away a few strides before launching himself upward and over the trees, Grimley the falcon in toe.

She closed her eyes as the fierce tornado formed from the winds pulled to his sides.

"Why did you save me?" Meleena asked when they came to a landing. She felt he'd taken her only a safe distance away, yet when she looked around, she saw they were at the edge of the mountain platforms which would carry her down to Sen'Prin.

"You opened a path for salvation for me when I didn't know there was one," he responded. "I'm very grateful and indebted to you."

"Please, stay. Talk to Arenay. Maybe you could join the Sen'Prin and help defend against the cruelty of Sen'Drorn."

"My place is in the wilds now. But will think about it. You know where to find me." He gave a half-nod, his horn tilting crossways.

"Thank you for defending me against your niece. Now, and before, in the forest."

He nodded and blasted off with a mighty wind-step.

Meleena took a deep breath and stepped from the forest to reveal herself to the confused Sen'Prin gondola operators.

CHAPTER THIRTY-ONE

It had taken just over a week to recover from the physical injuries of having her horns removed, though the humiliation would stick with her a lot longer. Yulah had managed to crawl through the forest, without wind power, until she hiked it to a place where she could use her wrist-com to call her elites and have them pick her up, and the group returned to Sen'Drorn to lick their wounds.

She had spent the recuperating alone in her room, seething mad. The anger and need to push on was a better catalyst for prompting her decision to push forward with her bold takeover idea, to rescue what was left of her pride. When the week was out, her horns were functional, wind power returned.

A plan had crystallized.

Yulah rushed off down the halls of Sen'Drorn fortress to meet with Emperor Ryogrim.

"The Meruyan have driven us out and the resources are low," he said in his guttural tone.

Yulah shook her head. "We can work with this. Look at this mess! We need to come back and strike with full vengeance."

"You are the General now, Yulah. I suggest you go and you fix it on the ground. That is how Malotus handled things."

She growled. Fine. Maybe she could use a vacation from the capital to get some of her anger out.

She bowed to her emperor. "Much obliged, it will be done."

Despite her unpleasant feelings about Emperor Ryogrim, the NHV was a great place to blow off steam. She chuckled at her own clever pun.

It didn't take long for her to get an airship together with a crew of elites. She brought with her a wound coil of copper chains, a new piece of tech her disciple had been working on. She couldn't wait to use it.

She and her troops bore down on them, following the coordinates right to Iringbon's hiding place. They had beaten her people back? What was the big deal?

She came in there in a whirlwind of smoke and wind, igniting her new technology, unfurling the ropes and snapping the whip as she shifted her wind energy into the hand chamber and lit it aflame.

A fire whip—perfect. Her attacks were like a dance, jumping and dodging the Meruyan rebels with a whir of metallic fire. They stood no chance.

They pushed the Meruyan rebels back, their unauthorized Kelpies fleeing under bodies of water in fear, their riders either captured, burned, or otherwise surrendered.

It wasn't long before the Hyish trade markets were in sight, and the entire market set aflame.

Yulah's heart soared with the victory. This could not have gone better.

The Hyish fled back through the tunnel. They are cowards. They even agreed to help with the cave-in, which Yulah didn't need. She had her own explosives, which detonated and blocked the tunnel once and for all. No more Hyish would be trading with her Meruyan workforce.

The whole thing did give Yulah a great idea, however. The Hyish on the other side of the mountain would be kept happy. They would trade with Yulah and the Sen'Drorn now, and she and her men would trade Meruyan products to them. A middle-man operation was born, which would bring inflation and wealth for the Sen'Drorn. If the Hyish wanted their pearls, so be it. Now the Meruyan would have to work twice as hard, to get more work together. Pearls and other desirables from the sea.

Sure, there would be more protests, but she would be in this place like Malotus had been back in his early days as General. Had the Meruyan such short memories? Did they already forget about the burnt lands?

Well, she'd make her workforce live there now. Expanding the operation was in order. No more off-limits land. She'd have them plow the fields and reseed it. If things wouldn't grow, she'd set up another business there, or make the Meruyan live there, more growing land in the lush NHV proper.

Celebrating her victory, she decided to take a second residence in the former Meruyan Council villa. A country home to relax and watch over things here, outside of the busy Sen'Drorn City, and once she became Empress, nobody would question her.

She'd put the Meruyan on, changing it to her liking, soon.

***

Yulah strutted through the halls of Sen'Drorn Fortress, head high, spirits soaring after her victory in those disorderly Meruyan lands. She had called a war meeting with Ryogrim to discuss the latest progress. The Meruyan would trouble the Sen'Drorn no more for a while after that. But this was not the only point of this meeting.

I have what I need now, she thought. *There are enough advisors on my side. Now is the time to strike.*

Yulah spoke to her most trusted council beforehand: "I need to show them what true strength looks like, remove them from fear and doubt. I will gain all the pleasures and power, they will see what it takes to enjoy this world. To truly know love is to provide for the self entirely, all may be sacrificed for this natural and beautiful order."

This is what she truly believed. The world had shown this to her, through its treatment.

"What is this all about?" asked Ryogrim.

"I am here to propose a motion," said Yulah from her seat.

Yulah continued. "All those on the honorable council in favor of deposing our current emperor in favor of someone new. Stand up and vote." She motioned with her head and Ranfaf the Fifth stood up.

Ryogrim looked around, angry and aghast as the other advisors followed, until there was a majority.

"How—how dare you! I will have all of you beheaded!" the emperor bellowed.

"Sounds like we have a majority," said Yulah from her standing position.

The Emperor scoffed. "This is unheard of! Who could you even choose to replace me, you are all a bunch of spineless cowards!" He laughed in half disbelief.

"And now, I propose, a vote. Who would we like to select to replace the Emperor?" Yulah said, continuing to hold firm and lead the flow of the meeting. "How about someone who will head the spear and lead Sen'Drorn into better, prosperous times. Someone with a plan to take out the Sen'Prin once and for all."

Her trusted lacky spoke on her behalf, just as they had rehearsed. "The General for our next Empress!" called Ranfaf the Fifth.

"Hurrah! To Yulah! I second this!" called the advisor of Engineering Technology. He was followed by the advisor of City planning, and the advisor of Finances. Then advisor of Hyish relations.

One by one, her allies rose again, until they formed the majority, and the shocked advisors out of the inner circle fell cowardly into place, mouths agape and eyes wide. They did just what Yulah had anticipated. Ryogrim had called it correctly, they were a bunch of spineless cowards. But if you swayed enough of them to your side, that was a very good thing indeed. They were all clay in her hands.

"This...this is treason!" Ryogrim shouted in rebuttal.

"It sounds as though they have come to a decision. They want Yulah for Empress," Yulah said, her heart pounding in her chest as the moment she had planned, scraped, and calculated for had actually just occurred. It felt like a dream, almost unreal. "If you won't go peacefully, which I know you will not... We have ways."

Ryogrim shot her the foulest look she'd ever seen. His face wrinkled up, teeth bared, beady silver eyes fiery with scorn.

"Guards!" Yulah shouted, looking directly at him.

Boots pounded the stone pavement and the guards quickly surrounded Ryogrim with their neck chockers held at the ready. He tried to struggle but they grappled him into a bowed position at the foot of the throne, and all the advisors watched in silence as they began to drag him away. He was in such flabbergasted shock, not enough even to shout.

It was as if they all held their breath. The only sound, the heavy footsteps of the guards and labored breathing of the emperor. The large chamber doors creaked closed, so loud in the otherwise silent room. There was a pause.

And then Yulah ascended the throne. Her heart welled up with self-love. She had been right. The other councilmembers were as selfish as her, and together they had done what needed to be done.

The strong, the wonderful, the powerful, had become in charge. She had done what even Malotus had never done.

Her heart bent, buckled, momentarily, for the pain. Loss of her uncle.

The weakness of it, feh! she thought.

She brushed the thought of him aside. Now it was her time. She stood and took a bow, her gossamer hair flowing, long and luxuriously. They cheered, worshiped her. She deserved it.

Her very flesh glowed from within as she took full love of herself. Finally. It felt good.

"My first order of business...." she said smiling at her loyal council. "Cut off the emperor's, I mean Ryogrim's, horns, and drag him to his new home in the prison cell. After this, I will tell you all a lovely story.

Then, you will show me to my new chambers in the highest towers of the fortress."

Ah, it's good to be the empress. All is right with the world. It's not so unfair after all. Only those who believe in themselves can be strong and take what they want. They must simply know what they want and go after it.

The panel leaned in for her attention. How they could wipe away the Sen'Prin once and for all. What technology had she been working on all this time, which granted such power, with limited manpower?

"I happen to know they are weak right now," she said. "And we have our chance to launch a strike directly upon them."

She put her feet up on the throne, leaning sideways and drinking deeply from a fresh, hot mug of spiced drink. In her fingers, she held a gold coin, with the head of Ryogrim staring back at her. Her fingers closed over it, pointed claws sharp over his smothered face.

She'd have to have new coins created with her face on them. Emperor Ryogrim would never be in charge around here again.

CHAPTER THIRTY-TWO

Meleena was almost pummeled over as she was met with hugs and cries of relief from the others and warm welcomes.

"Were so glad you are safe!" Naia called out.

"How did you make it out?" asked Thian.

"How did you get here? Really! Upala is safe, she found us..." explained a worried Kyra.

"How is everyone?" Meleena asked, gawking at the group. Zoltan's hair was a mess, many of their faces, shoulders, and elbows were full of dirt and scratches.

"We managed to find each other in different areas along the bottom of the gorge! There were some minor injuries, but somehow, we all made it back up safely," said Jessup. "We were so worried about you."

"We thought you were lost," huffed Zoltan.

"Yeah, we won't take you for granted ever again. It's real good to see you, squirt," said Riigs.

"I..." Meleena stuttered. "I guess this is a surprise."

Meleena was overwhelmed and joyful at the shock of it. She didn't realize the others cared about her much at all, in fact. They were a friendly enough bunch, but always kept at arm's length.

They hugged her in turns, Riigs patted her floating blue hair, and Upala came bounding up to her and she was on the ground in a heap rolling about.

They threw her a little party, with Meleena's favorite Warix foods.

"I think we all could use a break after this," announced Kyra, stuffed with sugar almond cookies. "Everyone is safe and the mission was, overall, successful. We don't know who's behind it, but we have the machine now. We just need to piece together what clues we have. I'll take the gunk and supplies to the tech lab, and all that. The rest of you can have a day to yourselves."

Meleena was just looking forward to a nice bath and a warm bed, but this was so much better.

***

The group was down by the river, swimming, playing ball, and lounging by the banks. Meleena had been looking forward to a day like this, especially after everything she'd been through with the others.

The pools were sparkling with emerald-green flora. As promised, huge red, yellow, and orange flowers, elongated, trumpet, multi-flopping spines, blossomed from the jutting forest undergrowth.

She took in the smell, fragrant and fruity, alive. Nectar sprigs buzzed about, drinking from the large flowers, disappearing into their depths, and emerging happily tooting. A perfect way to spend a day off. She shoved the idea of Malotus out of her head. How strange was that? Seeing him come by and save her, actually save her life! It was heroic, even if Yulah hadn't come around. Who would have thunk it... Malotus of all Warix. If this was possible, maybe there was good in everyone.

Then again, it was likely her that caused the gondola destruction in the first place and therefore all of it was on her. She and whoever she was working with...someone on the inside among them, which, was still gnawing away at her.

She was a bit miffed that, interestingly enough, Flax had not joined them. He had stayed at the lab and was helping with sample analysis. Funny how things go wrong like that. He can't be here, and yet we don't still know much...Meleena couldn't help herself. Her thoughts were crowding out the happiness. There was something that didn't add up.

Was Flax still contacting Yulah? She didn't know…but Yulah was certainly behind everything, personal and otherwise. And a lot of them getting away happened when Flax wasn't around. Maybe Flax wasn't at the lab when they went to the stakeout? Maybe he was out in the forest, doing her bidding…maybe he led her to them…how else would they know where they are?

Meleena sat up suddenly, the water dripping from her hair.

This was startling, if it were true…? But things just kept adding up. They never figured out where the automata had come from. Maybe this was by design?

Maybe Flax was sabotaging the results. That and using her technology to blow up Sen'Prin! Was Borak also in on it? A shiver of upset hit her at the very notion of suspecting them. But what else could it be, there was no choice. As much as she hated to, she would have to speak up about it soon, it really had become dangerous not to at this point. If nothing else, her suspicions had to be investigated. Yes, she would find Kyra and tell her, privately. Yes, that'd be a good plan.

A voice suddenly spoke from behind her, making her jump from the pool of water.

"Sorry to bother you like this," Kyra said in her usual matter-of-fact tone.

"Kyra! Oh I wasn't expecting you. Err, I have to talk to you about something actually." Then, seeing her concerned face, changed her tone. "What is it?"

"Again, I am sorry after promising you a day off, but Arenay requests our presence at headquarters. There is an issue of security."

Meleena gulped. What could this be about? Did they already suspect Flax? Did they think she was in on it perhaps? Her skin tingled with fear, all the way down to the tips of her extended arm fits. Her own ideas about this would have to wait.

She got out of the water and climbed to the sand, where Upala was napping, wings and tail blending into a lovely swoosh, while others were on the sand, lounging and reading, the boys had stopped playing with their ball and were getting ready, turning to smile and greet her.

Meleena felt a warm new sense of kinship towards her team. She put her things together and got dressed, hitched up her boots.

They returned together to headquarters, where Arenay met them on the ramparts. She looked nervous and shook her head, simply pointing at the crowds forming below.

"Time has run out! You must give us the perpetrator!" shouted the Hyish from below. There were crowds of them forming, tails swishing viscously from side to side, clawed hands at the ready for attack. Some sharpened weapons, spears, and slingshots to toss flaming pellets.

"What can we do?" asked Kyra, as one ripped through the air and passed her ear.

"Please, we need more time, we have almost found the culprit," Arenay shouted down below.

"You ignore us for too long. You never intended to give us what we ask!"

A storm of hissing from below.

They pushed each other until things were getting out of hand to the point of riot.

"We cannot meet your demands so soon."

The Hyish collective continued to push, more and more appearing from the wilderness, crowding the space, until many were up against the rampart walls, and they started to climb, but slid down again. Their claws were too thick for the spaces between the stones.

"We have to do something. I don't they are going to start a war here," Arenay confessed. "We must keep them out, but not in a way that harms them. It will look very bad." Her wristcom buzzed and as she looked down at it, her face turned to horror.

"It can't be..." she murmured, cheeks ghost white.

"What is it?" asked Kyra as the group stared.

"Our friends at the Meruyan council have informed us that Yulah has announced herself as the new Empress of Sen'Drorn. I can hardly believe it. Ryogrim has been deposed and is in the dungeons."

Meleena stared at her. This was a worst-case scenario and spelled disaster for them all. "How did she do it?" she asked, thinking it may have to do with all the technology she'd utilized as General. And yet, Ryogrim would never give up his position willingly, no matter how good she was.

"She must have gotten enough of the higher-ups in Sen'Drorn to turn against Ryogrim, somehow," Arenay said, knitting her brow. "But, one thing is certain, she is behind the explosions of our cities, and this is very dangerous for us."

Her wristcom buzzed again.

"Oh, no. It gets worse. Councilman Ives said she has reclaimed the Northern Hilly Villages and sewn destruction there. The Hyish have been banished, the tunnels closed, many Hyish and Meruyan there are dead."

The hissing from the Hyish below the fortress ramparts grew louder. Meleena looked over the wall to see flaming pellets were hitting the walls and creating small craters for the Hyish to start gaining foot-holds and climbing, ever higher.

"Uh, everyone…this isn't good." She indicated to it. "Someone in our very walls is responsible for killing the Hyish for their fire glands, to work on technology. And they are sharing it with Yulah! What are we waiting for?"

"Yeah! Enough talk! It's time to start cracking skulls in the tech lab, this much is certain!" said Naia, and Riigs nodded in agreement.

Zoltan and Thian agreed as well, and the whole group joined in, to follow Meleena as she set off into headquarters towards the tech lab.

She would find Flax and Borak and confront them. Her heart was pounding. It was all she could do. How did Flax know about this thing? She started to think she was right to suspect him.

Meleena burst into the tech lab, followed by the other team members. They had to reveal the guilty party and apprehend them now. Perhaps it would stop the Hyish's impending assault if they could throw someone down there.

Meleena's cheeks were burning hot, as she shouted, "Flax! It was you, wasn't it?"

His face went blank, a look of shock.

"Ah, don't pretend! You have been acting strange since I got here. Sneaking off, on the wristcom. I heard who you were calling! It was Yulah! She is a high up in the Sen'Drorn and…"

"Meleena!" Borak cried. "How you say that after all he's done for you?"

He looked crushed.

"I heard him on the wristcom, with Yulah!"

"It's true…" stuttered Flax. They stared at him. "I mean I'm not the rat!" his arms shot up as they closed in. "I have been calling Yulah…I can't believe you saw that." His cheeks flushed and he looked to the floor.

"Flax, how could you!" Meleena was desperate. After he'd been so nice to her, and now this!

Borak looked from one to the other. His eyes were wide but seeking to say something. "I'm sure it's something reasonable…"

Meleena wasn't so sure he wasn't in on it as well. Of course, he'd defend Flax. Maybe they'd worked out all kinds of deals. Her head was swimming.

"I can explain myself…it was nothing more than personal. I was trying to make amends, to apologize for being such a jerk and double-crossing her. I wanted to make her understand why I did it, but not enough to become a traitor. I felt she deserved that much, my explanation and…I don't know, maybe to understand I had real feelings for her, wasn't using her. Maybe even a part of me thought I could convince her to leave Sen'Drorn."

They stared, baffled.

"Of course, she wouldn't listen."

Meleena's mouth dropped open.

The others in the team shook their heads, looking disappointed at her.

"*Meleena* just has a thing for him, this is personal for *her.*"

"Just go back to your Meruyan village."

"Yeah, there's no place for her here."

"Only a traitor would even assume it was Flax."

"Leading us in circles."

"What did we even listen to her for? Why is she even here?"

How quickly their true colors came out. So, this was what they all truly thought of her. Her worst fears were coming true. She had suspected they weren't really her friends, speaking behind her back about their disapproval, how she didn't fit in. Now she knew it plainly.

Meleena flushed with heat. She took a deep breath to avoid the swelling tears. She removed her glasses. She was about to start running from the room when something caught her arm.

It was Borak.

She looked up at him, pleading, desperate. "Just let me go, alright!" she cried.

"Everybody, just hang on a second!" Borak roared to the group.

Meleena couldn't bear to look into his eyes.

They stood round in the lab, staring from one to the other.

"Was it you, Flax? Or was Borak also involved?" questioned Meleena, demanding to know. She held out the papers, which she had taken from Flax's room, proving they had known of the technology for some time.

The group closed in on them, looking for who to tie up.

Borak shouted, "WAIT, everyone! Meleena! Hear me out. I know what happened. Yes, Flax and I have had the ideas for some time. But we are not traitors. It is Yulah, in Sen'Drorn, we know that. And yes, Flax has a relationship with her."

They nodded in agreement, getting angrier.

"...But he's just been a silly fool in love. It's Phineas who's been leaking information and tech within these walls. Yulah and Phineas have been passing information, working together."

"Oh, pish-posh."

"It must be. While I was in the Sen'Drorn work prison," Borak explained. "It was me...I had told Phineas about the Hyish fire gland idea. We were just prisoners working on engineering, I thought I could trust him. I thought I wouldn't ever get out of there."

"Ach," Phineas waved it off. "No, that's silly. It wasn't me."

"Yes, even I must admit that also the clues fit," said Borak pensively. "You were there with us on the days in the lab, back when we discussed the fire lizard's theory. It can imagine you overheard us."

"Also, someone has taken pages from my journal, and then the whole thing went missing. Someone here has been getting ideas from my work," said Meleena.

"I don't need this," said Phineas.

"And the gunk, it's a byproduct of the fusion process."

Phineas' eyes twinkled. He swiftly picked up his gear, backpack, and mechanized vest. "I'll do it here," he said suddenly. "Nobody takes a step or I'll engulf this whole room in flame, with all of you in it!"

Shock through the group. They stood tense.

Phineas backed up and turned the dials on his front vest, his eyes clouding with wind energy usage. Thunderstorms cracked overhead. Instruments shook and fell off the table as beakers hit the ground with a smash.

He aimed his weaponized glove with the flamethrower trigger embedded in the palm at the group and moved with his back to the doorway, preventing escape, and strapping on Meleena's jetpack, which had been left there, possibly for days. She was surprised anyone would make use of it. It was clunky on her but suited him perfectly. It fit snugly atop his devices, long lanky limbs dangling.

"For my experiments in service of Sen'Drorn, I was banished from their laboratory, left to be experimented on in their dungeons—by my own brother, the head of the department! But Yulah has been kind to me! She saw my potential that day when you freed me from the fortress." He grinned at Meleena and Flax. "Even as I took Yulah hostage, she saw it. She felt the raw power of what I had created. The ability to manipulate the energy in the air beyond simple copper interaction. Thanks to Flax and Borak's novel idea, which they were too weak to execute—of adding fire glands from certain creatures, genius! I extrapolated the idea to include the Hyish, whose fire glands were much larger and better developed. It was worth it, to kill a few of them for, THIS. You will see its wonderful firepower soon."

He turned to Meleena. "But indeed, you are welcome for the help on this jetpack. It wasn't just Borak, I created the internal technology." He grinned. "It uses the fire-lizard tech as well."

He bowed low, the interwoven, wired bulk of the jetpack on his back visible.

"Yes, girl, I'm not all bad. That's the point! Great tech is simply that, progress for us all!"

"But your pulling water from the clouds and creation of the gunk has disrupted the whole system of wildlife, the whole balance of our land! And I never saw such gunk come out of the jetpack!"

Phineas laughed brazenly, like crackling fire coming to life. He shifted his shoulder and brought the jetpack around. One hand went to a side compartment. He kept one hand on the trigger of the flamethrower. Meleena felt sick to her stomach.

"You see this? Who do you think cleaned out the tank after you left every day?"

He pulled on the side compartment, and it opened, copious amounts of the gray fluid spilled onto the floor.

Meleena had never messed with the mechanics of it before. They had to start it after all, and she didn't want to touch or break it.

"Now if you'll excuse me, my mistress Yulah and I have big plans today."

CHAPTER THIRTY-THREE

Phineas ran from the lab, with long strides, jetpack clanking on his back. Meleena and the gang didn't hesitate, giving chase and bolting out the door after him towards the terrace, not letting him get away now that his back was turned.

Once they reached the ramparts, they ran into Arenay and her top advisors, looking concerned, peering over at the Hyish mobilizing below and discussing plans of action that didn't involve direct retaliation. Arenay was still trying to negotiate at this stage.

"Arenay, look out!" shouted Kyra, as Phineas dashed onto the terrace. Arenay turned just in time, but Phineas didn't strike, instead, running and pitching himself, to all their shock, off the ramparts.

The group followed to the edge to catch up with the situation. Nervously, they all peered over the ramparts to see where Phineas had gone, but it wasn't necessary. He rose and faced them using the thrust of the jetpack to hold him up, leaving his arms free to use the device in his copper-gloved hands.

"I've been working on this baby a long time!" he announced, projecting his voice loudly to the attention of the crowd. "It's my special toy!"

Arenay and her guards shot wind at him, trying to throw him off balance, but he shifted and dodged it, using one hand to redirect the energy around him and stabilize.

His other hand went to the dial on his arm, shifting its gears. As the next wind burst came at him, a torrent of icy wind exploded out of the nozzle of his hand. The group was knocked back in the torrent. Meleena ducked and shielded her eyes to protect her glasses, staying low as many were knocked off their feet.

More icy wind blasted at them. Icy shards shattered the windows of headquarters behind them with an earsplitting blast. Ice and glass flew in all directions, as Phineas cackled, entertained by his power over them all. It was hard to tell what was what, as the air between them sparkled with grim beauty.

He'd been there, at their side, kind, helpful, unassuming, for months now. Secretly he'd been sneaking out in his off-time to blow up the villages of those who so kindly took him in, just for a little glory and power, and above all else, revenge.

Now he'd won, hiding amongst them and making a clean escape.

Meleena seethed with anger amidst the fear of the moment, as she kept low, failing to see much of what was going on. There was another explosive sound. He must have changed settings as a blinding white light flooded and Meleena shut her eyes tighter through it all.

The stone floor tremored and a horrible crack and rumble made her instinctively look around. It smelled of burning. The rampart wall was cracking. It had been hit by concentrating lightning and a chunk was broken off and sinking.

"Look out!" Arenay cried as the others yelled and shouted, dispersing in all directions to avoid falling with the rubble.

The Hyish used this as a grim opportunity to finish their ascent.

Meleena started to slip as she rushed away on a slippery sinking stone. Naia, held up by Riigs, pulled her up as a chain.

"We'll pursue him as best we can, but go check on Flax, he and Borak are back in the lab! They went looking for gear to counter him with!"

Meleena ran back, to find things much worse than she thought possible. The room lie in ruins, glass shattered and tables turned over.

“Oh, thanks for coming back,” gasped Flax. Borak was been injured badly by glass and lay bleeding in his arms. “He needs medical attention.”

“Flax, we need to find an airship out of here, now!” Meleena implored. She realized she had not seen Upala in quite some time, and would not be able to say goodbye to her, or possibly see her again. She wondered where she was, and hoped she was safe.

“I’ll be alright,” said Borak, holding his bloody chest. “I’ll take the internal route down to Odella’s house. I should be safe to hide out there.”

Meleena and Flax helped hoist him up and bring him to the tube system, where he insisted they take an airship to flee the city. His eyes were so wide, concerned. “I’ve done enough runin’ in my life. I know where I have to be,” he said, coughing up blood and wiping it away with his forearm. “I can’t leave Odella alone in this city.”

Flax and Meleena, hoping for the best, reluctantly parted ways with him.

Back on the ramparts, the Hyish were running amok and hand-to-hand combat had ensued. They slashed Zoltan in the face, creating a scar over his eye, and he screamed in rage and blasted three of them back. Riigs grabbed a broken pillar and tossed it at them, and the group got together, forming a wind energy surge that knocked several back off the ramparts to the forest floor below. They returned, replaced immediately by the next wave, bolts of fire from their breath scorching like fire rain.

Flax and Meleena urged the others to flee. It was hopeless. The wind of the Warix attacks only entangled with the Hyish fire, and created explosions that further hurt and destroyed the structures, dealing heavy blowback which injured the Warix much more than the Hyish, whose scales made them immune to their own fire, no matter how much wind storm sent it flying. Phineas stayed involved, flying safely out of the way overhead, using lightning bolts to blast open areas to aid the Hyish in their destruction of headquarters.

The Warix were forced to retreat and many got on their knees, taken prisoner.

No wonder the Warix feared the Hyish and avoided war with them at all cost, thought Meleena as she and Flax ran for dear life. There was no winning. Tricking the Hyish into a conflict against his own enemies was brilliant, though, she had to admit. Yulah and Phineas, whoever had come up with that plan, were a deadly team. They were the first ever to solve the stalemate and penetrate Sen'Prin's mountain fortress city, in the name of Sen'Drorn.

Flax and Meleena ran back through the corridors of the inner headquarters, trying to dodge Hyish while looking to hijack an airship small enough to be operated by only two people. Meleena would have to handle the rudders, and Flax all the wind, but it still would be better than trying to carry her out. Arenay and Zoltan came from another corridor, looking disheveled, their hair partly singed off by fire. One of Zoltan's horns had cracked off, limiting his ability to use wind power.

As the four of them rose in a small airship together, Hyish chased and piled on to stop them, and they air-kicked them off with their boots one by one until they could obtain liftoff. Everyone was panting as they slowly rose.

"Nooo!" Zoltan cried, as one Hyish grabbed him by the leg and he slid from the side.

Now they were three.

From the air, they looked down at the ruins of the city, the tree cover of Sen'Prin had started to burn. Those marauders worked fast.

"The city is lost," said Arenay in a state of humbled shock. "We need to stay calm and figure out what to do now."

Flax and Meleena looked at one another, tears welling up in her at the very sight of him. How could she have accused him earlier? Ruined things between them, and in the face so much bigger threats.

Things would be uncertain now, moving forward. And they were alone with Arenay, with no place to go. The unthinkable had happened.

Empress Yulah had dominated them all.

She shook from the fear of the fate of the rest of them who had not made it out. Naia, Riigs, Zoltan, Kyra, Thian. Were they alive? The best they could hope for is that they had allowed themselves to be captured by Hyish. But who knew what that meant.

"And the other citizens of Sen'Prin?" Meleena expressed aloud to the *former* leader of these people. "They are at war and in the hands of the Hyish and Sen'Drorn now, without warning."

Arenay bit down firmly on her jaw, eyes glaring outward as she fought back tears. "I sent as many soldiers as possible, to each level to warn and evacuate the citizens. We have a protocol. In case this day ever arrived." She choked up.

Meleena put a hand to her mouth. The Sen'Prin had been at war with Sen'Drorn since their foundation. They had started as rebels who had escaped and founded this place.

"Does this mean the end of Sen'Prin nation?"

"We have sheltered locations in the mountains. It will be like when we were new," said Arenay with a troubled deep breath. "I don't think many recall those days, but they will have to lead. I am only sorry I am not with my people. There was such a rush."

"Where can we even go now?" Meleena asked. "Is anywhere safe? Dlawn'Edo?"

"There's no way Arenay can show up there. She would be immediately turned over to Sen'Drorn and executed," Flax said bitterly.

"Excuse me, but why are you here with us, escaping in an airship, to begin with?" asked Meleena, dawning on her. "I know you rushed away like the rest of us, but why not just go back? Flax and I can join you."

She didn't recognize which direction they were going, all turned around. They could have been going in circles for all she knew.

"We are going to find Malotus," Arenay stated flatly, to the utter shock of Meleena and Flax, who turned, gaping at her.

Arenay and Malotus were, of course, sworn enemies.

It was worse than their affiliations against one another in their careers. Their feud was personal and went back to their days together in the military, enforcing the NHV Meruyan workforce, well before the formation of the Sen'Prin nation.

"Why are we looking for Malotus?" asked Meleena, baffled.

"He's the only one who can fix this. I have not forgotten about Nushen'yu's mother seed, our former legendary weapon, which she said grew from the Navanax beast. If he has been living in the wild this long, I believe he has been looking for it, or else knows by now better than any of us where to find it," said Arenay, looking at the expansive wilderness below them.

Meleena agreed, and Flax looked at both of them, baffled. "Well, he's saved my life out there twice now," assured Meleena. "And he's become very close with the spirit of the forest, if ever there was such a thing."

"I believe there is, and he knows a lot more than the rest of us," said Arenay wistfully.

"How could you possibly know that, or where to find him?" asked Flax, still skeptical.

Arenay let out a sad sigh. "I've been having visions of him in the wilderness, flashes of light. They started as vivid dreams, but have been clouding my days lately. We are connected, him and I, somehow. I know it sounds strange, but feel it like a pull from the wind spirit Nushen'yu herself, calling me to find him. The blood in my veins, like a magnet, shows me the way. Now, are you with me?"

Meleena gaped, wide-eyed. It was not at all the answer she'd been expecting.

Flax put his hands to his eyes, let out a sigh, then shrugged. "I'm here, so I'll along for the ride, though I still don't like Malotus, or forgive him for what he's done."

"That's good enough for me," said Arenay, leaning in and turning the rudders of the airship around in a sweeping motion. Meleena and Flax held on tight.

Teaser:

Sen'Prin City lay in fiery ruins.

Meleena, Flax, and Arenay had barely escaped and now sailed on an airship deep into the eastern wilderness.

Her heart heavy, burning with longing to go back and find the others they had left behind. Yet she knew there was nothing the three of them could do. Their plan was to find Malotus, who may be the only one with the knowledge that could restore things to less-than-chaos.

If he knew the location, as Arenay surmised, of the origin of the Nushen'yu wind goddess seed. If there were more.

So much doubt circled inside Meleena. It seemed there was no way out of this. Helplessness, like fire in her veins, rose at the loss of Sen'Prin, as well as Yulah's rise to Empress of Sen'Drorn.

If we gave up and went back to Meruyan lands, it would be a pointless existence. Being in the seat of this conflict gave her life some meaning. Plus, she didn't really have a choice as they were already heading deep into the wilderness east of all known civilization, Meruyan and Warix alike.

As they flew over the treetops, it seemed the world had lost its brilliance and color. Somehow, everything appeared dull, flat, unappealing.

From what Meleena knew, generations of strife and minor conflicts had prevented the Warix from expanding. Their population stayed small, sustainable on its own, in harmony with nature. But what about the rest of the planet? What was on the other side? Were there more continents, perhaps containing unknown humanoid races, with different problems? Or was it empty of people and simply wild places full of strange ecosystems and creatures?

The wind blew through her blue woven hair. "Where are you steering us to, exactly?" Meleena inquired, noting how much land they covered. While she sat, pondering, helpless without wind powers to guide the airship, Arenay and Flax discussed where Malotus could be hiding.

GLOSSARY

RACES

Meruyan (People). humanoid race, originally creations of earth spirit, blessed by water spirit to become an aquatic people who can breathe underwater with rib gills. Live underwater and by the seashore. Their photosynthetic hair gathers energy from the sun and floats in air. Various shades of greens and blues for hair and skin. When they get wet, fins spawn from their forearms and legs. Those living underwater for very long acquire tube worms, barnacles, mollusks on their bodies, as well as webbed extremities and shoulder spines.

Meruyan Council: ruling members of the united Meruyan governance, headquartered in the Meruyan capital city.

Meruyan Nation Flag: blue-green wave, merging of land and sea.

Meruyan Council Historian: A village local representative, appointed by the Meruyan Council to document and report on notable happenings.

Warix (People): humanoid race, originally creations of earth spirit, blessed by wind spirit. Can manipulate the wind, and use it as a basis for their technology (*see wind-tech*). They have horns to sense the wind, and if cut, disables their abilities for up to a week until regrowth. Eyes, hair and skin colors resemble a fall forest, with shades of brown, bronze, reds, yellows, and shades of purples, white and black. A curious people, they often explore in search of better resource opportunities, and seek to dominate others they meet. The Warix people are currently split into two antagonistic nations (see Sen'Drorn and Sen'Prin).

Sen'Drorn (Warix Nation): larger, older/established Warix nation, exploits Meruyan for resources and dominates overall. Flag: flower-mane lion. Represents power. Led by former-war hero Emperor Ry-ogrim.

Sen'Drorn Emperor: the ruling power of the stronger Warix nation. Elected by the elite council, chosen for battle prowess, he decides on expansion plans with the aim of bringing prosperity and a high standard of living to the people of his nation.

Sen'Drorn Flag: depicts the flower-mane lion, strong and fierce, and represents power.

Elder-Advisors: the elite few who decide on the policies of the Sen'Drorn nation.

Sen'Prin (Warix Nation): smaller nation of Warix, split-off from the first, who fight for better Meruyan rights.

Sen'Prin Flag: depicts the Nectar sprig pollinating the resting flower-maned lion. Represents compassion as a balance of power.

Sen'Prin Governess: leads the small nation and its defensive military and spy network; current governess Arenay is also the first.

Hyish (People): humanoid race, originally creations of earth spirit, blessed by fire spirit. Reptilian, most numerous, live everywhere in tribal villages. Glass-blowing experts due to their spit-fire and resistant scales. Said to be unconquerable, due to their fighting spirit and ability to come together in large numbers. Loyal to other Hyish above others; also love shiny riches.

May'Fee clan: prominent Hyish clan, wealthy nomads on the pulse of inter-group politics. Their flag is a black and white serpent skull. (*see Hyish nomads*)

SIGNIFICANT EVENTS

Great Split, The: infamous event where a rebellious third of the Warix people left the Sen'Drorn Nation and split off to form the Sen'Prin Nation, triggering the current political instability. Eighteen years ago from present.

Journey of Future Leaders: a journey undertaken by the top few students chosen for the coveted Council apprenticeship, to learn more of their world and prove themselves worthy to join the governance in the top tier of society.

Light of the Meruyans Festival: event celebrating the start of summer and the end of study for young Meruyans coming of age; on this night, Councilmembers assign apprenticeships to determine their future vocations.

SPIRITS

Earth Spirit: unnamed fabled spirit, original creator of all the humanoid creatures.

Fire Spirit: unnamed fabled spirit who endowed the Hyish with their spit-fire ability and fire-resistant scales.

Noyade (Water Spirit): fabled water spirit, worshiped by the Meruyan, who Blessed them with water breathing, fins, to make them aquatic humanoids.

Nushenyu (Wind Spirit): fabled wind spirit who bestowed the Warix with their wind abilities, and in turn worshipped as a Warix goddess.

NOTABLE LOCATIONS

Arctic City: northern city inhabited by Meruyan and Warix.

Dlawn'Edo: capital city of Meruyan, in a forested mountain waterfall basin, protected from Warix attack. Historically was a monastery.

Fleeg Street: commercial center of Sen'Drorn city. Where Flax lives, working for Borak's engineering shop.

Gebuk'Desa: one of the northern hilly villages on Warix land, where Meruyan live and work.

Jade Desert: location for Hyish trading post where the Jade Hyish Clan dwells; Where Sen'Prin spies, Flax and Thian, are seen looking for the lost pendant.

Northern Meruyan Villages: Meruyan villages under Warix-dominion, more inland, tropical climate for best year-round crop growing (see Gebuk'Desa).

Pontai'Desa: one of the southern Meruyan villages, where our hero hails from.

Sen'Drorn City: largest city of the Sen'Drorn Warix. Built on a steep cliff, full of winding angles, with buildings of volcanic rock, designed to get around with wind energy. The fortress at the top is headquarters for the Emperor and his ruling elites.

Sen'Prin City: the city of the Sen'Prin Warix nation, established when the people fled. Built inside a steep forested gorge, on a series of bamboo bridges, it provides the natural protection from invasion that allows their survival.

Southern Meruyan Villages: Meruyan-sovereign land village in the southern bay, by the shore and undersea. (see Pontai'Desa).

Underwater City, The: last remaining large Meruyan underwater civilization.

Vendengire: a Warix town not far from Sen'Drorn, which was secretly taken as a Sen'Prin outpost.

OBJECTS

Blue root tea: common breakfast tea, native to the southern Meruyan territory with a Sweet-tangy pungent smell. Sentimental to Meleena's childhood.

Bronze (tech): secondary valuable metal alloy, used as a cheaper catalyst for wind energy, but less efficient than copper.

Copper (tech): valuable metal, sought after and mined by Warix due to its catalytic properties, enhancing wind-energy and serving as a basis for their technology. (see wind-tech).

Kelpweave: clothing material worn by Meruyan, allowing for easy transition between land and sea. Harvested by special fine-bred kelp, farmed underwater. In contrast, Warix wear leather and plant-based fibers. Meruyan wear Warix clothing only when living on their land, therefore can't easily go underwater, thus living unnaturally.

Wind Goddess Pendant: a legendary, ancient, carved pendant shaped like a ram's head, said to contain the trapped spirit of wind. The Warix nations seek it out, hoping she will help end their stalemate and fight for their side.

Wristcom: Warix tech, wind-up gadget that clasps to the wrist and uses radio waves to communicate afar. Standard in the military and council in all nations, otherwise not as common among civilians. Very few Meruyan own one; only top government Meruyan council-members.

Wind (Tech): tech based on copper as a catalyst, where wind is blown through small tubes to enhance its effect on the other side. Energy can be stored inside motors to generate electricity, powering lights and gadgets. The highest quality power comes from more intricate surface areas created, such as copper bent into spirals, therefore the most skilled engineers are masters of crafting delicate artistry.

PLANTS/ANIMALS

Algae-fur creatures: Any animal, often native in the forests, that has algae fur, which allows for nutrient-gain via photosynthesis.

Algae-maned Falcon: Like many creatures in this world, animal that has algae fur, which allows for nutrient-gain via photosynthesis. (Like Meruyan's hair). This falcon is used by Malotus as a loyal, intelligent pet.

Bulbub tree: tall forest trees with sheet-like (willowy) vines, night-glowing bark, and edible roots.

Bramble Sheep: docile, domesticated land creature farmed for the berries growing from its back, fibrous spiny outer fur, and meat.

Flower-maned lion: large land predator. Among Warix, symbolic of power. (See Sen'Drorn Flag).

Gommwood: a grazing creature that looks like an orchard of dead, leafless trees when gathering to graze in large, open spaces. Dangerous: loud sounds scare them into stampeding, earning them the name "quiet forest" and inspiring legends of missing people.

Kelpie: water-horse, hostile except to Meruyan, who share a bond and have domesticated them for riding and carrying loads. They bite Warix and won't permit them to ride, which is why the Warix banned them in the northern villages.

Muul'dre: harmless forest herbivore, thin legs, with scales that glisten to alarm if in danger.

Neutolyth: Giant, shelled semi-aquatic, tentacled beast of burden used in Meruyan farming.

Netic: cactus-lizard creature domesticated by the Hyish. The creature retracts its full body spikes only for a Hyish rider, due to their shared reptilian bond.

Nectar sprig: small flying pollinator of plants, nectar drinking griffon. Symbolic among Warix of altruism and collaboration. (see Sen'Prin Flags).

Pon-Urchin: giant sea urchins adapted to living on land, farmed by Meruyan for meat and carapace.

Rock Lobster: breed of lobster that never stops growing, said to live for hundreds of years. Said to make good companion animals for Meruyan, due to their strength and loyalty.

Vangrot: small, climbing, chattering creatures, dangerous for often stealing food. Live in a broad range of locations.

PHRASES:

Hyish Language:

Ahnn'yaeh: "get lost"

Arash'sha: "excuse me"

Desh'Ja: "we are"

Desh'Ju: "you are"

Desh'Ju Warix?: "Are you a Warix?"

H'th'ka'Ja: "thank you," literally: "we are gracious"

Na ga sshhek: "it is over there"

Ne Mayfee na lang?: "where is Mayfee's tent?"

Rash'Ju Warix?: "Do you understand Warix?"

Sssuhan: "Dirty liar"

Sssuh'Ju nels: "You cheated him"

Uhn, ghha: "yes, okay"

"Warm sands welcome": Hyish greeting, in the Warix language.

MERUYAN EXPRESSIONS

Meruyan Language: original language of Meruyan, used underwater and composed of clicks.

"Do fish have fins": Meruyan expression to relay obviousness.

"Fish-kisser!": Meruyan expression for one who overly flatters or humors someone for personal gain.

"Inhale the ocean": Meruyan expression for taking on too much to an impossible extent.

"Nushenyu's blessings!": Warix greeting or exclamation.

"Oyster-brain": Meruyan expression for calling someone stupid.

"Oysters!": Meruyan exclamation of surprise, shock, or dismay.

"Praise the waves": Meruyan expression for happiness, good fortune, or relief.

"The turnip calls the carrot dirty": Meruyan expression for hypocrite.

WARIX

"Storm and thunder!": Warix expression of disbelief or indignation.

“Sen’Drorn” (linguistic): Warix language, ‘sen’ meaning ‘loyal,’ ‘drorn’ meaning ‘to the state.’

“Sen’Prin” (linguistic): Warix language, ‘sen’ meaning ‘loyal,’ ‘prin’ meaning ‘to the people.’

“What in Nushenyu’s storms is going on”: Warix expression of surprise.

ABOUT THE AUTHOR

J.B. Lesel is a fantasy writer living in California and sometimes in the forests of Germany. She enjoys reading, writing, travel, being in the wilderness, and sometimes volunteering abroad on wildlife biology research projects.

She has a master's degree in business psychology and works for an ad agency in SEO/ data analytics.

Find her online:
Website: jblesel.com
Facebook: @jbleselofficial
Instagram: @jb.lesel

www.ingramcontent.com/pod-product-compliance
Lightning Source LLC
LaVergne TN
LVHW091109080826
845145LV00008B/1856

* 9 7 8 1 8 3 9 1 9 5 3 3 4 *